ISBN: 978-0-9559909-7-7

I0526024

A Witch Like No Other

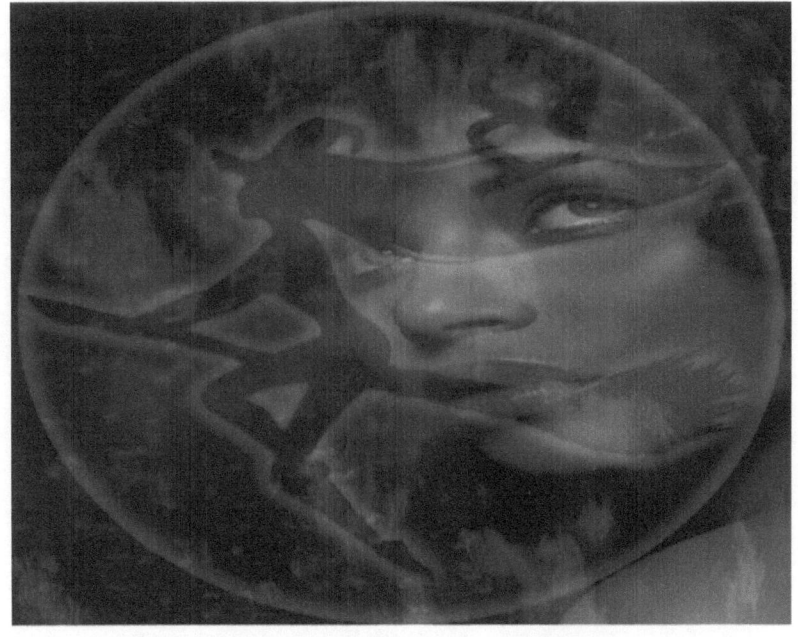

By Makala V. P. Thomas

For

Nathan Walcott

Sherene Williams

Shannon Thompson

Makeda Farrell

Joseph Smith

Madalene Aza

To the London Borough of Hackney. No matter how far I go in life, I will never forget where I came from.

x-x-x Mwah x-x-x

A Witch Like No Other

"I don't want to go college again."

"'Dora, you're eighteen years old. You need to go to college."

"I don't care," said Pandora stubbornly, not even looking at him. "Every time I go they think I'm weird from the very first day."

"That's because you refuse to communicate with anybody."

"Well I don't want to socialise, Dad. It gets on my nerves."

"You've been like this since you was fifteen, Pandora."

Pandora glared at him. "What does that mean?"

"Nothing," her father Ted said wearily. "Nothing at all."

"You think I'm weird too, don't you Dad?"

"I just think… if you had at least one friend-"

"I don't want any friends!"

"All right, keep your hair on."

Ted reached out to touch Pandora's curly hair, but she withdrew quickly. "Don't touch me."

Ted scowled at her. "I'm not allowed to touch you now?"

Pandora chose not to answer that, continuing her talk about college.

"They call me a *cool* know it all because I don't do work in class but I always hand my essays in on time-"

"Well, you're a very intelligent girl."

Her elder brother Marlon pretended to choke on his toast at that; Pandora kicked him under the table.

"I hate people who come up to me, wanting to be my friend."

"Pandora, listen to yourself. You can't not have friends, it isn't-"

"It's just how I want it," Pandora said flatly. "Because soon after a while they just… leave me. They decide I'm too much for them or they turn on me because I got better results than them, or for no reason at all."

"I know you're thinking about Janice, but-"

"Don't say that name!" Pandora burst out, making Ted jump. Marlon was glaring at him as well, swallowing his food before saying "She's a flipping barracuda, Dad. She turned on 'Dora and broke my heart."

"She was my best friend," said Pandora bitterly, Marlon just as bitter.

"She was my girlfriend and then she- she-"

"Ok, how about we change the subject," said Ted gently, hating to see his children looking like their world had been torn apart. Well, Pandora had changed ever since their mother died, but Marlon was the same.

"I remember how popular you was, Pandora." He sighed heavily, remembering. "You had more friends than Marlon."

Pandora smiled at the memories. For one tiny moment she missed her friends more than anything in the whole wide world… then she snapped out of it. She didn't need friends, or socialisation. But she couldn't help saying "If we didn't move so far away maybe I'd still have them."

"Don't try that," said Marlon, grinning at his sister. "My friends from Westport come here everyday, so that's not an excuse."

"Shut up, camel mouth. Where was I?"

"College," Ted said, picking up his cup of coffee. Pandora nodded.

"They'll find out I see a shrink three times a week because- because-"

Pandora swallowed hard. Images of her screaming, her mother and plenty of blood flashed across her eyes. Stile's evil face-

"Don't think about it," Ted said gently. "'Dora?"

Marlon was staring at her. Pandora realised she was shaking, making her mug rattle on the table. Gripping the mug and taking a sip of smooth hot chocolate seemed to calm her down. Ted smiled, relieved as she said "Then they find out that I'm taking medication for depression-"

"You don't need them," Marlon said grumpily. "I don't know why you take them anyway, you're fine just how you are."

Pandora raised an eyebrow and he smiled. She didn't smile back, wondering why Marlon was being nice to her. It was common knowledge they hadn't got along since Pandora hit sixteen, Marlon seventeen. She could cause an argument if she wanted, but decided against it.

"Maybe I do need them, Marlon. I mean I- I can't sleep without them, and I don't think about our mother when I take them, I forget about Stile-"

Ted gripped his cup of coffee as hot, bubbling rage swept over him. Damon Stile, his former neighbour, the man Pandora feared more than anything in this whole world- the only person she feared, he thought bitterly. If only he knew what was going on beforehand-

"I need them," Pandora said flatly. She needed to write something- write what she was thinking down- write anything.

Marlon swallowed the rest of his tea in one gulp, then he said to Ted "Father Teddy Bear, did you know Pandora's got a box?"

Ted's eyes nearly left his head. "A box?"

"I've got loads of boxes," Pandora said through gritted teeth. "Dad-"

"If you're doing some sort of witchcraft like your mother did Pandora-"

"I'm not!" lied Pandora. "I'm not, I swear it Dad!"

Her mother Dreamer had taught her a lot of things. If you have bad thoughts it was best to write them down and then burn the paper. That way you wouldn't get stressed over the thought, because it'd be gone.

Ted looked like he took his daughter's word.

His late wife Dreamer was a beautiful witch, and didn't hesitate to perform a trick if people asked her to. He loved Dreamer, but he hated anything out of the ordinary- magic first. Ted scowled at the memories as Pandora smiled at him. She was thinking the same thing.

He remembered the night he had come home from work with a splitting headache. Pandora was nine years old, Marlon ten. They were curled around Dreamer on the carpet, fast asleep as she read aloud from a book.

She shushed Ted gently as he opened his mouth, indicating to sit on the sofa. Ted obeyed, head pounding. Dreamer stood slowly and walked over to him- Pandora whimpered immediately, wanting her mother. She opened her eyes, Dreamer smiling at her as she said "Sleep, Pandora."

"I'm not tired anymore, Mummy. Can I watch?"

"If you want to that badly."

"My head," said Ted, in terrible pain. "I need an aspirin- I need-"

Dreamer placed her hands on his head, asking "How was work?"

"Work? Work was- was..." Ted stopped abruptly as swirling white mist circled his head. "Dreamer, what are you-"

"I asked you a question, Teddy Bear."

Marlon giggled, sitting up at that. "Teddy Bear, Mummy?"

"That's what I call your Daddy, sweetie pie. Ted?"

"Work was stressful. My client just won't accept the fact that he's going to be charged no matter what I do for him. I can help convince the judge to give him a short sentence, but we're looking at six months minimum-"

Pandora's mouth was hanging open, but Ted couldn't see why.

"What did he do, Ted?"

"Drug smuggling," mumbled Ted, as Dreamer massaged his head. "Wow, Dreamer. You could be a therapist if you-"

Ted stopped as he caught sight of them in the mirror across the room. No wonder Pandora was sitting like she was in a trance- Dreamer's hands were aglow! Ted leapt up immediately:

"Dreamer!"

"I wasn't doing anything wrong!" said Dreamer as she pouted at him.

"I don't want you doing any magic at all, do I make myself-"

Ted stopped as he lifted a hand to his head. "My headache's gone!"

"I can give it back if you detest magic that much," said Dreamer coldly, and Ted opened his mouth to tell her to do it, then he stopped. He hated making his wife angry or upset.

"No- don't. I... thank you."

"You're welcome," she said icily, then she smiled at Pandora. Marlon seemed unfazed by the fact his mother could do magic, but Pandora was the opposite. She loved it. She wanted to be just like her mother.

"Bedtime, Marlon and 'Dora," said Ted, knowing that a million thoughts must be zooming around his little girl's brain. He was glad that Marlon didn't care for magic, but he was concerned for his daughter. Pandora pouted as Marlon did, making their parents smile. They looked like twins. Pandora ran and kissed their mother goodnight as Marlon hugged Ted happily, then they switched places for Pandora to hug Ted and Marlon to kiss Dreamer, then they both ran upstairs to bed, Pandora tripping Marlon up mischievously so she could reach her room first.

Ted turned to Dreamer, worried.

"Did you see Pandora's face when you- you know."

Dreamer shrugged a shoulder. "She's fascinated by it."

"Exactly, and I really don't want her to be."

"Why, Ted?" said Dreamer sadly. "Are you ashamed of me?"

"What? No," said Ted, as she turned away from him. "Dreamer?"

"I'm going for a walk," she said, sighing. "Just a small one."

"I'll wait up for you."

"No- you need to get some sleep. I don't want you-"

"I'll wait up for you," Ted repeated firmly, kissing her hand. Dreamer smiled as she pulled on her coat, then she walked to the front door.

"I won't be long."

As soon as the door closed behind her Ted walked to the window and looked out. What he saw made his stomach drop three inches. Dreamer had entered his friend Damon Stile's house- the front door closed.

He had a mind to dash across the road and demand what was going on. But then he knew that Dreamer would never betray him, ever. She and Damon got on brilliantly, everyone knew that. In fact, Damon knew Dreamer first, and Dreamer's frightening mother Agnes had predicted her only daughter and Ted were meant for one another. It was also Agnes who had turned Damon into a toad, Ted thought ruefully, the minute he offered to baby-sit Pandora.

"I should have known," Ted muttered, and Marlon looked at him.

"Dad?"

Pandora was busy reading the newspaper. It didn't look like she heard him. Ted sighed as he looked at his daughter, not answering Marlon. Stile changed her forever. It was all his fault. Dreamer's murder, Pandora hating anyone who wasn't a relative, her refusal to socialise- it was all his fault. If only he could turn back time.

Ted shook his head as if trying to get rid of his thoughts. He couldn't think of that now. He needed to focus on his kids.

"What was I saying to you two?"

"Not me," said Marlon indignantly. "Pandora."

"The conversation ended," said Pandora coldly, looking at her brother. "Yes I do have a box, I've got plenty. I just use them to store things."

"Get you," said Marlon, grinning. "She couldn't stick to the legend, could she Dad? It's not Pandora's Box, it's Pandora's Boxes!"

Pandora rolled her eyes and went back to reading the paper. Ted smiled as he collected everyone's plates and cups, putting them in the sink.

"So what's on the agenda for today, kids?"

"I'm going out with the guys," Marlon said. "Er… can I, Dad?"

"Sure you can, son." Ted smiled at him. Even though he was nineteen, Marlon still had complete respect for his father. "Pandora?"

"I'm going to my room to pretend I don't exist," Pandora said without looking up. "Maybe if I wish it enough times it'll finally come true."

Marlon and Ted exchanged concerned looks at that, Marlon saying "Pandora, you know I can drop the guys; we can go out if you-"

"Go where, big brother?"

"Anywhere you want."

Ted nodded his approval: at least Marlon was trying.

Pandora closed the newspaper, looking thoughtful for a minute. Then she shook her head, saying "It's ok. I'd rather stay in my room."

Marlon looked at Ted, who smiled and shook his head. The smile meant *'You tried, son. Don't try and force her.'*

"Besides, I have to go see Shrinkabell," Pandora said, looking at Ted, who burst out laughing with Marlon. "It's Thursday, right?"

Ted nodded. "I won't be long at work, 'Dora, so-"

"You don't have to come, Dad. I'll be fine."

* * *

"Pandora darling, how are you?"

"Fine, Miss Hughes. Just fine."

Miriam frowned, concerned with how down Pandora sounded. She started counselling Pandora three years ago, and had come to love her like a daughter even though the first rule of her profession was *never get attached to the client.* Miriam found she didn't care. She was close friends with Dreamer at school, but had moved abroad in their last year. When she finally moved back home she found that Dreamer had a beautiful baby boy- in the blink of an eye. Miriam thought then that if she stayed Dreamer wouldn't have gone off track with this mystery boy. Her life was ruined- or so she thought. Dreamer wasn't letting a baby stop her from doing what she wanted: she returned to college, had fun with her friends and was still very popular. If Dreamer didn't care about the baby, then neither did they. So nobody really felt anything changed when the baby girl was born- but Miriam did. She hated whoever the father to these children was, for taking Dreamer away from her.

Bitter inside, Miriam told Dreamer she was leaving and never coming back. Her parents were moving abroad, for good this time. Miriam had a choice whether to stay with her aunt or go- angry, she chose to go.

Dreamer didn't care, she carried right on with her life, Miriam thought with a small smile. That was so typical of Dreamer. But then again, Dreamer must have missed her, because her mother called.

"Stop this nonsense, Miriam. You've no need to be jealous of Ted."

"That's his name?" Miriam said disgustedly. "Ted?"

"He's a lovely boy. His parents want him to wed Dreamer."

Over my dead body, Miriam thought furiously.

"She'd never marry him."

"Dreamer is in love," Agnes replied. "And she's not even eighteen."

"So?"

"So she may marry Ted. I leave the choice up to her."

Miriam demanded to speak to her.

"Dreamer, you won't marry him. Will you?"

"Now you want to talk?" Dreamer answered coldly. "What's the point?"

"Dreamer, I'm sorry for what I did- I can come back if you want-"

"But I don't want, so stay in America."

"Please don't marry him, Dreamer!"

"Why not?"

"You just can't! You'll forget all about me!"

Dreamer softened for a minute. "No I wouldn't, I promise."

"Just don't marry him," begged Miriam. "Please?"

"Why?"

"Because I..."

The remaining two words lingered on her lips, Miriam crying now.

"Oh boy," said Dreamer, amazed. "Why didn't you tell me?"

"We've been friends since forever," wept Miriam, ignoring the question.

"And now this- this Ted guy, and his stupid kids-"

"*My* stupid kids," Dreamer interrupted, though she wasn't really angry.

"We'll live happily ever after, exactly. I knew you'd understand!"

"That wasn't what I was going to say, and you know it!"

"Give me your address," Dreamer instructed. "That way we can write to each other or something. I'll send you a picture of my er... what was it again? Oh yeah, stupid kids."

"I didn't mean that, I just-"

"Forget it," Dreamer said firmly. "They're not the point right now."

Wiping her eyes, Miriam asked "What's the point, then?"

"Ted Stone is. I'm marrying him whether you love me or not."

"Fine!" shouted Miriam. "Fine, marry him! See if I care!"

"I won't bother seeing, because I know that you do."

Miriam slammed the phone down and ran to her room, throwing herself on her bed. She cried every night for a whole month. Two months afterwards Dreamer's mother Agnes called, telling her Dreamer did marry Ted, but refused to give up her last name. Miriam laughed: good. Dreamer Black sounded so cool. She couldn't imagine a Dreamer Stone.

Miriam begged Agnes for Dreamer's address, Agnes giving it without hesitating. Miriam wrote Dreamer a long letter of apology, though she wasn't exactly sure if Dreamer would reply. She wrote almost five pages, weeping as she did. She promised Dreamer she'd be there for her from now on, and wouldn't do anything to upset her. Miriam missed Dreamer so much it was starting to hurt. She wouldn't eat. She could just about sleep. She was always cold. Dreamer's absence had a tremendous effect on Miriam, and her parents were starting to worry. Miriam couldn't tell them the reason she was so depressed was because she missed her best friend, instead making up a feeble lie about a boy back in England.

Her father sympathized, her mother scolded.

Dreamer didn't reply to the letter, but Miriam knew she received it. She wrote another, asking Dreamer for a recent picture of her. Dreamer didn't reply until Agnes found the letters and forced her, Miriam thought as she smiled a little. Dreamer simply sent the picture as requested, with a picture of Ted Stone, and her two children.

When Miriam saw the photos she fell in love with Baby Pandora at once, her green eyes startling against her brown skin- she was the spitting image of Dreamer. Baby Marlon had brown eyes like his father, just as gorgeous as his sister. How could she have called them stupid?

Miriam called Agnes, asking her to give Dreamer her number. Dreamer took the number, but she didn't use it. So Miriam called Agnes again, frightening the woman as she demanded for Dreamer's contact details. Agnes knew how much Miriam loved her child, praying she loved Dreamer as a sister and nothing more as she gave the numbers.

Dreamer simply listened to Miriam speak, not saying a word.

"I'll come back, Dreamer- I promise. I won't leave again."

"You say it like I begged you not to go," Dreamer replied icily. "Did I?"

"No no, you didn't. But you had to have minded a little bit-"

"To be honest, Miriam, I did miss you a little. But I don't anymore."

"What?"

"I've moved on," Dreamer said coolly. "You're in my past, ok? Don't bother coming back here to mess up my present."

"But- but we're best friends!"

"I'm *your* best friend, but you're not mine."

"You- you liar!" said Miriam, voice cracking. "Don't lie, Dreamer!"

"I've got to go," Dreamer replied flatly. "Nice talking to you."

Miriam couldn't stop crying after that. Tears were a part of her now. Her parents consulted a doctor and her tutor at her college, both who came to see her. The doctor prescribed some depression tablets while her tutor helped Miriam get back on her feet.

"Why don't you try mentoring, Miriam? It does help."

"I'm not talking to a shrink!" sobbed Miriam. "I want my friend, Miss!"

"Where are they?"

"She's in England- and she hates me!"

"I'm sure she doesn't," her tutor said warmly. "And I meant studying the profession of mentoring, not going to see a counsellor. It does help you control your emotions- and you're very good at talking to people."

"Can I change my course? Will you be tutoring me?"

"No, but you can come to see me anytime you like."

After that Miriam knew what she wanted to do. She'd practice mentoring with her family, and then try the real thing when she got back to England. The only snag was her aunt lived far out in the country: it felt like Dreamer was on the other side of Earth.

Still, they had things to sort out. Agnes called Miriam over, much to Dreamer's surprise.

"When did *you* get back in the country?"

"About two weeks ago," Miriam said, gazing at her. "How are you?"

"Don't give me that," Dreamer said coldly. "Why are you back here?"

"Because I miss you," Miriam said slowly, carefully. "That's why."

Dreamer's mouth twitched as if she wanted to smile, and Miriam saw.

"Can we be friends again, Dreamer?"

Silence. Dreamer frowned as she thought, obviously wondering if having Miriam back in her life would benefit her in any way. Miriam waited anxiously, but Dreamer took her time.

Agnes handed Miriam a cup of tea, watching her daughter.

"Ok," Dreamer said almost five minutes later. "All right then. But I don't want you in my face all the time like before. I'd rather see you once every three months or something, because I have a new life and I have a husband and I go to college and I have new friends, and-"

"Dreamer!" barked Agnes, making her jump. "Don't be so immature."

"I'm not, Mama. I'm telling her how it is," Dreamer answered, then she looked Miriam straight in the eye. "Take it or leave it."

"Fine," Miriam said stoutly. "I've got studying to do anyway, so I wouldn't be able to see you much either. Actually, I just came to clear the air because I was a wreck in America, I missed you loads. And now I've seen you, so I'm fine now. That's all I wanted. Now I can move on with my life and leave you behind. Bye Agnes, I'll be going now. I won't bother calling to say I got home, it's not like she cares anyway."

Dreamer was impressed, as Miriam knew she would be.

"Well... it's going to take hours for you to get back to that place."

Miriam shrugged, feigning nonchalance. "So?"

"So stay here with me tonight. Mama, can Miriam stay?"

Miriam smiled broadly as Agnes nodded; Dreamer smiled back. Then they gave each other a massive hug and ran upstairs, talking and laughing as if they'd just got home after school like the good old days.

Dreamer wasn't joking about having a long distance friendship, but Miriam didn't care. They were friends again. At least she could pick up the phone and call Dreamer whenever she wanted, and Dreamer could call her. Miriam still resented Ted Stone for changing everything.

But there was something about Pandora that made Miriam determined to know her. She telephoned Dreamer in the middle of the night asking about her, and expected Dreamer to hang up and go back to sleep. But Dreamer did something very strange. She made Miriam promise- yes, promise- that if anything happened to her or Ted she would look after Pandora and Marlon. And Miriam promised. She didn't care if she was only eighteen and up to her knees in coursework.

Dreamer visited when Pandora turned one just a few days before.

"I want you to be Pandora's godmother, Miriam."

Miriam was overjoyed: Dreamer must have known what she thought of the beautiful little girl. Reverend John was more than happy to give a private ceremony just between Dreamer, Miriam and grandmother Agnes.

Miriam knew from that day on she would play some sort of role in Pandora's life, but then Ted and Dreamer had moved away to start their lives properly, now young adults. They'd done it on the sly, telling nobody, simply packing and leaving in the middle of the night. Nobody knew their address, not even Agnes, though Dreamer and the children visited every week and weekend.

Miriam remembered Pandora's fifteenth birthday. She was in America at the time, and she didn't know Dreamer's new address (they'd moved twice again in the years.) Still, she called. Dreamer let Pandora speak, though Pandora didn't remember Miriam.

"Hello?"

"Happy Birthday Pandora!"

"Thank you!" she said brightly, then she paused. "Um… who is this?"

Before Miriam could answer Dreamer took the phone.

"Go and look after your party guests, Pandora."

"Who was that, Mum? Do I know them?"

"Yes, but you can't remember them. Go on now."

"Why did you do that?" demanded Miriam, a little hurt.

"Because now isn't the time for you to meet. It will be later this year."

"Dreamer, I… you mean I get to see her in the flesh?"

"Yes, Miriam."

"Thank you, Dreamer! It's about time! Have you settled down, then?"

"Westport's lovely," Dreamer said nonchalantly. "Very nice."

Miriam could tell something was wrong.

"Dreamer, is everything all right?"

"No," Dreamer said, voice cracking. "I've done something very wrong!"

Startled as Dreamer cried, Miriam tried to soothe her while firmly reminding her that it was Pandora's birthday party, and it wouldn't do for her mother to be crying at the event. Dreamer didn't care.

"I betrayed Ted," she wept. "God knows I didn't mean to, but I did!"

Miriam opened her mouth furiously, then remembered her years of training and her brilliancy at her job. A mentor never loses their temper.

"Do you want to tall about it, Dreamer? Tell me what happened."

"His- his friend Damon Stile-"

"Ted's best friend? Wait- Dopey Damon from high school??"

"Yes, him! We were… talking, and-"

"Mum, Janice and Marlon!" said Pandora, sounding near tears. "They're kissing in the back yard, Mum! She's my best friend, how could he-"

"I'm coming, 'Dora. Miriam, can you call me back on my cell phone?"

"Of course," said Miriam, as if *she* made the call.

Miriam shuddered, remembering when she called Dreamer at eleven p.m. that night, knowing that the party would be over, Pandora and Marlon would most likely be in bed, and Ted would be watching the news.

"Dreamer, what's going on? You and Damon Stile, how-"

"It was an accident," said Dreamer calmly, much more in control than before. "We've been close for years, I never-"

"Why?" Miriam cut across, then she remembered her profession. *Never lose your temper with the client.* Miriam took a deep breath, then she said "You told me you and Ted are made for each other. What happened?"

"Ted's hates me being a witch now," Dreamer replied. "And Damon- well, he loves it. He can never get enough of a spell, Miriam, or a trick-"

"You wanted Ted to love you for who you are? What you are?"

"Yes! Oh Miriam, I'm so glad you understand."

"Tell me more," pressed Miriam. "That can't be all."

"Damon confessed he loves me after I turned his hair blonde," Dreamer said flatly, as if the fact meant nothing to her. "He told me he knows he's Ted's best friend but he doesn't care anymore. He loves me and 'Dora-"

"Pandora?" Miriam cut across sharply, eyes narrowing.

"As a daughter," Dreamer said, annoyed. "He was telling me he wanted us to move in with him, but I refused- it was meant to be a small kiss, nothing more, and then-"

"Don't," sighed Miriam. "Spare me the details."

"Then I found out I was expecting my third child-"

"Dreamer!"

Suddenly Dreamer was crying again.

"Damon was over the moon- he just knew without me telling him- it would be his first born- but I couldn't do it, Miriam! I couldn't!"

"I understand," said Miriam gently. "Does Damon know you got rid-?"

"Dreamer?" said a voice in the background. "Are you all right?"

"Teddy, I'm fine." Dreamer sniffed before repeating it. "I'm fine."

"Are you sure?"

"Yes," said Dreamer miserably. "I'm on the phone, Ted."

"Sorry."

Dreamer waited before saying "Miriam, I feel that I… I'm going to die."

"What?!"

"I've been having dreams," Dreamer said sadly, "Ever since I got rid of the baby. Damon thinks I'll give up everything and live with him, but I can't- I won't. I love Ted and I always will- I belong to him."

Miriam smiled, feeling a little jealous. "That sounded lovely, Dreamer."

"I've been having nightmares about Damon and Pandora," said Dreamer quietly. "He may have been- they could be just dreams, but-"

"What, Dreamer? What's been going on with him and my- Pandora?"

"He's been doing things to her," whispered Dreamer. "My little girl, and I didn't even know. He's been tutoring her since she was twelve- I didn't suspect, nobody did. Maybe there's nothing to suspect. But my dreams-"

"Ok Dreamer, ok. What does that have to do with you dying?"

"He'll find out I got rid of the baby, and he'll lose control."

"You mean he'll-!!"

"Promise me you'll look after my baby girl, Miriam. Promise me."

"Dreamer, you can possibly know you're going to-"

"Promise, Miriam!"

"I promise!"

Dreamer hung up then, not wanting to take the conversation any further. Miriam, mind spinning, tried calling back but the phone was turned off. A day after Dreamer's murder Miriam ran straight to the police and told them what she knew. Ted also happened to be there as she ran to the officer in charge of the case, saying "Dreamer had an affair with her killer. She called me- she knew she was going to die-"

The policeman pulled her into an office the same time Ted grabbed her other arm, frantically asking "What did you say? Dreamer and-"

But the officer pulled her into the office and slammed the door shut. Pulling out a notepad and pen, he said "Talk."

Ted did the same thing as soon as she left the station. Eyes brimming, Miriam told him who she was, what she was to Pandora, and what Dreamer had told her only a week ago.

"Where is Pandora?" she asked desperately. "Please Ted, tell me."

"She's in hospital," Ted replied, looking away. "It turns out Damon-"

"Yes yes, I know- will she be all right?"

"No," said Ted flatly. "She's in shock- she witnessed the whole thing."

"No," said Miriam, shaking her head in disbelief. "No! How? When?"

"I was at work. Marlon was at football practice, Dreamer was home with Pandora. Pandora's refusing to tell the police what actually happened, she just keeps saying it was him. He killed her."

Ted's eyes filled, Miriam's too. They walked in silence, then Miriam asked "What about Agnes? Does she know?"

"She called beforehand, telling me I must stay with Dreamer. I told her I couldn't, I had a very important meeting at work-" Ted's hands balled into fists; he was angry. "If only I did- Dreamer might still be here."

"You can't blame yourself," started Miriam, then she felt annoyed. Why did she always use her mentor technique? Why didn't she say that what Ted was saying might be true? If he had listened to Agnes Dreamer might still be alive. She'd been a mentor for so long it was now a part of her.

"Um… here."

She fumbled with her purse, pulling out a card.

"Please contact me as soon as Pandora leaves the hospital. I'm her godmother. I love her, Ted- like my own daughter."

"She'll immediately think you're trying to take her mother's place."

"I want to work with her as well," explained Miriam. "I'm a mentor-that's my workplace on the card, and work number."

"So we don't have to tell her who you are?"

"No," said Miriam painfully. "Not for a while, anyway."

"Why didn't Dreamer introduce you to the family, uh…" Ted peered at the card before saying "Miriam Hughes?"

"I'm not sure, but I did travel a lot. I was never in one place."

"I see."

"Promise me you'll call and let me see Pandora?"

"I promise."

"Earth to Miss Hughes," said Pandora, scowling. "I didn't come here to watch you gaze into space, you know. I could be at home in my room."

Miriam smiled at her, loving how feisty the girl was. "I'm sorry."

Pandora hesitated, then she smiled back. "Never mind."

"Pandora, I… sit down."

Pandora sat, looking curious. "Is something wrong?"

Miriam opened her mouth to say no, then she nodded. "Yes."

It had been three years. It was now or never: she had to know.

"Would you like to know what I was thinking, love?"

"Not really."

"I was thinking about your mother," Miriam said gently. "About you."

Pandora looked nervous now. "What about us?"

"Get a cup of water, Pandora. You may not like this…"

* * *

"I knew you was," Pandora said flatly, an hour later. "I could tell."

"You could tell I was your godmother?" said Miriam, bemused. "How?"

"I have dreams," Pandora said shyly. "Like my mother used to. Isn't that what you told me?" Miriam nodded. Pandora was eighteen now: there was no need to hold anything back. "I never told you, but you looked real familiar when I met you three years ago."

"Oh honey, you should have said."

"Yes, I know. I-" Pandora hesitated. "I have a box."

Miriam leant across her chair, interested. "A box?"

Pandora nodded. "It's made of pure gold; it was my mother's."

"Dreamer had a box… that's interesting. Is it a magical object?"

"Yes," Pandora said, nodding. "When I'm… upset or angry, I write."

"Yes, you did tell me that."

"I write it down, and I put the paper in the box. Then I light the candle."

"Candle? What candle?"

"That's just it, I don't know. When I write it appears in the box."

"And you light it?"

"Yes, and I put it in the box on top of the paper."

"Pandora, you could have started a fire."

"It's magic, I said," said Pandora impatiently. Miriam smiled at her, wanting to hear more. Pandora had never looked so exultant.

"Go on, love."

"And I put the candle on top of the papers, and I close the box and go to sleep." Pandora hesitated, then she whispered "It glows. Bright yellow, so I don't need my lamp on."

Miriam nodded understandingly: Pandora was afraid of the dark.

"But three nights ago Marlon barged in on me, and he saw it glowing."

"What did Marlon say?"

"Nothing," scowled Pandora. "He just stared at it. And I told him not to tell Dad and he stared at me too, then he backed out of the room and closed the door."

"Do you think he was scared?"

"Marlon's not scared of magic. Our mum was a witch, remember?"

"Yes, I remember."

"He doesn't take it seriously," grumbled Pandora. "This morning he was grinning like a Cheshire cat when he told Dad about the box."

"Oh no," said Miriam, though she was smiling. She thought Marlon a delightful boy, though Pandora was her favourite. She remembered when they had both come to meet her. Pandora didn't answer her when she said hello, but Marlon smiled and shook hands. Then he stepped back and said "No offence Lady, but I don't need a shrink. I'm all right without one, because I've got my Dad to talk to about my Mum and stuff."

He hesitated, then he asked "Is that all right?"

"Of course it is," Miriam said soothingly. "Would you like to leave?"

"Yes please. Come on, Pandora."

Pandora looked at him, then back at Ted, who was waiting. Then she looked at Miriam. Miriam thought nothing of it at the time, but now she knew that when Pandora's green eyes had scanned her face it was because she was experiencing some sort of déjà vu.

"Would you like to stay and talk?" Miriam asked her gently, hopefully.

Pandora opened her mouth, then she shook her head and walked away.

"You keep thinking," complained Pandora, as Miriam smiled. "I might as well go back home now, you're not even doing your job."

"I'm thinking three years back-" Pandora went rigid in her seat, Miriam quickly adding "When we met properly."

"Can we just start the session please, Miss Hughes?"

"Pandora, I'm your godmother." Miriam's smile was ravishing: it felt so good saying those words. "You don't have to- you can call me Miriam."

"I don't want to. I'm not used to it."

"Well, you don't have to be so formal now that you know."

"I just said I'm not used to it," Pandora said heavily, drumming her fingers on the chair arm. "Besides, I want to talk for once. Just because you're my godmother it doesn't mean you can start slacking, you know."

"Well said," smiled Miriam. "How are you, Pandora?"

"Fine."

"Can you tell me what's on your mind?"

"September," said Pandora, sighing. "I have to go to college."

"I think that's a very good idea."

"I'm going to drop out anyway," she said, shrugging. "You know I- I…"

"You have a problem with socialising since your mother died?"

"Say Dreamer," said Pandora sadly. "You was friends, right?"

"Very close friends, but love, you just told me I can't start slacking on the job." Miriam smiled as Pandora scowled at her. "Right?"

"Right, you flipping…"

Miriam burst out laughing, Pandora smiling grudgingly.

"So, Pandora. You have a problem with socialising."

"Yes. I hate it, and now I have to go back to college again. I dropped out of the last two courses," said Pandora, shrugging a shoulder. "I hated them. Why was I doing a load of Science? I don't want to be a scientist."

"Pandora, you're eighteen now. You know you can choose whatever you want to choose," Miriam told her gently.

Pandora shrugged, saying "I did choose them when Dad suggested Science. Nobody made me. I wish there was some sort of magic course; that's why I chose Science. Loads of experiments and stuff, right?"

"But Pandora, you also like to write."

"Yes Miss Hughes, I know."

"Would you like me to help you choose a course for September? If you'd like, I can gather some prospectuses and we'll-"

"Are you allowed to do that, Miss Hughes?"

Miriam knew she said it to goad her, but she couldn't help reacting.

"Pandora, I'm your godmother. Stop thinking of my job, ok darling? To be honest I'd really like to take you out one day, just us. Shopping, the cinema, you name it. In this office I am your mentor, but think of outside it. Wouldn't you like to know me a bit more? Your godmother? Right now all you have is Ted and Marlon. You can have me as well, love."

Pandora hesitated. "How do I know you won't leave me?"

"Pandora, I'd never leave on my own accord. I promise."

"What if we have a big falling out?"

"We'll work it out."

"What if I tell you something you wouldn't like?"

Miriam laughed. She couldn't stop herself- Pandora looked so worried!

"Pandora, remember I'm your mentor. For three years we've been talking, and you've told me plenty I didn't like."

"Oh."

"So how about it, Pandora?" asked Miriam. "Let me in your life?"

"No, I… all right then. But I bet ten pounds you'll leave me soon."

"Don't be ridiculous."

"I guess I'm getting there," said Pandora thoughtfully. "First I had just two people in my life for over two years, and now I've got three."

They looked at each other, and they both smiled.

* * *

Pandora didn't come home until eight that night. Ted was practically ripping his hair out with worry: she was always home by four latest. It wasn't his rule of course, but he had gotten so used to Pandora's ways that it hadn't occurred to him she might want to stay out later.

"Where've you been?" demanded Marlon, rushing downstairs in nothing but a towel around his waist, his hair dripping with water. "I've been worried sick, Pandora! You'd better be grateful I didn't call the feds..."

He trailed off in amazement, Ted staring at her as well.

Pandora's smile was so broad it lit up her features, revealing the girl they loved and lost the minute Dreamer was pronounced dead.

"Dad, I'm sorry you worried, but... first I had just you two, and now I've got a third person to spend time with."

"Who is he?" demanded Marlon, but Ted knew what she was going to say. Pandora shook her head at her brother, saying "Not a boy, idiot. I hate boys and I hate girls too. I hate people. I'm talking about Miss Hughes, Marlon."

"The shrink? What about her?"

"Her and Mum were friends. She's my godmother."

"What!" exploded Marlon. "Your godmother?? Since when?"

"She told me everything when I went there," said Pandora happily. "She even told me the church I had the ceremony in and everything, and she talked about Grandma for a bit too- and I never really spoke about Grandma... isn't it nice, Dad? Why didn't you tell me?"

"I didn't want you to think she was taking your mother's place, 'Dora."

Pandora's smile faded as she thought about that.

Marlon was seething. "Why didn't you tell *me?*"

"Come on son, I didn't know until your mother died."

Marlon's expression cleared immediately, then he scowled.

"You want to watch her, 'Dora. She's really attached to you. Remember what happened last time when certain people were attached to you?"

"Shut up, Marlon!"

Pandora shook her head, but the images were in her mind again. Stile hovering over her as she played the piano-

"Pandora," said Ted firmly, but she didn't respond. "'Dora, stop thinking about it. See what you've done?" he said to Marlon, who shrugged.

"I'm just warning her, Dad."

"Yes, and are you going to warn her if she makes new friends too?"

"No, I-"

"Get some clothes on, Marlon."

Marlon looked hurt by the dismissal, but he obeyed.
Before Ted could talk Pandora left as well, looking as moody and down as she did before she left the house this morning.

* * *

Pandora scrawled Damon Stile's name down frantically, placed it in her golden box and lit the candle. Closing the lid and watching as the box began to glow, she breathed deeply. Soon Stile left her mind totally, Pandora whispering "Thanks, Mum."

Dreamer had taught her so much. Pandora climbed into bed, wondering about her godmother. It wouldn't hurt to have a woman figure in her life, would it? And Miriam was very fond of her, for some wild reason. Pandora knew it was because she was friends with her mother, and had watched her grow from a distance, through pictures and letters from Agnes and Dreamer. How did she know that? She just did.

Ted knocked on her door, Pandora calling "Don't come in!"

"Will you come out, then? I miss my little girl."

"Dad, we've got tomorrow to talk. And Saturday too."

Ted laughed, saying "I only want a hug, 'Dora."

Pandora cringed. Physical contact was out of the question.

Ted knew that of course, but it couldn't hurt to try for the thousandth time. Pandora gritted her teeth before saying "I don't want one, Dad."

"All right then. Sleep tight."

"You too."

* * *

Pandora's alarm went off at ten a.m., Pandora rolling over in bed.

"Why do I even have a cell phone?" she muttered, sitting up slowly. "I mean, it's not like I get calls anyway. I should give it away."

She swung her legs out of bed into her slippers, yawning as she looked at her golden box. Where did Dreamer get it from? Grandma Agnes, probably. And the spell book as well. Pandora smiled, knowing that Ted would go berserk if he found out she stole Dreamer's dusty old book from her bedroom, along with the magical box and crystal quartz, and her wand. Her *wand,* Pandora thought hungrily.

Ted had burnt all of Dreamer's things in anguish, except her pictures. Marlon stole some of her things too, but Pandora didn't know what things. She didn't care. She had her mother's wand and spell book and box and crystals, and that's all she needed. Ha, thought Pandora smugly. Witch in the making.

* * *

"Pandora, I'm sorry for getting at you last night."

Pandora ignored her brother totally, appearing deeply immersed in her book as she drank her tea. Marlon tried again.

"I was being an idiot-"

"As always."

"And I'm sorry."

Silence.

Marlon looked at Ted, who said "Pandora, your brother's talking to you."

"Can't you see I'm reading, Marlon? Talk to me afterwards."

"I give up," said Marlon angrily, getting up. "I'm going to watch TV."

"Try getting a job," Pandora replied, turning a page.

"You're such a-"

"Nothing worse than you, big brother."

"Hey," said Ted warningly, when Marlon opened his mouth furiously. "It's still morning time. What are we doing today, then?"

"I'm staying home," Marlon said, looking daggers at Pandora.

"I'm staying in my room," Pandora said flatly, then she glanced Marlon's way. "Keep out of my way, Marlon."

"I've got nothing to say to you anyway."

Ted sighed, picking up his briefcase. "See you this afternoon."

"Bye Dad."

"Bye," said Pandora, not even looking at him. Ted smiled, feeling that they were getting somewhere. Before Pandora wouldn't even have acknowledged his leaving, and now... he knew he had to thank Miriam.

* * *

Pandora picked up the house phone a week later, then put it down.
"Just call her," said Marlon, annoyed. "Stop moping around."
Pandora glared at him. "Why are you still here?"
"I'm taking my time, little sister. And I want to see if you've got the guts to call your godmother."
"If you wasn't such a loser maybe I'd share her with you."
"If you wasn't such a freak I'd consider your offer."
Pandora's eyes flashed. "Why don't you flip James over and suck his-"
"Pandora!" said Ted, surprised at her. "Curb your tongue."
Pandora glared at them both and punched the numbers in the phone, waiting impatiently.
"St. Peter's Clinic. How may I help you?"
"Uh..." Pandora swallowed. "Is Miriam Hughes there please?"
"She's in a meeting right now. Can I take a message?"
"Well, I- um... I just..."
Pandora looked at her father for help, not used to speaking to other people. Ted took the phone, saying "Tell her Pandora Black called."
"Yes sir. Have a good day."
"See what being a loner does to you?" said Marlon, shaking his head. "You can't even talk to other people anymore."
"She was a stranger!" said Pandora, eyes filling. "I didn't know what to-"
"Never mind," said Marlon reassuringly, as the doorbell went. Ted opened it to James Henbit, Marlon's best friend.
"Wassup, Mr Black!"
"Hello James," said Ted wearily. James was one of those people who could do your head in just by smiling at you.
"Marlon, you ready to go?" James looked their way, then he exclaimed in surprise. "Pandora! Hey girl, how you doing?"
Pandora opened her mouth, but no sound came out. She hadn't seen James since she was fifteen, him sixteen. He was a guest at her birthday party... then they moved away. Marlon refused to lose contact with him, expectedly. They'd known each other forever. But Pandora changed big time. Now she couldn't stand people at all.
James frowned at her, wondering what the silence was for.
"Pandora?"
She shook her head and fled upstairs, slamming her bedroom door behind her. James looked at Marlon, amazed.

"You weren't kidding, bro?"

"No," said Marlon heavily. "Come on, let's go."

* * *

Ted got home a little late, due to train delays. "Pandora?"

Silence.

Ted knew she was in, she just didn't bother answering him. Marlon wasn't back yet. Ted dropped his briefcase on the kitchen table, then he sat down as he thought of his late wife. He felt angry that she had betrayed him, sad because she was gone.

Rubbing his forehead, he asked "What should I do about Pandora?"

Have a cup of coffee first, Teddy Bear. Then talk to her.

Ted gasped, falling out of his chair. The familiar whistling of the kettle made him scramble to his feet and look around fearfully.

"Dreamer?"

* * *

Pandora flicked through Dreamer's spell book, recognising her grandmother's handwriting, shortly followed by her mother's.

She heard the crash in the kitchen, but didn't go and check it out.

"Dad probably passed out," she joked to herself, then he heard Ted's footsteps on the landing. Slamming the book shut and pushing it under her bed, she grabbed a newspaper and sat innocently as he knocked.

"Can I come in?"

"If you have to."

Ted came in with a mug of hot chocolate for Pandora and a cup of coffee for himself. Pandora put the paper down, sensing his alarm.

"What's wrong?"

"Nothing, 'Dora. Nothing," Ted said quietly. He wasn't about to tell her anything. She'd get her hopes up and maybe try and do something silly.

Pandora accepted the chocolate, watching as he sat on her chair.

"Have you thought about college, Pandora?"

"Miss Hughes is going to help me choose a course."

"You didn't like Science, did you?"

"I hated it," said Pandora disgustedly. "I'm never studying it again."

"When you got an A-star in your Science GCSE?"

"I got As in most of my other subjects," Pandora pointed out. "Ok?"

"Ok. Did Miriam call you back at all?"

Pandora shrugged. "I didn't answer the house phone. I never do."

"Then how can you expect- does she have your mobile number?"

"No."

"Pandora," started Ted, then he decided scolding her wasn't necessary. He had learnt from Miriam that talking calmly and rationally was the best way to deal with Pandora.

"At least you're seeing her tomorrow anyway."

* * *

James sped down the motorway, saying "You've got to help her."

"Who?"

"Pandora," said James. "She's your sister, man. She needs you."

"You wouldn't say that if I told you what she said this morning."

James grinned, sparing a glance at his best friend. "What did she say?"

"She told me to flip you over and suck your... you know."

"Whoa! Are you serious?"

"Yep."

"So she's still Miss Feisty, then."

"Sure. She's the same really, but she hardly smiles or laughs, she stays in her room to pretend she doesn't exist and she hates socialising."

"I was close to her once upon a time."

"Yeah, when she was flipping ten years old."

"It's not my fault she met Janice at high school and forgot about me."

Marlon glanced at his friend. "Why do you say it like that?"

"Like what? Wait- no." James shook his head. "Don't get it twisted, Marlon, I'm not interested in Pandora. Nope. Never."

"You'd better not be."

"Hey, I've got a girl already. You know that already."

Marlon smiled. "I forgot. Cindy, right?"

"Yup. Cindy."

Though it had been six months since James had actually spoken to Cindy, six months since they last saw each other. They split up ages ago, and James didn't want to tell his best friend. Marlon would tease him and then suggest what went wrong. Nothing went wrong, not with him. Cindy was the one who cheated.

"Pandora, though. Is she going to college this term?"

"She is, but she'll probably drop out again."

James was glad the night hid his scowl.

"Don't you have faith in your little sister?"

"James, come off it. I love Pandora, but we have to be realistic. She left school with high grades and she ditched all her friends just before. She just wants to be alone; ever since Mum died she's been like that. I try with her, but she shrugs me off. She hardly speaks to me anymore, except at breakfast. Seriously James, I'm the one who has to start the conversations, like all the time. And it always turns into an argument."

"Maybe it's the things you say."

"She just doesn't want to socialise. Stile's lucky he's in prison, because I swear I'd have killed him. He told her things, James- I know it. She's scared of people because of what he said to her- did to her."

"It's sick, man." James shook his head. "It's sick."

"I won't give up on her," said Marlon heavily. "I promise."

* * *

Pandora sat writing in her notepad when she heard Marlon come home with James, saying "Dad, can James stay over?"
Pandora stopped writing as she listened.
Downstairs in the kitchen, Ted shook his head.
"Marlon, are you even thinking about Pandora?"
"She was friends with James when she was ten," Marlon pointed out, James nodding as he looked towards the stairs.
"But that was many moons ago," Ted said reasonably. "You know about your sister's... socialising issues-"
"It's ok, I understand," said James. "May I use the bathroom, sir?"
Ted nodded, James leaving the kitchen to let Marlon try and convince his father to let him stay.

* * *

"Pandora?"

She flinched at James'ss gentle voice, not answering.

Outside the door, James said "Can I come in?"

She didn't answer.

"Pandora, it's been ages. Remember the fun we used to have?"

Playing tag and hop scotch? Thought Pandora jeeringly. Sure.

"Um... I know you hate people and er... don't want any friends. You just don't want to socialise," said James, sitting down by the closed door. "But I uh... look, if anything remember I'm still here, ok?"

Silence. James, being optimistic, took that as a yes.

He scrawled his mobile number on a bit of paper he had and pushed it under her door as he said "That's my mobile number."

Still she said nothing. James understood, having counselled Marlon on Pandora many times. There was nothing he didn't know.

"Call me anytime you want. Do you know what college you're going to?"

Nada.

"Well, I'm going to Forest Academy. Maybe I'll see you there, yeah?"

Pandora hugged herself, simply listening to his voice.

"James!" called Marlon, making him leap up. "Hurry up!"

"Anytime you want to talk," whispered James, "Call me, ok? Bye."

He scrambled to his feet and backed down the landing as Marlon came upstairs, making out he just came out of the bathroom.

"Dude," said Marlon in mock disgust, "Never eat egg rolls again!"

James burst out laughing. "See you later, Marlon."

Marlon watched him go, then he knocked on his sister's door.

"I'm back, 'Dora."

"I'm glad," she answered sarcastically, making him laugh.

"Can you at least try and get along with me, Pandora? For once?"

"What's the point? Since my seventeenth birthday you've been a-"

"So have you," he said, prodding the door as if it was Pandora. "Yes?"

"I don't care. You're worse than me because you're a guy."

"Well thanks for letting me know," pouted Marlon. "Night, Pandora."

"Night."

Pandora crawled across the carpet, reaching out and picking up the piece of paper. James'ss number? Whatever, she thought amusedly, turning to her golden box. She placed the paper in there by itself, then she grabbed the candle that materialised minutes later, lit it and placed it on top of the paper, then she closed the lid down.

James Henbit was part of her past; there was no way he'd become her present. Never.

Pandora climbed into bed, wondering if he was always so patient.

* * *

When Pandora woke up she could tell straight away something wasn't right. She got up slowly as she always did, then went straight to her box on her desk. It felt warm. Curious, she opened it and looked inside.

Pandora shrieked, stepping backwards. Then she reached out and picked the box up, staring down at it's contents though there shouldn't be any.

The candle was gone, but the paper from James was still there.

"Great," muttered Pandora, then she looked at her mother's picture. "Am I supposed to keep it or something, Mum?"

Dreamer's ravishing smile seemed to grow: Pandora smiled back.

"I'd bet all my money you're still alive somewhere, not joking."

Elated, she saved James'ss number in her mobile phone.

* * *

"Pandora, can you pass the salt?"

Pandora glanced at her brother, then she looked at the salt.

"It's in the middle of the table, Marlon. You can reach it yourself."

"Why," demanded Marlon, "Are you so damn difficult?"

"Don't talk to your sister like that," said Ted warningly, as Pandora smiled before saying "Because that's how I like to be. Problem?"

"Go and see your shrink, you deluded little hermit."

Pandora slammed her glass down, making everyone jump as she stood.

"I'm going anyway."

* * *

Miriam eagerly waited for Pandora to arrive. She got the message from the receptionist, that Pandora called. That certainly was a first.

You really love my little girl, don't you?

"Yes," said Miriam happily, turning to whoever spoke. "I really-"

She stopped dead, staring at her closed door. "Hello?"

Silence.

My little girl… Miriam shook her head, trying to reason with herself.

"It can't be. There's no way Dreamer can be-"

She shrieked as Pandora slammed her fist on the door, furious.

"Can I come in, Miss Hughes?"

Miriam opened the door, shaken. "Good afternoon, Pandora."

"Sorry I'm late, but I went in the park for a bit and I- are you ok?"

"No, not really. I- never mind me, love. How are you?"

"I've decided I want to do a writing course at- at Forest Academy."

"Good for you," said Miriam, pleased as she turned to her desk. "I've got the prospectus here somewhere, with some others-"

"No, it's Forest Academy I want to go to."

Miriam looked at her, surprised. "Why that particular college, Pandora?"

"Because- this is embarrassing."

"No darling, sit down. Talk to me."

* * *

"I think he wants to be friends with you again, Pandora."

"What about my Mum?"

Miriam swallowed. "Well- you don't know it was Dreamer who-"

"It was her, I know it was," said Pandora, eyes sparkling. "That box hasn't ever done that before, and I swear her smile got bigger when I looked at her picture."

"Pandora, it's just wishful thinking." And unexplainable events, she added silently, hating Pandora's disappointed face. "That's all it is."

"But- but just say she was alive-"

"She isn't," said Miriam gently. "You went to the funeral, didn't you?"

"Yeah I did, but they kept the coffin closed," said Pandora, thinking. "And- oh gosh! Those guys carrying it said it was real light as well!"

Miriam cringed as she remembered, hidden by the public who had come to pay their respects. She'd never cried so much in her entire life that day. She'd lost her best friend, didn't even get to see her one last time.

What if all that was buried was the coffin, nothing more? Miriam felt sick to the stomach. What if Dreamer was alive?

"I mean, she's a witch," said Pandora. "You think she'd just go?"

"I don't want to have this conversation, darling."

Talk to her, Miriam.

"What?" said Pandora, when Miriam leapt up. "What is it?"

"Would you like to go for a walk, Pandora?"

"Ok," she said curiously, getting up. "How come?"

"Because I'm your godmother, love. Come on."

"Won't your boss be angry with you?"

"I'll handle him."

Sure enough, when Tony Pets left his office to see Miriam leaving with Pandora, he marched up to them immediately.

"What on earth is going on, Miriam?"

"Nothing," said Miriam flatly. "I'm just taking Pandora for a walk."

"To get some air," Pandora added, and Tony smiled at her.

"You would be good for my Alice, Pandora."

Pandora raised an eyebrow. "Who?"

"His daughter," Miriam said, amused. "Alice is your age, Pandora."

"Wow," she said dryly. "Can we go now, Miss Hughes?"

"Pandora, I've told you already you can call me Miriam-"

"No she can't," interrupted Tony, eyes narrowing. "Why can she?"

Miriam glared at him. "Because she's my goddaughter."

Tony stared at her, then he looked at Pandora. "She is?"

"She is," said Pandora cheekily. "Can we go now?"

"Yes we can," Miriam said, then she looked at Tony. "Unless you have an objection to me taking her for a walk in the park?"

"I... no," Tony said awkwardly. "No, not at all. But Miriam, if you're a relative I think it's best if we change Pandora's mentor-"

"No!" said Miriam, aghast. "You can't do that-"

"If you change Miss Hughes I'm not coming back," Pandora told Tony stonily. "My dad pays you big money, I know he does. If... if I have to change just because she's my godmother, that's out of order. I won't come back, and I'll bully your daughter until she has to come here too."

"Now really Pandora, you're overreacting-"

"So you think," Pandora replied flatly. "Can we go, Miss Hughes?"

"Of course."

* * *

"That wasn't very nice, threatening him about Alice."

"He's stuck up," Pandora replied. "He deserved it. Who is she?"

"She's a lovely girl, but she has some issues of her own."

They sat down in front of the lake, cross legged on the grass.

"What issues?" asked Pandora, and Miriam smiled at her.

"I can't tell you that, love."

"Are you her mentor?"

"No, of course not."

"Then tell me, Miss Hughes- please?"

Miriam shook her head, amused. Pandora pouted, turning to look at the lake.

"Swans," she said musingly. "Mum loved swans."

"Did she?"

Pandora nodded. "Especially the black ones."

Miriam felt her stomach drop. "There- there's black swans?"

"Sure," shrugged Pandora. "Only nobody really sees them."

"Maybe because they don't exist?" suggested Miriam, but Pandora shook her head as she said "They do, because Mum showed me one."

"I've never heard of or seen a black swan, Pandora."

"Because you haven't seen something with your own eyes, does that mean it doesn't exist?" asked Pandora, staring her full in the face. "Or because something seems impossible, does that mean it can't happen?"

Miriam opened her mouth, then closed it. Dreamer had done a lot of impossible things in her time, including turning an annoying boy who was besotted with her into a toad, making her pen write lines by itself when they were in detention, bewitching the Head so that they had an extra week off, giving her rival chicken pox at college- talking to Miriam even though she was dead?

Miriam shivered, Pandora gazing across the lake. Miriam looked too, smiling at the sight of the beautiful white birds.

"They're lovely, aren't they?"

Pandora nodded, eyes filling. "I want her back, Miriam."

"Dreamer? Of course you do- we all do, but-"

Miriam broke off, staring at the water. Swimming towards them was a beautiful, elegant black swan, it's beak ruby red.

"Told you," breathed Pandora, slowly getting to her feet. "I told you."

"Pandora, come back-"

Pandora ignored her, walking towards the graceful bird. Miriam cursed magic under her breath: that bird wasn't there ten seconds ago.

"Pandora!"

Oblivious to her godmother's calls, Pandora crouched down next to the bird as she whispered "Hi. See what happens when they don't believe?" The bird nodded. "You just appeared, didn't you?"

The swan crooned softly, Pandora reaching out to stroke it. Suddenly the bird made a weird rasping noise, like it was choking. Miriam leapt to her feet at that: "Pandora!"

The bird heaved, as if it was trying to force something up. Pandora's eyes grew wide as the swan began to sparkle, Miriam grabbing her arm and pulling her back as she said "We're leaving, Pandora-"

"We can't!"

"We have to! Something weird is going on-"

"It's my Mum, Miriam!"

"She's dead!" said Miriam angrily. "Dreamer's dead, Pandora!"

The bird gagged, something gold appearing in it's mouth. Miriam stopped struggling with Pandora as they stared at it- the swan heaved again, whatever it was dangling from it's beak- before Miriam could stop her Pandora darted forwards, grabbed the thing and pulled-

"Pandora, no!"

The bird shrieked, Pandora falling backwards- BANG!!

Miriam cried her name as smoke swirled around her- she couldn't see!

"PANDORA!!"

"I'm here, Miriam, I'm here!" Pandora grabbed her hand. "Look at this!"

Miriam didn't want to look, the smoke clearing. She stepped back in shock as she looked at the lake: the birds were gone. Every single swan and duck- gone. The black swan had disappeared as well-

Pandora shook Miriam frantically, saying "Look!"

Miriam dragged her eyes away from the lake to look at what Pandora was dangling in her face- she screamed. She couldn't help it.

"She's alive," breathed Pandora. "She has to be!"

Miriam shook her head, staring at the heart shaped locket with her friend's name on the front in swirly writing: *Dreamer.*

* * *

"Have some tea, 'Dora, and calm down."

"If she is alive she's got some explaining to do," said Marlon darkly, drumming his fingers on the kitchen table. "I'm not joking."

Miriam said nothing, very shaken up. Ted gently but firmly told her to stay the night, in the guest room. Miriam accepted the offer without hesitating: she didn't want to be alone.

Pandora had rushed home with Miriam hot on her heels, excitedly telling Ted and Marlon what happened at the park, and what happened with Dreamer's picture- but she didn't mention her golden box.

Ted said nothing, Marlon said a lot, Miriam couldn't speak. Ted made everyone some tea with biscuits on the side, deep in thought.

Could Dreamer be alive?

* * *

"Ted?"

Ted looked up, then he smiled. "Hi Miriam. What's the matter?"

Miriam hesitated, then she came and sat next to him on the sofa.

"I know you probably don't think she could be alive, but-"

"I didn't before," confessed Ted. "Now I'm not so sure."

"Well, this is going to sound crazy, but today before Pandora came, I..."

Miriam stopped, then she took a deep breath. "I heard Dreamer's voice."

Whatever Ted was expecting, that wasn't it.

"You... you heard Dreamer's voice?" Miriam nodded, looking down at her lap. Ted hesitated, then he said "So did I."

"You did?" she said hopefully, and he nodded. "So I'm not crazy."

"Far from it. What did she say?"

"I was looking forward to Pandora visiting..."

"Shh!" whispered Marlon, glaring at his sister. "They'll hear us!"

They were on the stairs, listening hard to their father and Miriam.

"And then she said 'you really love my little girl, don't you?' And I said yes, thinking someone came in, but only her mother could have called Pandora her little girl, nobody else in their right mind except you-"

"You breath stinks, camel mouth!" hissed Pandora. "Go floss!"

"Shut up, hermit!"

"What did she say to you?" asked Miriam shyly, and Ted hesitated. Then he said "I was wondering what to do about Pandora, and she said- these were her exact words, mind."

"I know, Ted."

"Have a cup of coffee first, Teddy Bear. Then talk to her."

Pandora's heart pounded as Miriam said "Was she right?"

"Oh yes, we had a talk about college. But before that, Miriam, I... look, I was so shocked when I heard her voice I fell out of my chair- and not just that," said Ted breathlessly. It sounded like he'd been dying to get it off his chest. "The kettle started boiling on it's own accord."

Marlon clapped a hand to Pandora's mouth as she gasped, whispering "Shut up, 'Dora! Do you want them to hear us?"

"She always used to make me a hot drink," said Ted sadly. "Coffee in the mornings before I went to work, and tea when I got back home."

"What about the locket?" asked Miriam. "Do you recognise it? Dreamer had it on after I came back from America- when I was eighteen."

"It was her mother's first," Ted answered heavily. "Before, it said Agnes. When she handed it down to Dreamer, the name changed... and Dreamer was eighteen when she got it. I guess if Dreamer was alive she'd have

given it to Pandora on her eighteenth birthday- and if she is alive then…
it's obvious she wanted Pandora to have it. Real obvious. She did say
Pandora would get it when she's old enough."

"And Marlon?" asked Miriam, and Ted smiled.

"Dreamer had a ring. Pure gold- unisex. That would be Marlon's gift."

"What will you do if the ring appears for Marlon, Ted?"

"I… I don't know, Miriam. I don't know."

* * *

Pandora bolted upstairs as the front door rang. Annoyed, Marlon called "It's just James, 'Dora! Jeez!"

"Ready for game, Marlon?" said James happily, holding a football under his arm. "You know we can't afford to mess up this time."

"Ready as ever," Marlon said determinedly, fastening his shin pads. "Dad, I won't be back till seven this evening."

"Ok," said Ted from the kitchen, not really paying attention. He was deep in conversation with Miriam about Pandora.

Marlon and James came into the kitchen, wanting to hear too.

"Does she always run like that when the doorbell rings?"

"Always," said Marlon bitterly. "If only she'd come out with me, I'd-"

"Go and ask," said Miriam. "Do you think she'd say yes?"

Everyone shrugged, Marlon saying "I'll try get her to come."

"I don't think football's her thing," started James, and Marlon answered "Tell the coach something important came up."

"But- all right. Can I come too?"

"No, idiot. It's a brother sister thing."

* * *

"No, camel mouth."

"Come on 'Dora!" whined Marlon. "Please!"

"No. I'm not coming out with you and your stupid boyfriend. "

"James left ten minutes ago- and he's not my boyfriend, Pandora!"

"Well you seem real close for just friends," Pandora said from inside her bedroom. "I'd bet all my money he's gay."

"Well he's not, he's got a girlfriend."

Pandora paused at that. "He- he's got a girlfriend?"

"Yep."

"Why does he want to help me?"

"He sees you like a sister, silly. He's always telling me to help you."

Pandora looked at her mobile, then she said "All right."

Marlon's heart sped up. "All right what? You'll come?"

"Yes."

"Dad! Dad, she said all right!" said Marlon happily, beaming at Ted, who was at the foot of the stairs. "She's coming!"

"So hyped," muttered Pandora as she grabbed her jacket. "Jeez."

* * *

"This is where we saw the black swan," Pandora told her brother as she pointed at the lake. "It just appeared."

"D'you really think Mum might be alive, Pandora?"

Marlon was the eldest. He'd always thought he had to set an example, be mature even though he wasn't. And missing Dreamer as much as he did, he couldn't help asking his little sister what she thought.

"I... I don't know. Miriam said it's just wishful thinking, but I don't think she meant it. She's as scared as Dad is."

"And you?" probed Marlon impatiently: that wasn't a good enough answer. "Are you scared?"

"No," Pandora said. "She's our Mum, remember? Why should I be?"

"That's what I think too," Marlon said, smiling. It felt so good to be out and about with his sister again. "Dad and Miriam can hear her."

"I know. It's not fair."

Marlon nodded as some girls walked past, smiling at him. Pandora rolled her eyes as he smiled back, and they giggled. Taking her brother's hand, she glared and said "He's taken already."

"What the- Pandora!" said Marlon, stunned as they all walked off with their noses in the air. "What did you do that for??"

"We're meant to be spending quality time together, remember?"

"Slipped my mind," grumbled Marlon as the sun revealed itself at last.

Something sparkled on the grass, catching his eye.

"What's that?"

"What's what?" said Pandora curiously, but he didn't answer as he left her side, staring down at the grass. Pandora looked at her mobile, at the only four names in her contact list. Ted, Marlon, Miriam, and James.

Pandora decided to text their father, knowing he'd be anxious.

* * *

"I hope she's having a good time," Ted said to Miriam worriedly. "Pandora and Marlon aren't compatible for more than an hour."

"Yes they are," said Miriam thoughtfully. "Marlon loves his sister very much. Pandora loves him too, she just enjoys being defiant."

Ted looked at Miriam, expression blank. "You know her well."

"She does open up to me," said Miriam, a little smugly. "After all, I am her mentor- and godmother. She does love her brother, Ted."

Before Ted could answer his mobile went off. Without taking his eyes off Miriam, he reached down and picked it up off the table. Miriam had no choice but to stare back until he lowered his gaze.

"It's Pandora."

"Is she all right? Where is she? Are they-"

Ted's broad smile stopped her sort as he said "Look at it."

Miriam took the phone to read the text.

> *Having a good time, Dad. I never thought*
> *it would be this fun hanging out with Marlon*
> *but it is. I just told some girls to get lost in the*
> *park, and he's riled for that, ha ha.*
> *Pandora.*

"Ted, that's lovely."

"It is, isn't it?" he said happily. "She's really coming along."

"Shall we go and meet them with some sandwiches?"

Ted smiled at her. "Sure."

* * *

Ted and Miriam both opened their mouths to call them, Miriam holding the basket of food and drinks. Then Miriam pulled Ted into the trees as soon as she saw Marlon's frightened face.

"'Dora! Pandora, come here!"

Pandora turned, expression deadpan. "What for?"

"You've got to see this," said Marlon as he bent and picked something shiny off the grass. "It's the... it's-"

Pandora rolled her eyes and walked over to her brother. "What?"

"The ring," breathed Marlon. "Mum's ring, look!"

Pandora stared down at the ring in his hands, amazed.

"No way."

"Yes way! What should I do with it?"

Pandora smiled, saying "I don't know, Marlon. Why not chuck it in the lake and forget all about it? We won't mention this ever again, all right?"

"I can't just-"

Then he realised she was being sarcastic, the way she was glaring at him.

"We'll tell Dad first, ok idiot? But whatever you do, don't let him take it off you. Mum wants you to have it, obviously. Try it on?"

Marlon hesitated, then slipped on the ring. Pandora's green eyes widened as it began to glow on his finger, Marlon staring down at it.

"It's a magic ring," he said amazedly. Without warning, he whirled round and pointed at the lake. The great circle of water rippled at once, the birds startled as they were buffeted around.

"Nice," said Pandora, impressed. "You're a wizard."

Marlon shook his head. "It's the ring, not me."

"Oh yeah? Take it off and do it again."

Marlon pulled the ring off and gave it to Pandora before flicking his hand at the lake. This time the water rose slightly, waves crashing against the bank. Marlon stumbled backward as the ducks and swans screeched fearfully, Pandora clapping for her brother.

"And you act like magic doesn't exist!"

"Shut up 'Dora," he muttered. "I thought it was the ring."

"It only glowed because it acknowledged your power, Marlon."

"You know a lot!" he said, then he paused. "What about you?"

"Me?" she said tonelessly. "What about me?"

"Don't play innocent. I know you've been doing magic in your bedroom," said Marlon, smirking at her. "I saw the box glowing."

"So?"

"So I want to see you do something. Come on 'Dora, I know you can."

Pandora hesitated. "Will you tell Dad?"

"And get in trouble? Hell no."

"Promise?"

"I promise, Pandora. Now show me the magic!"

Pandora pulled her wand out of her inside pocket, pointed it at a swan as she thought of that Disney film Bambi and said *"Alterio!"*

BANG!!

Marlon yelped, staring at the doe. "Whoa!"

Pandora smiled, waving her wand. Smoke swirled around the doe, soon clouding it from view. The wind blew seconds later, clearing the smoke. Marlon gasped as the swan stared at them haughtily before splashing back into the lake and swimming away.

"Marlon! Pandora!"

They whirled round, staring at their father's angry face.

* * *

"Give me the wand, Pandora." Ted held out his hand. "Now."

"No."

"Now!"

"No!"

"Give me the wand!"

"Don't shout at her!" said Marlon angrily, pulling his sister away from Ted. "Don't give it to him, Pandora. He's jealous."

"Jealous!" spluttered Ted. "You think I'm jealous of you two?"

"Yes!" said Marlon angrily. "What's wrong with being-"

"Nothing," said Miriam desperately, thinking of Dreamer. "Nothing!"

"Don't encourage them, Miriam!" said Ted angrily, glaring at her.

"I'm not, Ted." Miriam did her best to stay calm, using her mentor technique. "Dreamer was my friend at school and college; I've seen worse than what Marlon and Pandora was doing."

"You're not helping," he said furiously. "Give Dreamer's wand, 'Dora!"

"It's mine now, Dad!" Pandora pocketed the wand, backing away. "Mine, ok? You're not taking it away from me!"

"Pandora-"

"Stay back- stay back or I'll hex you!"

"Ditto," said Marlon, joining his sister's side. "Stay right back, Dad."

Ted stared at them, then he turned to Miriam.

"I've lost my kids in the blink of an eye."

"No you haven't-"

"Do you know why I can't stand magic? Do you?"

"No I don't-"

"Because their grandfather killed my parents!" spat Ted, Miriam recalling what Dreamer told her.

"It was an accident, Miriam! They jumped in front of the spy to save him-Ted nearly jumped as well but Mama dragged him back-"

"And if they think I'm going to let them follow his footsteps, they've got another thing coming!"

"It was an accident, Ted!"

"Accident my back foot! He never liked my parents because they didn't have an ounce of magic in them-" Ted took a deep breath, then he said "Then he just disappeared!"

Miriam tried to calm him. "Dreamer told me what happened already-"

"No justice!" said Ted angrily, stamping his foot. "When the police and ambulance got there they said it was a double stroke-"

"Ted-"

"And now they want to be just like Paul!"

Pandora recoiled, then she turned and sprinted away.

"Pandora!" shouted Marlon, but she didn't look back. "See what you've done?" he yelled at Ted, before he ran after his sister. "Pandora!"

Pandora sped up, turning a corner out of sight.

Marlon skidded on one leg, swearing violently. Passers by stared at him, alarmed as they quickened their pace. Marlon didn't care if he looked mad, he was furious as he stormed back over to his father.

"Now what?!"

* * *

Stuffing a pen and notepad into her rucksack with her golden box and spell book, Pandora added some clothes and her teddy.

Wiping tears of anger off her face, she looked at Dreamer's picture.

"Is that what he thought of magic- even when you met him?"

This time the picture didn't do a thing.

"It's not bad," said Pandora angrily. "It's wonderful. *You're* wonderful."

Suddenly Dreamer's voice rolled around her bedroom.

Where are you going, Pandora, when you fear people?

"I'm leaving!"

For how long?

"Two days!" she said furiously, noticing a frown on Dreamer's face in her picture. "Don't try and stop me either, Mum!"

Where will you stay, darling?

"I'll sleep in the park!"

And what will you do if a stranger wakes you up?

"I... I'll run away!"

Fine, what will you do if the police *wake you up?*

"I'll still run away," sighed Pandora, sitting on her bed.

Think about it, Pandora. You can't go anywhere.

"Did Grandpa really kill Dad's parents?" she asked, eyes filling.

It was an accident, darling.

"But that's why Dad hates magic, though. Right?"

He loved it before the incident, Dreamer replied. *Yes.*

"Well, he can't stop me from being a witch and Marlon a wizard."

I know.

"He hated you doing magic too, I remember."

Because it reminds him of your grandfather, that's all.

"That's all?"

That's all, Pandora. Now go and wash your face.

* * *

"You selfish git!" spat Marlon, Miriam standing between him and Ted with her arms held out. James was there as well, holding Marlon back as he said "She could be anywhere, thanks to you!"

"Me!"

"Yes, you! Trying to dump your burdens on us- why don't you go and talk to Miriam in her office or something?! Pandora was so calm and relaxed today before you messed it all up!"

She was? James thought to himself. That's good. She still hasn't called or texted me, though. Obviously she doesn't want to know.

"Let go of me, James!"

"Let's keep it cool, Marlon!" said James, scared that his friend would swing for his dad. "I've got a car, we can look for Pandora!"

Before Marlon could answer he, Ted and Miriam jumped at the same time, their beloved Dreamer's voice echoing inside their heads.

She's at home. Go to her.

"What was that?" demanded James, as they looked at each other. "You looked like frogs or something!"

Heart racing, Marlon said "Go home, James. I'll call you."

Breathing heavily, Ted added "Visit in a few days time- we need to be alone right now. There's things we need to sort out."

"I want to see Pandora," said Miriam quietly. "What if she heard…?"

They looked at each other, then they sprinted away.

James looked down at the picnic basket, picking it up as he called

"I'll just hold onto this for you, yeah?"

They didn't look back.

* * *

"Pandora!" yelled Ted, bursting through the front door with Marlon and Miriam behind. "'Dora, are you all right?" Silence. "Pandora!"

"I'm in the bathroom!" she called angrily. "Leave me alone!"

"Hurry up and come out!" said Marlon desperately- he dashed up the stairs as soon as the bathroom door opened and pulled Pandora clean off her feet, giving her a tight hug. "Are you all right?"

"I'm fine," she mumbled into his shoulder. "I heard Mum talking-"

"So did we, so did we- she told us you're here-"

"I thought you would run away," said Ted, relieved to see his daughter safe and sound even though it can't have been over an hour.

Pandora almost didn't answer him. He knew her well.

"I would have, but Mum stopped me."

"But she's dead," whispered Miriam. "I can't figure this out."

"Put me down Marlon," muttered Pandora, and he did. Tightening her robe, she said "She might be alive, Miriam. I told you already."

"And if she is," Marlon said like before as he rubbed his neck, "She's got some explaining to do. I mean serious explaining, mind you."

Ted opened his mouth to ask about the wand, then he closed it.

Now wasn't the time.

* * *

Two days later, Alice Pets walked into the clinic her father owned as Pandora was walking out. They banged into each other, both of them stumbling backwards. Steadying herself, Alice said "Sorry for that."

Pandora said nothing, staring at her. Alice hesitated, then she asked "Are you ok?"

Pandora nodded, backing away slowly. Alice stepped closer.

"Are you sure?"

Pandora's back hit Miriam's door- fumbling for the doorknob, she opened it and ran inside, quickly closing the door behind her.

Miriam turned, surprised. "Pandora, what-"

"There's a girl out there," said Pandora, panic stricken. "She was- was-"

"What?"

"Talking to me!"

Miriam laughed. She couldn't help it as she opened the door and looked out. Alice had a confused look on her face as she came over, asking "Is she ok? I didn't mean to scare her, I-"

"She's fine," said Miriam soothingly. "How are you, Alice?"

"Never mind me- what's wrong with that girl?"

"She's not used to socialising with people," Miriam explained. "Pandora's been through a lot- but really, under the shyness she's a wonderful girl to know."

"I'll bet," said Alice, already intrigued. "Pandora's such a cool name."

"Would you like to come in and say hello?"

Pandora shook her head, but Alice said "Can I?"

"Miriam, please don't let her in!" hissed Pandora, but Miriam ignored her. Pandora backed away as Alice walked in. Smiling, Miriam said "Pandora love, this is Alice Pets. She's Tony's daughter."

"Hello," said Pandora nervously, and Alice said hello.

"Pandora's a really cool name, you know. I wish I had it."

"Oh- thank you," said Pandora shyly, and Alice smiled at her.

"Who gave it to you?"

"My mother," said Pandora, nodding at a picture on Miriam's desk.

Alice looked, then she gasped. "That's Dreamer Black!"

"You know her?" said Pandora, amazed. "From where?"

"She's been on the telly before on her mother's show-"

Pandora was confused.

"Grandma had a show?"

"She still does," said Alice. "You know, one of those clairvoyant shows. Last week it was Agnes versus Mystic Meg-"

"You're kidding!"

"No no, I'm serious! Dreamer was there, and-"

Miriam choked on her coffee, Pandora looking frightened.

"My Mum was on the show?"

"She's always on the show," said Alice, shrugging. "Sometimes she takes over. I can't believe she's your mum, she's so cool and-"

"She's alive," said Pandora weakly, and Alice frowned at her.

"Who said she wasn't?"

"Alice love, how long has Dreamer been on the show?" asked Miriam.

Alice thought about this. "About six months now."

"Six months," said Pandora. "She's been around for six months!"

"Pandora, I'm sure Alice would like to know what on Earth you're talking about," said Miriam gently, and Alice nodded. "How about you two go for a quick walk in the park? I'll meet you there in half an hour: I need to lock the office and tell Tony not to worry about Alice."

"I'm eighteen," pouted Alice. "You don't have to explain to Daddy."

"Yes I do," smiled Miriam. "Go on, both of you."

Pandora hesitated. "But... I don't know her."

"You do now," said Miriam firmly. "Pandora, Alice has just told you Dreamer is alive- you owe her a conversation. She wants to know you."

"Be your friend," corrected Alice, and Pandora sighed her ok.

* * *

"I witnessed the whole thing," said Pandora, tears falling down her face.
"Stile killed her. He- he wouldn't stop stabbing her- maybe he couldn't
stop. I was screaming at him to stop and he- he-"
Alice's eyes filled over as she handed her new friend a tissue.
"I never knew, I-"
Pandora shook her head, understanding.
"They covered it up big time, because she was a witch. They couldn't let
that get out, the stuck up little gits."
Alice thought about this, then she said "But Pandora, listen for a minute.
Dreamer's a witch, right?" Pandora nodded. "You can't seriously have
thought she was gone forever. A while maybe, but not forever!"
"I know, it's stupid now." Pandora wiped her eyes, then she said "There's
some other things I want to tell you, if you're not scared."
"I'm not scared of anything," said Alice boldly, and Pandora smiled.
"Neither am I."

* * *

Alice was totally impressed. "So you're a witch like Dreamer?"
"Yep." Pandora paused. "I'm not as powerful as her, though."
"And your brother's a wizard- his name's Marlon, right?"
"Uh-huh."
Alice counted everything off on her fingers. "You're a witch. Your big
brother's a wizard. You've got a wand, a spell book and a box."
"That's right."
"Your father hates magic because your grandpa killed his parents-"
"When he loved it before," Pandora added. "Go on?"
"Dreamer's been talking to all of you, Miss Hughes included," said Alice.
"And you lot was all scared because you thought she was dead, but she's
alive- she's been around for six months-"
Pandora didn't respond to that. She still couldn't believe it.
"And you and Marlon performed magic right here in this park, in this
spot- in broad daylight," said Alice, frowning. "Are you nuts?"
"We wasn't thinking," mumbled Pandora, and Alice looked at her. Then
she said "How many spells do you know, then?"
"There's hundreds in the spell book," Pandora said cautiously, not
wanting to give an actual number. "I just haven't practiced a lot of them."
"Ok, how many have you practiced?" probed Alice, and Pandora
mumbled something. "What?"

"Just one," she muttered. "I'm only really good at one of them."

"Can I see it?" Alice asked eagerly, and Pandora smirked at her.

"In broad daylight?"

Alice pouted. "I only said that to sound mature."

"Yeah, sure."

"Come on, let me see it. What does it do?"

"It changes something into something else."

"Like bread into toast?"

Pandora rolled her eyes. "Did I say I've got a toaster?"

"No," said Alice, face growing hot. "Sorry."

"My Mum turned a guy into a frog once, at college."

"Wow! Stuff like that?"

"Stuff like that."

Shaking her head, Pandora pulled out her wand. Then she smiled.

"What's your favourite animal?"

"Bunny rabbit," said Alice happily, then she stopped as Pandora stared at her. "What? Come on, they're cute! And I love Bugs Bunny."

"I stopped loving him when I turned thirteen- but I love Disney."

"So do I!"

"Are you sure it has to be a rabbit, Alice?"

"I'm sure. Wait!" Alice looked around, then she said "A blue one."

Pandora smiled at her, saying "Now we're talking. Ok, here goes."

She looked at the swans and ducks, then she pouted.

"They're all in the water!"

"I've got some bread right here," said Alice, rummaging in her bag.

"Alice. Why exactly do you have bread in your shoulder bag?"

Alice smiled innocently. "To feed the ducks."

Pandora couldn't help smiling back. "I like you."

"Ditto," she said happily. "I think we're going to be real good friends."

"Don't throw all of it in the water," instructed Pandora, deliberately not answering that. "Leave some pieces by the edge, let them come out."

Alice obeyed.

Pandora's green eyes sparkled as she watched the birds swim over.

"Suckers."

As soon as a swan hopped onto the bank she flicked her wand, saying *"Alterio!"*

BANG!!

Passers by ducked immediately, while Alice squealed "It's mine!"

Pandora casually slipped her wand back in her jacket as people looked over curiously, Alice scooping the rabbit up and cuddling him.

"Can I keep him? Oh Pandora, let me keep him!"

"Ask your Dad, not me," said Pandora through gritted teeth: people were beginning to stare at her. "Where did you find it, Alice?"

"What? Oh- by the water," she said, catching on. "Over there."

Looking at the rabbit as it twitched it's purple nose, Pandora suddenly wanted one too. Alice sprinkled more bread a few minutes later, tricking the birds into coming back.

"Alterio!"

BANG!!

Pandora smiled at the rabbit, jet black with blue eyes. "Gorgeous."

"I'm calling mine Barclays," said Alice happily. "Because he's blue."

"Barclays?" said Pandora, amused. "Shouldn't it be Sky?"

"Nope! You know that bank Barclays, it's theme colour is blue, right?"

"Oh, right."

Pandora cuddled her bunny, Alice saying "What about yours?"

"I'm calling him Shadow," Pandora said fondly, then she saw Miriam.

"Uh oh. What's Miriam going to say when she sees them?"

"Tell her like it is," said Alice determinedly, and Pandora laughed.

"Miriam, I just turned two swans into baby bunnies."

"Did you really?" said Miriam, not really focusing on the rabbits in their arms. "We need to go to your house now, Pandora. Right now."

"Why?"

"We have to tell Ted and Marlon Dreamer's alive."

* * *

"Six months ago? SIX FLIPPING MONTHS AGO?!!"

"Dad, calm down!"

"I can't believe it," said Marlon weakly, staring at the screen. "Mum…"

Dreamer Black laughed on screen, Agnes as well.

"Mama, stop that."

"Now now Dreamer, don't tell me to stop. Take a break."

"But Mama-!"

The audience laughed, Agnes as well.

"No buts, Dreamer Black- go and make me some coffee."

"We've got a phone call, Mama. Hello?"

"Hello Dreamer, this is Mark."

"Hello Mark," Dreamer said warmly. "How can I help you?"

"I've been feeling really depressed lately, and-"

"You fell out with your close friend?"

"I- yes," he said shyly. "Good riddance-"

"No darling," said Dreamer gently, Agnes scowling at her. "She's your soul mate, Mark. It's not me you should be talking to, it's her."

"But-"

"You both said some things you didn't mean, but the truth is you need each other the same way I need my…" Dreamer paused, then she said "What you need to do, Mark, is hang up right now and call Sarah before it's too late. The clock's ticking. At eight o clock on the dot she'll get a phone call from a previous lover- time isn't on your side."

"Thank you so much, Dreamer."

"You're welcome. Goodbye now."

"Bye."

"Isn't she great?" said Alice happily as she cuddled Barclays.

"Yeah she is," said Marlon wistfully. "Can we call them up, Dad?"

Ted didn't know what to say. Yes, and talk to the woman he'd almost gone mad over he was so in love, or no and let the kids hate him? Instead he glanced at Alice, saying "Thank you very much, er…"

"Alice," she said, at Pandora's side. "You're welcome."

"I don't know how much longer I could have-" Ted stopped abruptly, looking from Alice to Pandora and back. "Friends, Pandora?"

"I met her at the clinic," said Pandora shyly, and Marlon cheered.

"Everything's going from good to brilliant!"

Alice blushed, saying "I hope I can see Pandora again."

"Of course you can," said Ted warmly. "Pandora?"

"We had fun today," started Pandora, "And I'm glad I met Alice, but-"

"But?" said Marlon, heat rising. *"But?* 'Dora, she just gave us the key! Now we know Mum's alive, ok? What more you do want?"

"She might not like me after a while," said Pandora flatly, as if Alice wasn't even in the room. "You can't say she will."

"You can't say she won't," Marlon shot back. "Hermit."

"Camel mouth."

"Enough," said Ted sharply, as Marlon opened his mouth. "Alice?"

"I- I really like Pandora," stammered Alice. "She gave me Barclays."

"She did?" said Ted, eyes narrowing. He knew what that meant.

Pandora hugged Shadow fiercely, stepping away from him.

"So I cast a spell. So what?"

"Don't take that tone with *me,* young lady."

"Pandora, I'd really like to see you again," said Alice cautiously, and Pandora's green eyes flicked onto her. "If that's ok?"

"Well, I... I mean I just-"

Ted glared at her. Marlon glared at her. Miriam pouted.

"Take my number," sighed Pandora, and everyone smiled.

* * *

"Welcome to the Amazing Agnes cabaret. You will be put through to Agnes in exactly thirty seconds. Please choose now whether you'd like this call to go live or be private."
"Private!" hissed Pandora and Marlon at the same time, anxious.
"For a private talk, press one. For a live-"
Ted pressed one before the operator could finish, heart racing. This was it. In seconds, he would be speaking to his wife.
"Agnes speaking. How may I help- oh Lord."
"Agnes, put Dreamer on the phone," said Ted desperately, knowing she was shocked to find him calling. "Please- we need to talk."
"Of course, darling. How are you and the children?"
"We've been better," said Ted, as Miriam pulled Alice's arm.
"It's time to go, darling."
Alice nodded, whispering goodbye to Pandora. She hardly heard, not that Alice cared. The front door closed softly as Dreamer spoke.
"Hello?"
"Mum!" burst out Pandora, as Ted said "Dreamer, how could you-"
"You're alive!" said Marlon furiously. "Come home right now, Mum!"
"Marlon sweetheart, you don't under-"
"Oh yeah I do! You'd rather talk to strangers than your family!"
"How could you be around for six months and not call?" asked Ted, while Pandora said "Playing with our minds as well- that was mean."
"I wasn't playing with your minds, Pandora-"
"We thought you was dead," whispered Pandora. "I had nightmares six months longer than I needed to-"
"Pandora-"
"I'm just glad you're alive," she muttered, more to herself than to her mother. "You'll come home now, right Mum?" Silence. "Right?"
"Sweetie, I'm helping your grandmother with her work-"
"Do you need money, Dreamer?" Ted asked. "I can give you whatever-"
"It's not about money," started Dreamer, but she was cut off again.
"Come home." said Marlon sadly. "Stuff the work, just come home."
Pandora turned and left as he spoke, going upstairs.
Her bedroom door slammed shut as Marlon got up, leaving too.
His door slammed shut seconds later.
"This is why I didn't come," said Dreamer sadly. "Ted?"
"I'm here," he said quietly. "Dreamer, I... we need to talk."
"The past is the past," Dreamer said just as quietly. "We need to put it behind us if we want to look to the future."
Ted smiled at that. Dreamer was full of logic.

"But… I just want to know why."

"Why what?"

"You know what, Dreamer. How could you betray me? I thought I was a good husband, I thought you loved me."

"You sound like a woman, Ted. I don't want to talk about it."

"I- I sound like a woman?" spluttered Ted. "Dreamer, I-"

"Be man enough to put it behind you," Dreamer said. "Ok Teddy Bear?"

"I will if you come home."

"I don't have a key to your new house."

"You can get one when you get here."

Dreamer laughed. "I *am* here, Ted. Open the door."

Ted whipped round, staring at the front door fearfully. "Seriously?"

"Seriously. Open the door, it's cold."

Ted hung up right there and then, Marlon and Pandora walking down the stairs slowly, almost trance like. They could sense their mother's presence.

"Dad, open the door," said Marlon, Pandora as well. Her eyes were red.

Ted took a deep breath, then he opened the door.

Though he had a deep voice, Marlon's scream was high pitched. Dreamer Black laughed at his face, opening her arms.

"Come here, Marlon."

Marlon sped down the stairs immediately, lunging for his mother. Dreamer held him like he was still ten years old, shushing him gently.

"I thought you was dead!"

"I was, darling."

"But you're here! How?"

Dreamer smiled. "A powerful woman never reveals her secrets."

Pandora hugged Shadow, backing up the stairs. She was dreaming. Dreamer's eyes locked on hers, making her freeze.

"Come here, Pandora. You're not scared?"

"I'm not awake," mumbled Pandora, and Dreamer laughed.

"Come here this instant, young lady."

Pandora handed Shadow to Ted before she did a Marlon, rushing at her mother. Dreamer held her children as they wept, her eyes filling over.

"I'm here now," she said softly, kissing them both. "I'm here."

Across the road, Miriam watched her friend reunite with her family. Dreamer was back after three years and one month, and one day.

Miriam couldn't help feeling bitter. It was all going so well! Now Pandora would forget all about her, and Dreamer would most likely keep her away just as she did before. And Marlon seemed to like Miriam too, but he'd forget as well. And Ted. The bitter feeling grew as his front door closed, Miriam walking away slowly. There could have been a greater

friendship between them, but now Dreamer was back from the grave...
Miriam chastised herself for thinking such selfish thoughts.

"I should be glad," she said to herself. "Glad for Pandora especially."

The words meant little to her right now. Miriam's eyes filled as she walked back to the clinic in time for her six o clock meeting.

When she got there Alice was arguing with her father.

"I'll keep him in my room, Daddy! You won't know he's there!"

"No pets for the last time, especially furry ones!"

"Why not??"

"Because I'm al- al- *atchoo!* Allergic and *atchoo!* I don't like them!"

Alice shielded Barclays as her father sneezed, Miriam handing him a tissue glumly.

"Thank you, Miriam. How is your godchild?"

"Pandora? She's fine," said Miriam sadly. "She won't be coming back."

"What!" exploded Tony. "Why not?!"

"Because she's just reunited with her mother," sighed Miriam. "And her mother was the reason she had to come in the first place."

Tony frowned at her. "Dreamer Black is dead."

"Not anymore," said Alice smugly. "She's back."

"Nonsense," scoffed Tony. "All of it. She died three years ago!"

"She's a witch," said Miriam miserably. "Meaning she wouldn't have been gone forever. It's a pain, isn't it?"

Tony knew she was thinking of Pandora, and he let her go into her office without another word on the subject. Turning to Alice, he said "You can keep the rabbit if you go to college this September."

"I was going anyway," smirked Alice. "Thank you Daddy!"

"I want to see Dreamer," said Tony, almost to himself. "I'll call."

"Dreamer's got a man," Alice reminded him. "Don't forget, Daddy."

Tony glared at her. "You sound like your mother, Alice. Get ready to go."

"I'm ready, Dad. Oh, wait! Can I call Pandora?"

"No," said Tony, thinking about the money he made from Pandora's coming to his clinic. "If what Miriam says is true, then she needs to be alone with her family. Hopefully she'll want to talk sooner or later."

* * *

"Kids, go to your room," Ted said a few hours later, and Pandora and
Marlon got up obediently. Then they scowled at each other, thinking the
same thing: now that Dreamer was back, they couldn't listen on the stairs.
Dreamer watched them go with a smile on her beautiful face.
"They've grown so much."
"I know," said Ted. "Dreamer, we need to talk."
"What about?"
"Well... I- you-"
"Ted, if I could go back in time and stop myself from doing what I did, I
would." Dreamer sighed longingly. "Mama won't teach me."
"It's not that." Ted hesitated, then he said "I've missed you."
"I've missed you too."
"Why didn't you come six months earlier?"
"I was afraid of giving one of you a heart attack," smiled Dreamer, and
Ted smiled back. "The days turned into weeks, then months."
"And Agnes didn't even call."
"You told her you don't want her near Pandora or Marlon, Ted."
"It was the magic phobia all over again," said Ted, looking away as she
frowned at him. "I'm sorry I offended your mother, Dreamer."
"She forgives you," Dreamer replied. "Do you forgive me?"
Ted knew the question was much deeper than it sounded. Dreamer waited
patiently as he looked at her, not breaking the silence. Then-
"Yes," he said softly. "I forgive you."
Dreamer's eyes filled over. "I'm sorry, Ted. I'm so sorry."
Ted pulled her close to him and held her, saying "It was partly my fault.
Miriam told me everything-"
Dreamer stiffened in his arms at her name. "Miriam?"
"Yes, Dreamer. Your friend from school and college?"
He waited fearfully, wondering if Miriam was a fraud.
"Pandora's godmother," Dreamer said, sighing as she let him go. "She
told you everything about Damon?" He said yes. "Everything?"
"Yes," he said painfully. It still hurt like heck. "Everything."
Dreamer decided not to take the conversation further, turning to look
around the living room self consciously.
"You have a nice house."
"We couldn't stay in Westport," Ted replied, a little colder than he meant.
"Yes, I know," said Dreamer. "A lot happened to the family in that
town."
"To Pandora especially. Too much things happened to her there."

Ted stopped as Dreamer looked at him, pain in her expression.

"I had dreams about it- what Damon was doing to her. I tried to tell myself they were just horrid nightmares, Ted- I tried."

Angry tears coursed down her face, Ted listening silently.

"The dreams were getting worse, and then- then-"

Ted knew Dreamer had suffered as much as their daughter did.

"You don't have to go on, Dreamer. But… I really want to know."

"Mama called me. She had the dreams too."

"Dreamer, I'm your husband. Why didn't you tell me about them?"

Dreamer gave him a look so cold Ted shivered.

"Tell you, Ted? You, when you hate anything like that?"

Ted immediately felt a twinge of regret. Glaring at him, Dreamer continued "It all came to me the minute Mama called. Why he was always asking for Pandora. Why he always wanted us over- just us two, never Marlon or you after a while. I came just in time: Pandora was against his wall. I was so angry, Ted- I shouldn't have done it."

"Done what?"

"What Papa did that night when we had dinner with your parents."

"Good," said Ted fiercely, making her start in surprise. "What else?"

"I was in such a rage I told him I never cared for him, a fling is a fling and nothing more." Dreamer smiled, an evil smile. Ted swallowed as she said "I knew I was going to die that night- I even conjured the machete for him. I gave him a sporting chance, wanting to infuriate him- but suddenly he grabbed the knife and went for my baby."

"Pandora," whispered Ted, Dreamer's face still stone cold.

"He was mad enough to slice and stab her, Ted. That angry."

"Pandora was…"

"On the verge of death," Dreamer said bitterly. "He had his chance to kill me right then."

"What happened?"

"She was on the floor," Dreamer said coldly, then she stopped as she sensed her children just outside the living room door. Pandora and Marlon had been listening since their father said Miriam's name.

Pandora was weeping silently, in her brother's arms. Hearing her mother's voice again brought the tears on, but having to relive the horror of Westport made everything worse. Marlon hugged her fiercely, desperate for her to stop trembling, but her body wouldn't oblige.

"Go on Dreamer," urged Ted. "She was on the floor. Then what?"

"I turned my back on him- I had to. She would have died before my eyes if I didn't heal her- and then Damon stabbed me in the side."

Ted winced, as did Marlon and Pandora. "Then?"

"Magic left my body for a split second," said Dreamer sadly. "I lit up,

Pandora screamed because she knew what just happened, and Damon realised if he kept stabbing me I'd be mortal for longer and longer-"

"I told him to stop," sobbed Pandora, not caring if they heard. "I told him, Marlon- I swear I told him not to hurt her- he wouldn't listen-"

"He wouldn't listen," Dreamer repeated smoothly, holding up a hand to stop Ted from rushing to their child. "He knew exactly what to do. He was so angry and hurt for what I did and said, and I was livid about what he was doing to Pandora, right under my nose. But I couldn't defend myself anymore. My... my last thought was to help my little girl."

Pandora broke down, sobbing. Dreamer continued to talk as if she couldn't hear her child, and Ted had no choice but to listen.

"So I healed her with the last ounce of magic I had left: I knew that was it. I looked at my body, and I couldn't do a thing. I was mortal."

"And Damon?" said Ted disgustedly. "What did he do?"

"He stared at me, then he screamed like a girl." Dreamer laughed derisively. "He realised what he just did, and he called an ambulance straight away for me and Pandora."

"What happened to Pandora?"

"She passed out," Dreamer answered, Ted saying "And Damon...?"

"Kept telling me he loved me and he was sorry." Dreamer laughed again. "He was saying he loved me, he'd make it all better and he was sorry for what he did to Pandora. He kept telling me to forgive him for everything..."

* * *

Far across the country, Damon Stile lay in his cell, staring up at the ceiling. Thinking about the love of his life and what he did to her.

"Dreamer, I'm sorry!" cried Damon, grabbing her hand. "I'm sorry!"

She didn't respond, though she was still conscious. Damon squeezed her hand, saying "I love you so much, Dreamer! I love you!"

"P-Pandora-"

"Her as well, I shouldn't have done it-"

"H-how could you, Damon?"

"I'll make everything better, I promise," he wept. "I'm sorry, Dreamer!"

"S-sorry won't exactly h-heal me now, w-will it?"

"I know, but... doesn't it make the situation a little lighter?"

If Dreamer had the energy she would have slapped him senseless. Instead, she glared at him as she said "You, Damon... are sick."

Damon flinched. "Dreamer-"

She winced, but otherwise ignored him. "D-deluded tosspot-"

"Don't, Dreamer!"

"Blasted evil s-son of a-"

"Stop it!" he said, shaking her, making her cry out in pain. "Dreamer?"

Dreamer turned her head to look at her child, who lay motionless on the floor. Her fingers twitched: she was coming round.

"I thought you loved me," wept Damon, and Dreamer looked at him.

"This is i-ironic. There's an- an album Marlon has..."

Damon rocked back and forth, holding her hand as he listened.

"Called... Pain is Love."

She gathered enough energy to smile at him, a cruel smile.

"You... you love me and I'm in s-so much pain. Get the joke?"

Pandora's scream made Damon jump as Dreamer's eyes closed.

"You killed her!"

Before Damon could retort the front doorbell rang: Dreamer was unconscious. Pandora was too weak to get up: Damon staggered to his feet. The bell rang again, more urgently as police sirens sounded in the distance.

"Ambulance! Is everything all right in there?"

"Help us, help! Mum, wake up," sobbed Pandora. "Wake up!"

Dreamer didn't respond.

Seconds later paramedics surrounded Dreamer's punctured body, some around Pandora. She was greatly distressed. Damon couldn't answer anything, nothing at all. He stumbled into his bathroom, looking into the mirror- only it was Dreamer staring back at him.

And she smiled viciously.

"I've got you right where I want you, Damon Stile."

Damon stared at her, mouth hanging open. Then he ran back onto the landing to stare at Dreamer's lifeless body, being lifted onto a stretcher. She was unconscious. Heart racing, he ran back into the bathroom.

Dreamer was still there, looking very much awake.

"You hurt my child, Damon."

"You're going to die," he said miserably, not caring about Pandora. He'd stopped caring the minute Dreamer's lips touched his. "I murdered you!"

"You think?" she said sarcastically. "The police are waiting for you."

"What should I do?"

"You've no choice but to let them arrest you: Pandora said it was you."

"That little-"

"Don't insult my daughter!!"

Damon's mouth snapped shut. Even though she was gone and this was just some sort of magical hoax, he still thought Dreamer could hurt him.

"I could deny everything, say it was a burglar."

"You think you could live with it?" Dreamer asked icily. "Knowing you murdered someone and got off free? Knowing you killed me?"

"You killed our baby," said Damon, tears falling. "Our firstborn!"

"I already have a firstborn," Dreamer said nastily. "And it wasn't a baby, Damon. Just a small group of cells. I practically starved myself hoping for a miscarriage, did you know that? I'm a cruel Mummy, aren't it?"

Damon stared at her, shocked. "You- you're just angry right now."

"I'm having the time of my life," Dreamer answered. "Now, as I wait to be placed in another realm, I can watch you suffer like you deserve to."

There was a knock on the bathroom door: Dreamer's face dissolved. Damon stood staring at his stunned reflection, merely nodding to every question the police asked him. He didn't try and bolt, or lie about anything. He let them handcuff him without a fuss, revelling in Dreamer's cruel words. He actually thought he'd be safer in prison.

Now, as he lay in on the top bunk in his cell, he shook his head.

"I must be nuts to love that witch."

"She's dead," his roommate George muttered thickly from underneath him: for three years he'd had to endure Damon's talk of Dreamer Black, every day and night for the first year. Beating Damon every night wouldn't stop him, but reminding him she was gone would.

And it always worked: Damon fell silent.

Yes, Dreamer was dead and gone. All because of his uncontrollable rage, everything hitting him hard. She got rid of his baby. She didn't love him. She knew about what he'd been doing to Pandora. She swore she'd kill him on the spot even. So maybe he was defending himself...

Damon laughed and shook his head. It was hard coming out of denial- it took two years and George to help him. He wasn't defending himself, not when Dreamer wasn't even looking at him, when her back was turned towards him. Not when she was seeing to her daughter.

Damon smiled, rolling over. "I really must be mad to love her, George."

"She's dead, damn it!"

"I know," sighed Damon, closing his eyes. "I know."

* * *

Pandora stood at the door, holding Shadow the rabbit. Dreamer was fast
asleep; Ted was wide awake in an armchair across the room. He was
staring at his former wife, deep in thought. Pandora wondered whether to
go back to bed, but something told her she should stay.
"Dad?"
Ted jumped, looking at her. Then he smiled at her.
"Come here, 'Dora."
Pandora hesitated, then she stepped into the room. She felt light headed
just for a few seconds, then she carried on walking. She knew it was her
mother's energy that made her body feel weird, so she didn't respond to
the sensation. Pandora made sure she sat on the carpet, away from her
father. Just because Dreamer was back it didn't mean Pandora changed.
Ted realised that, because he asked "No goodnight hug?"
"No."
"What did you want to say, then?"
"I um... I just wanted to ask-"
"Dad," mumbled Marlon, walking in. "We need to talk about all of this."
"Camel mouth had a nightmare," Pandora translated, trying not to laugh
at Ted's puzzled face. "He's trying to cover it up."
Dreamer slept on, Marlon looking at her.
"What if she goes away again? Did you lot sort it out properly?"
No, Ted answered silently, but he said "Of course we did."
"So we're a family again?" asked Pandora, looking at Dreamer as well.
"We was always a family, whether your mother was here or not, 'Dora."
"I told James everything," Marlon told Ted. "If that's ok."
"Some people must have known she was alive," Pandora muttered as she
put Shadow down. "Come on, she was broadcasted all over the world."
Marlon nodded, watching as the rabbit scurried around happily.
"True."
"What did you want to ask, Pandora?" Ted asked his daughter.
"I... well, now that Mum's back-"
Pandora stopped abruptly as Dreamer rose, almost in slow motion.
"Hey Mum," said Marlon softly. "Have a good sleep?"
"Fine, darling. Why aren't you in bed?" asked Dreamer curiously,
looking from him to Pandora and back, then at the clock. "It's almost-"
"Five," said Ted quickly, and they smiled at him. He so wanted to be in
Dreamer's good books, but there was something holding him back a little.
Excusing himself, he went downstairs.

* * *

The phone rang right next to Miriam's head, making her jump. Fumbling for her lamp, she turned it on and grabbed the phone before it gave her a splitting headache. Swallowing to moisturise her dry throat, she whispered "Hello?"

"Miriam, it's Ted."

"Ted?" she said, not sure if she heard right. "Pandora's Ted?"

"Yes. I needed to talk to someone."

"Well why don't you talk to your wife?" she said coldly. "After all, she is back- why would you talk to me when she's in your life again?"

"I know you think she'll take us- I mean, Pandora away from you again-"

"Go figure."

"But she won't this time, I promise she won't. I won't let her."

"Do you forget who your wife is, Ted? Or did the three years apart deflate your brain?" Miriam asked in mock concern. "She's a witch, remember? And in the background, I've watched and listened to how she plays you like a puppet on a string. I know so much about Dreamer, you'd be surprised. Maybe she doesn't even love you." Then she covered her mouth. "Ted, I'm sorry. I didn't mean it to come out like that-"

"It's fine," he said reassuringly. "It makes a nice change from the mentor composure, anyway. I didn't know you were hurting inside, Miriam."

"I'm not," she lied. "I... fine, I'm a teeny bit jealous of Dreamer, because she has Pandora- and she *will* keep her away from me, Ted. I know it."

"But why?"

"Maybe she thinks she'll lose her, I don't know."

"I'm coming to your office today, Miriam. I really do need to talk."

"Never mind the office," she said, knowing the clinic was ripe with gossip. They knew Dreamer was back now. If they saw Ted visiting and entering her office without Pandora, rumours would spread.

"Where, then?"

"The café in town?" suggested Miriam. "We can go there."

"Later on today?"

Miriam peered at the clock on the wall. It was twenty past five.

"In the afternoon. I need to catch up on my sleep."

"Ok. Thanks."

"Anytime."

Miriam put the phone down, yawning.

Would Ted tell Dreamer what she said? Miriam thought as she laid down. Then she decided she didn't care.

* * *

Dreamer stared out of the kitchen window, deep in thought.

She was back with her family, with who she belonged. So why didn't she feel satisfied? Yes, she was glad she was back with her children and Ted, but... something wasn't there like it was before. Something was missing. Agnes? She wondered, then she smiled and shook her head.

"Not Mama. What is it?"

She drummed her long nails on the kitchen counter, gazing outside still. A raven landed in a tree opposite the window, Dreamer looking at it.

"What's missing, Spirit? Tell me."

"You feel cold towards Ted for no reason."

"But I love him."

"Yes you do."

"What should I do?"

"Talking always helps, Dreamer Black."

Before Dreamer could retort the raven vanished.

"Dreamer?"

She turned to look at him. "Yes Ted?"

"You know Miriam's Pandora's counsellor, don't you?"

"Yes I do."

"And you and Miriam- well, you were friends."

"I know."

"Do you think Pandora should stop going to her now that you're here?"

Dreamer shrugged a shoulder, turning back to the window.

"It's up to Pandora, not me."

"But... don't you even-"

"Even what, Ted?"

"You almost sound like you're not bothered."

"I'm not."

The words were out before she could stop them. Ted stared at his wife's back, amazed.

"What the hell happened to you?"

"Something died in me the night Damon killed me. It's as simple as that."

Dreamer didn't know what was wrong with her. Neither did Ted.

"Did you even want to come back, Dreamer?"

"I don't know anymore, Ted."

"So it was all lies, then. What you said to me when you got here."

"No it wasn't."

"Something's holding you back from me, Dreamer. What is it?"

"Ted, if I knew I could tell you." Dreamer didn't even turn around. "I'm back with you at least, isn't that good enough?"

"No, because the Dreamer I knew and loved isn't back."

Hurt, Dreamer looked at him. Ted stared back at her, ready for it. Pandora and Marlon traipsed downstairs happily, then they stopped dead as Dreamer said "Maybe I should go until I find myself."
"Where will you stay?"
"That's my problem, not yours."
Ted's eyes flashed: in three strides he was right in front of her.
"Your problem is my problem."
"No it isn't."
"I'm your husband," he said angrily, hurt now. Dreamer shrugged.
"Not if the certificate was cancelled as soon as I died."
Ted stared at her. "What did you say?"
Dreamer couldn't help smirking. "You're a widower."
"Not anymore," he said heatedly. "Because you're alive."
"That's true. Now get out of my way."
"No."
"Move, Ted!"
"No!"
Dreamer pulled out an incredible wand, made of pure gold studded with diamonds. Pandora gasped at it: hers was made of silver. Obviously Dreamer was even more powerful than before she died.
"I'm not going to tell you again."
"Go on then, do it," said Ted heatedly. "Go on!"
Dreamer's wand sparked at the tip as she smiled.
"You think I won't?"
"I think you will," Ted shot back, "And I don't care. Kill me if you want, stash my body in a ditch. Cast the spell, Dreamer!"
Dreamer stared at him, then she said "It'll hurt, but it won't kill you."
"Go on then!"
"I won't if you get out of my way and let me leave you."
Ted shook his head, arms held out. "Never."
"You asked for it. *Conscendio!!"*
BANG!!
"Dad!" yelled Marlon and Pandora, smoke swirling everywhere. Coughing, they ran into the kitchen- only they soared back into the living room.
"This isn't your argument," Dreamer said softly. "Stay there."
Pandora and Marlon obediently sat on the sofa, waiting fearfully.
Behind the wall of smoke, Dreamer knelt next to Ted. "Ted?"
His eyes flickered. Blood poured from his mouth. Dreamer sighed, muttering a spell to heal him completely.
"You idiot. You really thought you could stop me, right?"
"Right," mumbled Ted, sitting up. "Because I love you, Dreamer."

"Don't," she said, emotion tearing at her. "I'm leaving."

"No you aren't."

"Yes I am, and I'm never returning."

"Follow in your father's footsteps, then," he spat, sitting up. "Come in, wave a few hexes and then leave, not caring about the damage you made. Never mind me or the kids, Pandora especially."

"Don't compare me to Papa, Ted. This isn't like that."

"No? Well Dreamer, enlighten me. Tell me what it's like."

Dreamer looked away from him, running her index up and down her wand. Ted eyed it warily, asking "Did Agnes give that to you?"

"Mama? No," Dreamer answered, looking at it. "It appeared for me as soon as I'd been with Mama for a week- after my power returned to me."

Holding cushions to their mouths, Pandora and Marlon tried to listen in the living room, on the other side of the thick wall of smoke.

"Can't hear anything," said Marlon sulkily, and Pandora moved away and sat on the sofa again. Remembering Shadow, she ran upstairs.

"Dreamer, please don't leave."

A soft smile curved Dreamer's mouth as she looked at Ted. "Why not?"

"Because it'll just drive me insane. I hear from a stranger you're alive, you turn up, and then you leave as if you didn't care about us. Like you just came to let us know you're fine before going again."

"That wasn't my intention, but now that you say it-"

"Dreamer!"

She laughed at his face. "I'm joking, Ted."

"Good," he said huffily. "You're staying, do I make myself clear?"

Staring at his angry face, Dreamer felt the aloofness leave her body. Ted pushed himself up, glaring at her.

"I asked you a question, Dreamer Black."

Lord, how she loved him. But she also loved to tease him.

"What's in it for me if I stay, Teddy Bear?"

"I'm not playing games with you, Dreamer. I-"

She kissed him before he could finish, surprising him.

* * *

Upstairs, Pandora was staring at her phone ringing. Someone was actually calling her other than Marlon or Ted. Shadow squeaked impatiently, as if trying to say "Answer it!"

Pandora reached for the phone as it stopped blaring. She smiled at Shadow, saying "Missed call."

Miriam put the phone down and picked up her cup of tea, wondering what Dreamer was doing right this minute.

* * *

Dreamer and Ted were laughing, still in the kitchen. This time Pandora and Marlon were with them, smiling broadly as they finally had breakfast at the table. Trying to sound serious, Ted said "Pandora, what was it you wanted to tell me last night- I mean, this morning?"
Pandora didn't answer him for a minute.
"Well... I just um... you saw me and Marlon in the park, right?"
"Right," said Dreamer, smiling at her children. "That was beautiful."
Pandora silently thanked her mother for boosting the situation. Dreamer winked as she picked up her cup of tea, waiting for the rest of it.
"And- and Mum's got a new wand," said Pandora. "So... can I keep-"
"Yes," said Dreamer, while Ted said "No."
"Ted!"
"Dreamer!"
They glared at each other, Dreamer saying "It was my wand, Ted."
"Was?" Pandora repeated hopefully, and Ted scowled at her.
"You are not keeping that wand, Pandora."
"Yes you are," said Dreamer, still glaring at Ted. "It's my gift to you."
"Wow! Really?" Then Pandora realised. "You made me take it."
"I certainly did."
"Me too?" asked Marlon, though he didn't say what he took.
"You too," said Dreamer, nodding. Ted wasn't having any of this.
"Kids, it's inappropriate for you to go around casting spells-"
"We won't, we swear," said Marlon, Pandora nodding. "That's a promise."
"Spells in the house and that's all," said Ted. "None in public, ok?"
"Ok," they said together, eyes shining. "Thank you, Dad."
Ted didn't respond to that, though Dreamer smiled at him.
"Look who's softening."
"Dreamer, you- I... oh, I'm going to work," he said huffily, as everyone laughed again. Sipping her tea, Dreamer said "You have a day off."
"No I don't, silly. I've got to hand in a load of paperwork and if I'm completely honest with you, I didn't even start any of it-"
The house phone went off, Marlon picking it up. "Morning."
He listened for a moment, then he said "Dad, it's your boss."
"You're fired," joked Pandora, and Ted smiled at her before taking the phone and saying "Morning John."
"Ted, this paperwork is extraordinary! Where did you find the time to..."
Ted's eyes widened as he listened to his boss rant and rave excitedly.
"We thought we'd have to let our client down, but Ted, you really went

for the kill, didn't you!"

"John, I-"

"It's amazing stuff! We'll give it to Darius to use in court-"

"But-"

"The best I've seen this summer by far, no joke about it!"

"Thank you John, but I didn't-"

"You've earned yourself a few days off for your hard work, Ted-"

"Thanks again, but I'm trying to tell you I-"

"We might just use this as an example for the trainees too-"

"John, will you listen to me for a-"

"How is the family, by the way?"

"Never been better John. About that paperwork-"

"Sorry Ted, I've got another call. Thanks for the hard work!"

"Wait!"

The line went dead, Ted placing the phone down.

"But… I didn't do any paperwork. I didn't even hand it in-"

Dreamer smirked. "Told you have a day off."

"Whoa," said Pandora, Marlon as well. "That's really cool!"

"Don't ever do that again," Ted told Dreamer sulkily. "I wanted to do it."

"Even if you did do the paperwork it'd never be as good as mine, Ted. You know that," Dreamer said smugly, and Ted scowled at her.

* * *

Pandora gazed across the lake in the park, deep in thought. Six boys walked past her, grinning broadly.

"Hi Pandora." Pandora didn't react. "Where's Marlon?"

"Leave her alone, she's crazy," another boy advised his friend. "Did you know she has to go see a shrink?"

"A shrink??"

Pandora tried her best to pretend they weren't there, but it was hard.

"A shrink and she's eighteen, can you believe that?"

"Well I don't know why she's going- shrinks are for losers and-"

"Mad people. Yeah, we know."

Pandora got to her feet, the idiots smirking at her. They only wanted to rile her because she'd blown each and every one of them off at her house, going up to her room when they tried to make conversation. This was their way of payback.

"You should've come with me when I said, Pandora."

"Never mind him," another guy interjected. "When I tried talking to you, you shunned me off. You shun off everybody."

"Because she's mad," chorused the other five. "Right Pandora?"

Taking a deep breath, Pandora turned and walked away, ignoring the boys as they whistled and called after her.

"We'll stop by later, Pandora!"

* * *

Miriam sat inside the café, waiting anxiously. Ted was almost forty minutes late- if it became an hour she was leaving.

"Can I tempt you with yet another tea?" the waiter asked, smiling at her. Miriam smiled back, saying "Make it two this time please."

"Expecting company?"

"That's right," she said, turning to look out the window.

"Miriam," a voice said softly, and she looked at the speaker.

It took all of her willpower not to scream her name.

"Dreamer!"

"That was weird," mumbled Pandora, holding her mother's hand. Both were seated at Miriam's table. Pandora was in some black jeans and a black t-shirt, already looking bored to death. She didn't acknowledge Miriam's presence, didn't even say hi. Miriam masked the hurt she felt.

"Hello Pandora."

Silence.

Dreamer looked stunning in a silver gown, as if she were attending a ball. Her diamond earrings sparkled with her bracelets and wedding ring- she looked amazing. Miriam suddenly felt very small in her comfortable jogging suit- small and unattractive.

"Don't be ridiculous," said Dreamer, reading her mind. "You look fine."

"Everyone's looking at you," mumbled Miriam, and Dreamer shrugged.

"Ignore them. How have you been?"

"I've been... ok. Pandora made up for what wasn't."

Pandora smiled but said nothing, looking at her mother.

"About Pandora," started Dreamer, and Miriam blurted "Don't! I know what you're going to say, I know it! You'll keep her away like before!"

Dreamer pretended to gaze out the window, oblivious to Miriam's voice. Pandora smirked as she finally realised how much Miriam cared for her.

"I didn't know you cared so much, Miss Hughes."

"Pandora, of course I care for you, I'm your godmother- Miss Hughes??"

"That's your name, isn't it?"

Everyone looked over- only at Miriam. Miriam suddenly realised she must look demented, as if she was talking to herself or something. The waiter nervously came and set the two cups of tea down, asking "Anything else you'd like?"

"No thank you," said Dreamer, smiling at him. "We're fine."

Feeling jealous as the waiter blushed, Miriam said "I'm hungry, actually."

Dreamer's green eyes locked on hers.

"Are you?"

"Yes I am. I'm very hungry."

"In that case bring my friend your lunchtime special," Dreamer said coolly to the waiter. "That would be your steak and kidney pie with fries, right?" The waiter nodded. "Please give her baked beans on the side and salad as well, and a large glass of cranberry juice. And a slice of your chocolate cake for dessert if there's any left when she's finished."

"Yes Ma'am."

The waiter walked away with his notepad, still red in the face.

"Why did you do that?" hissed Miriam, and Dreamer smirked at her.

"What kind of friend would I be if I let you starve, Miriam?"

Pandora laughed quietly. "Mum, you're wicked."

"Thank you darling."

Very hot in the face, Miriam said "I wouldn't have starved, Dreamer-"

"You said you were very hungry."

"I was only-"

"Be quiet."

Miriam obeyed, closing her mouth. Pandora smirked, Dreamer smiled.

"Good girl."

"This isn't like before, Dreamer!" said Miriam angrily. "I'm not tailing you like a lost puppy anymore like I did at school and college, doing everything you said-"

"Did I make you, Miriam?"

"No, but I'm letting you know things have changed!"

"I've been gone for three years," Dreamer answered. "Obviously things have changed, Miriam. You're stating the very obvious."

Pandora laughed as her mobile went off. Answering happily, she said "Pandora."

"Hey Pandora, it's Alice!"

"Hi Alice," she said tonelessly. "I didn't expect you to call so soon."

Dreamer looked at her daughter. "Have a bit of tact, Pandora."

Pandora shrugged, saying "I'm not used to callers."

"Was that Dreamer Black?" said Alice excitedly, and Pandora said yes.

"How come you're calling me, Alice?"

"Well... I thought we were friends."

Dreamer snatched the phone off her daughter, knowing full well Pandora was about to say something cutting, like "You thought wrong."

"Pandora's feeling very under the weather," she said gently. "She's just about to have her lunch, Alice, so maybe you'd like to call back?"

"Ok then. Yes Miss," said Alice humbly. "Welcome back."

"Thank you," said Dreamer, warming up to Alice instantly. She sensed Alice would be a good friend to Pandora, felt good vibes.

"Would you like to come over for dinner, maybe six o clock?"

"Yes please!"

As Dreamer and Alice conversed Miriam and Pandora stared at each other, Pandora's expression ice cold. Frightened by the look on her face, Miriam whispered "What have I done, Pandora?"

"I don't want to see you anymore. I don't need you."

Miriam fought the hurt welling up inside her. Mentor technique!

"Why is that, Pandora?" she asked as calmly as she could. "Because Dreamer's back in your life, you want to kick me to the curb?"

"Exactly. I only needed the counselling because she was gone."

Startled, Dreamer ended the phone call.

"What was that, Pandora?"

"I don't need her," said Pandora, looking at her mother. "Not anymore."

"Darling, she's your godmother."

"I don't care, and besides," sniffed Pandora, "It's not like I actually need her. More like the other way round."

Miriam's mouth hung open: this wasn't Pandora speaking.

"What happened to her, Dreamer?"

"I'm not sure," Dreamer replied, frowning at her child. "Pandora?"

Pandora's eyes filled over. "It was Marlon's friends."

"What about them?" asked Dreamer, concerned.

"They said I'm mad because I have to see a shrink."

"When was this?"

"When I went for a walk in the park after breakfast."

"Really," said Dreamer, while Miriam said "Did you tell Marlon?"

"No."

Dreamer wondered whether a curse was the solution to the situation. It would make them both feel good, but...

"Why don't we forget them for now," she said gently. "Pandora?"

Pandora said nothing, staring down at her lap. Then she nodded.

"Good girl," said Dreamer, as a large plate was set down on the table. "Now then, let's see if Miriam eats all of this food."

Miriam stared down at the plate, feeling sick.

"I- I can't eat-"

"You said you were hungry," Dreamer cut across, smile gone now. "So eat, Miriam. Or are you going to waste my money and upset me?"

Miriam didn't want to upset Dreamer at all. It felt so good being with her again, and apart from that she'd been on the receiving end of Dreamer's hexes when she was in a very bad mood for as long as she could remember. Sighing, she picked up her fork.

Pandora was amazed, but she held her tongue. She'd always seen Miriam as an independent sort of woman, who'd never take an order unless it was what she wanted. And it wasn't, but she was taking it anyway.

Dreamer couldn't help feeling smug. Good.

"So Miriam, you planned to meet my husband here?"

He's not your husband anymore, Miriam wanted to blurt out, but her mouth was full of steak and kidney pie. Swallowing hard, she gasped "That's why you're force feeding me, right? As punishment!"

"Don't be ridiculous," smirked Dreamer, as Pandora laughed. "Did you?"

"Well… yes, but it's not what it looks like-"

"What do you want it to look like?" Dreamer quipped, still smirking.

Miriam foolishly opened her mouth to say she wanted it to look like Ted was having some sort of affair with her, then she closed it. Instead she said "What it is. Just me mentoring Ted away from the clinic."

"Whatever problems he had this morning are gone," Dreamer replied. "We sorted things out, which is why he didn't bother to come."

"Oh."

Anger bubbled in the pit of her stomach. Ted didn't bother calling to say he wasn't coming- didn't even care that Miriam could have been waiting a long time for him to show up. To make things worse, Pandora said "Do you have a crush on my dad or something, Miss Hughes?"

"Don't be ridiculous, Pandora," said Miriam through gritted teeth: for the first time ever, she wanted Pandora elsewhere. "That's absurd."

"Not really, I mean you-"

"Hush," Dreamer commanded softly, and Pandora closed her mouth. "Miriam, I hope you're being honest with me."

Miriam swallowed, the she said "I am- I'm being honest-"

"Look me in my eyes and tell me you're being honest, Miriam."

Dreamer's eyes became the only things she could see, dark green whirlpools glittering in a void of darkness.

"If you aren't, I'll know. If you're planning to get your hands on Ted, I'll find out."

"I… I…" Miriam felt like she'd pass out. "I'm not… he's a friend."

"I can see that. You've helped him with Pandora."

"Yes I have," said Miriam, heat rising. "While you-"

"You know nothing about what I've been through," hissed Dreamer, making Pandora and Miriam recoil. "Nothing."

"I know enough," Miriam said bravely. "You don't deserve Ted."

The green eyes vanished, leaving Miriam staring into darkness.

"Miss? Would you like your bill?"

"What?"

Miriam blinked: she was back in the café. Dreamer was sitting in front of her, Pandora playing with her phone.

"I'm paying," Dreamer said quietly: the waiter blushed again as he handed her the bill, hands shaking. Dreamer took the paper and looked at it, then she snapped her fingers. A crisp ten pound note appeared with five pound coins, the waiter yelping. Smiling at him, she said "There you go. Keep the change for putting up with my friend here."

"T-thank you Ma'am," he gasped, taking the money and backing away. Dreamer frowned, thinking.

"Miriam had four cups of tea, each ninety pence, the lunch special is five pounds, plus baked beans on the side which cost seventy pence, and a large glass of cranberry juice cost two pounds…"

Pandora's jaw dropped. Dreamer wasn't even looking at a menu, and it was her first time here in this town. Miriam was gaping as well.

"That makes eleven pounds thirty," said Dreamer, looking at the waiter. "Three pounds seventy isn't much of a tip, is it?"

"What? Oh no Ma'am, it's fine," blurted the waiter, his face bypassing red and turning purple. "Please, it's the biggest tip I've got here-"

"Really?"

"Yes, I promise you- it's no problem at all. Thank you," he gushed, Dreamer still frowning at him.

"Are you sure that's all you-"

"Yes Ma'am it is. Thank you very much, I-" he tripped over a chair as he backed away, then he said "Please come again um… Miss Black!"

"How do you know my-"

Dreamer's eyes landed behind him, her jaw dropping. The television in the corner of the café had her beautiful face on, and her mother's as they took a call. Dreamer's name streamed along the screen, a voice saying "Please do not attempt to call Dreamer's hotline, for she is unavailable for the time being. For further information, please go to AmazingAgnes.com."

Everyone turned in their seats to stare at Dreamer, then talk broke out.

"Call the press, call the press!"

"We've got a celebrity in our town!!"

Miriam was pleased to see the pained look on her friend's face as she said "I don't want any publicity- I'm on vacation."

"Vacation?" said Pandora, hurt. "I thought you was here to stay, Mum?"

"Darling, I-"

Dreamer wanted to say she was staying, but she couldn't.

"Mum?" said Pandora anxiously. "Aren't you staying?"

Dreamer chose her words very carefully.

"I will stay, Pandora, after I do one more thing."

"What's that?"

"Never mind for now," she said, Miriam scowling at her. She knew that look on Dreamer's face: she was up to no good.

"And they needn't know I'm staying either," Dreamer said under the

babble of excited people looking her way. "Ok sweetie?"
"Ok."

* * *

"Yo Stile, it's lunchtime."

"I'm not hungry," Damon answered, making the officer laugh.

"What, so you gone starve up in here?"

"That's right."

"My Mama always say who don't eat, dead. Who dead, bury."

Damon glared at him. "Get lost, Dwayne."

"Hey, come eat. You still gone be a murderer after some turkey ham, and your woman still gone be dust. Come have some."

"I should knock you out, you spangled little-"

"Knock me out if you will, just don't prick me with a knife now."

"You-!!"

Dwayne slammed the cell door shut just in time, locking it back.

"Darn it, Stile! I lost ma stud again. When you gone stop attacking me like this, man? Am a black dude trying to help y'all survive up in here, and this is the thanks I get? Fine fool, starve. No turkey ham your way."

"I don't eat turkey anyway," Damon replied. "I'm a vegan."

"Now shut yo trap, Stile. You in *prison* now. You aint getting' no menus up in here, you feel me? I bin telling' you dis for three years an' you *still* aint listenin'. When you gone understand you got another..." Dwayne chuckled. "Another what, Stile? Ha, another what's the name now... lemme see. It's comin' to me like dogs an' meat- just like these prisoners wid their turkey ham!"

"Get lost, Dwayne!"

"Don't worry man, I got it now. Another *twenty two* years, right? Oh darn it Stile, why didn't you tell me? Why didn't you lemme know?"

"GO AWAY!!"

"Easy Stile!" said another voice, a pair of blue eyes peering at him through the tiny cell window. "What's going on?"

"P.C. Jones won't leave me alone!"

"Sarge, am jus' tryin' to get some food up in his bony butt, and he yellin' at me like I'm his woman." Dwayne snapped his fingers to add effect. "Am jus' doin' ma job. What happen to his woman again?"

Damon slammed his fist against the cell door furiously, imagining it to be Dwayne's face. It felt good, so he repeatedly threw punches at the metal door: "Take that, you son of a-"

"Oh help us all," said Dwayne amusedly. "He finally cracked, Sarge!"

"Stile, stop that or I'll have you sedated," the other officer said firmly, but Damon didn't. Now he imagined the door was Ted Stone, his former best friend. A punch for stealing his girl. A punch for having Marlon so he couldn't get her back. A punch for being the reason why Dreamer got rid of his firstborn. A punch for everything.

Only when he saw blood on the door did he stop, surprised.

"I'm bleeding!"

"Oh, for Heavens sake- P.C. Jones , go and consult the nurse."

"How 'bout *you* get the nurse and I'll stay here?"

"Now, Jones!"

"Yes Sarge."

* * *

"What happened to *you?*" said George, the cell door slamming shut behind him. Damon shrugged, nursing his bandaged hand.

"That idiot Dwayne made me lose my temper."

George grinned: he liked P.C. Jones. "What did he say?"

"He got to me about Dreamer."

"Oh," said George, smile fading. "Damon, remember she's-"

"I know. But sometimes I feel... like she's alive."

"What?"

"It's just a feeling," said Damon, almost to himself. "It's crazy, I know- but I felt like I had a hole inside my heart up to three days ago... and now I'm whole again. Do you think she's alive?"

George didn't know what to say.

"She was powerful," Damon continued. "She might be back."

"It- it's not possible, mate."

"Why not?" Damon demanded, heat rising.

"Yes, why not?" a voice echoed smoothly, making them jump and whip round to stare at whoever spoke.

Dreamer Black was leaning against the wall in the corner of the cell, highly amused as she listened to their conversation. Damon stared at her, then everything spiralled into darkness.

* * *

"Stile, wake up! Where's the ambulance, for crying out loud?!"

"It's on its way, Sarge-"

"Don't call an ambulance!" said Damon groggily, opening his eyes. He was lying on the cell floor, at least six officers around him.

George was standing behind them, petrified as he looked around. He shook his head violently when Sergeant Brown demanded again what happened in the cell, scared that he'd throw up if he spoke.

"Smith, you were right here! *What happened??"*

"Come on Damon," a female officer said gently. "Up you get."

Damon sat up, wincing as he looked at his hand. It was aching.

"He needs to be checked by the doctor-"

"I need an ice pack," Damon said throatily. "I... please."

"What happened, Stile?" said Sergeant Brown for the umpteenth time.

"I passed out because I saw..." Damon stopped, looking at George. Beads of perspiration trickled down his forehead, his large fist in his mouth. George shook his head, Damon saying "I saw blood."

"Blood??"

Damon pointed at the cell door, then he glared at P.C Jones.

"It's Dwayne's fault."

"Someone get that cleaned up," another officer said disgustedly. "Now!"

"Who's the Sergeant, me or you?" Brown said coldly, then he repeated the line. "Someone get that cleaned up."

"Yes Sarge."

Half an hour later it was just Damon and George in their cell again. Damon swallowed, staring at the corner Dreamer had stood in.

"George, did you...? I mean, I wasn't-"

"I saw her, mate," said George in a weird voice. "You wasn't dreaming."

"I knew she was back," said Damon, looking at him. "I knew it."

George hesitated, then he said "She's beautiful, Damon."

"I know. But she's got Ted and two kids and-"

"You told me already," George interrupted, having heard Damon ramble on about the woman for three years straight. "I know everything."

"I won't be able to sleep," Damon muttered, rubbing his forehead. "Damn that woman. She did it on purpose, knowing I'd wait up hoping for her to come back or something- trust me. I know how her mind works."

"How long have you known her for?"

"Since high school, George. Since flipping high school."

"Longer than this Ted moron."

"Exactly. She met the idiot when we was fourteen. I knew him because he was my next door neighbour and that. You know what, though?"

"What?" said George, suddenly eager to hear more about Dreamer.

Damon stared down at his hands, saying "I don't think she wants him in the same way."

"How do *you* know?" demanded George. "You saw her for a split second- you don't know she doesn't want her husband."

"Why not?" said Damon, secretly hoping that Dreamer would repeat the words like she did before. George waited but nothing happened, so he said "Because that was your first time seeing her in three years- and I think she'd prefer this Ted guy to you any day, especially since you assaulted their daughter for no reason-"

"Maybe she came to finish me off," said Damon, suddenly afraid. "We didn't exactly sort that part out- any part actually. We was screaming at each other and then I went crazy with the knife-"

George snorted with laughter.

"You know Damon, you've been so normal here I can't imagine you going crazy with anything, I'm sorry. Was it a pen knife?"

"Ha ha," said Damon dryly, as George roared with laughter. "A machete."

"You? A machete?" spluttered George. "Never!"

* * *

Ted smiled as Dreamer appeared in the living room, Pandora and Marlon clapping enthusiastically. Marlon smirked at his sister.

"Bet I'll be able to do that soon, 'Dora."

"In your dreams," Pandora retorted. "All you can do is splash water."

Marlon ignored her, saying to Dreamer "Where was you, Mum?"

"I was on a walk," Dreamer answered, unable to stop a smirk appearing on her beautiful face. "I startled a lot of people, though."

"Why?"

"They either saw me as a celebrity or they thought I was dead," Dreamer said, amused as she left the room. "I'm going for a shower."

* * *

The doorbell rang, Pandora rising to her feet pronto.
"It's only James," said Marlon like he did before, though his voice was real gentle this time. "He doesn't even have to come in, I'm going."
Pandora hesitated, then she sat back down. Marlon reached out and batted her curly hair, saying "See you later. Dad, tell Mum I said bye."
"Five days, ok son? That's what you said."
"Five days?" said Pandora, startled. "Where're you going?"
"We're playing loads of teams in different areas," Marlon explained. "I'll be staying at James'ss place till everything's over."
"Oh," said Pandora, disappointed. "Well… you'd better win."
Marlon smiled, knowing his sister really meant "I'll miss you."
"We'll win, I promise. I'll bring the trophy back for you."
The doorbell rang again, Marlon picking up his bags.
"Oh, and try and talk to Alice," he added. "She looks really nice."
"So did Janice," Pandora retorted, making him cringe.
"True. Just have a good time. And apply for college too, ok 'Dora?"
"Which one are *you* going to?"
"Forest Academy."
"That's where I want to go."
"Great! Gotta go," he said as the bell ran a third time. "Bye!"

* * *

Dreamer picked up her mobile, dialling her mother's number.
"Agnes speaking."
"Hello Mama," she said breathlessly. "How are you?"
"It hasn't even been three days," huffed Agnes. "Why would you call me, little one, unless you want to get something off your chest?"
"I do. And Mama, don't call me 'little one.' I'm a grown woman."
"Thirty three years old and still giving me heart attacks," said Agnes, a little fondly. "You haven't grown up yet, Dreamer. Pandora is more grown than you are."
"That may be so Mama, but I still don't like to be called 'little one.'"
"Well you will be," Agnes retorted, amused. "What is your reason for calling me, then?"
"You already know, Mama."
"Tell me anyway."
Dreamer hesitated, then she said "I saw Damon Stile today."
Agnes tutted. "Just couldn't resist, could you?"
"We have a lot of things to sort out, Mama."

"They're over with," scolded Agnes, wishing she could pull Dreamer's ear and yell the words inside it. "Over with, Dreamer. He hurt both you and Pandora and he's suffering for it. Leave it at that."

"He still hasn't told me why he did it, Mama. I have to know."

"No you do not, young woman. Don't even think about-"

"I have to go back," Dreamer decided. "We need to talk."

Agnes was silent for a moment, picking everything out of those nine words. The tone of voice, the words 'have to' especially. No she didn't have to. She *wanted* to. There was a big difference.

Dreamer listened anxiously, saying "Mama? Are you still there?"

"You're playing with fire, little one." Agnes spoke calmly. "I think you have developed feelings for Damon Stile."

"I have not, Mama!"

"Don't lie to me," said Agnes wearily. "I hate the lies, Dreamer."

"We were friends. I met him when I was just eleven, Mama."

"Yes, I know that. He was round the house with that Miriam for as long as I can remember. Nearly everyday for years." Agnes couldn't help smiling as she remembered. Then she scowled. "Then you met Ted when you was fourteen, got landed with Marlon at sixteen, Pandora seventeen-your life was ruined in the blink of an eye."

"It was not," Dreamer argued, "Because I still did what I liked while you and Ted looked after them-"

"Oh yes, I forget." Agnes chuckled. "You're a handful, my girl."

Dreamer smiled. "Should I see Damon or not, Mama?"

"My girl, my advice is to let things be. But if you simply have to see him to put your mind at ease, then go. As long as you're going for Pandora."

"That's all I'm going for," said Dreamer uncertainly. "I mean... I can't live not knowing what made him hurt my child, Mama."

"I agree," said Agnes solemnly. "When will you go?"

"Not for a while."

"That's my girl."

The doorbell rang downstairs, Dreamer staring through the floor at Ted opening it to Alice Pets, who looked very excited.

"Oh no- Mama, I forgot all about Alice coming over to see Pandora."

"Well then go," urged Agnes. "That child needs a friend right now."

"What should I make for dinner, Mama?"

"Your mind is on that boy in the cell," said Agnes forlornly. "You have never asked me what to cook in all your life, Dreamer."

Dreamer was startled as she realised that. But her mind wasn't on food.

"Just tell me, Mama!"

"Why don't you try some spicy rice with curried chicken-"

"And jalapenos with vegetables! Thanks, Mama!"

* * *

"Shall I call the fire brigade?" said Pandora dryly, making the table erupt
with laughter. Dreamer handed Alice a glass of cold water, saying "You
don't have to eat those, Alice. Some people can't handle them."
"I'm ok," said Alice, gulping water. "I'm fine."
"Are you sure?" asked Ted, and Alice nodded.
Pandora's plate was empty like her father and mother's. Alice's was
empty too, with the exception of jalapenos.
As much as she hated to admit it, Pandora enjoyed Alice being here. She
couldn't help smiling at her friend as she slowly ate another hot chilli.
"What college are you going to, Alice?"
"Whatever you're going to," she gasped, reaching for her water.
"I think I'll go to Forest Academy," Pandora said, looking at her parents.
"Miriam's got the prospectuses in her office."
"Haven't you got an appointment with her, 'Dora?" said Ted, frowning.
"Tomorrow," Pandora said, feeling guilty. "I'll go early though, and...
well, say sorry to her."
Dreamer nodded, saying "Good girl."
"Sorry for what?" asked Ted curiously. "Dreamer?"
"It's over with, Ted. It doesn't matter anymore."
After everyone was finished and seated in the living room, Pandora
hesitated. Then she said "Alice, do you want to see my room?"
"Good girl," said Ted, smiling broadly as Alice nodded.
As she and Pandora ran upstairs, Ted turned to Dreamer happily.
"This is all because of you."
"What is?"
"You know, her socialising a bit more. She would never have asked Alice
to see her room if you didn't come back."
Dreamer knew this, but she said "She would have over time."
"Don't count on it."

* * *

"That's Dreamer's box?"

"My box," Pandora said, though she wasn't really annoyed. "Yep."

Shadow the rabbit squeaked at Pandora, stomach rumbling.

"Oh no- I forgot to feed him!" said Pandora, stricken. "I need bread-"

"Bread?" said Alice, puzzled. "What for?"

"Remember he's really a bird," Pandora told her. "He just looks like a rabbit. Birds like bread, remember?"

"No wonder Barclays didn't eat his vegetables!"

Pandora smiled as she left the room, Alice looking around at her drawings stuck on the wall.

"Cool."

* * *

"And where is Pandora going with that hard dough bread?" said Dreamer amusedly, not even looking at her. Pandora laughed at herself for thinking she could sneak past without her mother knowing.

"I'm going to feed Shadow. He hasn't eaten since this morning."

"Ok."

Pandora looked around. "Where's Dad gone?"

"He's in the bathroom," said Dreamer, just about focusing on her child. Pandora wanted to ask if she was ok, but she didn't want to hold Shadow up. She ran and kissed Dreamer on the cheek before rushing upstairs.

* * *

"Enough, greedy!" said Pandora, amazed. "Jeez!"
Shadow pushed her finger with his tiny paws, squeaking in protest as she handed the other half of the bread to Alice, who put it back it it's bag and tied it tightly.
"Leave it in the corner for tomorrow," Pandora said, Alice obeying.
"I'll come with Daddy to the clinic if you want, and we can go to the park and hang out after your meeting."
Pandora thought about this, then she nodded.
"Ok."
"What time is your appointment?" asked Alice, picking up her jacket.
"Four o clock."
"Ok then, I'll see you there."
Pandora got up to see her to the door, saying "Thanks for coming."
"Thanks for having me," Alice returned shyly, and Pandora smiled.

* * *

"Damon?"
"Yeah?"
"You sleeping?"
"No."
"Me either."
"I figured."
"Do you think she'll come back?"
"Yes."
"When?"
"I don't know," sighed Damon, rolling over. "I don't know, ok George?"
It was pitch black in the cell. George was silent for a minute. Then he said "Does she always affect people like this?"
"Yep. She's in your head for life, mate."
"Oh. Ok."

* * *

"Dreamer?"

"Yes Ted?"

"I've been thinking. It'll be great for us to get away sometime."

"I'm not sure about that," Dreamer said slowly. "I'll be going soon, Ted."

"Going where?"

"Away for a while. Don't worry, I'll come back."

Damon Stile's boyish face slowly materialised in front of Dreamer's eyes. Little did she know he was the first thing Ted thought of.

"Damon."

"What did you say?" said Dreamer, startled as she turned to look at him. It was dark in the bedroom, so she turned on the bedside lamp to get a good look at him. Ted stared at her, face revealing nothing.

"Damon, Dreamer. You heard what I said."

Dreamer felt like a deer caught in the headlights.

"What about him?"

"Are you still attracted to him?"

"Ted-"

"Just answer the question."

The way he handled her just made Dreamer love him all the more.

"No."

It wasn't exactly a lie. And it wasn't exactly the truth, Dreamer thought as Ted surveyed her in silence. He knew it wasn't the truth.

"We didn't exactly talk about you cheating on me, Dreamer."

"I don't want to discuss it, Ted."

"Are you leaving for a bit to see Damon?"

"No. I'm leaving to check on Mama."

"You've just come from her, though."

"Well... I miss her so I'm going to see her for a few days."

"Why don't you take Pandora with you then," Ted said lightly, annoying her. "She hasn't seen Agnes for three years."

"I'd rather take Pandora with Marlon," Dreamer countered. "Yes?"

"Fine. I know it's Damon you want- I can tell."

"It might be Damon I'm thinking of," Dreamer answered, "But trust me when I say all I want is you."

Ted relaxed at that. It must be revenge for Pandora.

Dreamer quickly turned off the lamp so he couldn't see her smirk. Laying down, she said "Goodnight Ted."

"Night."

* * *

"I'm sorry for yesterday," Pandora said, looking at her knees. She looked like she was a six-year-old being severely told off. Miriam sat across from her, wondering if she meant it.

"Let's forget about it, love. How was dinner with Alice?"

"Nice," said Pandora truthfully. "I liked having her over."

"Pretty soon she'll have you over, and so on and so forth."

"Mmm."

Pandora's mind was elsewhere. Miriam saw that.

"What are you thinking of, Pandora?"

"College."

"You definitely want to go to Forest Academy?"

"Yes. Can we look at the courses?"

"Of course."

* * *

"Hi Pandora," said Alice happily, leaving her father's office. Pandora struggled not to smile back as she said hi.

"What are we doing again?" she said, though she knew already.

"Walk in the park," Alice said brightly. "I've got Barclays with me."

"Atchoo! Atchoo! Alice, is Pandora out yet?"

"Yes Daddy!"

"Then get this- atchoo!- rodent out of my office!"

"Barclays isn't a rodent," said Pandora, when Alice looked hurt.

"I'm allergic," sniffed Tony, rubbing his neck. "Hello Pandora."

"Hi Tony."

"How is er… your mother?"

Alice scowled at him but said nothing, simply going into her father's office to retrieve her precious rabbit.

"She's fine," said Pandora tonelessly. "Why?"

"I was just inquiring because she's the reason you've been coming here…" Tony trailed off as Miriam looked at him, amused. She knew what he was thinking. "And I've decided we need to talk."

"Talk to my father," Pandora answered. "Ready, Alice?"

"Yep! Bye Miss Hughes," said Alice, walking through the door with Pandora. Then she ran back to smile at her father. "Shame, Daddy."

* * *

Shadow the rabbit stared at Barclays haughtily, not leaving Pandora's side. Barclays squeaked merrily, running around in circles.

"I guess they represent us," Pandora said. "You're happy and full of life, while I'm withdrawn and don't trust easily. What do you think?"

"Very true," said Alice, amazed as she looked from Shadow to Barclays and back. "We're the rabbits. I mean… you know."

"Sure," said Pandora, picking up Shadow. "And when I start trusting you a little, I'm more open and I communicate more."

She placed Shadow in front of Barclays as she spoke. Barclays stopped his play and tottered over, Shadow backing into Pandora's arms.

"Well obviously he's not ready for friendship," said Pandora, amused. "But he could do with the fresh air, right Shadow?"

Shadow snuggled into her happily, Pandora pleased.

"I'm glad I've got Shadow. He's something I can care for, and love."

"That's real sweet," Alice said. "Ditto Barclays."

"Shadow probably would've been my only friend, if I didn't meet you."

"You're in a real strange mood, aren't you?" said Alice jokingly, and Pandora smiled at her as she nodded.

"I'm glad we met. I might have been a loner for life."

Alice beamed at her.

* * *

Dreamer hugged and kissed Denise, downstairs in her restaurant.

"How's Ted?" Denise asked, chewing gum. "Still the same?"

"Fine, Denise. Just fine."

"Uh oh. Come come come," said Denise eagerly, ushering Dreamer through the restaurant and into a private parlour. "Sit sit sit!"

Dreamer sat, looking around. "It's beautiful, isn't it?"

"The restaurant?" said Denise, uninterested. "Sure, sure. Now talk!"

"I love Ted," Dreamer said carefully. "But I've been thinking about-"

She broke off, staring through the wall at a tall man dressed in a suit. He smiled at the waitress as she walked over, showing perfect teeth.

"A table for one again, sir?"

"Yes please. I'll have the usual- you already know what that is."

"Yes I do sir."

"Who's that?" demanded Dreamer, Denise turning and looking at the wall behind her.

"It's Mr Concrete, darling. You noticed we had the parlours done over?"

"No- that man in the suit. Who is he?"

"Probably Antonio. He's always in a suit."

"Antonio?" Dreamer repeated. "Is he a regular?"

"He's in everyday around this time," Denise said uninterestedly. "And don't even bother with him: all he cares about is making money."

"Really."

"Yes. So what's going on with you and Ted?"

"Who? Oh, Ted. I love him," said Dreamer slowly, "But..."

"You're not in love with him," Denise finished, Dreamer's nodding.

"Exactly. I don't love him like I did before I died." She sighed, asking "What am I going to do, Denise? It's going to tear the family apart!"

"Call your mother," Denise said soothingly. "She'll know what to do."

"What do *you* think I should do?" asked Dreamer, looking at her.

"Well... Ted's still the most gorgeous guy I've ever seen," Denise said, smiling at her friend. "Maybe you should talk with him about this."

"Just tell him I don't love him as a lover but more like a brother?" asked Dreamer, amused. "Just like that?"

"No, silly. Actually, yes. I mean no. I don't know!" said Denise, as Dreamer laughed at her. "Don't laugh, this is about your future."

Dreamer shut up.

"Good," smirked Denise. "I don't think Ted will take it too hard."

"Why not?" demanded Dreamer, stung. *Everybody* takes Dreamer hard.

"Because he's got on fine without you for three years," explained Denise.

"And it's only been three days. The longer you leave it, the more it's going to hurt. I say you just sort this now. Tonight."

"Tonight?" Dreamer repeated, then she shook her head. "My children."

"Wow," said Denise, loving it all. "This keeps getting better!"

"Excuse me Miss Jessica, Mr Antonio is asking to see you," a waitress said meekly, popping her head round the door. "What to do?"

"Tell him I'm unavailable," Denise said, waving her away. "Go on."

"Yes Miss Jessica."

"Being the manageress rocks," said Denise happily. "They love me."

"They tolerate you because they want to get paid," Dreamer countered, and Denise pouted at her.

"You tell it like it is."

* * *

Marlon sank down on the sofa, bones aching. He was exhausted. He'd just finished playing ball with James in the fields, after an entire morning of training, a match at noon and then more training afterwards, in the early evening. After losing their first game, it made Marlon and James even more determined to win. He and James stayed in the park after training, challenging each other one on one at football. Now it was eight p.m., and they were starving.

"Let's order pizza or something!" called Marlon, and James said ok.

Marlon picked up the house phone, then he put it down and picked up his mobile. Pandora hadn't left his head today: he needed to hear his sister.

"Hello?"

"Hi Pandora," he said, feeling warm. "Did you have a good day?"

Pandora was amused. "You miss me, big brother."

"Yeah I do. How was your day?"

"You lost the game, didn't you?"

"I... yeah," said Marlon, scowling. "Yeah, we lost."

"Well there's still more games, so cheer up."

Marlon was surprised. "We lost our first game, that's not good."

"Yeah, but if you lose again and win the other three you'd still get the cup. Use your brain, camel mouth!"

"Who are you, and what have you done to my sister?"

Pandora laughed at him. "In answer to your questions, I had a really nice day. Meaning I'm in a really nice mood."

"I see," he said, thinking hard. "Did you meet a guy or something?"

"I spent the day with Alice," Pandora said, "And I've decided to be her friend because... she's quite fun. I like her."

"Oh my," said Marlon, highly amused as James walked in holding a can of Sprite for him. "Pandora actually wants to socialise? It's a new day!"

"Pandora?" said James before he could stop himself, and Marlon nodded. "She's finally making friends again, J. This is brilliant."

James smiled and nodded, glad Marlon didn't find anything strange about his expression or tone of voice when he said her name.

"What are you doing, camel mouth?" asked Pandora, stomach fluttering a little. "Getting wasted?"

"No I'm not, actually."

"Well you're about to. On junk food or something."

"So what?" he said, more amused than annoyed. "It's not a crime."

"Mum's back," said Pandora, voice full of love. "I'm going."

"Don't you dare hang up, 'Dora! I want to speak to her!"

"Speak to her when you get back," Pandora answered, amused. "Bye."

Cursing as the line went dead, Marlon dialled the house phone instead.
"She's so annoying! You're so lucky you're the only child, James!"
James didn't answer, pretending to be immersed in a pizza leaflet.
"Hello, good evening."
"Hey Dad," said Marlon, deciding against asking for Dreamer straight away. "Guess what happened- we lost."
"Ah well," said Ted, not disappointed. "You had fun, that's what counts."
Marlon smiled. He loved his old man.
"Exactly. What did you do today, then?"
"Lazed around."
"You?" snorted Marlon. "Ted Stone? The workaholic?"
Ted laughed, saying "Since Dreamer came back things haven't quite been how they used to be, Marlon. Pandora didn't bother looking out the window for passers by before she left the house. I haven't thought about work either- I feel like I'm flying. And Pandora smiles a lot more too."
"And I'm real happy," Marlon added, smiling. "This is great."
"It sure is. But… have you noticed anything different about Dreamer?"
"She's the same with me and 'Dora," said Marlon carefully, "But it's like she's got a problem being alone with you now, Dad. She leaves the minute it's just you two in the room- don't lie," he said, when Ted started to talk. "You two need to sort everything out properly."
"Maybe you're right. Son, just between me and you-"
Marlon stood straighter, listening.
"I think your mother doesn't love me anymore."
"Aw, Dad." Marlon felt real sorry for him. "She does, I promise."
"Not in the same way."
"How can you tell, Dad? Get lost," he added sharply to James, who was trying to listen. James glared at him and picked up the house phone to order their pizza.
"I just can. She basically admitted it when she said something died in her the night she was killed." Ted drew a deep, ragged breath. The hurt he felt was beginning to show, and it frightened Marlon.
"Dad, don't you dare get depressed over this. If she doesn't love you then… get over it. That's the best thing. Oh!" A horrible thought struck him as he stood there. "She isn't seeing someone else?"
"She wants Damon Stile," Ted said, angering Marlon.
"What?"
"I think she's seen him already."
"Dad-"
"After she got back- maybe the day after or-"
"Shut up, Dad! Shut the hell up! She can't want that psycho- not after everything he did to her and Pandora! You're talking crazy!"

"I'm being serious, Marlon. She's got her eye on someone else."
"You don't know that."
"How long have I known Dreamer for?" asked Ted wearily. "I know."

* * *

Miriam cursed violently, hating herself for longing to see Dreamer Black. She thought those days and feelings were long gone- but they were back with a vengeance. It had taken all of her strength and willpower to get over Dreamer's dismissal of their friendship, over her death, over their friendship. It had taken all of her friends and family and a psychiatrist to help her forget the past; the mornings she'd meet Dreamer everyday to go to school, forget the messing around in class, and the weekends they'd spend together having fun- forget how much she loved Dreamer. And now... Miriam threw a cushion across the room in anger. Everything she'd worked so hard for was slowly slipping away. The independence, the ability to get on without her friend. Miriam slowly picked up the house phone, then she slammed it down. She was *not* calling her.
Agnes.
Agnes would help her. As soon as Miriam reached for her diary it vanished. Miriam shrieked, then she heard Dreamer's laugh.
"Scared you, didn't I?"
Miriam turned to look at her best friend, heart racing. "Dreamer!"
"Hello my friend," said Dreamer amusedly, and Miriam smiled.
"What are you doing here? Nobody comes to my house."
"I'm not nobody," Dreamer replied smoothly. "Or am I?"
"No," said Miriam quickly. "No you're not."
Dreamer looked around the living room interestedly.
"A bungalow. I always thought you'd go for a mansion, Miriam."
"That's more your style," Miriam said, suddenly embarrassed of her home. "Um... would you like a drink? Can I get you anything?"
"I'm fine," Dreamer replied, picking up a photo and looking at it closely. Miriam hovered about, watching her breathlessly.
Dreamer flashed her a smile, saying "I mean a lot to you."
It wasn't a question, it was a statement.
"Yes," Miriam said before she could stop herself. "Yes you do."
"I take back what I said: I'm pretty thirsty."
Miriam rushed into the kitchen, gushing "Hot drink or cold?"
"Hot please," Dreamer replied. "It was pretty nippy outside."
Miriam rushed to the kitchen and boiled the kettle, pulling out two mugs, tea bags and sugar. Dreamer looked around the house while she waited, taking in every tiny detail. Miriam knew she didn't bother asking because

she knew what the answer would be.

"You have three bedrooms?" said Dreamer interestedly from the passageway, and Miriam called "Two are for visitors really. One of them hasn't been used yet, and the other one's for my parents when they visit from America. They came last year."

"Interesting."

Miriam set the coffee table carefully, wanting to impress her friend.

"I always wonder where Papa is," Dreamer said as she looked in the bathroom. "I'd love to have both he and Mama over."

Miriam smiled. "Why do you speak like that, Dreamer?"

Dreamer was offended. "Like what?"

"So perfectly. 'Both he and Mama...' wow."

Dreamer smiled as she walked back into the living room, stopping when Miriam's jaw dropped.

"What are you looking at?"

"I didn't notice your gown," Miriam mumbled, embarrassed. "It's lovely. And it looks very expensive too."

Dreamer smiled, looking down at it with pleasure. "It cost me five hundred pounds. A lady in the country has them made for me, all the time. I tell her the colour and she makes lovely gowns, all for Dreamer."

Miriam smiled, repeating herself. "It's lovely, Dreamer."

"Strangers thought so too," Dreamer replied, amused as she sat down. "Just before I came here an Italian man ran across the road, nearly getting hit by a bus." Her smile grew. "Then he did this:"

Dreamer placed a hand over her heart, saying in a deep voice, *"Amore."*

Miriam burst out laughing as she handed Dreamer her cup.

"You're lucky he didn't try and abduct you, Dreamer."

"I'd have liked to see him try," said Dreamer, placing her wand on the coffee table. It sparked menacingly, Miriam looking at it in wonder. The gesture was made on purpose, Dreamer clearly meaning that nobody could trouble her in any way.

Swallowing some tea, Miriam asked "How's Pandora?"

"Pandora is fine," Dreamer said with a smile. "Much happier."

"I knew she would be."

Dreamer nodded. "I knew Alice would be good for her."

"It's more you than Alice, and you know that," said Miriam, amused. Dreamer never wanted to hog the limelight. She preferred to blend in the background, though with her that just wasn't possible.

Dreamer shrugged a shoulder, Miriam saying "You know it."

"Alice has helped too," Dreamer said in Alice's defence. "She has."

"Yes, by ten percent. You're the other ninety."

Dreamer chose not to answer that, simply sipping her tea.

"How's Ted?" Miriam asked bitterly.

"Ted's fine," Dreamer said, sighing. "He's just fine."

Miriam frowned as Dreamer stared into her cup. "Dreamer?"

"No. Please don't ask me anything."

"What's going on with you and Ted?" Miriam asked, and Dreamer scowled as she looked at her. Were her ears not working?

Miriam waited, Dreamer suddenly remembering she was a mentor. Her personal counsellor through the years, she thought amusedly. Maybe talking to Miriam would feel better than the talk with Denise Jessica.

"I love Ted," Dreamer said slowly and clearly, enunciating each word. "Don't think I don't, because I do. But-"

"You don't love him in the same way," Miriam said, and Dreamer nodded. "Well, at least you know what you feel."

"That is true," Dreamer answered, and Miriam smiled. Perfect English again. "I feel as if he is my brother, not my lover. I'm... not the same."

"Yes you are," said Miriam firmly. "You just don't feel the same."

"I suppose," said Dreamer heavily. "I don't know what to do, Miriam. I guess I've become bored of Ted now. I've been his lover for eighteen years- fifteen if you exclude the last three. I'm not satisfied anymore."

The words were unkind, but honest... and Miriam loved them. She was sixteen again, and she'd first heard of Ted Stone. She hated him more than anything for taking Dreamer away from her. And then she was back in the present, thirty three again... Miriam was shocked to find she was still hurting over everything that happened. Though she tried not to, she felt glad Dreamer felt this way about Ted, who had once been her sun, moon and stars. Without Ted Dreamer felt she was nothing- once upon a time. She'd finally gotten through that phase- finally!

Miriam saw this as a payback opportunity for Ted's taking Dreamer away from her all those years before. If Dreamer meant what she said, then Miriam could finally be back in her life- properly.

Dreamer didn't think anything of Miriam's silence. She sipped more tea, then continued "I know it's not good-"

"Why- I mean, of course it isn't," Miriam said, catching herself just in time. She was just about to demand why it wasn't good Dreamer was over Ted. "No it's not good, not on Pandora and Marlon. But- but don't think it's not good for you," she pressed on quickly, Dreamer looking at her. "Don't even think about forcing yourself to stay with him for their sakes, because you'll be unhappy. Pandora and Marlon will know you're unhappy and it will make them unhappy too. Same with Ted."

Dreamer didn't answer that. She didn't look as if she'd even heard. Miriam watched her curiously, wondering what was going on inside that head of hers. Dreamer didn't speak for almost ten minutes, her tea cold by then. Hesitating first, Miriam asked "Are you ok?"

"Hmm? Oh. Me? I'm fine," said Dreamer, smiling at her.

Miriam smiled back as she raised the cup to her lips, made a startled noise, then she picked up her wand and tapped the side of the cup with an annoyed expression. Miriam's smile grew as steam rose from the cup, Dreamer saying "Tea grows cold too quickly."

"I agree," Miriam said, putting her own cup down. "Um…"

Dreamer looked at her questioningly. "What?"

"When are you going back home?"

Dreamer glanced at the clock; it was only six thirty.

"Maybe at eight, if you don't mind me staying."

"No, of course not, why would I mind if you- you can stay, I…" Miriam trailed off, embarrassed as she realised Dreamer was frowning at her sudden speech impediment. Swallowing, she shook her head. "Sorry."

"Don't be," said Dreamer, amused. "I suppose it's been too long."

"So long," sighed Miriam, nodding. "We've been apart for ages."

Dreamer nodded, thinking to herself.

Really and truly, they hadn't been together properly since they were sixteen. Miriam was in America half the time, she was besotted with Ted. Miriam had all the time for her, but she had none for Miriam. Dreamer recalled telling her friend she wanted to see her once every three months.

"I've been cruel to you, haven't I Miriam?"

Miriam started to say no, then she nodded. "Yes you have."

"I didn't mean to- well I did," Dreamer said as an afterthought, making Miriam laugh. "I meant every word at the time, but-"

"Now you regret it," said Miriam, and Dreamer scowled at her.

"Do you always know the answer, Miriam? What to say?"

"It comes with the profession," Miriam answered as a yes. "Why?"

"It's nice, but… annoying. Very, very annoying."

"Hey, I helped you a lot of times," Miriam said defensively. "Every time you called with a problem or for advice, I gave you a good answer."

"True. We only stayed in contact because of the phones."

"If we didn't have phones we'd never have stayed in contact," Miriam said, shuddering at the thought. "I'd be a wreck."

"Mmm. How was you when you heard I died?"

Miriam's smile faded as she remembered. Dreamer waited, interested.

"I… I cried every night for a year and a half. It near enough killed me, Dreamer." Miriam's eyes filled as she looked at her friend. "I wasn't eating much, I was scared of sleeping because I'd dream of you."

"Hence my name," said Dreamer amusedly, but Miriam didn't smile.

"Tony helped me get through it. Alice's father," she added, when Dreamer looked puzzled. "He was dealing with divorcing his wife and getting custody of Alice at the time, but he didn't get to have her."

"What a shame," said Dreamer dryly, not really interested.

Miriam nodded, saying "Alice loves her father, though. As soon as she turned eighteen she came to live with him, because she was of age and she had a choice. She never really got along with her stepfather."

"So this man helped you get over my death?" said Dreamer, wanting to keep the subject on target. Miriam nodded again.

"He didn't want me to fall ill from depression, he was worried. He didn't let me carry on working, but I still went to the clinic to see him."

Dreamer sat up straighter, eyes sparkling. "Really."

"Yes, and I- no," said Miriam, as Dreamer smiled at her. "No, Dreamer! He was never a lover of mine; he's not really interested in love since Elizabeth left him. We're just friends. Friends! *Friends,"* she repeated in a spooky voice, and Dreamer burst out laughing.

"You're so funny sometimes, Miriam. I missed you when I came back six months ago, when I was staying with Mama."

Miriam looked doubtful. "Did you?"

"Yes. I missed all of you."

"I'm glad, then."

"So you should be," Dreamer answered, getting up. "I should go."

"What? So soon?" said Miriam disappointedly, looking at the clock.

"It's almost eight," said Dreamer, looking around for her shawl. Miriam reached to pick up her wand for her- "Don't!"

Miriam froze, Dreamer picking her wand up.

"I'm sorry, I was only-"

Dreamer shook her head, saying "Never touch the wand, Miriam."

Miriam pouted, remembering their days at school, Dreamer's brilliant silver wand. She said the same thing back then, and nearly went mental when Damon tried using it as a pencil at a homework club.

Dreamer smiled, saying "Glad you remember."

"Will you come again, Dreamer?"

"Yes."

"Promise?"

Miriam knew she sounded childish, but she didn't care. Dreamer pulled her into a tight hug, Miriam inhaling her sweet vanilla scent with delight. She even laid her head on Dreamer's shoulder like a baby.

"I promise I'll come again," Dreamer told her, letting go. "Ok?"

"Ok," said Miriam, feeling much better after the hug. Much happier anyway, because Dreamer Black never broke a promise. "Call me as soon as you get home. Tell Pandora I said hello too."

"I will."

Before Miriam could say something else Dreamer vanished in a flash of white light, startling her: it looked like a firework went off in her living room. Tiny lights shimmered before fading into darkness, Miriam sitting on her chair and smiling. What a way to go.

* * *

Pandora sat cross legged on the carpet cuddling Shadow, downstairs in her living room. She wasn't going to bed until Dreamer came home. Ted brought her a mug of hot chocolate, placing it on the coffee table.
"There you go, 'Dora."
"Thanks, Dad."
Pandora put Shadow down and picked up the mug, sipping slowly. Ted watched her, a warm feeling spreading all over. That was his little girl right there. Pandora noticed him looking, pausing self consciously.
"What?"
"Nothing," smiled Ted. "Nothing at all."
Dreamer appeared, Pandora instantly putting the mug down and getting up to give her a hug.
"Hello sweetheart," said Dreamer warmly, as Pandora squeezed her tightly. "Did you have a good day?"
"It was ok. I missed you," Pandora replied, standing on tiptoe to give her a kiss. "Where've you been? You're always out these days."
"These days?" Dreamer repeated, amused. "I've only just got back."
"You know what I mean," pouted Pandora, sitting back down. Shadow scampered up to Dreamer happily, looking up and twitching his nose.
"Aren't you a cute little bunny-wunny?" said Dreamer adoringly, reaching down and picking him up. "Yes you are. You're gorgeous!"
Ted smiled as Dreamer snuggled Shadow, then suddenly he felt jealous. Dreamer was giving the rabbit more affection than him. She hadn't even acknowledged his presence. Trying not to sulk, he drank his tea as he looked at his daughter. Pandora was gazing at her mother as she sat, holding her mug. Shyly, she said "Do you want him, Mum?"
"Hmm? No darling, he's yours." Dreamer smiled at her. "Keep him."
"You can have him you like him so much."
"Keep him," Dreamer repeated gently, putting Shadow down and walking into the kitchen. "I need something to eat."
Shadow squeaked, running after Dreamer happily. Ted watched the woman he thought of as his. Her gown was beautiful, he remarked. Black silk, clinging to her body as if it was part of her. Dreamer's brown skin shone as she moved around the kitchen, making Ted's mouth water. She was his, definitely. His own Galaxy chocolate.
Ted chuckled at his thoughts, Pandora looking at him.

"What's so funny?"

"Your mother," Ted answered, hoping Dreamer would look up, but she didn't. Her back was toward them as she made a sandwich. Pandora waited curiously, and Ted said "Never you mind, 'Dora."

"Fine."

Inside the kitchen, Dreamer smiled to herself. In the living room, Ted's face fell. How in the world was he going to win her heart again?

Dreamer walked into the living room and sat down with a tray, staring down at her sandwich as if wondering what to do with it.

"You eat it," explained Pandora, and Ted and Dreamer burst out laughing as they looked at her serious face.

"'Dora, she knows what to do with it," chortled Ted, and Pandora pouted.

"I'm only trying to help. What's in that sandwich, Mum?"

"Cheese and ham, but... I don't want it cold," Dreamer replied thoughtfully, then she smiled and pulled out her wand. Pandora nearly dropped her mug, eager to see her mother perform a trick.

Ted opened his mouth to protest, then decided against it.

Dreamer whispered something inaudible to their ears, tapping the sandwich with her wand. Pink smog furled from the tip of the wand, covering the sandwich totally for a good four seconds before unfurling. Soon it became part of the living room air, completely transparent. Pandora gasped as Dreamer smiled at her plate, satisfied.

"A cheese and ham toasty is much better."

"Dad, isn't she great?" said Pandora happily, and Ted nodded.

Dreamer bit into her toasty slowly, thinking of Miriam now. She really was cruel to her in the past, wasn't she?

Shadow was tired. He wandered about the living room looking for a place to sleep, finally settling on Ted's feet.

Pandora laughed, saying "He did that earlier as well."

"Are you sure Shadow's a boy?" Ted said jokingly, making her laugh again. "Because a lot of girls like your old man's feet, 'Dora."

"Not me," Pandora said, smiling at him. "Never your feet, Dad."

Dreamer didn't take part in the conversation, her mind on Miriam. Remembering she had to call, she quickly finished her food and got up. The plate slid off her lap and hung suspended in the air, Pandora wowing again. Even Ted seemed impressed, though he tried to hide it. The plate followed Dreamer into the kitchen as she dialled on her mobile.

* * *

"Hello?"

"I'm home," Dreamer said, making Miriam smile.

"I didn't think you'd really call."

"Well I did, and-" Dreamer paused, saying "Miriam says hello, Pandora."

"Tell her I said hello back," Pandora said in the background, Dreamer saying "She says hello back, Miriam. What are you doing now?"

"I'm curled up on the sofa with hot chocolate and a bag of cookies."

"Isn't that nice."

"Yes it is, Queen of Sarcasm. What's wrong with that?"

"Nothing, I just wish I could relax like that sometimes."

"Well, you can always come over one day- maybe stay over."

"Really?"

"Yes," said Miriam, amazed. "Dreamer, what's the matter?"

* * *

Pandora mouthed *goodnight* to her mother, who smiled and held an arm out. Pandora rushed into her warm embrace happily, Dreamer kissing the top of her head.

"Sweet dreams," she whispered, Pandora nodding with a smile as she left the kitchen. Stopping by Ted, she reached down and picked Shadow up.

"Night Dad."

"Night," Ted said vaguely, Pandora stopping to look at him properly. Ted stood slowly and smiled at her, but his eyes were troubled.

"Dad? What's the matter?"

Dreamer looked up as she spoke to Miriam, seeing her daughter's concerned face as she looked at her father.

Ted shook his head, saying "Nothing's wrong, 'Dora."

"Don't believe you."

"Trust me, it's nothing. But I'd really like a goodnight hug."

Pandora put Shadow down and ran and gave him a hug. Surprised, shocked and amazed all at once, Ted hugged her back.

"Only because you looked so down," Pandora mumbled into his shoulder.

"Tomorrow night I'm not hugging you."

"I'd better be down tomorrow night then," said Ted amusedly, making her giggle as she let him go.

"See you tomorrow, Dad. Have you got work?"

"I've still got two days off," Ted said, smiling at her. "Remember?"

"Yep. Night!"

"Night."

"What happened just then?" Miriam asked Dreamer, who answered "Pandora just gave Ted a hug goodnight."

"No."

"Yes."

"That's excellent!" Miriam exclaimed happily, and Dreamer nodded. Then, remembering Miriam couldn't see her, she said "Yes it is."

"You don't sound too pleased."

"I am, honestly. I'm just tired, and-" Dreamer broke off as she noticed Ted leaning against the doorframe, watching her talk. Noticed his shirt was undone, showing his sculpted chest; smooth and brown. "And…"

Miriam waited, but Dreamer said zilch as she stared at him.

"And what?" probed Miriam, after minutes of silence. "Dreamer?"

Ted cocked his head to one side, a smirk playing on his face. He knew Dreamer couldn't resist him, whether she loved him or not.

Swallowing, Dreamer whispered "What are you doing?"

"Watching you. Is that a crime?"

"Yes, because I'm on the phone and you're… looking like that."

"You don't like the shirt? I'll take it off then."

"No!"

But Ted already pulled his shirt off, revealing his beautiful muscled arms and broad shoulders. Dreamer almost dropped the phone. Ted grinned.

"Bet you missed this body while you was with Agnes."

"I- I…"

On the other end of the line, Miriam was furious.

"He's doing it on purpose to win you over, Dreamer! Ignore him!"

Dreamer nodded, shaking herself as she said "You can't win me over with your body, Ted. I'm going out."

"Scared of being alone with me now?" Ted asked, smirking at her.

"I don't need this right now: I'm tired. My bones ache."

"Tell him you'll sleep in the guest room," whispered Miriam, and Dreamer said "Exactly: I'm sleeping in the guest room, Ted."

"Why?"

"Because that's all I am here: a guest."

Ted's eyes flashed just like before: he wasn't in the mood for her games.

"I'm your husband, Dreamer."

"You are not my husband," Dreamer said coldly, pleasing Miriam.

Ted shrugged, turning to leave- but he couldn't. Not yet. Looking back at Dreamer, he said "You don't love me anymore, do you?"

"I do, just not in the same way."

"What the *hell* does that mean?" he exploded, startling her. "It's a straight question, so give me a straight answer. Yes or no?"

"Tell him like it is, Dreamer. Don't let him intimidate you."

Ted moved closer, Dreamer stepping backwards.

"Tell me, Dreamer, and I'll know where I stand. Yes or no?"

"Say no," said Miriam firmly, but Dreamer was frozen. "Dreamer!"

"I- I need fresh air!" she said to both Ted and Miriam, but neither of them

was having any of it. Ted grabbed her arm while Miriam said "Tell him!"
"Tell me," he said firmly. "Don't leave me hanging in the kitchen."
"Ted, let go of me," Dreamer said, cursing herself when she realised she
left her wand in the living room. "Let go!"
"Give me an answer, Dreamer!"
"I can't give you a yes or no!"
"Why not?!"

* * *

Pandora heard shouting in the kitchen, getting up.
Ted shook Dreamer angrily, now holding her with both hands.
"Tell me how you feel, Dreamer!"
"Ted, let me go," sobbed Dreamer. "Let go of me!"
"Why did you come back? What was the point of it?!"
"Let go of me!"
"Answer me!"
Miriam was shouting down the phone at him, but Dreamer's mobile was
on the kitchen floor by now. Pandora crept downstairs slowly, listening.
"Do you love me or not?! ANSWER THE QUESTION!!"
"I can't!" cried Dreamer, tears falling. "Ted, please- Pandora-"
"What about her?"
"She's coming down the stairs- let me go-"
Ted moved to close the kitchen doors, pulling Dreamer with him. Pulling
them shut, he used the key hanging on one door to lock them.
"There," he said furiously. "She can listen, but she can't see a thing."
"Let go of me," sobbed Dreamer. "Please!"
"No! Tell me what you feel, and be honest about it!"
Dreamer couldn't breathe anymore.
"Talk to me, Dreamer!"
"I can't!"
"Yes you can! How can you do this to me? I gave you my all, damn it- I
gave you my heart! Why are you doing this to me?!"
Without realising it, he pushed her with such force she lost her balance.
Dreamer slammed onto the kitchen floor, crying still.
Staring down at her in shock, Ted backed two steps. Then he decided she
deserved it: "You deserve to be treated this way, Dreamer. You're right:
I'm not your husband. You are definitely not my wife."
Dreamer shook her head, sobbing. She didn't answer him.
Ted dropped to his knees a few feet away from her, head in his hands.
Without caring that Pandora was outside the door, he said "I hate you."
Dreamer flinched, tears falling. Ted looked at her, eyes filling over.

"I hate you, Dreamer!" His voice cracked. "You hurt me so much!"

They both cried their hearts on the kitchen floor, Ted shaking his head. Dreamer didn't love him. She didn't deserve him anyway.

Pandora listened to their sobs, confused. She didn't understand why they turned on each other like that- didn't know why.

She sat on the carpet with her back to the kitchen door, listening. Dreamer's wand sparkled on the chair she sat in, but Pandora didn't dare touch it. Hugging her knees to her chest, she listened and listened and listened until she fell asleep. Then she snapped awake and quickly went back to bed before one of them found her there.

* * *

At six in the morning, Ted woke up. It was dark in the kitchen- and cold. He shivered, remembering he had no shirt on. Dreamer lay motionless across from him, sleeping. Ted's anger at her vanished: she looked so innocent when she was sleeping. Innocent and beautiful.

Ted got to his feet quietly, unlocking the kitchen doors and pulling them apart. They didn't make a sound. Ted turned to stare down at Dreamer, eyes filling immediately. Was it over between them?

Reaching down, he gently lifted her into his arms. She was freezing. Pandora peeked out of her bedroom door just in time to see Ted walk past with Dreamer in his arms- she smiled. They'd make it up.

Now she could go back to sleep after worrying about them all night.

Ted laid Dreamer down, then he lifted her up. She was not sleeping in the guest room, not in this stupid little double bed. She was staying with him. Once inside his room, he held her in one arm and used the other to remove her gown. Not thinking anything except he needed her to be comfy, he let the gown drop to the floor and lifted her out of it. Then he carried her to his wardrobe, opened it, selected one of his t-shirts and took extra care pulling it over her head, pulling each arm through the sides. There. That was her done. Dreamer stirred as he laid her under the duvet, whispering "What are you doing?"

"Believe it or not, I'm not angry," Ted whispered back. "I love you."

"I love you too…"

Dreamer closed her eyes and went back to sleep. Ted stood there, smiling broadly. Did she say what he thought she said? Did she mean it? Yes to the first question, probably no to the second. Still, he didn't care. Ted slipped under the duvet after removing his work trousers, cautiously moving closer to her. Dreamer opened her eyes to look at him: Ted stared back.

She remembered last night. She had meant to stay strong, tell him like it is, and then get the hell out of the house without looking back. But she didn't. She couldn't, because it wasn't what she wanted.

She was still unsure about how she felt about Ted, but at this moment she didn't care. Bravely moving closer, she wrapped her arms around him and laid her head on his warm chest. Ted held her tightly, whispering the sweetest words imaginable, knowing by evening Dreamer would be head over heels in love with him again if he played his cards right. Dreamer listened to him, eyes filling over. He loved her so much.

* * *

At eleven they woke up, still in each other's arms.

"I'm sorry," they whispered together, Ted saying "Forget about it."

Dreamer shook her head. "I'll leave as soon as I talk to Pandora."

"You're not going anywhere," he said firmly, holding her tighter, afraid if he let go of her she'd get up and go.

"Ted, if I stay I'll only hurt you even more-"

"I don't care, Dreamer. I'm not losing you."

"Ted-"

He pressed his mouth to hers desperately, not wanting to hear it. Dreamer responded slowly, as if unsure where she wanted this to lead. Ted gripped her hair hungrily, making her hand shoot up and grab the back of his neck, pulling him closer as she kissed him passionately.

That's more like it, Ted thought. He knew which buttons to press. Dreamer pressed every inch of her body against his, suddenly fired up. Ted broke the kiss reluctantly, panting "Is this what you want?"

Dreamer didn't bother answering him, pulling him closer. Their lips met again as their bedroom door opened, but they didn't notice.

Pandora coughed loudly, making them break apart and look round.

"Breakfast in bed," she said meekly, and they smiled at her.

* * *

Miriam knew that if she didn't get to the house quickly Dreamer would be tricked into staying by Ted's side. She didn't know what she wanted, and that made her vulnerable. If Miriam had her way Dreamer would leave with her, and stay with her at her bungalow.

* * *

Ted massaged Dreamer with skill and ease, feeling her tense muscles relax. Dreamer kept her eyes on the mirror in front of the bed, simply watching him work. Pandora sat on the carpet with Shadow, reading aloud from one of Dreamer's favourite books.

"And she scowled at him, answering 'This is your way of winning my heart, Kane? With gold and not love?' Kane laughed at her, lowering the sack of gold coins. 'Erica, you are too sentimental. I look not for a woman to love, but a woman to promote my image.' 'You disgust me, Kane.' Erica shook her head. 'I am not the woman for you.'"

"Tell him like it is," mumbled Dreamer, making Ted and Pandora smile.

"Kane could feel his temper rising. He-"

The doorbell rang, making her stop reading. Ted didn't stop his massage, though he smiled at her.

"Get the door, Pandora."

"But- but- I can't- oh, all right then," she said huffily, getting up. "You're taking the Mick now, making me do all this weird stuff. I'm still not used to socialising, Dad! And touchy huggy stuff unless it's Mum, and…"

Ted and Dreamer laughed as she grumbled to herself, jogging downstairs.

"She'll be fine in two weeks," Dreamer said musingly, Ted nodding as he ran his hands down her back. Then he leant down and kissed her shoulder, whispering "Are we all right now, Dreamer?"

Dreamer shook her head, then she nodded. Then she shrugged.

"I don't know. I think so."

Ted sighed, then he smiled. "That's better than 'I don't think so.'"

"Exactly."

Pandora took a deep breath, then pulled open the door.

"Alice!"

"Hi Pandora!" she said breathlessly. "I'm sorry I didn't call or anything-"

Pandora smiled and pulled her inside, surprising her.

"How've you been, Alice?"

"I've been great! Is Miss Black here?"

"Call me Dreamer," Dreamer called, and Alice giggled.

"Dreamer. I'm glad you're home!"

"I'm glad you came," Dreamer replied, Alice taking off her coat and shoes. Pandora took them and put them in the closet for her like a good chauffer would, Alice beaming at her so brightly it unnerved her.

"Um… would you like a drink or something?"

"No thanks," Alice replied happily. "I've just had lunch with Daddy."

"Ok, let's go up."

* * *

Alice took over reading while Pandora brought Dreamer hot chocolate and marshmallows with two cupcakes.

"I hope you don't leave now," she told Dreamer ruefully. "Dad's the best guy in the whole wide world. You can't give him up, Mum."

Dreamer smiled at her child, choosing not to answer. That was Pandora, eighteen with the mind of a thirteen-year-old. Ted grinned at her, mouthing *"Thank you."*

Pandora winked before sitting down next to Alice on the carpet.

"What part are we at now?"

"Erica calls the guards on Kane," Dreamer said before Alice could answer. Pandora took the book off Alice, saying "My turn."

"Go it, 'Dora," smiled Ted, sitting down next to Dreamer and flexing his fingers. Smiling at her, he said "You're all nice and soft now."

"I feel it," Dreamer answered with a smile. "'Dora?"

"Kane let the guards pull him away, knowing it wasn't the end." Pandora paused for effect, everyone smiling at her. "Erica watched him thoughtfully, thinking he did and said the things he did for show. She was sure Kane was kind underneath, sure of it. As if he knew what she was thinking, Kane looked back and smiled at her, saying 'You will be mine, Erica!' Erica shook her head and went inside.'"

"She loves him really," Alice said, intrigued by the tale. Ted nodded, surprised at himself. He should be downstairs watching football, not hanging out with the girls listening to love stories. Before Pandora could continue Dreamer's mobile went off, Dreamer reaching for it.

"Dreamer talking."

"Dreamer," said Miriam in a choked voice. "Is everything ok?"

"Everything's fine," said Dreamer, Ted laying next to her and resting his head on her back. "Ted- get off me, I'm on the phone."

* * *

Images flashed before Miriam's eyes, unwanted.

"He's on top of you?"

"I didn't mean- he's got his head on my back."

"I need to talk to you," Miriam said quietly, and Dreamer said ok.

"Are you all right?"

"No! I thought you was going to leave him last night, Dreamer!"

"I was going to!"

"No you wasn't! You said everything for show, didn't you?"

"That's not true, ok?"

Dreamer rolled off the bed and got up as Miriam rose from her sofa.

"And even if you couldn't go, you could have told him you don't love him, Dreamer!"

"I couldn't do that to him!"

Ted glanced at her sharply, realising he was the subject on the line.

"You've done worse to me in your time, haven't you?"

"I was upset! How could I go anywhere when-"

Pandora and Ted leapt up at the same time, startling Alice.

"Come now," Miriam said firmly. "Tell him you have to go."

"But-"

"Now, Dreamer!"

"Ted, I- I... my friend needs to see me," she said, turning to look at him, then she took a step backwards in alarm. His face was murderous. "Ted?"

"That's the person who was speaking to you last night, isn't it?"

"Yes. I- no. Fine, yes."

"They was telling you what to say, wasn't they Dreamer?"

Dreamer opened her mouth to say no, then she nodded. Ted shook his head in disbelief: someone wanted him and Dreamer apart. Dreamer probably did love him- now he was sure she did. Pandora thought so too.

Ted looked Dreamer right in the eyes, saying "Who are they?"

"Ignore him and teleport," Miriam said, knowing if she didn't she'd never be able to leave. "Do it, Dreamer!"

Temper rising, Dreamer obeyed.

* * *

"You'd better explain what the hell is wrong with you!" she screamed, appearing in a flash of red light. "Now, Miriam!"

"Have a cup of tea," Miriam answered, infuriating her. "It's still hot."

Dreamer looked at the coffee table, tempted by the little cakes and biscuits laid out for her especially. Sighing, she sat down.

Miriam sat too, watching her every movement. Dreamer refused to make eye contact, unable to believe what was happening. Miriam had never been like this with her before in her life. Giving orders etcetera. Dreamer guessed she had taken too much, like filling a glass with wine without stopping. Eventually it would spill over the edge of the glass. The glass was Miriam, and the wine was Dreamer. Miriam had taken too much of her crap and it was time to take control for once.

"What happened, Dreamer?" she asked calmly. "You was all set to leave Ted while you was here yesterday, but you suddenly got cold feet when you got back- probably when you saw him with his shirt off."

Dreamer chose not to answer that, sipping her tea in silence.

"You know I would have let you stay here, Dreamer. You still can."

Dreamer reached for a cupcake in reply, refusing to speak.

Her mobile rang, and she answered it quickly. "Dreamer."

"Mum, is everything ok?" said Pandora worriedly. "Where are you?"

"I'm with a friend, darling."

"Are you coming back?"

Dreamer looked at Miriam, who stared back at her coldly, silently daring her to say yes. Unnerved, Dreamer said "Put Ted on the phone, Pandora."

"You aren't, are you?" Pandora's voice cracked. "Why not?"

"Pandora-"

"Is it another guy you're with?" Silence. "Mum, say something!"

"Put your father on the phone," Dreamer said quietly, but she didn't.

"We tried hard to make you stay, and you still went!"

"Pandora, I'm not going to ask you again." Dreamer spoke calmly. "If you don't put Ted on the phone I'll hang up, then turn my mobile off."

"Mum, don't say that! I just want to talk to you!"

"And we will talk, darling, but I need to speak to Ted even more."

"I heard you in the kitchen," Pandora said sadly. "You don't love him."

Dreamer shot an accusing glance at Miriam, as if blaming her. Miriam suddenly felt a surge of guilt, and she opened her mouth to apologise but Dreamer shook her head angrily.

"It's done now, isn't it?"

"What's done now, Mum? Who are you talking to?"

Dreamer opened her mouth spitefully, about to let Pandora know that it her godmother who wanted to tear the family apart. But she knew better, knew she wasn't as low as that.

"That doesn't matter, Pandora. What matters is you've disobeyed me."

Pandora flinched at her tone, and handed the phone to Ted silently before leaving the room and joining Alice in her own.

"She's with another man," she announced bitterly, making Alice's jaw drop. "Her and Dad had an argument last night, and both of them were even crying and stuff- but they were kissing this morning so I thought-"

"I don't think she's with another man," Alice said, shaking her head. "Dreamer's not like that."

"How do *you* know what she's like? You've only seen her twice!"

"But I've watched her for six months," argued Alice, "And everyone got to know her through the telly. She's not the cheating type."

Pandora scowled at her, saying "You don't know a thing."

"If she doesn't love your dad you can't be angry with her for that. People fall out of love all the time," Alice said matter-of-factly. "She's been with him for ages and a half, so-"

"Listen, people stay together for like fifty years," Pandora said furiously. "And before my Mum met whoever she was talking to-"

"Shh!" hissed Alice, hearing Ted's raised voice. "Listen!"

* * *

"Who is it, Dreamer? Who are you with?"

"Ted, if I tell you you'll lose your temper-"

"Lose my temper?" Ted repeated. "Lose my *temper*? Dreamer, my temper got lost in the woods the minute you vanished. Where are you?"

"I can't say that either."

"Don't play games with me, Dreamer!"

"Don't shout at me!" Dreamer's voice cracked. "I hate it, Ted!"

Miriam put an arm around her as she listened, Ted saying "Who is he?"

"Who?"

"The guy you're with!"

"I'm not with- you don't know him," Dreamer said, when Miriam shook her head. "I'm staying with him, Ted, and there's nothing you can do about it."

"You don't mean that."

"I do," said Dreamer, eyes filling. This was going horribly wrong. "I do."

"I know you don't, because your voice is so soft." Ted shook his head. "If you meant it you'd be cold as ice, Dreamer, and you know it."

Dreamer swallowed, tears falling. "I... I'm hanging up."

"When I find out who's making you do this," Ted promised her, "I'm going to kill them with my bare hands."

"Try it," Miriam said coolly, making him stop dead.

"It's a woman you're with?"

"She's a friend," Dreamer said, unable to stop the tears. "A friend!"

"Is she making you do this, Dreamer? This friend of yours?"

"Ted, I have to go, I'm sorry."

Ted took that as a yes. Pandora slowly entered the room as he said "When you're ready, Dreamer, come home. You know I can never stay mad at you for long. Tell this woman I'm going to-"

Miriam snatched the mobile and pressed the red button before he could finish, shaking her head as she said "To think we were friends."

"I don't want to choose between the two of you," said Dreamer sadly.

"So I'm leaving both of you for good. I'm going back to Mama."

"You can't!" blurted Miriam, shocked at how desolate her friend looked. "Don't get depressed over this, Dreamer: you said you don't love him."

"I said I don't love him in the same way," Dreamer corrected, "And after today, I realise I was just looking for attention. I do love Ted."

"Dreamer, don't-!!"

But she'd already teleported.

* * *

Ted paced back and forth in the living room, unable to relax. Pandora was drumming her fingers on the arm of her chair, as worked up as her father. They were waiting for Dreamer to come home, or at least call.

It had been an entire week, a miserable, gruelling week. Marlon was back home, but he stayed shut in his room all day and night, refusing to communicate, just like Pandora.

Ted slumped on the sofa, saying "This is hopeless."

Marlon stomped down the stairs angrily, storming into the living room.

"I can't eat, Dad! I can't sleep properly! I want my mother, ok?"

"What am I supposed to do, Marlon?" said Ted wearily, looking at him. "Her mobile phone's turned off. She's not with your grandmother. I've even asked Miriam but she hasn't seen her either."

"Everyone's real worried," Pandora said, averting her gaze to her lap before they saw her eyes fill. "Nobody knows where she is."

"Don't cry, 'Dora," said Marlon gently. "She'll come back soon."

Pandora shook her head, not answering him.

The family tried getting back to the life they had before Dreamer came home, but it was impossible. Ted's boss suggested he take time off, but Ted refused. He needed to work to keep his mind of Dreamer. Alice came over in the day to keep Pandora company, both of them speculating over Dreamer's whereabouts, their guesses becoming sillier and sillier. Alice suggested she was the couch in the living room while Pandora argued that she was definitely Shadow the rabbit. They both laughed until they cried, Marlon angrily telling them to cut it out. He even told Alice to get out the house- only yesterday. He was taking Dreamer's absence very hard, as was Pandora, but Pandora seemed to be dealing with it better than he was... on the outside. Ted and Marlon both heard her sobbing into her pillow every night since Dreamer left, but they didn't dare confront her about it.

Marlon was still towering over Ted.

"Try her mobile again."

Ted stood too, Marlon stepping back a little. His father was over two feet taller than he was, his face miserable as ever.

"Marlon, you know I've been trying. It's turned off."

Marlon nodded, eyes welling. "I miss her so much, Dad!"

"Don't, Marlon!" said Pandora, tears falling. "Don't cry, ok?"

"Dad, do something!" said Marlon desperately. "Call Grandma!"

"She doesn't know where Dreamer is, Marlon. I've called already."

* * *

"Look at you," scolded Agnes, placing a bowl of warm soup in front of her daughter. "You look terrible, Dreamer Black."

"Mama, please." Dreamer shook her head. "I don't want to hear it."

"You *will* hear it," said Agnes, heat rising. "Running away isn't the way to deal with this, Dreamer. You have to go back."

"No."

"Why not?"

"Miriam and Ted love me too much, and I can't handle it."

"That much I agree with, but what about your children?"

"My children are young adults, Mama. Eighteen and nineteen years old."

"They're still children, even if they're forty one and forty two," Agnes said firmly. "How do you think they're dealing with this?"

Dreamer shrugged, pushing the bowl away from her.

"You will have your dinner, Dreamer, or I'll take the wooden spoon and lay it about you until you'll be desperate to get back to Ted Stone, and leave this very evening!"

Dreamer hastily pulled the bowl towards her and picked up her spoon.

"Why can't Miriam understand?" she said between mouthfuls of soup. "We can work this out properly; me, her and Ted."

"How about we get Miriam over here instead?" asked Agnes, but before Dreamer could protest she clapped her hands.

BANG!!

Miriam appeared, looking knocked for six. She blinked several times before everything swam into focus- Agnes standing there, beaming at her, and Dreamer- *Dreamer.* She refused to look at Miriam.

"You may feel a little giddy, dear." Agnes led her to a chair. "Sit down."

Miriam sat slowly, eyes on Dreamer. Dreamer determinedly stared down at her bowl of soup, Agnes saying "Speak up, Dreamer."

"She can share me, Mama. But she wants me to herself."

"You've neglected her for a very long time," Agnes replied. "From her point of view, it's always been Ted this, Ted that."

"But-"

"She's sick and tired of being second best," Agnes said firmly. "Which is why she behaved that way. I would have too, Dreamer Black."

"Thanks for the support, Mama." Dreamer was furious. "I'm the victim!"

"Miriam and Ted are the victims," Agnes said, glaring at her daughter. "They've been topsy-turvy since you came back into their lives."

"I could wipe their minds and leave again," Dreamer shot back, hurt. "Pandora's and Marlon's too."

"You'll do no such thing," Agnes said, temper rising. "Apologise to her!"

"I'm sorry Dreamer," Miriam said quickly, but Agnes shook her head.

"I meant Dreamer, Miriam."

"Me!" Dreamer burst out. "I did nothing, Mama!"

"Exactly! And in doing so you've hurt not only Ted, but Miriam as well!"

"I visited Miriam," said Dreamer hotly, glaring at Agnes. "I'm not lying!"

"You visited Miriam while you ignored Ted, and then you smooched with Ted while forgetting about Miriam!" barked Agnes, making Dreamer recoil. "You apologise to Miriam right now, and Ted afterwards!"

Dreamer stubbornly remained silent, Agnes glaring at her. Miriam looked away, glad Agnes was on her side, but she wanted Dreamer to be happy.

"You see?" said Agnes, reading Miriam's thoughts. "She doesn't even care if you don't apologise, as long as you're happy!"

"Then what's the fuss about?" said Dreamer cheekily, then she stood swiftly as Agnes pulled out a magnificent wand, jet black. Miriam nearly smiled as Dreamer pulled out her golden wand too, ready as ever. That was Dreamer all right. Not afraid of anyone or anything.

Agnes blinked, surprised. "You'll duel with your mother?"

"You'll duel with your daughter?" Dreamer countered, and Agnes laughed as she lowered her wand. Dreamer only lowered hers when her mother placed her wand inside her robe, laughing still.

"You get your bravery from your father."

"Papa is a coward," Dreamer said coldly, sitting back down. "If he were brave he'd return home- don't you agree Miriam?"

Miriam jumped, startled at Dreamer talking to her so suddenly.

"Well, I- I... he has his reasons for staying away, I think-"

"Well said," said Agnes, sharply adding "Now apologise, Dreamer."

"Sorry."

"Properly!"

"I'm sorry, Miriam!"

"Good," smirked Agnes. "Now, Miriam, you'll stay the night."

"Oh, I- I couldn't stay," said Miriam, looking at Dreamer. "I don't want to intrude or anything, Agnes- this is um... mother daughter time."

Dreamer and Agnes both burst out laughing, Dreamer saying "Stay."

"Ok," she said quickly, and they laughed again.

* * *

"Remember when you made Miss Minis' wig fly off her head?" Miriam burst out laughing in her bed, Dreamer as well. "That was hilarious!"

"I did a lot of things at school," Dreamer answered, across the room from her in another double bed. "But the best time was when-"

Agnes rapped on the door sharply, saying "Girls, quieten down."

"Sorry Mama," Dreamer called, then she shook her head. "We're grown women and she's treating us like we're still thirteen."

"Because you act it," said Agnes, popping her head round the door. "Running away and trying to control each other, jealous of your best friend's husband while the best friend forgets her children- that shut you up, didn't it?" Dreamer and Miriam were both looking shamefaced. "Good. Now go to sleep, or at least whisper. Turn out the lights."

"Yes Mama," Dreamer said resignedly, obeying. Smiling in the dark, Miriam said "Goodnight Agnes. Thanks for having me over."

"Anytime, dear."

Dreamer waited until the passage lights went out and Agnes's bedroom door closed before muttering "Suck up."

They both burst out laughing again.

* * *

"Hey Pandora," said Alice brightly, coming in. "Hear from Dreamer?"
Marlon glared at her as Pandora shook her head, saying "Not yet."
"She'll call," said Alice reassuringly. "Today, I bet you five pounds."
"You're on," said Marlon angrily. "And I'll be laughing when you hand it
over- and then I can take Emily to the cinema like I promised."
"Who's Emily?" Pandora said curiously, but Marlon shook his head.
"I made her up, but that's not the point. I just want Mum back."
"And she will come back," Alice said gently. "I promise."
Something stirred inside Marlon as he looked at her, not answering.
Alice, feeling likewise, averted her gaze.
Pandora, not noticing the connection between her brother and friend, said
"Maybe she won't call today, but-"
"I'm back!" called Ted, entering though the door in the kitchen- the back
door. "Did you two survive without arguing?"
"Yeah," said Marlon, a smile forming now. "We didn't argue at all."
"Good. Hello Alice," said Ted, shaking his head at her. "You'd think this
is your second home; you're here almost everyday."
"It's only been two weeks, Mr Stone," Alice said shyly. "I'll be out of
your hair when Dreamer comes back, I promise."
Ted smiled at her, saying "We wouldn't want that, would we Pandora?"
"No," Pandora said grudgingly, and Alice beamed at her.
Marlon watched her as he set about making his father a cup of coffee. He
found Alice annoying, too happy. A girl version of James really. He
wouldn't mind a girlfriend who was just like his best mate. Two James's
in his life would be awesome. But there was Pandora to think about here,
Marlon thought as he poured the water into Ted's cup. He remembered
her reaction to his seeing Janice, her ex best friend, his ex girlfriend. She
hadn't spoken to either of them for almost four months- and with most
people that would've been hard, especially when one person lived with
you and /the other you saw everyday at school. But not for Pandora,
Marlon thought with a small smile. She treated me like nothing, and-
"Camel mouth." Pandora interrupted his thoughts. "You're making a
mess, look." She pointed at the counter. "Clean that up, ok?"
Water sloshed over the side of the counter, splashing on the floor-
scorching Marlon's bare feet.
"OW!!" he yelled, dropping the kettle. "Dad!"
"Baby," said Ted amusedly, getting up and picking up the mop. "Go and
sit down, I'll make the tea myself. Thanks, though."
"No problem," Marlon muttered, feet stinging. "Least I tried."
"You could've tried making it by magic," Pandora told him smugly.

"Then nobody would've gotten hurt, don't you think?"

"Shut up, Pandora!"

Now that she said it, making the tea magically would have been the best thing to do, especially when he needed to practice using it.

"Dad, my feet hurt," mumbled Marlon, looking at Ted. "I want a hug."

"Go and sit on the sofa," Ted answered, and Marlon obeyed.

"Can you believe him?" Pandora said, amused as she looked at her brother. "You'd think he's still a baby."

Alice found it sweet that Marlon still needed his parents to comfort him, as if he was only six years old. Still, she nodded in agreement. Marlon glared at her and turned away, picking up the television remote.

Not so much like James- James would've stuck up for him. The doorbell went, Ted sighing as he said "That'll be James."

Pandora pulled Alice away and up the stairs as Marlon got up, saying "Think of the devil!"

"Don't you like James?" Alice asked her curiously, after Pandora shut and locked her bedroom door with them inside. "You always run when he comes over, did you know that? But when other people come, like your dad's clients from work or neighbours or Marlon's other friends, you-"

"I chose Forest Academy because he was going," blurted Pandora, making her stop short. "I didn't choose it because it was a good college."

Alice tried not to smirk. Pandora was human after all: she had a crush on James. Sitting down on Pandora's bean bag, she said "Spill."

So Pandora told her everything about James, that they were best friends at primary school and even in secondary school- up to Year Nine. James hardly spoke to her afterwards: he was besotted with everything she wasn't included in.

"It wasn't like I liked him then anyway," she said flatly, shrugging a shoulder. "I had my friends, especially Janice, and a boyfriend as well."

Alice sat up straighter, asking "Who was he?"

"An idiot. Marlon and Janice got together at my fifteenth birthday party, James had some other girl, I had Jonathan (the idiot), and we was all happy. Even when Mum got killed, Janice and Jonathan helped me and Marlon and even Dad. Everything was all gravy until Jonathan cheated on me with Janice-"

"No way!"

"Yes way," said Pandora bitterly. "Two best friends gone in ten minutes."

Alice couldn't help herself. "Was Marlon ok?"

"No. You might have noticed he's a real emotional guy," Pandora said, smiling a little. "He's got girls on the side, though, but he-"

"Never mind that," said Alice quickly, not wanting to hear that Marlon was a playa. "We was talking about James."

"I still haven't spoken to him," mumbled Pandora, feeling guilty. "Since he gave me his number ages ago- where's Miriam, Alice? I need to talk to her about a lot of stuff, but she's been off for two weeks. Does your dad know where she's gone?"

Alice shook her head, saying "She probably needs a break. You know, she talks to a lot of people but nobody talks to her. Does she even have any friends? A social life, I mean?"

Pandora opened her mouth, then closed it. She'd never thought of Miriam outside the office, not properly. Even though she was her godmother- godmother!

"Her and my Mum!" said Pandora, mind racing. "They was best friends."

"Probably still are," Alice answered, wondering what she was thinking.

"They might be together," Pandora said excitedly. "I mean, how come as soon as my Mum disappears she does too?"

"She didn't," Alice argued. "Miss Hughes was around for a whole week."

Pandora closed her mouth, thinking hard.

"Something still isn't right about her leaving."

* * *

"Smart girl, my Pandora," Dreamer said to Agnes amusedly. "She thinks Miriam might be with me, Mama."

"And she is," Agnes replied, smiling at Miriam. "Before her manager thinks she's slacking she must go back home- you as well."

"That place isn't my home," Dreamer said huffily. "It's just... Ted's."

"Call the boy and ask how they are," Agnes answered, stirring the broth in her cauldron with a giant wooden spoon. "Go on, little one."

"Mama, I've told you to stop..."

Muttering darkly, Dreamer sauntered into the living room and picked up the house phone.

* * *

"Shouldn't you be going home?" Marlon asked coldly, as Alice came downstairs jauntily. "This isn't a youth centre, you know."
"I'm hanging until eight o clock," Alice answered just as coldly. "If Dreamer doesn't call by then, you'll get your five pounds."
James looked up from the sofa as they glared at each other.
"Where's Pandora, hiding upstairs still?" he asked lightly, and Alice smiled at him. Marlon immediately felt his stomach writhe with jealousy as she said "I don't know why she keeps doing that."
"Maybe I scare her," joked James, and Alice's smile grew. Annoyed, Marlon said "What did you come down for, Alice? You're not wanted."
"I came to talk to James," Alice shot back, "So *you're* not wanted."
James burst out laughing. "Shame, bro! She got you."
Marlon glared at him, saying "You want to talk, go in the garden."
"Fine," Alice said blithely, pushing past him even though there was plenty of space to pass without touching him. "Come on James."
James obeyed, to Marlon's anger.
"Be right back."

* * *

"Did you know Pandora's going to Forest Academy?"
"No," he said, surprised. The house phone rang inside as he said "You're not joking with me, Alice?" Alice said no. "How come she's-"
"Maybe because it's a good college," shrugged Alice, but James waved that away as he said "She's going because I'm going."
Alice raised an eyebrow. "Isn't that a bit arrogant?"
"No it's not, because I…"
Alice pretended to be deeply interested as James told her what she already knew.
Meanwhile, inside the house, Marlon was speaking so fast into the telephone the caller couldn't understand a word he was saying.
"Sweetheart, calm down for me. Where's Pandora and Ted?"
"Upstairs, and I'm not getting them," Marlon said stubbornly. He rarely had a moment alone with his mother, and he was going to use this time whether Dreamer liked it or not. Ted jogged downstairs with his daughter as Marlon said "I'm packing up, Mum. I'm coming to you right now."
"Give the phone!" shrieked Pandora, startling him. Before Marlon could react Pandora socked him in the stomach, winding him completely. Marlon dropped the phone, gasping for breath as Pandora picked it up.
"Mum, are you all right? Are you angry with me?"

"Why would I be angry with you?" said Dreamer, puzzled at her.

"Because I didn't give the phone to Dad when you asked me to-"

"Oh," said Dreamer, vaguely remembering the incident. "No I'm not."

"Promise?"

"I promise, love. How are you?"

"Rotten," Pandora said, eyes filling. "Ok on the outside, but-"

Ted took the phone, saying "She's been crying every night since you left, Dreamer. We've all been miserable as heck- where are you?"

"I'm with Mama right now," Dreamer said cautiously. "I…"

She trailed off, not knowing what else to say. Ted listened to her silence, Marlon and Pandora behind him. Finally Dreamer said "I'm sorry."

"What for?" said Ted, Marlon and Pandora in unison, startling Ted as he turned to look at them. Grinning, Marlon said "Inner hearing, Dad."

Dreamer laughed, Ted saying "They are definitely your kids, Dreamer."

Just then Pandora caught sight of Alice and James outside through the kitchen window. Nudging Marlon, she whispered "What are they doing?"

Marlon looked too, then he said "They're probably getting together."

Pandora heard the bitterness in his voice, but she let it go because she was feeling just as bitter.

"I'm going to my room."

"Ditto."

Ted frowned as his kids traipsed upstairs, but he didn't call them back. He was focusing on the love of his life.

"Are you coming back home, Dreamer?"

"I- I-"

* * *

Agnes prodded her in the back, hissing "Say yes!"

Dreamer ignored her, pleasing Miriam.

"You can't stay away," said Ted, pleading in his voice. "You can't."

"Ted, I just need a few more days."

"Are you with that woman who was making you say everything?"

"I'm with Mama," Dreamer said quietly. "I told you already."

"A few more days." Ted drew a deep breath, then he said "Then will you come home? Back to me and Marlon, and Pandora?"

Dreamer didn't know what to say. Miriam was looking at her, her brown eyes cold and dark. For the first time in her life, Dreamer was afraid of her best friend. She knew if she went back to Ted Miriam would never forgive her. She'd been with Ted for so long, practically ignored Miriam for years. She couldn't do it to her again.

Miriam looked down at her feet, waiting to hear Dreamer tell Ted she loved him and was coming home soon. Taking a deep breath, Dreamer said "Ted, I can't."

Miriam's head shot up in surprise, Agnes shaking her head at her.

"You're lucky Dreamer has a good heart, my girl."

Miriam nodded, Ted saying "She's with you at Agnes's place??"

"Yes she is," Dreamer said softly. "She needs me, Ted."

"Who the hell is she?" demanded Ted, angry tears welling up. Alice and James entered the house as he said "Dreamer!"

"Tell him," urged Agnes, and Dreamer whispered "I can't, Mama!"

"You can," said Ted gently. "Do I know them?"

"Yes- you'll lose your temper and do something to them-"

"No I won't," lied Ted. "I won't touch them if they're a woman."

"You're lying."

"I'm not!"

"Yes you are," said Dreamer flatly. "I can hear it in your voice."

"Dreamer, just come home- please!"

"I'm staying with my friend, ok Ted?"

"Where do they live? Can I at least visit you?"

"I'll visit you instead," Dreamer replied, and Miriam scowled. Smiling at her, Agnes whispered "You can't have it all, Miriam."

"I suppose," Miriam whispered back, then a sudden thought struck her.

"Dreamer-" Dreamer looked at her. "Don't come to mine."

"What?"

"Don't come," Miriam repeated, then she drew a deep breath. "Unless it's what you want. I don't want you to come unhappy."

Agnes's smile grew as she looked at Dreamer, who was surprised.

"Now you want to go back to your old self?"

"I don't want you to come unhappy," Miriam repeated. "Against your will. I'm being selfish- I'm only thinking about myself. "

Ted frowned as he listened. The woman's voice sounded a little familiar.

"If it's not what you want," Miriam said slowly and clearly, as if Dreamer couldn't understand a word, "Don't come. Is it what you want?"

"Say no," Ted said angrily, not touched at all. Dreamer was.

"I thought you wanted me to leave Ted and stay with you?"

"She what!" exploded Ted, but Dreamer wasn't listening to him.

"I do, but… I don't want you unhappy."

"You can't stay with her, Dreamer. She's a fricking queer!"

"Be quiet, Ted!" snapped Dreamer, feeling uneasy in her stomach. Miriam smiled at her, saying "It's your choice."

Ted wanted to shout "Come home!"

But he knew he had to play it smart, just like this mystery woman. She was using charm on *his* woman, and he could feel her slipping away.

"She's right," he said smoothly. "It's your choice, Dreamer."

Surprised, Dreamer said "What did you say?"

"You heard me," Ted said calmly. "If you want to stay with your friend, I won't stop you. I just realised I shouldn't order you about- it's your life."

Agnes smiled broadly: the boy was smarter than she thought. Dreamer had a confused look on her face as she said "Are you sure?"

"Sure as ever. She's right, it's your choice."

* * *

Alice tapped him on the shoulder, whispering "Tell Pandora bye."
Ted nodded, mouthing *"Bye."*
James walked her to the front door, feeling light hearted. As Alice turned
to say bye he gave her a hug, saying "Thanks for the info."
"Anytime," she said, pleased as she hugged him back.
Little did they know Pandora and Marlon was watching from Marlon's
bedroom window, which overlooked the street their house was on.
"I'll kill her," muttered Pandora, as Marlon said "I'll kill him."
Then they looked at each other, surprised.
"What're you killing him for, camel mouth?"
"What're you killing *her* for?" Marlon retorted, and she smiled.
"I won't tell if you won't."
"Deal."

* * *

"So what do you want to do?" Ted asked lightly, angering Miriam. She
knew what he was up to. Dreamer didn't *know* what to do. Innocent as
ever, Ted said "How about you come back home?"
"Ted-"
"Just listen," he said gently. "You come back home, and you can see your
mystery friend anytime you like. Everyday for all I care, I'm not joking.
You can sleepover if she means so much to you, it's no bother."
He's good, Agnes thought impressively. Way good.
Miriam thought so too, but she wouldn't let him win so easily.
"Or the other way round," she said just as gently. "You can come home
with me and visit *him* anytime you like."
Fury exploded in the pit of Ted's stomach, but he said "Or that too."
Dreamer was stuck. Agnes was highly amused. Wanting to join in the
fun, she said "How about I flip a coin, Dreamer?"
"I can't see the coin," Ted protested, and Agnes said "You have my word
I won't cheat- both of you."
"I'll take tails," Miriam said quickly, angering Ted. When he found out
who she was…
"I'll take heads, then."
"Wait- wait!" said Dreamer, feeling isolated. "I'll make the choice, ok?"
"Yes," said Ted and Miriam at the same time, amusing her.
"I'm going home- wait," she said, as Miriam's jaw dropped. "I'm going
to do this fairly. Two weeks with Ted and two weeks with you."

"No!" shouted two voices, startling Ted. "No, Mum! No!"

"Who the hell is this person?" demanded Marlon, storming down the stairs with Pandora in tow. "Dad! Who are they?"

"Some woman who's forcing your mother to do the unthinkable," Ted answered bitterly, Pandora saying "What's her name?"

"I don't know, 'Dora. Boil the kettle for your old man- his head hurts."

Pandora pulled out her wand and flicked it in the direction of the kitchen; Marlon grinned as the kettle started to boil.

"Cool."

"Ask your friend if that's what she wants," Ted said blithely. *"Fairness."*

Miriam opened her mouth furiously, then she closed it. Dreamer's green eyes sparkled as she said "What do you think?"

"Anything you want," Miriam said smoothly, making Dreamer smile.

"Ted?"

"Anything you want," echoed Ted calmly. "Good thing it's the first of August, huh? Or we'd be working out the dates."

He knows how to play the game, Miriam thought, Agnes too.

"And at the end of the month you decide where to go," Agnes told Dreamer, Miriam and Ted saying "Ok," fast as lightning.

"Settled," Agnes said triumphantly, beaming. "Oh, you both are good at this sort of thing. It's almost some sort of game."

"A game I'll win," Ted said loudly, knowing the mystery lady would hear. Cringing at his cockiness, Miriam said "In your dreams."

Dreamer and Ted spoke for a bit more, Dreamer telling him she'd be home in an hour. Already Ted was working out what they could do for Dreamer in that hour. Run her a bath, lay out little treats...

Dreamer whispered goodbye and put the phone down, then she smiled.

Miriam smiled back, saying "It's a win-win. Are you happy?"

"Yes. Are you?"

"I'm happy if you're happy. That's a yes," she added warmly, and Dreamer's smile grew.

"Mama will send you back for me, won't you Mama?"

"Where are *you* going?" said Miriam, startled. "You said an hour!"

"I'm not going home, I'm... going somewhere else."

Miriam recognised the mischievous glint in her eye, as did Agnes.

"Don't even think about going where I think you're going," Agnes said firmly. "Leave that boy alone, Dreamer- let things lie."

"I can't, Mama. I still need to know what I need to know."

"You'll only confuse yourself even more," Agnes replied, shaking her head. "You're just like your father- reckless."

Dreamer smiled and teleported.

* * *

"Enough!" yelled the officers, five holding Damon back and another five holding George back.

"Tell them she's alive!" Damon shouted at George, but George refused.

"We was hallucinating, Damon! Hallucinating!"

"We wasn't ha- let go of me!"

The officers refused, saying "Detention, Stile!"

Seconds later he was sitting in a tiny room, all alone.

"How long am I in here?" he yelled, an officer calling "One hour!"

"But I didn't- I'm not lying to you!"

"Well if your magical girlfriend really is back from the dead, let her rescue you! Let her take you for a walk in the park, Stile!"

Laughter erupted at the officer's comment, Damon sighing as he muttered "She's not my girlfriend. And she really is back."

"Frustrating when they don't understand, isn't it?" a voice said softly, and Damon turned to look at the speaker, knowing who it would be.

Dreamer looked stunning in an emerald green gown, bringing out her eyes, with matching bangles and earrings.

Damon swallowed hard, scanning her face fearfully. Dreamer stared back at him until he let out a breath, assured she wasn't angry.

"Yeah, it's frustrating," he said hoarsely, then he swallowed again. "Um- I..."

Dreamer waited, but he shook his head.

She stood in the corner of the room, watching him struggle to say something- anything. But he couldn't. Dreamer let five minutes of silence pass before she said "How are you, Damon?"

"Fine," he croaked. "You?"

"Never been better."

"Good- that's good."

Dreamer said nothing in reply, Damon realising he had to talk fast or she might leave again, and this time not come back.

"When did you- you know. Come back to life?"

"About seven months ago."

"How did your family take it?"

"As I expected them to," Dreamer answered coldly. "Speaking of my family-" Damon flinched, knowing what was coming up next. "Tell me what possessed you to assault my only girl, my youngest child."

Damon shook his head, saying "I don't know."

He drew back as Dreamer pulled out a magnificent wand- it wasn't the silver wand he was accustomed to seeing, the nice silver one he'd seen since the age of eleven. This golden wand studded with diamonds looked much more deadly- and that meant *Dreamer* was more deadly than before she died. She was more powerful.

Dreamer moved closer, kneeling down so they were face to face. Her wand sparked as she pointed the tip right between his eyes, her green eyes darkening with fury. Damon swallowed hard, staring into them.

"Either you tell me or I'll plague this entire prison," she said icily. "You'll all die within six months, officers included."

"Dreamer, I- please," he said desperately, as her free hand reached for his neck. Seconds later he was choking.

"You'd better talk to me, Damon." Her voice was just above a whisper. "Tell me why you did it, and if you tell me you don't know again…"

She didn't finish her sentence. She didn't have to.

Swallowing with difficultly, he choked out "You'll be disgusted."

"I already am disgusted," she snapped. "You've got five seconds to talk before I set this plague off- one."

"Dreamer, please-"

"Two."

"I can't tell you!"

"Three, Damon!"

"No!"

"Four!"

As her wand started to emit some foul coloured gas, Damon realised she wasn't kidding- he was stupid to think that she was. Dreamer would murder over a hundred people without thinking twice or looking back.

"I don't do halves and quarters, it's not my style. Fi-"

"All right!" he screamed, and the gas cleared immediately.

Dreamer raised an eyebrow as he swallowed, shaking like a leaf- then she tightened her grip on his neck as she said "Start talking!"

"I was your friend first," said Damon, willing his eyes not to fill. "I was there before Ted- I was."

"So?"

"I wanted you," said Damon bitterly, "But you wanted *him.*"

"So?"

"Pandora looks just like you," Damon said, swallowing hard. "Spitting image." Dreamer didn't answer this time. "So when I- did I what I did, I guess I was pretending-"

Dreamer released him and got up, wiping her hand as if he was something repulsive.

"Pretending she was me? Damon, that is- that's… it doesn't even have a name it's so disgusting!" she said angrily, as he hung his head in shame. "What were you thinking?"

"That she was you. Didn't we just cover that?"

His sassy remark earned him a powerful slap in the face- SMACK!! Damon crashed onto the cold concrete floor, tasting blood in his mouth. Wow, he thought as he got up slowly. What a woman!

Outside, an officer just happened to be walking by when Dreamer said "If you ever cheek me like that again I'll rip your head off, understand?!"

"Understood!"

"I should murder you like you murdered me, you filthy son of a-"

"Dreamer, please!"

The officer pulled back a tiny bit of the metal slate, eyes widening in shock at the beauty glaring at one of the prisoners.

Stumbling backwards he whispered into his walkman "I need backup right away- don't reply. I need Sergeant Brown up here especially- the detention room on the top floor. Come quietly."

* * *

"Well I'll be damned," whispered Sergeant Brown, watching Dreamer rage at Damon with no intention of stopping soon. "He wasn't lying."

"She's gorgeous, Sarge."

"Look beyond the gorgeousness," hissed Brown, glaring at his officers. "We're dealing with Dreamer Black here- she's a witch. You've heard of Agnes and Paul Black, right?"

"Dangerous evil magic beings," an officer mumbled. "Especially Paul."

"No, Agnes is the worst," another officer whispered, but the first officer argued "Dreamer's husband said Paul murdered his parents at him and Agnes's place, with a couple spells. He made it look like they had some sort of fit or stroke or something- remember he's a sorcerer."

"Where is he now?"

"Word has it he's in the Bahamas. But their daughter, she… she's…"

"Even worse," whispered P.C. Jones. "'Cause she pretty, look at her."

"Not even that," said Brown, shaking his head. "Stile was telling the truth- and you're right. She's even worse because she came back from the dead- and can't you see that thing in her hand?"

Everyone took turns looking through the tiny crack in the door at Dreamer's wand, which was sparking in her fury. Damon was practically begging her to stop; he was terrified of what she might do.

"Don't tell me what to do either, Damon!"

"Dreamer, I'm sorry for what I did to Pandora- I'm sorry I killed you-"

"Sorry?" Dreamer's voice was suddenly quiet, so quiet the officers shuffled forwards to hear it. "Sorry? My baby's been scared of people for three years and all you can say is *sorry*? She hadn't even socialised properly until I came back to her, Damon. She had to see a shrink."

Damon wisely stayed quiet, wringing his hands in his lap.

"Maybe I *should* plague the prison and let you all die in here. You've all done something repulsive- you don't deserve to live."

"And- and the officers?" squeaked Damon, and Dreamer smirked.

"Let them die with you if they care for you so much."

Hell, no! Brown pulled out his gun, whispering "She's a demon! Get ready men... one... two... THREE!!"

He burst into the room with his men behind, holding up his gun and yelling "Freeze!"

Then they stopped dead, staring around.

"What- where is she?"

Damon sat on his chair as they looked about the tiny room, innocently asking "Is it time for me to go back to my cell?"

"You've got another forty minutes," snapped Brown, temper rising. "Oh, I should've known better than to try and corner the witch- she's the child of Agnes and Paul Black, after all. What was it, Stile? Teleportation?"

Dreamer watched as Damon smiled, saying "I don't know what you're talking about, Sarge. Why did you come in here? To see if I was ok?"

"To get your girlfriend!" roared Brown, reaching for his neck in agitation. "You stupid little... didn't you tell us she was alive?!"

Very Homer Simpson like, thought Dreamer amusedly, as Damon choked "Yeah I did Sarge, but that still doesn't tell me why you're here!"

"She was in here!" shouted Brown. "Talking to you!"

"Let him go, Sarge!"

Brown realised what he was doing and released Damon quickly. Taking a deep breath, he said "She was here. Wasn't she?"

Damon cocked his head to one side in mock concentration.

"Let me think... was Dreamer Black here in this prison?" He smirked and shook his head, saying "I don't think so. I would've yelled my lungs out, Sarge- I think you're hallucinating."

Dreamer smiled. He's got guts. He hasn't changed one bit, has he?

Brown realised Damon was getting his own back for the countless times he and the others had teased him about Dreamer's being alive for the past few weeks, prisoners and officers alike.

"Stile, you're being irrational."

"Very irrational," another officer said, and Damon shrugged.

"If Dreamer was here she would've gotten me out."

"Wishful thinking," Brown said cruelly. "Let's not forget what you did to little Pandora Black, Stile. Oh yes," he said quietly, as Damon froze. "It's all there Damon, in your files. You killed the mother and ruined the child, it's all there. And from what I made out, Dreamer isn't a very happy bunny. Plaguing the prison, killing us all... she's just like her father."

Dreamer was so close to cursing this man she knew she had to leave. Damon could feel the heat radiating from her body, and he knew she stood between him and Sergeant Brown; she wasn't protecting him, though. She was about to do something to the man.

"Go," he said, looking Brown in the eyes though he was talking to Dreamer. Brown folded his arms across his chest, saying "We're not going anywhere until we get an honest answer. Was that witch here?"

Dreamer's wand was out, pointing directly at his face. Sensing her fury, Damon repeated himself: "Go! We'll talk another time."

Dreamer refused. Brown stared through her body at Damon angrily, saying "We'll talk now, Stile! Is she planning an attack on the prison?"

Dreamer nearly laughed out loud as Damon shook his head.

"I don't know- please, just go. Come back at one in the morning."

Damn right I'll come back at one in the morning, thought Dreamer as she finally left the building. The cool night air was welcoming to her boiling skin. Dreamer inhaled deeply as if the air was water; she needed to calm down before she went home. Ted and the kids would see the anger on her face straight away, even if she smiled. It would be an evil smile.

Dreamer started walking slowly, twirling her wand between her fingers. She didn't care how many people she startled, her anger hadn't burned out yet. Seconds later she stopped and looked back at the tall grey building, thinking I'll come back and deal with *him*. That filth you call a Sergeant.

* * *

Marlon got the first hug, expectedly. "I missed you, Mum!"

"I missed you more," Pandora said, jealous as Dreamer kissed her son on the forehead. "I love that gown you're wearing, Mum."

"Thank you darling."

Dreamer let Pandora hug her as well, her eyes on Ted. He was standing in the doorway, watching the warm scene with even warmer eyes.

Marlon let go of Dreamer reluctantly, Pandora as well as they slowly exited the room, taking their time to go upstairs. Ted waited until both their doors snapped shut, Dreamer as well. Now they were alone.

"I've run your bathwater," Ted said softly, and Dreamer smiled shyly.

"Thank you. I need a bath after today."

"You look brilliant," Ted said, still in that quiet voice. "How's Agnes?"

"Mama's fine as usual," Dreamer replied, and Ted said "Maybe we can go and visit her- the four of us. Later on this week?"

Dreamer's small smile grew. "You mean that, Ted? You as well?"

"Me as well," Ted answered, nodding. "If she doesn't mind that."

"Of course she doesn't, but it can't hurt to ask."

Ted nodded as Dreamer looked away, anger creeping up on her. She was still furious, both at Damon and Sergeant Brown. Ted watched her take slow, steady breaths, and knew something was wrong. Taking a step forward, he said "Dreamer?"

"Mmm?"

"What is it?"

"A man compared me to Papa," she said truthfully, looking at him. "You don't know how angry I feel at him- and another person I know."

"How would they know your father?" Ted asked, then he realised what he was saying. Everyone in Europe had heard of Paul and Agnes Black, and rumours about their only child Dreamer. Even America had heard about Agnes and Paul- they were feared. Outcasts because of what they were- considered evil. Ted thought so too, when he was a small boy- only because of what his family had taught him growing up. They weren't meant to be in this world, he thought. Agnes and Paul terrified him, as they did everyone else- and he vowed if he ever met them he'd tell them how much he despised them and their magical selves.

Much to everyone's fear, Paul and Agnes moved close to Ted's area- high on a hill overshadowing the small town. Nobody remembered there ever being a house on a hill, which frightened them all the more.

Dreamer watched him as he stood deep in thought, then she decided to join him wherever he was.

Ted was all set to fulfill his promise, and he boldly marched round to the house- all alone. He took a deep breath, then he rang the doorbell. Nobody answered. Thinking of pleasing his father, he bravely rang again.
"Who is it?" called a soft voice, catching him off guard.
"Er... Ted Stone. I want to talk to the witch."
"What?"
"The witch," Ted repeated angrily. "Open up right now."
He braced himself as the door opened slowly, then his jaw dropped. Fourteen-year-old Dreamer stared at him curiously, Ted staring back. Minutes passed as they scrutinized each other's every feature, then Dreamer said "What do you want to talk to me about?"
"Come off it," Ted croaked, stunned by her beauty. Swallowing, he tried to remain in control. "Stop being stupid. You're not a witch."
"Yes I am. I am," she repeated, when Ted shook his head. "Not lying."
"Where's your magic, then?"
Dreamer stared at him as if he was crazy. "What do you mean?"
"See, I knew you was lying." Ted smirked at her. "You're normal, like me. You've got on your school uniform."
"So? I could've been in my robe."
"Your what?"
"Robe," Dreamer repeated amusedly. "What I normally wear."
"People don't wear robes."
"Witches do."
Ted realised he was being led astray, and he glared at her.
"Just get the witch out here, ok? Or the warlock."
"My father is a sorcerer," Dreamer said coldly, "And my mother-"
"Is a demon," Ted said lazily. "Yeah, I know."
"She's not a demon!"
"Where's your magic?" Ted said, trying to stay on target. "Tell me, if you really are a witch. Where do you keep it?"
"I was born with power, if that's what you mean," Dreamer said coolly.
"And yes, I really am a witch."
"Oh yeah? Show me a trick!"
Before he could react Dreamer pulled a shining silver wand out of her blazer pocket, then she said *"Repento!"*
"I'm sorry," Ted gushed immediately, mind spinning. "I didn't mean to offend you, I really didn't. I was only- hey!"
Dreamer burst out laughing, saying "I forgive you."
"That's a spell to make someone sorry?" Ted asked, and she nodded.
"That's quite cool, just- just don't use it on me next time."
"Ok," smiled Dreamer, "But you did owe me an apology."
"All right, you're a witch. A *little* witch," he added, smirking. "I'd like to

speak to your mother Agnes Black, or your father Paul Black."

"Mama isn't home right now- neither is Papa."

"Well can you take a message?"

Dreamer nodded, saying "Come inside."

"Never," Ted said fiercely, though that was what he was dying to do. Tomorrow he'd tell his mates he actually went inside the weird house. "I'm not coming in there to have my eyes ripped out of their sockets or get dipped into a giant cauldron, or be force fed rats and stuff-"

"What's your name?" Dreamer interrupted, making him stop.

"Ted. Ted Stone. What's yours?"

"Dreamer," she said, almost shyly. "How old are you?"

"Sixteen," he said proudly, then he frowned. "I haven't heard of you."

"Mama and Papa don't want me to have publicity," Dreamer answered, holding the door open invitingly. Ted hesitated, wondering whether to bolt and leave her. But she was so pretty! Doing what any boy would have, he stepped inside. Closing the door, Dreamer continued "So nobody really knows they have a daughter- well, people who don't know us. Only I know."

"Duh," said Ted, and she giggled. Ted liked the sound, but he also realised what she just said. "Only you? Where's the rest of you?"

"They rest of my family are mortals," Dreamer answered casually, "And they hate Mama because they gave birth to a witch- I mean her when I say that. They hate me even more, because of my father. Papa's family are mortal like Mama's- they hate me because of her too."

Dreamer's beautiful green eyes had filled over, both in Ted's memory and in the present.

"Oh," said Ted, not knowing what to say. "But... why you? You didn't do anything to hurt them: it's not your fault you're a- a witch-"

Tears coursed down Dreamer's face as she said "They're mortal, my relatives- they hate magic. They think we're evil and we're not, we're normal people just like they are but we still get treated like dirt-"

Ted pulled her into a hug before he knew what he was doing, feeling guilty. He rested his chin on top of her head, holding her close to him.

"I'm sorry," he mumbled. "I didn't know you felt like that- I just-"

Dreamer smiled into his shirt, saying "If Papa answered the door and you got rude to him, you wouldn't have made it home."

"Really?" smiled Ted, letting go of her. "What would he have done?"

Before Dreamer could answer a loud bang sounded behind them with a flash of bright green light, making them both spin round in shock. Agnes and Paul Black stood there, looking royal in robes of black and gold. They were laughing at something, though the minute they saw Ted and Dreamer the laughter died out instantly, their smiles vanishing.

Dreamer stood in front of Ted, saying "Papa, Mama- you're... early."

"Wrong choice of words," muttered Ted, as they stared at her disbelievingly. Paul, at least two feet taller than Ted, said "We're only thirty minutes early, little one. Who is this boy?"

"He's-"

"My name is Ted Stone," Ted said strongly and clearly, surprising Paul. "Please sir, I mean no harm. I was coming to um... er..."

"Give us a piece of your mind?" Agnes said coldly, and Ted nodded.

"He apologised," said Dreamer quickly, taking Ted's hand. "Mama, he apologised. Please don't be upset with him."

"You're not upset with him?" Paul asked his daughter, and Dreamer said no with a shy smile.

"He wasn't afraid to touch me, Papa. He gave me a big hug just now."

"Really," said Agnes, looking at Ted thoughtfully. Ted squeezed Dreamer's hand nervously: Dreamer squeezed back. "Tell me, Ted Stone. What did your parents teach you about people like us?"

"That you're evil," Ted answered, "And other things. But they're wrong." Paul joined his mistress's side with a weird smile. "Are they, Ted?"

"Yes sir. Well... I think so anyway," he said uncertainly, staring at Paul's expression, mirrored by Agnes's. "I think so."

"What makes you think they're wrong?"

"Dreamer," Ted replied, looking at her, and Dreamer smiled at him.

"Can he stay for dinner please Papa? Please, Mama? Please?"

Agnes and Paul smiled at their only child, and Ted suspected she had never been so earnest about a boy. Score one!

"I don't see why not, as long as Ted calls home and says where he is."

Ted froze, Paul adding "Whose house he's at, who he's with."

"Can you do that, Ted?" Agnes asked, though Ted knew it wasn't out of concern. She wanted to know if he had the guts. Ted nodded slowly, saying "Yes Ma'am, I can do that. No problem."

"Good," said Dreamer happily. "Papa, can I show him my room?"

Paul hesitated, then he nodded. Agnes glared at him, and he said "Agnes, I trust my little Miss Magic."

"I'll do nothing to breach your trust, Papa." Dreamer kissed him on the cheek before smiling at Ted. "Right this way."

After that first day Ted couldn't get enough of the Blacks. Even though his mother and father had giant fits after that first day, his father threatening him even, he still went round there as often as he could. It wasn't long before he and Dreamer had their first kiss, much to Paul and Agnes's delight, because they knew Ted would become family.

After three years and a heated row with his father, Dreamer finally came home with him to meet the dreaded parents. Ted felt proud as he introduced her, smirking at their shocked faces. He knew they were expecting a monstrosity with a wart on her nose and green skin, but Dreamer was beautiful.

The feel of Dreamer's mouth on his brought him back to the present, surprising but pleasing him all the same.

"What was that for?" he asked breathlessly, when she released him.

"I can't ever get used to you thinking of me like that."

"Can we come down now?" called Marlon sulkily, Pandora at his side.

"Sure you can," Ted called back, "But Dreamer's going up."

"Surprise tea?" Marlon asked his sister, and her face lit up.

"Yes!"

"Come on then!"

* * *

Miriam picked up the phone, then she put it down. If she called the very night Dreamer got home, Ted would lose the plot.

And besides, she had a lot of paperwork to do. After having so much fun with Dreamer for a whole week, she was kind of off track. She had to go through her notes about her clients, get herself back on track. Miriam cursed violently when she realised all she wanted was to be in her best friend's company, not sit at home doing paperwork.

"Damn it!"

She knew Dreamer coming back would muddle her mind! Furious, Miriam packed her briefcase for work and retired to bed even though it was barely eight o clock.

* * *

The long soak in the bathtub helped Dreamer relax. She felt her anger at Brown leave her body, yet her fury at Damon stayed there. She knew it would never leave her, knew she had to stop thinking about it at least for these two weeks she was home. Miriam was a mentor, she'd talk to her when she left here.

Dreamer dressed slowly, wondering why it was so silent downstairs. She didn't bother to psyche anything, because she knew if she was the reason for the silence she didn't want to ruin the surprise. Not wanting to dress for bed just yet, she pulled on an emerald green robe over a normal shirt and trousers, bringing out her beautiful green eyes.

Ted's eyes widened as she entered the living room, Pandora and Marlon's yell of surprise never leaving their mouths.

"What's the matter?" smiled Dreamer, Marlon stuttering "We haven't seen you in one of those since… since-"

Dreamer's smile grew as they stared at her, then she looked down at her robe, saying "Robes or gowns I'll always wear, Marlon."

"Can we watch a movie?" asked Pandora happily. "Us four together?"

Ted started to say that was a good idea, then he stopped himself and looked at Dreamer. She nodded, so he said "All right then. What kind?"

"Horror," Pandora said quickly, but Marlon said "No, hermit."

"I'm not watching a stupid sports movie, camel mouth, so-"

"A family film then," Marlon said decisively, but Ted said "Pandora hates that kind of thing."

"Well she's so freaky," said Marlon, grinning at his sister. "Who else apart from Pandora can watch horror on a daily basis?"

"I haven't watched a horror for ages," pouted Pandora. "Besides-"

"How about we let Dreamer choose?" Ted suggested, making them stop short and look at their mother. Dreamer stood deep in thought about something- instantly they thought she might leave them.

"Dreamer?" said Ted cautiously. "Are you ok?"

"Hmm? I'm fine," smiled Dreamer, then her eyes fell on the table in the kitchen. "Did you make that for *me?* "

* * *

"Mum, do you want some more hot chocolate?" Marlon whispered in the dark, Dreamer whispering "We'll all have some after the film."
"Ok then."
Ted put his arm around Dreamer as she lifted her legs on the sofa, disturbing Marlon, as he had his head rested on her knees. Dreamer reached down and stroked his hair before he could grumble, making him relax again. She smiled and rested her head on Ted's shoulder, to Ted's delight. Holding her close, he whispered into her ear "You ok?"
Dreamer nodded, and Ted kissed her brow softly.
"You don't look like you're into the film."
"I'm thinking about..." Dreamer trailed off, shaking her head. "Nothing."
She was doing it again, Ted thought painfully. Drawing away from him.
"You can tell me, Dreamer. I-"
"Shh!" hissed Marlon and Pandora at the same time, making Ted smile as he said "You sound like a bag of snakes."
"Shh!"
Dreamer snuggled up to Ted, closing her eyes. Ted pulled her closer, not knowing she'd fallen asleep.
"What are you doing tomorrow?" Silence. Ted shifted to look at her, then he smiled. "Never mind. We'll talk about it tomorrow."

* * *

Dreamer woke up, startled. It was silent in the living room. The movie had begun to display the credits, but nobody was watching. Marlon was sprawled out on the living room floor, snoring softly. Pandora was curled up in Ted's armchair, sleeping soundly with Shadow the rabbit on her lap. Ted was fast asleep too, arms around Dreamer.
Dreamer checked the time, stifling a yawn behind her hand. It was almost one in the morning. Dreamer knew Ted would wake if she tried to get up, so she simply teleported to the prison instead of moving first.

* * *

"I'm losing patience, Stile. *Where's the witch's headquarters?!*"
"I told you, I don't know!" said Damon, desperately trying to keep his
eyes open. He was still in the Detention Room at the top of the prison;
Brown refused to let him go back to his cell. The man was acting
demonic: he'd leave Damon be for half an hour, only to go to his office
and think up more random questions to ask him. Damon clapped a hand
to his burning eyes, the he said "Sarge, it's one in the morning! I need to
sleep! I'm shoveling all morning tomorrow- I won't if I haven't-"
"You will!" snapped Brown, glaring at him. "You'll shovel until you
drop, Stile! And then you'll have one glass of water before I bring you
back into this room, and you'll talk!"
Dreamer was disgusted. Damon slumped in his chair, rubbing his head
wearily. This is what he got for opening his big mouth and letting these
idiots know Dreamer was alive and kicking. He should've kept it on a
low, like George told him. Damon gritted his teeth, cursing silently as he
realised George wasn't on shoveling duty in the morning. The big guy
could sleep for a good twelve hours with no worries.
Brown stood, saying "I'll get it out of you before dawn."
"Yeah right."
Brown moved as if he was about to hit him, then he turned and left.
Damon glared at his back, wincing when the door slammed.
Dreamer appeared, saying "What's wrong with that man, Damon?"
"Looks like he's going crazy over you," Damon answered, Dreamer
staring at the iron door as if it was Brown. "He's got mega issues."
"It's your fault," Dreamer said coldly, and Damon shrugged.
"I know."
Dreamer tightened her robe, shivering in the cold of the grey building.
"This place is awful."
"I know. I deserve to be in here, still."
Dreamer nodded, looking around.
Suddenly Agnes' voice punctured her brain, sharp as heck.

Why on earth are you with that boy, Dreamer? You've no need to be with
him, especially at this hour! He told you what you wanted to know, so get
yourself right back home to your family!

"He said to come back at one in the morning," Dreamer said feebly, as if
Agnes was glaring at her right this minute. Damon frowned at her as
Agnes answered *Never mind what he said! GET BACK HOME!!*

Dreamer jumped and teleported before Damon could ask what the matter was. Then he smiled as he realised she was wearing a robe. She was the spitting image of Paul in that robe.

* * *

Back in her living room, Dreamer looked around. Nobody had moved, still fast asleep. Smiling, she went to Marlon first.

"Sweetie? Wake up."

Marlon mumbled in his sleep, rolling over. "Mum..."

"You fell asleep," Dreamer said gently, as he opened his eyes. "Time to go to bed, ok?"

Marlon nodded, Pandora stirring in her armchair. Marlon stood, looking up at his mother. He pouted, wondering why he was so small- or was it because she was real tall? He was five foot six, Pandora almost as tall as him. But Mum and Dad- whoa. Marlon smiled at Dreamer as Pandora stood, Shadow squeaking angrily as he thudded on the carpet. Pandora bent to retrieve him, but the rabbit scurried away furiously.

"Fine," yawned Pandora, stretching in her black pyjamas. "Night."

Ted rose as Pandora left the room, mumbling "We didn't even finish watching the film."

Ted smiled, saying "Next time we'll stay up, right son?"

"You bet, Dad." Marlon grinned at his father. "Night."

* * *

Dreamer woke to Ted's handsome face, transfixed as he watched her.
"What is it?" she asked, and he smiled and shook his head.
"Nothing. You look so innocent when you're asleep."
Dreamer smiled back, pulling the duvet over her shoulders.
"I don't want to move."
"You don't have to," Ted replied softly. "Breakfast in bed?"
"Yes please."
"What do you fancy?"
"What 'Dora brought us last time."
Ted smiled at her. "Shall we take it back to then?"
Dreamer smiled back. "All right then."

* * *

Dreamer was in her own world, Ted noted. The house was theirs for the
day, but she hardly said a word. Was she thinking about her friend? That
mystery woman who supposedly needed her more than he did?
"Dreamer, what are you thinking about?"
Dreamer opened her mouth to say nothing, then she frowned. She'd never
kept anything from Ted before she died. Why start afterwards?
"Damon Stile," she said heavily, sitting down on the sofa. Ted joined her,
angry already. Just hearing the name had him furious.
"What about him?"
Dreamer averted her gaze, not answering. Ted touched her arm gently,
acknowledging the guilty expression on his woman's face.
"What about him, Dreamer?"
Dreamer bit her lip before she murmured "I spoke to him."
"You what!" The words exploded from his mouth, Dreamer flinching.
"When was this? What did you talk about?"
Then Ted felt sick to the stomach as he remembered Dreamer's affair
with the man they were talking about.
"You want to go back to him?"
"I wanted to know why he hurt Pandora," Dreamer said softly, looking at
him. Ted melted down a little at her innocent expression.
"He didn't tell the police why," he muttered, rubbing his forehead.
"Pandora's scared stiff if you even say his name- she won't talk about
him for gold dust. I don't know why he- what did he say?"
Dreamer took a deep breath, then she spoke.

* * *

"Stile! Get up!"
"What for?" said Damon angrily. "I don't want to talk to the Sergeant again, ok? I told him already I'm not talking-"
"You've got a visitor," snapped the officer. "Up."

* * *

Damon stared into his former best friend's murderous face, shocked.
"T-Ted? What are you doing here?"
"Sit down, Stile!" called an officer, and Damon sat quickly. Ted was his first visitor in a whole year- his mother was away to cope with the stress. Damon felt bitter as he remembered Mom asking him why he hurt Pandora, and when he told her she broke down in tears, slapped him hard across the face, was restrained by security, and then she left. She didn't come back after that.
Ted didn't even *blink*. Damon swallowed, knowing this wasn't good. Suddenly he found himself reminiscing about the past, having Ted Stone as his next door neighbour. Ted, two years his senior, saw Damon as the little brother he never had. Damon remembered asking Ted something that was really important to him.
"How do you tell girls you like them?"
Ted, who was busy reading a sports magazine, said "Talking to them in private is rule one. Girls have too many friends who love gossip."
"True," said Damon, thinking of Miriam and her trying to get Dreamer to tell her about some mystery boy Dreamer met a while ago. Personally, Damon thought she was just making it up so the guys could leave her alone. How would he tell Dreamer she was his sun, moon and stars?
"Rule two," said Ted without even looking up, "Don't start blubbering when you tell her. You know, the whole 'I'm just telling you because blah blah blah, I've liked you for ages and blah'. Wait for her to answer you."
Or hex you, Damon thought, wondering if Dreamer would hex him when he confessed how he felt about her.
"Give her ten seconds," Ted said. "Count the seconds too. If she talks by then and she says she likes you too, invite her to the movies. If she just stares at you but in a good way, ask her if she's all right. If she gives you a dirty look give her one back and walk off. If she stays quiet the whole time, kiss her."
"Kiss her?" Damon repeated amazedly, and Ted grinned at him.

"That should make her snap out of it."

Damon burst out laughing. "You're so silly, Ted."

"Only to you, little brother. Who's the girl?"

"Someone in my class," mumbled Damon, not sure he could tell Ted that she was the sorcerer's daughter. He knew what Ted thought about magic.

"Bet she'll love you," Ted said confidently, making Damon smile shyly.

"You think so?"

"Course! Hey, can you keep a secret?" Damon nodded. "I've got a girl."

Damon frowned. "You've *always* got a girl."

"Not like this one," Ted said, finally putting the magazine down. For the first time he was real serious. "She's a witch."

Damon's jaw dropped. "What did you say?"

"A witch," Ted repeated. "Agnes and Paul Black's daughter."

Damon felt his eyes pricking. "Dreamer?"

"Yeah, you know her! How?"

"She's in my class at school," Damon said, looking at his feet. "She's one of my best friends."

"Great, so I don't have to introduce you when I bring her over. My parents are going mad over me seeing her; you know, fraternizing with the evil." Then Ted frowned at him. "She's your best friend?"

"After you, Ted. But I've known her since Year Seven," Damon said defensively. "And I'm not scared of magic like *some* people. Me and Miriam go to Dreamer's house all the time."

"Oh," said Ted, picking up his magazine again. "You should've said."

"I didn't say because you hate magic," Damon said, feeling guilty now. "I'm sorry, Ted. But at least you like Dreamer, so-"

"I *love* Dreamer," Ted corrected, looking at him. Damon's jaw dropped again, Ted nodding. "Yep, I love her. And I'm going to marry her as soon as I'm old enough, whether my parents like it or not."

Ted's icy stare seemed to cut through his thoughts. Damon shivered, then he said "It- it's nice seeing you again."

"You're lucky Dreamer made me calm down," Ted answered, "When she told me the reason you abused my child. Because I was so close to purchasing a gun and coming here to kill you, Damon." He put a hand in his inside jacket and pulled it out, saying "That could've been a gun in my hand. One shot and you would've been gone. I would've gone to prison- not that I'd have cared. At least I got something out of it."

"Ted, please- we're friends," Damon said painfully, making Ted smile.

"You got nerve, haven't you? You slept with my wife and repeatedly abused my child right under my nose, across the road from me- you *killed* my wife. And you've got the audacity to try and worm out of this with that lame excuse? We're not friends, Damon. Not anymore."

"Ted, I'm sorry- I really am. If I could go back in time-"

"You wouldn't have hurt Pandora?" sneered Ted. "I believe that part. You wouldn't have killed Dreamer, I believe that too. But tell me you wouldn't have had an affair with her, Damon- tell me."

Damon closed his mouth. Ted nodded, hands clenched into fists. Damon watched as he took deep, steady breaths to calm himself down. An officer watched them from across the room, knowing full well who Ted was.

Finally Ted said "Is it true?"

"Is what true?" Damon asked nervously, Ted saying "The reason you hurt Pandora. You was pretending she was Dreamer. Is it true?"

Damon hesitated, then he nodded.

"Damn!" Ted slid backwards on his chair, shaking his head. "No."

"Yes."

"No!"

"That's the truth," Damon said calmly, Ted's head in his hands. "Remember when I asked you about girls that day you told me about seeing Dreamer?" Ted lifted his head, Damon nodding. "She was the girl I was talking about. I wanted her for ages and she would've been mine, but you stuck your foot in it. You took her away from me."

"That's not true," spat Ted, glaring at Damon. "You're talking crazy."

"Oh yeah?" Damon leant forwards across the table, his anger matching Ted's. "Before you came along I had a chance with her- before you went marching round to her house like an idiot. Paul should've blasted the frown off your face."

"Paul wasn't there," Ted shot back. "Dreamer was by herself. And if you actually *was* clever you would've told me you fancied Dreamer- I would've backed off."

"Yeah right."

"I would have," Ted said angrily. "No girl was worth us breaking up."

Damon decided not to answer that. Maybe it *was* his fault?

"Anyway, it's all said and done now," Ted said, getting up. "Bye."

"Wha- you're leaving?"

"Did you think this was a social visit?" Ted asked coldly. "Well it wasn't. I just needed to hear you confirm the reason you hurt my kid. I needed to hear it from your mouth. And now I have-" Ted swallowed, hardly able to believe what jealousy had done to his best friend. It pained him to see him in this place, just like it pained him to see what he'd reduced his child to. "-So now I can go."

"Ted, don't go. I know you don't hate me- I can see it."

"I don't care," Ted answered, turning and walking away.

"Ted, don't go! I'm sorry!"

Ted didn't look back. Damon slumped in his chair, crestfallen. Then he

yelled "You can't forget the old days, Ted! You can't!"
Ted stopped, looking back over his shoulder.
"The old days are dead, Damon."

* * *

Dreamer was waiting for him outside. As soon as Ted saw her he pulled
her into a tight hug, then he kissed her fiercely. Passers by wolf whistled,
grinning at the beauty in the gown and the hunk in the suit. They looked
like they were about to attend an awards ceremony.
"Give it to her, Mister!" yelled a group of teenage boys, eyes wide as an
old woman batted her husband grumpily, saying "You *never-"*
"I'm too old for that!" snapped the old man, glaring at the couple across
the road. "They're not even forty, the youngsters. Look at them!"
Dreamer was stunned when Ted let her go.
Staring at him, she lifted a finger and let his tear drop onto it. Ted wiped
his face hurriedly, saying "Can you um... take us back now?"
Before Dreamer could answer Sergeant Brown braked hard, startling
them.
The witch!
"Freeze!" he yelled through his window, then Ted waved merrily at
someone behind the car. Brown turned his head automatically to look-
there was no one. Frowning, he looked at Ted- then he gasped.
The witch was gone.
"Freeze, Stone!" Brown shouted, stumbling out of the car. "Where's the
witch?" Ted frowned at him. "Don't play innocent either! Where is she?"
"Don't have a clue what you're talking about," said Ted breezily, walking
off. Brown followed furiously, saying "She was right next to you!"
"Who was?"
"The witch!"
"What witch?"
"Dreamer Black!"
Ted gaped. "She's alive?"
"Where's my gun?" said Brown furiously, realising he left it in his car.
"Stay there, Stone!" Ted smirked at him. "I mean it- stay there!"
Brown backed across the empty road, Dreamer watching him curiously.
She didn't understand why the man was slowly becoming obsessed with
her. Touching Ted's shoulder, she whispered "He's nuts, Teddy."
Ted nodded, brow furrowed. "I know. Why?"
"I'm not sure- should I teleport now?"
"Wait until he turns his head."
Brown quickly turned and grabbed his gun out of the passenger seat-

whirling around, he stopped dead.
Ted was gone.

* * *

Laughing, Ted and Dreamer fell onto the sofa.
"He's going to come to the house next, Ted. Trust me."
Ted laughed, saying "He might try and arrest me for... obstruction."
"He might if he gets real obsessed- *why* is he obsessed?"
"Europe hasn't changed much, Dream. Everyone's still scared of Agnes
and Paul- and there's been more and more rumours about you."
"Saying what?"

* * *

NoNonsense.Com Chatroom

PeachyPat: Agnes and Paul combined- a power combo.

DaveBrown: She's evil.

PeachyPat: She's evil and powerful. Worse than her father.

DaveBrown: Nobody's worse than Paul Black.

PeachyPat: Nobody's come back from the dead either.

Brown shivered, jumping as there was a knock on the door.
"Sarge? Can I come in?"
Brown quickly shut the computer down before snapping "In!"
The officer came in nervously, saying "About Ted Stone."
"Yes?"
"He came to the prison today, Sarge- visiting Damon Stile."
Brown frowned, asking "Did he throw a punch at him?"
"Er... no Sarge. He left pretty angry."
"He was with the witch," Brown said slowly. "No doubt she calmed him
down- wait! Blonde, I need someone to watch Ted Stone's house."
"What for, Sarge?"
"I want this witch caught. I want her chained up. I want the evil woman's
wand in my hands- both of them. She has two, did you know that?"
"N-no Sarge." P.C. Blonde stared at him. "Is everything ok?"
"No!" bellowed Brown, startling him. "She's evil!"

"I know Sarge, but-"

"I want her burned at stake, Blonde! Europe's just about got through the dark times. I remember everyone fearing Agnes and Paul Black-"

"We still do, Sarge- but nobody knows where Agnes lives, or Paul."

"I know that!"

"And their daughter- nobody really knows much about her. We only know about the showdown with Damon Stile; apart from that-"

"We know enough. She came back from the dead."

"What about their grandchildren, Sarge?"

"Pandora's harmless," Brown muttered, rubbing his forehead. "So is Marlon. No, it's their mother I want. Get a private detective up here right away. Call the best we have."

* * *

"There's a car across the road," Pandora said flatly, looking at her brother. "It's been there since lunchtime. I swear it was there yesterday."

Marlon bit into his sandwich as he walked over, frowning.

"Maybe they're tourists?"

"Or feds," Pandora answered, twirling her wand musingly.

* * *

Click!

Cruise lowered the camera, saying "That's what we need for Brown."

Jules frowned at him, saying "It's just a stick."

"It's a wand," Cruise corrected, shaking his head. Why did he always get goons for partners? The last idiot nearly cost his career chasing the target. Cruise Tyler knew exactly who Dreamer was, and wasn't at all stunned by her beauty. He was a little, but the fact she was a witch kept his head screwed on tight. He wanted to see her burn as much as Brown did, and was determined to get both wands before making his move.

"Come on," whined Jules. "Let's just forget it. We've been here a week and there's no witch about- just her bratty son and daughter."

"And her boyfriend," Cruise added. "I know, but don't forget she's Agnes and Paul Black's child. I bet she's invisible or something."

"You can't get invisible, Cruise. Use your brain," snickered Jules, and Cruise slapped him across the head, snapping "She's a witch!"

"I forgot!" howled Jules, as Cruise pulled his ear furiously. "Sorry!"

"You'd better be!"

* * *

Dreamer wrapped her arms around Ted from behind, murmuring "Are they still there?" Ted nodded. "They're not going to go away."

"Yeah they will," Ted answered flatly, as she rested her head on his shoulder. He stared down at the car through their window, saying "What do they want, anyway?"

"Me."

"Well they can't have you," Ted said roughly, and Dreamer laughed as she raised her head to kiss his neck.

"I know."

* * *

"There!" screamed Jules, pointing upwards. "Get the camera, quick!"
Cruise glanced upwards, eyes widening in shock.
"Damn it- where's the camera?"

* * *

"They're going to- to see us- Dreamer, stop-" Ted's voice was smothered by Dreamer's tender kisses. Little did they know a camera clicked with each kiss she gave.

"Mum!" howled Marlon, at the foot of the stairs. "'Dora ate my muffin!"
Without letting her man escape, Dreamer pulled out her wand and flicked it carelessly.

"Another one on his plate?" asked Ted, and she nodded.

"You got it."

Below, Cruise started clicking like mad.

"Atta girl Dreamer!"

"Cast a spell, cast a spell!" said Jules excitedly, bouncing about in his seat like a baby. Peering upwards excitedly, they saw Dreamer pull Ted away from the window. Cruise smiled broadly, satisfied. Finally they got something worth showing Brown!

"Cruise, did you see the stick? I mean the wand?"

"Yeah."

"Gold," said Jules greedily. "Pure gold!"

"Shut up, Jules. You'd be crazy to steal it," said Cruise, shaking his head. "That'd be your whole career gone in a moment of madness."

* * *

"Dreamer, stop. I have to go to work," Ted said desperately, feebly trying to pry her wanting body off his. "Pandora's leaving soon to go to Miriam-I have to see her off. So do you."

"Mmm," was only Dreamer's response to his statement. She loosened his tie mischievously, Ted unable to stop a smile spreading across his face.

"You're something else, Dreamer. I'm going to be late!"

"Dad, are you leaving yet?" Pandora called. "Can you drop me to the clinic on your way to work please? You don't normally start late afternoon. Can you, Dad? Please?"

"I'm coming," Ted called back. "Oh- and leave the wand inside!"

Pandora pouted but did as she was told, placing the wand on the living room table. Marlon immediately picked it up, saying "Mine now."

"Ha ha," Pandora said sarcastically. "Stick to the psychic stuff, ok?"

Marlon grinned, saying "I will, don't worry. There's things about me you don't know, 'Dora. I know exactly what you're thinking."

"Whatever," Pandora shot back, surprised at how jealous she felt. "Get ready to go out with your boyfriend, camel mouth."

"James isn't my boyfriend," Marlon said hotly, glaring at his sister as the doorbell rang. "We're best mates, that's all."

"Well the way you smile at him is a bit off," Pandora answered, casually backing out of the living room and jogging upstairs as Marlon went to open the door to his friend.

"Coward," he grinned, and Pandora scowled at him.

* * *

"Who's this guy?" Jules demanded, as Marlon smiled broadly at James.
Cruise gaped at the silver wand in Marlon's hand.
"What's the kid doing with it??"
James's jaw dropped as he reached for it, but Marlon shook his head.
James shrugged as if he wasn't even interested, Marlon letting him inside.
Cruise grabbed the binoculars, focusing them before peering through the
front window. Marlon and James were hitting each other playfully, the
wand still in Marlon's hand.
Grinning, Marlon pointed the wand at James- BANG!!
"Wow!" yelled Jules, awestruck.

* * *

Dreamer threw Ted off her, grabbing her wand and dashing downstairs.
"Marlon!"
Ted and Pandora was right behind her.
"Mum, I'm sorry! I didn't mean to- I was only-"
Dreamer stared at James's body, then she glared at her son.
"Give me the wand, Marlon."
"Nice one," Pandora added, Marlon holding out the wand.
"Mum, I... I didn't mean to-"
Dreamer took the wand and pocketed it, using her gold one to siphon
James's blood off his face as she knelt beside him. Her jaw dropped.
"What on Earth...?"
James stirred, everyone staring at him as he sat up dizzily.
"Wow, man."
He grinned at Marlon, who stared back at him in horror. Ted's stomach
churned, but he knew he couldn't turn away.
"Cool," said Pandora, unable to hide her smile. "That's really cool."
"It isn't," Dreamer said softly, cupping James's chin in her hand and
staring at his face. His pupils expanded as he stared into her green eyes-
Dreamer was so beautiful. Dreamer breathed out, relieved. He seemed
fine, apart from the fact that... James inhaled sharply as he tried to
memorize every inch of Dreamer's face. Her eyelashes, her lips... Ted,
knowing full well what he was thinking, coughed loudly the same time
Pandora did. Father smiled at daughter lovingly, then they looked at
James again. Dragging his eyes away from Dreamer's face, he looked at
Marlon.
"Did you send me to another planet or something?"

"He sent your *nose* to another planet," Pandora said flatly, and James laughed.

"Nah, he just knocked me out. Now you want to talk to me, Pandora?"

"I wouldn't be talking to you if you had a nose," Pandora snapped, folding her arms. "Touch it if you don't believe me."

"Touch my nose? Sure I'll touch it!"

James lifted a hand to touch his cute nose, as girls called it. Everyone held their breath, Marlon still horrified by what he saw. Pandora was the only one who was seriously fascinated. She watched amusedly as James'ss smile faded, his chin still in Dreamer's hand. Feeling smooth flat skin instead of his nose made him scream like a woman.

"Where is it?!!"

"Man, I'm sorry!" said Marlon, as James began scrabbling at his face frantically. "I didn't know it would blow your nose off, did I? I was just messing about!"

"Messing about!" cried James, the same time Dreamer said it.

Marlon flinched under his mother's stern gaze, saying "I'm sorry!"

"Sorry!" yelled James, eyes welling. "I've gone from good looking guy to good looking monster in under ten minutes, Marlon!"

"Mum can fix it," Marlon started, but not before James's body went limp. He passed out. Dreamer let his face go, James thudding back on the floorboards. Pandora burst out laughing, saying "Wow."

"Ted, you'll be late for work," Dreamer said softly, looking up at him. "And you'll be late for your appointment, Pandora."

Both recognised the dismissal, Ted glad to get out of there while Pandora wanted to stick around and watch her mother perform surgery on James.

"I'll be home by eight latest," Ted said, as Marlon hung his head. "Call me if you need anything, Dreamer. You too, Marlon."

Marlon nodded, mumbling "Yes Dad."

"Bye Mum," said Pandora brightly, making Dreamer smile and Marlon scowl at her. "Take your time putting the nose back. Can you film it?"

"Freak!" said Marlon disgustedly, as she laughed her head off. "Get out!"

"I'm going, don't worry. Come on, Dad."

* * *

Miriam smiled as Pandora walked in slowly, saying "Hello Pandora."
"Afternoon," Pandora replied flatly, sitting down opposite her.
Miriam found she didn't want to go on with this formality anymore.
"Would you like to go to the park, Pandora? We can talk there."
"Tony's going to swing for somebody if we go," Pandora said, amused.
"Besides, I've got something really funny to tell you."

* * *

James shivered, hands trembling as Dreamer handed him a mug of tea.
"Please Dreamer, I don't want to stay at home alone." James looked up at
her, eyes brimming. "I'll have nightmares or something."
"Who's at home with you, James?"
"Nobody," Marlon answered for him. "He lives by himself."
Dreamer was amazed. Despite her circumstances, she didn't believe a
parent should make their child leave before they were twenty-one,
whether they wanted to or not.
James sipped his tea, trembling as he said "Don't make me leave- can I
please stay here with Marlon? For the night?"
"I don't see why not-"
"Let him go!" Pandora burst out from the kitchen, making them jump.
"When did *you* get back?" Marlon said, surprised. Pandora decided not to
answer that, glaring at James. He was huddled up on the sofa. She didn't
think she could sleep under the same roof as him. No way.
Dreamer shook her head at her child. "Don't be so rude, Pandora."
"Mum, he's sucking up to you," said Pandora, heat rising as James
looked at her. "I don't- I can't stay with a stranger."
"Oi! James is my mate," said Marlon from across the living room, glaring
at her. "And he's not a stranger. You *know* he's not a stranger. If you
didn't act like he'd breathe fire if you went near him-"
"He's got his nose back, hasn't he?" said Pandora, scowling at James.
James thought she looked real pretty when she was fired up. "He wants
sympathy, look at him! Shaking and all of that snap."
"We're not all like you, Pandora!" said Marlon as he started laughing.
"He's traumatized! What would *you* do if you couldn't feel your nose?"
"Streak in the park," Pandora answered amusedly, making everyone
laugh. Smiling at her, Dreamer said "Let him stay for tonight, 'Dora."
"Fine. But I'm staying in my room!"
"If you want to you can- but you'll be down for dinner at half seven."

"Why so late?"

"Dad's home by then," Marlon answered for his mother. "We can all have dinner together- ooh, he's going to love it when he finds out James is staying."

James grinned, saying "I always give him a headache."

Dreamer burst out laughing, going upstairs.

"I'm going upstairs for a nap."

"Ok."

* * *

"Now?"

"Give it another half hour," said Cruise, checking himself in the mirror. The uniform they wore represented an electricity company from somewhere in the city.

Cruise licked his lips, nervous. He was about to enter the witch's home. He couldn't guarantee they'd come out alive. He was terrified of Agnes and Paul, Dreamer even more. Everyone he knew had an account at NoNonsense.Com, everyone shared stories about the sorcerer and sorceress. But with Dreamer, stories were limited. All they knew was that she came back from the dead. This made her even more dangerous because nobody knew much about her. She seemed nice enough on TV, but looks can be deceiving. Everyone read Sergeant Brown's blog: she'd threatened mass murder on a whole prison.

Nobody cared about her children, because they knew their father was one of them. Normal. That meant the kids' powers were restricted.

"Ready, Jules?"

"Yes boss."

"Ok, let's go."

* * *

The doorbell rang as Pandora jogged downstairs. She decided not to act as if she was afraid of the idiot in her own home.

"I'll get it," said Marlon, as she walked in the living room. James smiled at her as he got up. Pandora hesitated, then she smiled back.

Marlon pulled open the front door, staring at the tall men.

"Hello young man," Cruise said pleasantly. "We're from Vivid Electricity- a company from the city. Perhaps you've heard of us?"

"No," shrugged Marlon, staring down at the toolbox. "Who're they?"

"Electric company," Jules said earnestly. "Can we come in?"

"Dad's not home right now," Marlon answered, looking at his watch. "Come back in about an hour, ok?"

Cruise used his foot a wedge, wincing in pain as he said "We only want to check if everything's in working order, and you to fill in a survey-"

"I said Dad's not home," Marlon repeated, growing angry. "Move your foot, ok? There's nobody home!"

"Come on kid, be reasonable," said Cruise desperately. "We'll only have to come back from such a long way- we're here now."

Pandora walked into the passageway, saying "What's wrong, Marlon?"

"These guys! They won't let me shut the door."

"I'm calling Mum," Pandora answered, going upstairs. "Mum!"

Dreamer's eyes opened at the sound of her child's voice.

"Mum, there's these guys at the door and they won't get lost!"

Dreamer sat up, rubbing her forehead. "What do they want?"

"I don't know," said Pandora, "But they're trying to come inside!"

"All right, I'm coming."

Dreamer stood, smoothening her body-hugging t-shirt with one hand while she picked up her wand with the other.

Cruise's eyes widened as Pandora came back downstairs, Dreamer behind her. He couldn't believe it. He was actually looking at the witch everyone was going mad over. And she looked so ordinary in those jeans and t-shirt, even if they were black. Ordinary and beautiful.

"D-Dreamer Black," he stuttered, Jules's mouth hanging open.

"Can I help you?" Dreamer asked curiously, and Cruise nodded.

"We need to check everything is in working order, Miss. We're from an electricity company."

"Really," said Dreamer coolly, looking at the toolbox Jules was holding. "Where's the base of your company? Who are you representing?"

"I- I..." Cruise swallowed, Marlon glaring at him as he let the door go and stood behind his mother. Dreamer waited, James coming out of the living room to join Marlon's side. Cruise cleared his throat.

"We represent Vivid Electricity-"

"Never heard of you," Dreamer said breezily, tapping her wand against her thigh forebodingly. Cruise eyed it warily before he said "And our branch is in London city."

"London city," Dreamer repeated evenly. "Why come all the way out here to this town?"

"We're trying to get other towns involved in-"

"There's at least three more towns before this one," Dreamer cut across. "Did you go to those before you came to this one?"

The witch was smart, Cruise thought as he swallowed.

"Uh… your address was selected especially. Three from each town we pass- we've got the papers back at the branch."

"You must have a terrific memory," Dreamer said icily, making him step backwards with Jules in alarm. The sudden coldness in her voice frightened them. Was she going to curse them?

"Why do you say that, Miss Black?" Jules said nervously, Dreamer answering "Because I can't see you remembering over twelve addresses on your way here, or you knowing exactly where to go each time."

Before Cruise could think of a good reply a car door shut behind him, making them turn around. Cruise suppressed a groan: Stone was back.

"Hey, my wife and kids and James."

"Dad!" said Marlon and Pandora happily, Marlon saying "Back already?"

"The case went smoothly," Ted said, smiling broadly at them. "I won."

"You always win," Pandora said impressively, Ted frowning as he noticed the expression on Dreamer's face, then the two men.

"Who're you?"

"Some people who tried to force their way in," Dreamer answered, when Cruise and Jules remained quiet. Ted was no man to mess about with.

Ted's eyes narrowed. *"Force* their way in?"

"They wouldn't let me shut the door," Marlon said angrily. "This guy-" He pointed at Cruise. "-stuck his foot in the door so I couldn't close it."

Ted turned his brown eyes on Cruise, who stepped backwards.

"We didn't mean anything by it-"

"Ted, go inside with the rest," Dreamer said smoothly, and Ted scowled at her. "Go on, I want to ask them about this company."

Ted stepped inside, James eagerly taking his briefcase and tailcoat for him. Dreamer waited until talk started inside before smirking at Cruise.

"Nice try, cop. You're lucky I'm feeling very mellow today, or I would have turned your friend into a frog and let you take him to Brown."

Cruise gasped: she knew!

"Tread carefully," Dreamer said quietly, before she closed the door.

* * *

Alice called Pandora happily, asking "How's it going?"

"All right," Pandora said carefully. "James is staying over."

"Oh," said Alice, unable to stop a smile forming. "How come?"

"Marlon blew his nose off, and he's scared to stay at home alone."

"Marlon *what?*"

Pandora burst out laughing before she told Alice exactly what happened.

"He was messing about with my wand, and it went off when he pointed it at James's face."

"You're kidding."

"I'm dead serious- even Mum was shocked. It looked so cool, though."

"Pandora, you're so freaky sometimes. I swear you're a Goth."

"So what if I am?" Pandora said amusedly. "I wish Mum filmed it- you should've seen James's face when he tried to feel his nose- hilarious!"

"Boy," said Alice, shaking her head. "You really are weird sometimes."

"I know," said Pandora, suddenly wary. "Um... you're ok with that?"

"What?"

"It's just that a lot of people realise I'm weird and then they stay away."

"Not me," said Alice fiercely. "I like weird."

"Promise?"

"I promise," Alice said firmly. "Can I come over?"

"Tomorrow," Pandora said with a small sigh. "I have to deal with James today- hopefully he'll stay out of my way. He normally picks up Marlon and they go off somewhere- and if he stays around I'm usually gone. The last time he stayed over... I think I was in Year Seven."

"Go do your stuff," Alice said, amused. "Hopefully you two go out."

"No way!"

"Pandora, you've got a crush on this guy!"

"I have not!" lied Pandora, then she sighed. "Not a giant one anyway."

"Talk to him," Alice said firmly, stroking Barclays. "Tell me everything when I come tomorrow, ok?"

"Ok."

"See you tomorrow, then."

"Bye."

* * *

Exactly one hour after the lights went out in the house, Pandora got up. Taking a deep breath as her box glowed brightly, she walked to her door. Opening it slowly, she turned and looked around before backing out of the room, crashing into someone. Pandora suppressed a shriek as she stumbled, the person catching her quickly.
"Are you ok?" they whispered, and Pandora turned to look at them.
"James!" she hissed. "What are you doing?"
"I had to see you," he whispered back, letting go of her. "And you?"
"Bathroom," she lied, wringing her hands. "Um…"
James raised an eyebrow, whispering "You sure it's the bathroom?"
Pandora started to nod, then she shook her head. "No."
"What, then?"
"I was coming to watch you sleep." Heat stung her cheeks as she spoke. "I didn't think you'd be awake- it's two in the morning."
James said nothing for a minute, thinking to himself. She liked him. He knew it! She was fronting when she was with people, but when she was by herself like now… James smiled at her.
"What now?"
"Come in my room," Pandora whispered, looking at her parent's door, then her brother's. "They'll hear us out here."
James swallowed, Pandora realising he was as nervous as she was.
"Or I can come to your room…" she trailed off nervously, for he hadn't reacted to her words. "Are you ok?"
"Let's go downstairs," James said slowly. "We can have a hot drink."
"Ok."

* * *

Pandora kept her eyes on the screen, though she hardly saw a thing. They were watching her grandmother's show. James seemed calm enough as he drank his hot chocolate, but Pandora's fidgeting proved she was anything but calm. James sensed she wasn't used to this kind of thing, not since that jerk Jonathan anyway.

On screen, Agnes received a phone call. James marvelled at how much she looked like Dreamer, like Pandora. Though Agnes's eyes weren't green, they were grey. Paul Black's eyes were green.

"You've got Paul's eyes," murmured James, looking at Pandora. She frowned at him, and he added "Your grandfather."

"Oh." She smiled shyly, saying "Mum used to tell me that all the time."

"Yeah?"

"Yeah," she said, putting her cup on the coffee table. James faked stretching to yawn, resting his arm behind her. Then he put it around her and drew her closer to him, half expecting her to resist his arms. But Pandora welcomed the embrace gladly, shifting closer to him. James let her rest her head on his shoulder, Pandora wrapping her arms around him bravely. James was pleased: she was finally loosening up.

Pandora lifted her legs onto the sofa, sighing as she whispered something. James looked at her, asking "What did you say?"

"I said we could've done this ages ago."

"What, cuddle on your sofa?"

"Stuff like that. I was just being stupid."

James nodded in agreement, holding her closer to him. Pandora inhaled his familiar scent, remembering when she was ten, James eleven. She was upset about being left behind in primary school.

"Who's going to play cops with me if you're going?" she said, eyes filling as she looked at James. "I don't like the boys in my class."

Eleven-year-old James hugged her then.

"I'll still come over everyday, don't worry. We're still best friends?"

"Yes," wept Pandora, and he let her go as he ran after Marlon.

Pandora blinked hard to stop herself from reminiscing about James, back when they were best friends. James stroked her hair softly, Pandora enjoying the sensation. Then another thought struck her.

"James?"

"Yes Pandora?" he said quietly, Pandora looking up at him.

"Why did you stop speaking to me in high school? After high school as well?"

"I... hey, don't try and pin it all on me," James said, frowning at her. "You stopped coming up to me, remember that?"

"Because I thought you didn't want to speak to me."

"I was wrapped up with other stuff, that's all."

"You forgot about me."

"Yeah," he said truthfully. "Yeah, I did."

Pandora said nothing for a moment. At least he was honest. Then she said "I wasn't bothered about it then, but now I wish we carried on talking."

"Well, why don't we catch up on what we missed out," James suggested softly, but before Pandora could ask how his soft lips met hers.

* * *

Dreamer smiled, Ted muttering "I knew him staying was a bad idea."

"It wasn't," she said softly, and Ted glared at her.

"Just because you believe in romance-"

Dreamer kissed him before he could finish, Ted melting immediately. Suddenly he realised what she was doing, but he didn't want to break away. Seconds later Dreamer pulled back, smirking at him.

"You don't believe in romance, Ted?"

Ted was out of breath. "I hate when you kiss me like that."

"Liar."

"Look, it's nice Pandora and James are um… you know, getting along. But we can't leave them down there, Dreamer. I mean, what if-"

"Don't you trust our daughter?" Dreamer asked, frowning at him. "Pandora's just like you, Ted- her head is screwed on way too tight."

"She's like you too," Ted shot back. "She goes all dreamy when it comes to romance. All he has to do is say 'I love you' and she'll-"

He broke off, realising what he was saying. It wasn't Pandora he was talking about, not anymore. He was talking about the woman staring at him. Swallowing, Ted said "I didn't mean-"

"She knows what she's doing," Dreamer said, unable to keep the frostiness out of her voice. "Is there anything else you want to say which implies what I've done with Damon Stile?"

Ted shook his head.

"Good, because I'm going to sleep."

"Dreamer-"

"Goodnight, Ted."

* * *

James marvelled at how comfortable Pandora felt in his arms.
"You're so warm."
She smiled, eyes closed. "I know."

"Agnes will be back next week Thursday, ladies and gentlemen. Please do not attempt to call Dreamer Black's hotline number, for she is unavailable. To book a private meeting with Agnes, please apply online at www.AmazingAgnes.com."

"I want to see her," Pandora said, nestling closer to James. "I'm going to ask at breakfast tomorrow if we can go visit her."
"Mmm," James said. "You know, I don't know why Europe's so hyped over your family- well, Agnes and Paul. And Dreamer too, these days."
"What've they been saying about my Mum?" Pandora asked curiously. "I mean, nobody even knew they had a daughter until-"
"Apparently one idiot went out of his way to find out," James answered, not a bit tired. "It was on the news- Paul got him good and proper when he found the guy at his window looking at Dreamer- and apart from that he was drunk. Apparently he killed the guy and two more people, but they haven't got any proof. The guy just went missing, and the two people... the papers just said they had a stroke."
Pandora swallowed, thinking *Dad's parents.*
"Paul Black was just... I mean, wow." James shook his head. "He had Europe wrapped around his little finger. Still has, actually. Nobody can stop talking about him and Agnes, I'm not joking."
"You're not scared of him?" Pandora asked, and James shrugged.
"I'd be lying if I said no. I mean, he's a sorcerer. Powerful. And Agnes..." James shivered. "She's as powerful as he is. They've done loads of things in their time, seriously. They've even got books on them."
"Books?" said Pandora, mystified. "How long have they been around?"
"Centuries, I heard-"
"Centuries?!"
"Yeah," James said, frowning as he remembered the history lesson at high school. "In history at school (before the teacher got sacked), I learnt they'd been around for centuries. It was only... nearly thirty four years ago they calmed down."
Pandora counted back, then she clocked. "My Mum."
James nodded, saying "Exactly. I can't believe I'm telling you about your family, Pandora. You should know all of this already."

"I bet my mother doesn't know the half of what everyone's saying, and about all these books you're talking about."

"She must know," James said uncertainly, then he thought about this. "Actually, maybe she doesn't. I mean, it is centuries of storytelling."

"Exactly," Pandora said. "I don't think my grandma or grandpa would've sat her down and told her everything."

"True."

* * *

Marlon stared into the glass orb, unable to believe what he was seeing. Pandora smiled shyly at James, who smiled back at her. They leant closer to each other hesitantly-

"Don't you dare!" shrieked Marlon, gripping the ball.

And kissed each other, downstairs on the sofa.

"I'M GOING TO KILL YOU, YOU SON OF A-!!"

Pandora and James leapt apart the same time Ted and Dreamer sat up in bed, Marlon crashing through his bedroom door like a madman.

Pandora ran into the kitchen before James could stop her, through the back door and into the garden. James ran after her.

"What are you *doing?"*

"Go back inside!" she panted as she took a leap at the apple tree.

"JAMES!!"

James watched in awe as Pandora scrambled up the tree like a little monkey, pulling herself higher and higher up until she reached a window. Before James could make a noise of impression she vanished through the window, gone.

"Wow," he said, just as Marlon burst into the living room. Ted followed slowly, in a daze. It was only six in the morning!

"Where's Pandora?" spat Marlon, looking around furiously.

James made sure he was far back before saying "What do you mean?"

"Pandora!" said Marlon angrily, Dreamer joining Ted. "She was with you just now, I know she was! You- you was- you was-"

"Bro, I only came to get a drink," said James innocently, leaning against the fridge. "I haven't seen Pandora since dinner last night."

"But- but I saw-"

"Son, it's too early for this." Ted yawned, Dreamer softly adding "It's not even seven yet, Marlon. Pandora's fast asleep."

"What!"

Marlon rushed upstairs and, without knocking, entered his sister's room. Pandora laid under her duvet, Shadow the rabbit under her arm.

Heart banging against his ribs, he reached down and stroked her hair.

Pandora slept on, oblivious to whatever was going on in the world. Marlon looked back at his parents and best friend, embarrassed.

"I um... don't tell her anything, ok? Sorry about that."

"No problem," said James offhandedly, yawning. His eyelids were closing on their own accord; he and Pandora had thrown away the thought of sleep or even a small nap, instead spending the rest of the night and start of day talking to each other, both amazed at how easy it was to confide in one another.

"Bed," said Dreamer softly, and James nodded. He knew she knew what had transpired between him and Pandora, and he wasn't about to try lying to her either. But Ted was a different story... unless he knew too?

"Goodnight- I mean, morning."

"See you later," Marlon answered, following him back upstairs.

Dreamer started to go up as well, but Ted grabbed her arm.

"Are you mad at me?"

"Let go of me," Dreamer replied coldly: a straight yes.

"Look, I'm sorry about what I-"

Dreamer pulled her arm away and carried on walking, giving no indication that she'd heard a word come out of his mouth.

Ted sighed, glad he had a day off today. It would take at least an hour of his time to get Dreamer to forgive him.

* * *

Miriam fumbled for the phone, eyes heavy. "Hello?"

"Morning," said Dreamer, and Miriam smiled. "Were you sleeping?"

"Seeing as it's just gone six, yes I was. How are you?"

"I'm fine, you?"

"Fine. How's the family?"

"All right. Ted's being a pain in the neck, though."

"You should've stayed with me," smirked Miriam, not bothering to ask why he was being a pain. "We could've been trying to make breakfast together or something like that if you was here."

"Not really. I'd just flick my wand and breakfast is served."

"Mmm," said Miriam, yawning. "So how come you're calling so early?"

Dreamer paused, wondering that herself.

"I don't even know."

Miriam burst out laughing, sitting up in bed.

"You know, I've been hearing things about you at the clinic. Why did you threaten mass murder on an entire prison?"

"Those idiots at NoNonsense.Com need to get a life," Dreamer replied. "I only said it to make Damon Stile talk."

"Damon Stile?!"

"I spoke to him," Dreamer said, then she paused as she looked over her shoulder, sensing she was being watched. Ted was watching her, looking pretty angry. Deciding she didn't care, she continued "And yes, I threatened to murder him along with the whole prison, and after that about ten officers burst in with their guns yelling 'freeze'-"

"Wow," said Miriam amazedly. "You vanished, right?"

"Sure, and Sergeant Brown started making snide remarks about my father- oh, I would have hurt him so badly."

"But you didn't."

"No," Dreamer answered. "I left- and now he's obsessed with me. He had private detectives watching my house and everything."

"Which is why you should've stayed with me," Miriam concluded smartly. "If you did Sergeant Brown wouldn't be obsessed."

"He'll calm down," Dreamer said, shrugging a shoulder though Miriam couldn't see her. "Actually, I take that back. *Hopefully* he calms down."

"Mmm," Miriam said again. "He's a regular on NoNonsense."

"You've joined that site?" Dreamer asked icily, and she gushed "No! I'd never join something like that!"

"Because it was made especially for my parents," Dreamer said coldly. "And if what I'm hearing is true, me as well."

"Dreamer, your parents kept you a secret for as long as they could." Miriam spoke with plenty of reason. "Thirty years of secrecy- that was excellent. Until that stupid spy came to Agnes' house-"

"And Papa found him," Dreamer answered, nodding. "You're right."

"I know," Miriam said smugly. "Remember parent's day at school? Agnes and Paul came disguised each time- it was so cool."

"Nobody knew who my parents were," smirked Dreamer. "It was great."
BANG!!

* * *

Dreamer dropped the phone, whipping round.

"What was that??"

"Freeze!" yelled a dozen voices, footsteps pounding the stairs. Ted stepped backwards in alarm as the officers stormed into his room, holding their guns up. Sergeant Brown stepped forwards, smiling broadly.

"Hello Dreamer!" He stepped backwards as she glared at him, suddenly in one of her stunning gowns. He didn't even have time to take in the petite nightdress she was wearing.

"What do you want, Brown?" Ted said harshly, glaring at him as well. Brown smiled, looking at him as he answered "Your woman."

"You-!!"

"Hold him back!" snapped Brown, as Marlon, James and Pandora left their rooms curiously.

"What's going on? Mum? Dad?"

"Ah, Pandora and Marlon. And whoever he is," Brown said, waving James away. "Kids, I'm here for your mother."

"What?!"

"She's a witch," spat Brown, glaring at Dreamer. "A filthy, disgusting demon who shouldn't be here on this planet- an outcast! She doesn't deserve to live, and neither does her parents. We already have her mother, kids- your grandmother. She's going to be burned at stake at noon."

Dreamer gasped, unable to believe what she was hearing. Marlon made a dash for Brown furiously, but he was restrained along with his father. Brown looked around angrily, then he spotted them.

"Aha!" He darted for the bedside table, scooping up the two wands. "Mine! Finally, I have the wands! And the wand of Agnes Black!"

"You're mad," Pandora stated, making him turn around.

"Silence, Pandora. Or do you want to share a room with Damon Stile?"

This time James was restrained, Brown saying "Take them down to the van, all four of them! Leave me and Dreamer to talk."

Dreamer felt like she was going to faint. Her mother had been captured along with her lover and children, and would die at the hands of these mortals in stupid costumes. And now *she* was about to be captured.

"Dreamer, you're wandless!" said Brown triumphantly. "Defenceless! And now, now you'll die at my hands! At your mother's side!"

"W-why are you doing this?" whispered Dreamer, staring at him. "Why?"

"Because you're a witch!" snarled Brown. "You don't deserve to live!"

"So you're going to murder me and my family?"

"No," smirked Brown, shaking his head. "Never your children. Pandora and Marlon are only third class magical beings. *You-"* Dreamer flinched, Brown finishing "Are the real thing."

Dreamer was glad of that. She didn't think she'd make it to the stake if she knew Pandora and Marlon would die with her.

Brown pulled a tiny ball from his pocket, speaking into his walkman. "Take them to the stadium. Half of the town's there already."

Dreamer's mind was spinning. Brown smiled at her, saying "There is a way out of this sticky little mess, Dreamer." She looked at him through dazed eyes, making him frown. Her eyes were hardly focused. "Dreamer?"

She didn't answer him, Brown waving a hand nervously. He wouldn't be surprised if she was about to self-destruct.

"How many of me can you see?"

"Three," she whispered, swaying on the spot. Brown's reflexes were quick: he ran and caught her as she fell, saying "This isn't how it was meant to be!"

Then he realised that telling Dreamer her mother would die at noon and capturing her family would be a bit much, even if she *was* a witch. Still, he could make his proposal. Staring down into her face as she struggled to stay awake, he quietly said "Marry me, Dreamer. Choose me, and this can go away. All of it."

Dreamer's unfocused eyes suddenly locked on his, making him yelp. She didn't seem so dazed now. Glaring at him, she said "Never."

"Fine!" He slammed her onto the carpet, righting himself. "Die at noon!"

He threw a tiny black ball at her side before running out of the room, slamming the door shut behind him. He'd used a similar ball on Agnes- it would only take thirty seconds.

Dreamer stared as the ball hissed, a blue coloured gas streaming from it's centre. She gasped as she laid there, unable to get to her feet. Then she saw the mobile. Reaching for it, she whispered "Miriam, help…"

Miriam listened fearfully as Dreamer passed out, hanging up and dialling nine nine nine. Then she remembered it was the police who was behind it all anyway. Who would help her? Maybe she could go next door…?

Grabbing her jacket and car keys, she ran outside, crashing into an officer. She gasped, stepping backwards. Were they here for her too?

Staring at Miriam in her pyjamas, the officer gruffly said "Bryant Stadium. Now. Get dressed properly and go. I'll be back in an hour to make sure you've gone."

Next door people were running to their cars excitedly, saying "Finally we'll see the witches burn! What about the sorcerer?"

"They'll never catch Paul," a guy across the road called as he ushered his family into his car. "Miriam! Isn't this great? Agnes Black and her daughter Dreamer- we'll actually watch them die!"

Miriam stared around at her neighbours clambering into their cars. To think she found them nice people! They were cruel, just like Brown. Cruel!

Tears falling, she ran back inside to get dressed.

* * *

"Let us out!" yelled Marlon, kicking the steel door. "Oi! Let us out!"

"They're not going to let us out," Pandora said flatly, sitting in a chair. "Stop shouting, you're giving me a headache."

Marlon wheeled round to glare at his sister.

"They're going to kill Mum and Grandma Agnes!"

Pandora shook her head, eyes filling. "They can't- they just can't."

"They can! And they will," said Marlon angrily. "Don't you get it? *They've got Mum and Grandma Agnes!"*

"Don't shout at your sister," Ted said wearily, rubbing his hands together. The room was cold, even at ten thirty a.m. They'd been in there for at least three hours, stomachs rumbling. James wanted to wrap his arms around Pandora, keep her warm. She was shaking with cold. But if he did Marlon would make sure he broke at least six of his bones.

"Can't believe they got Grandma Agnes," muttered Pandora. "How?"

Marlon kissed his teeth. "What d'you mean, how?"

"Come on, you know who she is," Pandora answered, looking at her brother. "She's real powerful- you know the stories about her and Grandpa Paul. What did they do to capture her? It must have been big."

"You ok, Mister Stone?" James asked, and everyone looked at Ted.

He looked calm enough, but his eyes were anything but.

"Dad?" said Marlon uncertainly, and Ted looked at his kids.

"I'm not going to lie, you two. I'm scared. Petrified. I don't think I'll be able to handle it if a police officer told me Dreamer was dead a second time round."

That's when it hit them.

Hard.

Dreamer was going to die.

Pandora leapt up with James, joining her brother. The three of them screamed "Let us out!!" and "Open the door!!" or "You don't know what you're doing!!"

Ted just sat there, head in his hands.

Pandora pounded harder than any of them, tears falling. She didn't get her mother back just to lose her again, no way.

No way.

* * *

"Dreamer. Honey, are you all right?"

Dreamer opened her eyes slowly, in a daze. Immediately the thousands below started screaming, awestruck.

"She's awake, look!!"

Helicopters dipped low for a better look at her, Dreamer blinking slowly.

"What- what's... I don't under-"

"We're tied up, sweetheart." Agnes spoke softly. "Tied to these stakes."

That's when Dreamer realised she couldn't move. Thick, rough rope surrounded her body, hiding her brilliant clothing. Her hands were tied tightly behind the pole she was fastened to... Dreamer was furious.

"Mama, this gown cost almost six hundred pounds! It's not refundable!" Then she caught sight of them on a giant screen. "Look at me! I look like something ate me up and spat me out again!"

Agnes chuckled. "My girl, only you would think of your image at a time like this."

"Yes, well- Ted!" she gasped, staring at the many officers surrounding Ted, Marlon, James and Pandora. They were handcuffed, guns pointed at them to make sure they wouldn't move. "Mama, look at what they did to my family! They're being held like criminals!"

"Yes, I know. Now Dreamer, listen to me. Listen," Agnes said firmly, when Dreamer continued to stare at her family, who stared back helplessly. "Look at me, darling."

Dreamer dragged her eyes away from Ted's and looked into her mother's. "Flames aren't something to think lightly about, Dreamer. They are the only way to kill a witch or wizard, properly. No coming back."

Dreamer swallowed, listening hard.

"You were stabbed but you returned. If they shot at us today we'd probably die, but we'd return. Flames are the only way to do it right, and don't they know it." Agnes glared at the crowd. It looked like the Mexican Wave, the way they all shrank backwards row by row. "What I'm saying, little one, is don't be afraid. Embrace the flames."

"Embrace- Mama, I think the pressure has reached your brain."

"It's an old trick," Agnes replied thoughtfully. "What will truly kill a magical being is their own fear of dying. Listen to what I say, Dreamer. Embrace the flames, and they become a gun or knife."

Dreamer thought about this, finally understanding.

"If I welcome death, I'll come back?"

"Certainly."

"Then what are they waiting for?" demanded Dreamer, glaring at the massive crowd. "Let them light us!"

Across the stadium, Pandora was talking quietly to her father and brother. James listened, though he had nothing to do with anything.

"We have to call Marshmallows."

Ted and Marlon looked at her blankly. "Marshmallows?"

"I can't say their name," said Pandora through gritted teeth, as the officers watched them coldly. "But you'll get who I'm talking about soon."

"How can we call them?" asked Marlon. "We don't have a phone."

"Too right you don't," sneered an officer. "And you're not about to get one. So calling this little hero of yours isn't possible, I'm afraid."

Pandora ignored him. "Maybe I can try and get Mum to-"

"Hello kids!" said Brown cheerfully, stepping through the circle jovially. "Guess what Uncle Dave is going to do for you!"

"Don't talk to us like we're six," said Pandora icily, and Brown nodded.

"I forgot about that. You're still kids as far as I'm concerned."

"What are you going to do for us?" Marlon asked irately. "Let Mum go?"

"Oh no, she's going to die regardless of what I'll do for you."

"And what's that?" said James angrily, Brown looking at him.

"I'm sorry, who exactly are you?"

"He's my brother," Marlon said furiously. "My best mate James."

"Really? Then I guess James doesn't mind Dreamer being a witch?"

"Don't answer him," said Pandora quietly, looking at James. "He's setting you up: he'll throw you in a cell or something."

James obeyed, Brown smirking as he said "Your girlfriend is smart."

"She's not his girlfriend," spat Marlon, glaring at Brown. "James is like another brother to Pandora, and she's like a sister. Right James, 'Dora?"

"Yeah," they said quickly, avoiding his angry eyes. "Yeah."

"What's your offer to my kids?" Ted asked coldly, and Brown smiled.

"You're included, Ted. We wouldn't want Daddy to feel left out, even after his little vanishing stunt at the prison."

Ted scowled at him.

"When the witches are good and dead I'll let you go," Brown said, taking on a serious note. "You didn't need to get wrapped up in this, you lot. All I want is Agnes and Dreamer."

"What about us?" spat Marlon. "Me and Pandora? We've got magical blood running through us too, from our mother!"

"Yes, but there's only so much you can do," said Brown gently. "You are third, even fourth class magical beings. You don't need to get hurt."

"Thank God," said Ted, relieved. Brown nodded, understanding.

"Look, you must know what's at stake. I can't let them live."

"Ok, I know Agnes has done a lot of wild things in her time." Ted was shaking with rage. "But she's calmed down since Paul left, Brown! She's been at peace with Europe for almost thirty four years!"

"And Dreamer?" Brown said roughly. "She threatened mass murder!"

"Dreamer hasn't done a thing to hurt anyone," spat Ted. "She was actually a secret, and she might still be if your father didn't send an ignorant spy snooping round Agnes and Paul's home, knowing he probably wouldn't live to tell the tale-"

"My father knew what he was doing!" snapped Brown, glaring at him. "When you join the police force you're almost signing your life away-"

"He was foolish to send him- my parents might still be alive!"

"They had a stroke!" said Brown furiously, Marlon saying "Dad, don't!" The cutting answer that his parents had actually jumped in front of the spy to save his life as Paul released a deadly curse which killed them almost left Ted's mouth. He took a deep breath and closed it, Brown saying "Unless there's some information the police didn't-"

"Get lost!" snapped Pandora, Brown stepping backwards. Then he said "Well, I'm just telling you that when this is over you are free to go back to your uh... normal lives. Think of this as a fresh beginning," he added, smiling wryly. "No magic- nice and normal..."

Smiling still, he left them. Officers immediately raised their guns again, forming a tight ring around them.

Pandora locked eyes with her mother, saying "Pa."

Dreamer frowned, Pandora repeating herself frustratedly.

"Pa, Mum! That's all I can say!"

Ted clocked what she was trying to do, Marlon as well.

"Pa, Dreamer!"

* * *

"Pa?" Dreamer repeated, looking at her mother. "Mama?"

"They're trying to tell you something," Agnes said, staring at her former son-in-law and grandchildren. "Pa, Dreamer. What does that mean?"

"I don't know, I-"

"LIGHT THE WOOD!!" boomed a voice, and cheers went up.

"YES!!"

"Mama, I'm scared," said Dreamer, voice shaking as flames erupted almost magically around them. "I can't welcome death a second time-"

"Dreamer, you have to!" said Agnes, fear clutching her heart. "I'm not coming back to find my only child gone for good, I won't!"

"I can't do it, Mama! I don't want to die again!"

"Dreamer, you must stay calm! I know you're scared, but-"

"Scared! I'm tied to a pole, Mama! I'm scared for my family, Pandora especially! She'll most likely take her life when I die-"

"Which is why you must stay strong, Dreamer!"

"Mama, I- ouch!" cried Dreamer, staring down at the flames licking her feet hungrily. "It hurts, Mama!"

Agnes was crying now. She truly believed she would lose her child.

"Dreamer, you must stay calm- stay calm!"

"Mama, I- there's Miriam!" said Dreamer, staring down at the crowd. Miriam had fought her way to the front for over two hours, claiming she was going to take pictures when she was pushed back.

Panting, she stared up at Dreamer. There was no way she was losing her best friend a second time round. Holding her side, she mouthed *Paul.*

Dreamer clocked, looking at her children, who were still saying "Pa."

"Paul," murmured Agnes, eyes closed as Dreamer said "Pa- it's short for Papa! Papa, I need you! Help us!"

"What did she just say?" Brown spat, though he read Dreamer's lips perfectly. Shaking with fear, an officer said "She said Papa, Boss."

Realising what was about to go down, Brown grabbed the microphone.

"GET OUT OF THE STADIUM!!! NOW!!"

The wind blew harshly, dropping several degrees as the sky turned dark. Lightning flashed across the sky with an ear splitting shriek, thunder rumbling as everyone's hats flew off their heads, people screaming. Those who were closest to Dreamer or looking at the giant screen could see or hear exactly what she was saying.

"They're trying to murder me, Papa! Please help me!"

"Run!" screamed a woman, beside herself. "It's Paul Black!"

"TOO RIGHT IT'S PAUL BLACK!!" boomed a voice, which reverberated nicely with the thunder and lightning. "YOU MORTALS CHOSE THE WRONG TIME TO PULL THIS KIND OF STUNT!!"

Miriam smirked, then her neighbour grabbed her arm.

"Come on, Miriam! Do you want to die?!"

"YOU REALLY THINK YOU CAN HURT MY CHILD? SO HELP ALL OF YOU, FOR NOW YOU SHALL FEEL MY WRATH!!"

Forked lightning stabbed the ground at his words, everyone screaming. Dreamer passed out, Agnes screaming as she looked at her only child.

"Dreamer!"

The flames weren't even hurting anymore, she was that frightened.

"Dreamer, wake up!"

She wasn't dead- she couldn't be! The flames hadn't even reached her waist yet- Pandora saw as well.

"Mum!"

"Mum!" yelled Marlon, as everyone rushed for the stadium exit.

The officers surrounding them wanted to run, shaking in their boots as they looked at Brown. Brown was frozen stiff, staring up at the sky. Everyone looked up, gasping.

The clouds had joined each other and were swirling in a circle, different coloured lights flashing in the centre.

"James!" cried a woman, James whipping round.

"Mum!"

"That's my son!" she screamed, attacking an officer with her handbag. "Let him go this instant! He has nothing to do with this!"

The officer obeyed, the woman grabbing her son's arm and pulling him with her. James stumbled, looking back desperately.

Pandora and Marlon stared at him incredulously, then they looked away as he disappeared inside the mass of frightened people.

"Coward," muttered Pandora, Marlon saying "To hell with him."

Paul Black materialised in front of his sobbing wife, Brown yelling.

"Aaaargh!! *Paul Black!"*

"She's dead," sobbed Agnes, looking at him. "Our only child- gone forever!"

Paul flicked his wand, the flames dying immediately.

"She was calm at first, but then she grew frightened! Paul, help her!"

Paul cupped Dreamer's face in his beautiful hand, staring at her.

"Dreamer." She didn't react. "Little one... wake up."

Her eyes flickered, then opened. Agnes screamed again.

Dreamer stared at her father through jet black eyes, Paul staring back.

"P-Papa..."

"Shh," he said gently, as black tears fell down her face. "I'm here now."

He stroked the rope with one finger, the rope crumbling before him. Holding Dreamer to him, he freed his wife.

"Agnes. You look beautiful."

"Where have you been?" Agnes said furiously, as Dreamer sobbed into his shoulder. "Your child needed you more than ten times in the past-"

"Hush," Paul commanded softly, and Agnes fell silent. "Hold her."

He let Dreamer go, Agnes catching her as she fell.

Paul turned at looked around the empty stadium, amused at how quickly the crowd had evaporated.

"Hmm... they didn't even get to feel my wrath."

Agnes held Dreamer tightly, whispering into her ear as he spoke.

Paul Black towered above them, looking no older than thirty years old. Agnes indeed looked the same as she watched him look down at the bags of popcorn and hot dogs disgustedly, then he said "It's revolting. They actually would have watched you die without a second thought, carried on with their lives- perhaps even have gone to work afterwards. I will never understand why the mortals hate us so much, Agnes. Never."

"They fear us," Agnes replied softly, black patches on her grey robe. Paul remembered his child, pulling her out of Agnes's grasp.

"Dreamer, look at me."

She appeared not to have heard him, Paul repeating himself firmly.

"Look at me, little one."

Dreamer lifted her head, Pandora, Marlon and Ted cautiously climbing the platform. They stopped when they caught sight of their mother's face, then they ran over desperately.

"What happened to her?!"

"Be quiet," Paul said, glaring at them. "It will go away."

"Are you sure?"

Paul decided not to answer that. If he said it will go away, then it will. He didn't feel the need to comfort and reassure them.

Ted watched him put his index under his daughter's chin and tilt her head up, saying "Repeat after me, little one. I will be fine."

Dreamer opened her mouth, but no sound came out.

Agnes took her hand, saying "I will be fine, Dreamer."

"I- I will be fine..."

"Nothing can hurt me," Paul said gently, Dreamer swallowing as she looked at the stake she was tied to. Then she said "Nothing can hurt me."

Paul made her repeat similar lines, Pandora watching in awe as her mother's eyes lightened, the black tears ceasing as she spoke. Soon Paul was staring down into his own eyes it felt like, dark green and beautiful.

"There," smiled Paul, and Dreamer smiled uncertainly. Then the smile faded away as she looked at her father, saying "Don't leave me again."

"I won't," Paul said gently, as her eyes filled. "I won't ever again. I promise."

"I don't want to stay here. I'm coming with you, wherever you're going."

Paul was pleased, because he said "Now that saves an argument, because I was going to take you without your consent."

Dreamer smiled, everyone's hearts racing as they looked at her.

She was going again?

"Dreamer," said Ted desperately. "You can't- you won't go?"

That's when Dreamer remembered her family. They was gazing at her earnestly, begging her with their eyes not to go.

"For a small while," Agnes told them gently. "You'll have her back."

Pandora didn't believe that, looking at her brother. He thought the same thing, but he shook his head. Grandfather or not, this was *Paul Black*. The last thing they wanted to do was anger the sorcerer.

Ted thought the same thing, because he stepped back in defeat. Then he said "How long is a small while?"

"I have issues to sort out with my daughter," Paul replied, looking at him thoughtfully. The boy really did love Dreamer more than anything. "What I want you to do is stay strong, Ted. For your children's sake."

Ted looked at Pandora and Marlon, then he asked "What issues?"

"That I can't tell you."

"My parents?" asked Ted desperately. "I forgive you. It was an accident, I know it was- she doesn't have to go-"

Paul smiled and shook his head. "It's not about your parents, Ted."

"Then-"

"Dad," said Marlon and Pandora at the same time, making him stop short. "Listen to him, ok?"

"Smart children," smiled Paul, but before they could look at him he vanished, along with his wife and child.

* * *

Dreamer stared up at the fortress, amazed.

"It looks like our first house!"

"It *is* our first house," Paul replied amusedly. "Let's go inside."

* * *

Pandora and Marlon both held their sides, furious. Home was still miles away... and they both decided they hated their grandfather.

"He acts like he owns the planet! He can't just take her away from us!"

"Calm down," said Ted wearily, stomach gnawing. He didn't have his wallet on him, so he couldn't buy the kids something to eat. He didn't know how long it would take for them to get home either.

Pandora and Marlon glared at him.

"You should've told Paul she wasn't going anywhere, Dad!"

"Didn't you hear her? She said she wanted to go with him!"

"Then you should've told *her* she wasn't going anywhere!"

"And get blasted by Paul for ordering his daughter about?" Ted laughed bitterly. "I didn't have a choice in the matter, and neither did you."

Pandora and Marlon scowled at him, closing their mouths. They trudged on in silence, the cold wind blowing mercilessly.

Pandora shivered, then she scowled. "This is so embarrassing- we're in our pyjamas! And I swear we're not even halfway-"

Miriam's jaw dropped as she drove, then she slammed her fist on her car horn. Ted and his kids whipped round, staring as she pulled over.

"Miriam!" breathed Pandora, relieved as they ran to the car. "Hi!"

"Get in," she said, leaning over and opening the passenger door for Ted. Marlon and Pandora got in the back, thankful for her arrival.

"I'm so glad you're my godmother," said Pandora, rubbing her arms to get warm. Miriam looked back at her with a smile, saying "Even if I wasn't I'd have told you to get in, silly."

"Not really, because loads we knew drove past us-"

"Including James," spat Marlon, but Pandora said "Come on Marlon, he was with his mother. He wasn't driving, was he?"

"Ok, fine. But he still could've told his mother he wasn't coming!"

"I know," Pandora said, looking out the window as Miriam pulled away. Miriam watched her through the rear-view mirror, knowing the girl had a crush on James. Had anything happened between them since their last talk? She'd have to find out another time.

"Miriam, I can't thank you enough," Ted said, as Miriam turned up her heater for them. "We would've either starved or frozen to death."

"I can't believe nobody helped you," said Miriam angrily, stopping at a traffic light. "How can they be so cruel? Especially to Dreamer!"

"It's because she's a witch," Ted answered bitterly. "She can't change who she is, Miriam. I know some of them didn't want this to happen, I can tell. Some people weren't cheering, just standing there looking sick. They're probably the ones who called Dreamer's hotline."

"Exactly," Pandora burst out. "Magic lovers undercover."

"That nearly rhymes," said Marlon, smiling at his sister. "Cool."

Pandora slumped in her seat, Ted looking at her.

"Don't worry, 'Dora. Everything's going to be ok."

"He took my mother," Pandora spat, looking at him. "And she's not coming back unless she wants to, and even if she did he mightn't let her. You heard what he said, he would've taken her without her consent."

"Paul said they've got issues to sort out," mumbled Marlon, Miriam listening silently as she drove. "Maybe when they're sorted-"

"It depends what the issue is," Pandora snapped, Ted saying "That might just be an excuse, 'Dora. Remember, Paul's been away for years. Maybe he just wanted to catch up with his wife and child."

"True," muttered Pandora, then she scowled. "It's still not fair! Who the hell does he think he is? Just because Europe and the rest of the world is dead scared of him, it doesn't mean I am!"

"Ok 'Dora, ok," said Marlon, grinning at his sister. He loved it when she lost her cool. "You can't do anything, all right? But I say if she doesn't come back in two months we go get her. Two months is long enough to sort issues, right Dad?"

"Right," Ted said, smiling at him as Miriam spotted KFC across the road. Minutes later they sat in the car park, enjoying a family bucket.

"Good thing is Dreamer doesn't have to go to that woman," Ted said between bites of food. "I'd rather her be with her parents than her."

"What woman?" asked Miriam, though she already knew.

"Some friend of Dreamer's who wants to take her away from us."

"Her!" Marlon burst out angrily. "When I find out who she is-"

"What about Denise?" asked Pandora. "Remember Denise Jessica, Dad? She's got that fancy restaurant in the city, loads of adverts on screen."

Ted thought about this, then he shook his head.

"Denise would never do that to us, 'Dora. Remember how close we all was to her before she became the restaurant owner?"

"I'd like to see her," Pandora said broodingly, sipping her Coke. "Maybe you should ask her if she knows anything about all of that, Dad."

Ted nodded, saying "I'll give her a call."

Miriam felt a little guilty as she watched the man seated across from her eat, knowing he didn't have a clue that *she* was the mystery woman who'd corrupted Dreamer's mind.

Almost an hour later they were back on the road, Miriam biting her lip.

"I'm so tired," muttered Pandora, and Marlon said "Ditto."

"Sleep," Ted said gently, Miriam adding "We've got about two hours to go. When you wake up you'll be at home."

* * *

Agnes opened her mouth to scream, Paul clapping a hand over her mouth quickly as he hissed "Don't, Agnes! I need you to help me tell her."
The baby slept on, looking like a beautiful doll.
Agnes pulled Paul's hand away, suddenly furious.
"After you made vows to me in a church, you still went and-"
"No." Paul shook his head. "It's not mine."
"Well then whose is it? Don't tell me you kidnapped a mortal baby and-"
"No," Paul repeated. "It's Dreamer's baby."
"Impossible," spat Agnes, glaring at the love rat she thought was her faithful husband. "She's been back for seven months, and was only with Ted for one month in that time. It takes nine months to produce a child, Paul, and you know that. She hasn't had time to have a baby."
"You're right," agreed Paul- SMACK!!
The baby jumped in his sleep as Paul stumbled, holding the right side of his face in pain. Furious, Agnes said "So it is your child, then."
"No," Paul said for the third time. "It's Dreamer's."
Agnes raised her hand again, but this time Paul grabbed her wrist.
"Listen to me," he said firmly. "Three years ago, Dreamer was murdered by Damon Stile. We know this."
Agnes nodded, then she scowled. "Why didn't you do anything to him?"
"Stile? Don't worry, I will. I was a little busy... with Julian."
"Julian?"
"That's what I decided to call him," Paul said, then he looked uneasy. "Well, Dreamer wasn't there and I wasn't sure whether to tell you-"
"I'm your wife!" spat Agnes, and the baby whimpered. Taking a deep breath, she whispered "I'm your wife, Paul!"
"I'm sorry," said Paul, looking remorseful. "I should have told you."
"Yes you should- but this doesn't make sense!" hissed Agnes. "Dreamer was killed, and she certainly didn't have Julian then, so-"
"Dreamer was one month pregnant," Paul said quietly. "But she got rid of the child- of Julian. By magic, you see. It was so wrong of her."
"Yes," said Agnes confusedly. "Yes it was, but I still don't under-"
"You said it takes nine months to produce a child," Paul said quietly, looking at Julian. "When Julian appeared here he was almost nothing. Just a ball of light, Agnes. I nurtured this light for eight long months; I didn't leave home at all. When Julian took his first breath, I was the happiest man in the world, sad because Dreamer couldn't share the moment with me- thanks to Damon Stile."
"Yes, but I was there." Agnes didn't bother trying to mask her hurt. "I

was still there, mourning her death alone. Alone, when you should have been there with me."

"Yes, I know." Paul wasn't going to apologise a second time. "He's got her green eyes- my green eyes. He's a beautiful baby."

"How old is he?"

"Two years four months."

They stared at the baby in silence, for a good ten minutes. Then Agnes said "This is going to give Dreamer a heart attack."

"I know," agreed Paul. "But she has to know, Agnes. She also has to know she was wrong to try getting rid of Julian in the first place."

"You have to look at it from her point of view, Paul." Agnes spoke calmly. "She didn't want to lose Ted or her children over Damon Stile. I'm certain she'll lose Ted now, for he didn't know she was pregnant."

"He didn't find out?"

"No. I didn't tell him. I didn't think I had to," Agnes said, looking at him sharply. "I thought the baby was here no longer. And now-"

"Don't," said Paul, temper rising. "It isn't the baby's fault."

"True. We'll tell Dreamer tomorrow."

"Tomorrow?"

"She's exhausted," snapped Agnes. "She's been scalded by flames, which left a curse on her because of her fear-"

"I got rid of the curse," Paul said arrogantly. "Her eyes are fine."

"Yes, but she's been drained of her energy. Let her sleep, Paul. Please."

Paul knew he still had a hold on his wife. What he said still went. If he wanted to wake Dreamer she'd throw him a dirty look, but she wouldn't argue with him. Rubbing the side of his head, he decided to let Dreamer sleep. She *had* been through quite a bit.

"Fine, she may sleep. By tomorrow night, she'll know of the boy."

"All right," Agnes said reluctantly. "Will you tell her?"

"No. *We'll* tell her."

* * *

Dreamer frowned in her sleep, certain she could hear a baby wailing. Before she even thought of it properly she decided she was hearing things, and went back to sleep.

* * *

Ted yawned, rolling over to wrap his arms around Dreamer. The feel of the cool bed sheets made his eyes snap open, made him sit right up. He opened his mouth to whisper her name, then he remembered she wasn't even *in* the house. He didn't know where she was.
Marlon fell out of bed, banging his head on his desk on the way down.
"Ouch! *Mum!*"
"Mum's not here," Pandora said, at his door. She didn't bother wiping her tears away as Ted left his bedroom. "She's with Paul."
"Yes she is," said Ted, as Marlon got to his feet. "She's with Paul."
"I didn't mean to call her, I just-"
"Don't be embarrassed," Ted told his son. "You're lucky you didn't hear me running through the house calling her name, because I almost did."
Pandora smiled, going into the bathroom as she said "Two months, that's all. Then we'll *really* give him a run for his money."

* * *

Paul looked at his daughter as she ate her breakfast, wondering how to tell her. Agnes stood by his side, thinking the same.
Dreamer lifted her fork to her mouth, then she lowered it curiously.
"Mama, Papa- why are you staring at me? It's unnerving."
"Oh, Dreamer." Agnes's eyes filled. "We don't know how to tell you-"
Dreamer pulled a piece of tissue out of thin air, picking up her wand and pointing it at her mother. The tissue zoomed towards Agnes, Agnes catching it and wiping her eyes. Paul looked at his wife, speaking quietly.
"You're scaring her, Agnes. Stay calm."
Dreamer did looked a bit scared.
"Tell me what, Mama? What is it?"
"Sit down," Paul instructed, Agnes obeying. "Dreamer, you mustn't... freak out. I need you to stay calm for Ju- for our sake."
"Yes Papa," she said, looking at him. Paul smiled at her, then he looked at Agnes. She seemed a little more in control now. He didn't want to continue if she was going to weep. It would makes matters worse.

"When I said we had issues to sort out-"
"You weren't joking?" asked Dreamer, and Paul shook his head.
"No."

* * *

Dreamer dropped her mug of tea in shock, Paul raising a hand. The mug hung suspended in mid air, a bit like the silence.
Paul had told everything, Agnes helping here and there. He'd told Dreamer *everything*, not leaving anything out. First he'd made sure she knew how wrong it was to get rid of a child, which went nicely with the story he told next. But now it was silent.
"Dreamer, talk," urged Agnes, looking at her. "Say something."
Dreamer's head was spinning. The baby she heard this morning... Paul watched her, nodding. Dreamer took that as a yes. It was real. Swallowing hard, she finally managed to whisper "Where is my baby?"
"Asleep," Paul said, rising to his feet. "Come."

* * *

Dreamer didn't scream, like Agnes would have. She stared at the child as if she was looking in a mirror, her face expressionless. This was her child. Baby Julian Black looked like a little angel, innocent... and so small. Dreamer stepped closer to the crib as Paul and Agnes retreated, her eyes filling over. Reaching down, she touched the baby's tiny hand.
Baby Julian coughed, his fingers closing around one of Dreamer's. Dreamer smiled as her tears fell, then she looked at her parents.
"He's quite strong for a baby who's asleep."
Paul and Agnes smiled, Agnes asking "Would you like to be alone?"
"I... yes. Yes please."
"We'll give you some space. Come, Paul."
Paul looked like she'd told him to jump off a cliff, Agnes glaring at him.
"You've been with the child for two years, Paul! Dreamer needs to bond with her son!"
"Yes, but they've just met! Both of them might start screaming or-"
"Don't be ridiculous, Paul!"
"I'm not being ridiculous!"
Dreamer looked as if she couldn't hear a word, already in love with her baby boy. The baby tightened his grip on Dreamer's finger, eyes opening at the sound of raised voices. Dreamer gasped softly, staring at him.
"He has my eyes," she said, looking at her squabbling parents, who immediately fell silent. "You didn't tell me he had my eyes, Papa."

Baby Julian let Dreamer's finger go as he rolled over, using his hands to push himself into a sitting position. He was gorgeous, with his jet black curly hair and green eyes, outlined with long black lashes. Baby Julian scratched his head as he looked at Dreamer curiously, wondering why there was a stranger standing where Paul normally was.

"He's used to me being there." Paul spoke from the doorway, Julian looking around at the sound of his voice. "Don't be upset if he-"

Baby Julian suddenly giggled, stopping him short. He smiled shyly at Dreamer, saying "Hello. Where Paul-Paul?"

Dreamer reached down slowly, Julian lifting his arms. She picked up the infant, staring at his face. Baby Julian stuck his thumb in his mouth, staring back at her. They were both taking in each other's image, making sure they never forgot what the other looked like. The baby lifted a hand to Dreamer's long ringlets, which fell past her shoulders. Then he spotted Paul, shrieking happily.

"Paul-Paul!"

"Hello son." Paul's smile was ravishing. "Know who that is?"

The baby looked back at Dreamer, who smiled at him. Baby Julian giggled, saying "She my Mummy, Paul-Paul. See?"

Dreamer held him close to her as her tears fell, kissing him gently.

"How could I have decided to rid of you?" she wept, Paul and Agnes moving closer. Puzzled, the baby said "No cry, Mummy."

He placed his tiny hands on her cheeks, wiping her tears away.

"Paul-Paul, Mummy cry! Why Mummy cry, Paul-Paul?"

"He's beautiful," Agnes said softly, as Paul moved to take the baby.

Dreamer held on to him for a moment, then she let him go.

Paul held Baby Julian in one arm, then he said "Dreamer, you realise Ted isn't going to be able to deal with this." Dreamer didn't answer. "I have foreseen all of it, little one. He may try to harm the child if his anger gets the better of him. The same goes for his children. You can't go back to that house, do you hear me? Dreamer."

Dreamer closed her eyes, images flashing before them. Ted with a gun. Pandora with a knife. Marlon scheming on paper. They thought if they got rid of the baby things would go back to normal…

"Dreamer," Agnes said softly. "Dreamer, open your eyes?"

Dreamer obeyed slowly, looking at them. Then she said "I understand, Papa. Please let me call Miriam, and stay a while longer."

Paul nodded. "Of course."

"At the end of the week I will leave with Baby Julian. Mama, I want you to stay here with Papa. You have catching up to do."

Agnes nodded while Paul frowned, wondering if he missed something. She was going to call Miriam, he understood that. And she was going to stay for a while. Where did leaving in four days come from??

"So... a while longer." Paul's voice trembled as he tried to stay calm. "Your idea of a while longer is four days?"

"Papa, I can't let anything happen to my baby."

"If you stay here nothing *will* happen, Dreamer!"

"I know that, Papa."

Paul was confused now. "You know- and you still want to go?"

"I have to fight my demons someday," Dreamer said quietly, and Paul shook his head furiously.

"You want to fight them little one, fight them. Without Baby Julian!"

"I appreciate everything you've done for me, Papa." Dreamer spoke calmly. "But he is my baby and I intend to look after him the way I should have the minute I found I was carrying him. Ted will never forgive me, and neither will Marlon and Pandora- but it's fine. I'll deal with it. Please don't make this any harder than it has to be- please."

Agnes's eyes filled as she looked at her husband. "Paul?"

Paul hated feeling angry at his child. He wasn't going to give her a reason to be angry at him. Sighing, he nodded.

"Thank you."

"I hungry," said Julian, eyes filling. "Mummy, I hungry!"

"Mummy will feed you, sweetie."

Dreamer reached for her son, Paul handing him over slowly. As they left the room, he turned to look at his wife.

"Don't say one word," said Agnes firmly. "She knows exactly what she's doing."

"You really think so?"

"Yes. Come, I want to watch her feed my baby grandson."

* * *

Miriam's eyes nearly left her head.

"This is a joke. You- you're lying!"

"Julian, say hello to Miriam."

The tiny voice on the other end of the line made Miriam scream.

"Hello Minnyam!"

Dreamer gently took the mobile out of his hands as she lifted his spoon. Baby Julian opened his mouth, Dreamer feeding him slowly as she spoke. "Satisfied?"

"Dreamer," was all Miriam could get out. "Dreamer!"

"Yes, I know my name. I'm going to move two towns after yours, Miriam. That way I'm not so close, but not so far either."

"Of- of course, but if Ted does something to Baby Julian-"

"He may try," Dreamer answered thoughtfully. "But if he manages to hurt one hair on his head then so help me...."

Miriam swallowed while Agnes and Paul smiled, Paul saying "That's my girl right there. It's about time she started using the spells we taught her."

"Mummy, can I have 'nana?"

"Please," Paul said firmly, and Baby Julian giggled.

"Peas."

"He's so cute," murmured Dreamer, using her wand to peel the banana. She cut the banana into thin slices, the baby clapping as the pieces rose in the air and landed in one on his little bowls. Baby Julian reached for it eagerly, Dreamer smiling at his earnest little face.

"Say ta, baby."

"Ta, Mummy! Ta! See? I say two tas!"

Dreamer burst out laughing with Paul and Agnes, and Miriam on the other line.

"He sounds so sweet, Dreamer!"

"He is," Dreamer said lovingly, stroking the baby's curly hair. "He is."

"I'd love to meet him."

"You will, Miriam. Just not for now."

"When you come back?"

"Not then either- maybe in a few months."

"Oh, but- maybe I could visit you? I could help with Baby Julian."

Dreamer hesitated, already protective of her baby boy.

"I'll visit you instead, how about that?"

Miriam sighed. "Dreamer, stop being so difficult."

"I'm not, I just don't want anyone to know where I'm living yet."

"Two towns after me, I know already!"

"Calm down," Dreamer said firmly. "Me coming to yours with my baby

is better than you not seeing me or him at all."
Miriam closed her mouth. That was true.
"All right, you win. When can I see you?"
"In a few months."
"Make it one."
"One and two weeks."
"Deal."

* * *

Denise Jessica's eyes widened, Miriam nodding.
"It's true."
"I knew she was pregnant, but... wow. How is she dealing with it?"
"She loves him, and who wouldn't." Miriam smiled. "He's only two, Denise- he sounds so cute. She'll be back in Europe by evening."
"Dreamer," said Denise, as if Dreamer would answer her. "Wow."
"Excuse me Miss Jessica, we've run out of ice cream." A waitress popped her head around the door meekly. "What shall I tell the customer?"
"Apologise for the inconvenience and ask them to choose another dessert, then offer them a free slice of cheesecake as part of the apology."
"Yes Miss Jessica."
"You're really good at this," Miriam said impressively, Denise nodding.
"I have to be. The Prime Minister's coming for a meal next week, and so are the critics and followers. I have to be the best I can be."
"Don't stress yourself out, though."
"Are you kidding? Stress comes with the slightest thing. Cutlery out of place even- I'm not joking," Denise added, when Miriam's jaw dropped. "Last week the waiters set the tables like this: fork first, then spoon, then knife. It was chaos- the queue outside was getting so long and we had at least a hundred tables to fix- it was hell, Miriam."
Miriam laughed, saying "Good thing I'm a mentor."
Denise nodded. "One of us has to be a good listener."
"And advisor. I'm going to call Dreamer. Do you want to talk?"
"Course! I want her to tell me all the juicy details."
Miriam rolled her eyes. "I've just told you them."
"You can never hear a good story just the one time," Denise said with a smirk, and Miriam burst out laughing again.
"You're right. I'll put her on speakerphone."
Denise waited eagerly, but Dreamer's mobile went straight to voicemail.
"That means she doesn't want any calls," Miriam said amusedly, and Denise pouted.

* * *

"Paul-Paul want you, Mummy." Baby Julian stacked his bricks carefully, frowning in concentration. Dreamer looked at him curiously, and he giggled at her. "Paul-Paul call you now."
"Dreamer!"
Agnes clapped her hands, impressed. "He's definitely a Black."
"Good boy, baby." Dreamer rose to her feet, calling "Yes Papa?"
"Are you sure you've thought this through?" Paul asked, turning into the living area. "I don't want to take you all the way to England just to bring you all the way back. Make sure you've thought about this properly."
"Yes Papa, I have. The baby's things are packed and ready to go."
"What about his bricks?" demanded Paul, and Dreamer sighed.
"Baby Julian, it's time to put the bricks away."
"Mummy, I not finished!" he said, eyes filling. "Look!"
He still had about five more bricks to stack.
"Well, Papa says they need to be packed away for when we leave."
"We no leave yet," Baby Julian said smartly, making Dreamer laugh. Paul's eyes narrowed as the child giggled.
"He's been real cocky since you've come, Dreamer. I don't want you spoiling him, do you understand? If he comes back here on a visit throwing tantrums and all sorts, I'll-"
"Don't be so silly, Paul." Agnes laughed at him. "Pandora and Marlon was never spoilt. Dreamer knows what she's doing, yes? And Baby Julian is just showing off for his Mummy."
"Hmm. Well son, are you ready to go to your new house?"
Baby Julian nodded, his tiny tongue sticking out of his mouth in concentration. He finally placed the last brick on top of the stack, then he beamed at Paul, Dreamer and Agnes.
"Paul-Paul, look! I finish! See Mummy? See Nanny?"
They nodded, Dreamer flicking her wand. A tiny pair of shoes appeared with a miniscule puff coat, and a small teddy bear.
"Come and put these on, sweetie."
"Yes Mummy." The baby obediently got to his feet. "I coming."
Dreamer knelt in front of her tiny son, lifting him onto the sofa so his feet were at a decent level. While she put his shoes and coat on Paul said "I think you should stay for a few more days, little one. Just a few."
"Papa, I can't." Dreamer sighed as she said it. "If I stay a few more days I'll never want to leave- I don't want to leave even. But I have to."
"It's too soon!" Paul said desperately, but Agnes laid a hand on his arm.
"Don't, Paul. You've done wonderfully with the baby, but-"
"Agnes, it's not about Dreamer taking the child with her. It's about

Dreamer going full stop. Five days with her isn't enough. There's so many things I want to talk about- we need to catch up properly."

"Papa, you can visit every day if you have to." Dreamer picked up her son, handing him the teddy bear. "There you go, sweetie."

"Ta, Mummy."

"I'm not leaving never to return," Dreamer said, eyes filling. "We can come and stay every other weekend and you can stay with Mama at mine on the first ones. We'll see each other all the time."

Paul looked like he was thinking up another excuse, Agnes shooting him an angry look as she said "I'll take you instead, Dreamer. Papa's acting like a madman."

"We'll go to Golders Green in London city," Dreamer said, holding her son close to her chest. Agnes frowned, saying "But you live outside of the city, why would you-"

"I want to take Baby Julian home on a coach," Dreamer said with a shy smile. "It will be very nice, for me as well as for him."

Paul chuckled, saying "You were always a dreamer, Dreamer."

"Hence my name," smiled Dreamer, as he held his arms out.

"Come here, little one."

Agnes took the baby as Dreamer walked to her father, falling into his arms and hugging him fiercely. Paul kissed the top of her head, saying "Just remember, if there's an emergency call my name. Like you did at the stadium, little one. You know Papa will always be there for you."

"Yes Papa," she whispered, the baby puzzled at the sight of them.

"That goes for me as well," Agnes added, and Dreamer nodded.

"Don't cry," Paul said firmly, wiping her tears away. "I raised you better than to cry at every emotional situation. What happened to you?"

"I weakened when you left," mumbled Dreamer, and Paul laughed.

"Well now I'm back, so toughen up. Julian, my boy!"

"Paul-Paul!" squealed Julian, reaching for him excitedly. "Paul-Paul!"

Holding him in one arm, Paul kissed his soft cheek.

"Now you be a good little boy for Mummy, yes? Or Paul-Paul's going to come down and let you have it."

Baby Julian giggled, saying "I be very very good."

"I hope you keep your word, son. Ready to go on a coach?"

"Yep!"

"Yes," Dreamer corrected softly, and he giggled.

"Yeees."

"Call as soon as you reach," Agnes said as she kissed her daughter. "Don't stay up too late with the baby. Make sure he has a good night's sleep, and don't forget to give him warm milk before bedtime. And one day take him shopping in that mortal shop, Mothercare World. They've got some nice little outfits in there for Baby Julian."

"Yes Mama."

"Make sure you get a good night's sleep yourself," Agnes added, following Dreamer and Paul to the door. "Oh, and make sure you eat. I've packed some sandwiches in Julian's backpack for him, and some fruit. Yours are in your handbag, so make sure you eat that on the coach."

"Ok Mama," said Dreamer amusedly. "Anything else before we go?"

"Yes. Remind Papa to come straight home."

Dreamer laughed as Paul pouted, Julian giggling.

"Goodbye, Mama."

"Goodbye, darling. Bye-bye, sweetie!"

"Bye-bye!" said Julian happily, holding onto Dreamer tightly as Paul took her hand. They vanished, Agnes smiling.

She hadn't felt this happy in a very long time.

* * *

Strangers rushed to Dreamer at Golders Green station, tearful.

"Dreamer Black, we're so sorry for what happened at the stadium. We didn't know you was going to be burned too, we thought it was just Agnes!"

"You're so different compared to your parents, so gentle-"

"We've seen you on TV Dreamer, you're so nice to everyone who calls-"

"We didn't know that horrid policeman would do such a thing to you-"

"Your father should have hurt him!"

"We're really sorry, Dreamer!"

"It's fine," Dreamer said wearily, Julian staring at the strangers curiously from her arms. Paul was invisible, watching the mortals suck up to his daughter as if they really didn't want her to perish as well. Then he realised what they just said. They thought it was just Agnes? Hmm...

"What are you doing in the city, Dreamer?" a lady asked, and Dreamer replied "I'm getting a coach home."

"Oh, the coaches aren't going anywhere for about two hours," she said eagerly. "Would you like to come with me and my family?"

"No thank you," Dreamer said politely. "I'm going to visit my friend Denise Jessica. I need to get my son out of the cold."

"Ooh, he's adorable. How are your big kids, Pandora and Marlon?"

"They're fine, I think. They're with their father."

Paul coughed loudly, thinking that these people were a bit too nosy. And was that a photographer taking flashless shots of his daughter?

Hearing her father's warning sound, Dreamer detached herself from the people beaming at her.

"I really need to get going."

"Well ok, if you're sure you don't want to stay with us-"

"I'm sure," Dreamer said as politely as she could. "Thank you for offering."

"She can get our coach still!" a man said eagerly, looking at the lady. "Come on Barbara, ask her if she'd like to get the coach with us at five."

"The coach leaves at half five," Barbara said, sensing Dreamer's discomfort. Taking a step closer, she gently said "I know you don't trust us, Dreamer. But believe me, everyone doesn't hate you for what you are. I don't. I would really like to be your friend, if you'd let me."

Dreamer hesitated, saying "I'm not sure I can trust you."

"I know. Getting burned at stake was awful, thank the gods for your father. Having to see that on screen was terrible. But," Barbara said firmly, "We're not all like that."

"The majority of you are."

"Ignore that fact," Barbara said dismissively. *"I'm* not like that."

Baby Julian sneezed. "Choo!"

"Oh sweetie, I forgot all about you." Dreamer kissed his soft cheek. "I need to buy you some gloves or something-"

"Here," Barbara said quickly, producing a tiny pair from her handbag. "My daughter bought these for her son, but they're too small."

Dreamer didn't know whether to take them or not, everyone feeling sorry for her. That policeman really did his work, didn't he? Now she didn't trust mortals.

"Take them," Barbara said gently. "They won't explode."

"Thank you," Dreamer said quietly, taking the tiny gloves and gently pulling them on Baby Julian's miniscule hands. "There, baby."

"Ta, Mummy." Baby Julian shivered. "I cold."

"We're going now, sweetie."

"You're still going?" Barbara asked, everyone pouting at her. "Now?"

"Yes. I'll be back to get the coach... with you and your husband."

Barbara smiled, knowing she'd just made an excellent friend.

"Promise?"

"I promise."

Before anyone could ask anything else Dreamer vanished with her son, Paul smiling at the mortal woman. Now *she* was one of a kind. And she lived in Dreamer's town too. She would make a nice neighbour.

Sure Dreamer would be ok, he teleported back to his fortress in Spain.

* * *

"Oh my gosh!" shrieked Denise, reaching out to Baby Julian. "Wow!"
The baby hung onto his mother, startled as he stared at Denise.
"Hello baby!" said Denise happily, gazing at him. "Dreamer-"
"Can we sit down?" Dreamer asked. "Everyone's staring at us."
"Because we're famous," Denise said dismissively. "Look, they're taking pictures as usual."
Dreamer scowled at her, repeating herself. "Can we sit down, Denise?"
"Come to my office," Denise answered excitedly. "Forget a parlour."
 Dreamer followed her through the restaurant, ignoring the people calling her name and apologising on Sergeant Brown's behalf. If they truly didn't want her to burn they wouldn't have been at the stadium. Dreamer recognised a lot of faces, most of which had jeered at her and Agnes five or six days ago.
"So," said Denise breathlessly, once Dreamer was seated with her baby on her lap. "This is Baby Julian, then."
Baby Julian smiled shyly, hiding his face in Dreamer's jacket.
"He's so sweet!" said Denise happily, then her smile faded. "I heard about the stadium thing. How are you feeling?"
"Nervous of mortals," Dreamer answered, sighing. "Some ambushed me at Golders Green Station, apologising for everything."
"Like the people out in the restaurant?"
Dreamer scowled, heat rising as she said "They didn't mean it, Denise. They was at the stadium, shouting things at me and my mother. I recognised some of them," she added angrily, when Denise opened her mouth to defend her customers. "They were there, trust me."
"I'll bar them," Denise said disgustedly. "And the people at the station?"
"They weren't there, I don't think. The woman called Barbara said she saw it on screen- she looked really sorry. Her apology was real."
Dreamer told Denise everything the woman said, Denise listening silently. Then she said "Well, she's right. We're not all cruel like that."
"I know," muttered Dreamer, then her stomach rumbled.
Denise's eyes narrowed as she looked at her friend, then she asked "When did you last eat, Dreamer?"
"Noon," Dreamer said truthfully, and Denise glared at her.
"Do you think it's good to starve yourself?"
"I didn't feel hungry until just now," Dreamer said defensively. "I just-"
"What about Julian?" demanded Denise. "Did he last eat at noon too?"
"I should slap you, Denise! Of course he ate after noon!"
"Well, I have to check," said Denise, getting up. "I'll order you a hot

meal, ok? Stay right there."

"No, it's ok. I've got some sandwiches in my handbag."

Denise raised an eyebrow. "Cold sandwiches."

Dreamer wanted to laugh her head off. She knew her friend was offended, being the manageress of a thriving restaurant where there was plenty of delicious hot food waiting to be eaten.

"Yes."

"Save those for the coach. Stay put, Dreamer- I'll go order your meal."

* * *

Denise walked up to a waitress, some people clapping.

"Lovely food, Miss Jessica!"

"Thank you," she said, her smile plastic as she looked at the man who had called an apology to Dreamer. So he was at the stadium? "Would you like a drink to go with that, sir?"

"Your finest champagne, if you please."

I should spike it with poison, Denise thought as she nodded.

"Coming right up. Did you get that?" she added to the waitress, who nodded as she scribbled the order down.

"Yes Miss Jessica."

"And bring meal thirty two to my office, with a glass of fruit juice."

"Yes Miss Jessica." The waitress paused, then she whispered "Is it for Miss Black?" Denise nodded. "What about the baby boy?"

"Oh, snap! I forgot," Denise said, picking up a menu and looking at the children's section. Baby Julian was too small for burgers and chips and things like that... "Um... he's just a baby, really. I don't know what-"

"Maybe Miss Black can um..." The waitress looked round, scared someone would hear what she was about to say. *"Conjure something."*

"Exactly," Denise said, relieved. "Thanks, Bella."

"Anytime, Miss Jessica."

Smiling, Denise turned to go back to Dreamer, then she screamed.

"Ted!"

Ted stood there with his children on either side, smiling at her.

"Hi Denise. It's been a while, hasn't it?"

"It sure has," Denise said weakly, then she smiled and pulled Marlon into a hug, Pandora as well. "You look so well, you two!"

"You do too," Marlon offered, and she smiled at him as she gave Ted an air kiss on either cheek.

"Come, I'll get you a parlour."

* * *

Pandora and Marlon looked at their menus while Ted and Denise spoke, Denise fidgeting as she looked at the clock.

"Ted, what... what are you doing here?"

Ted frowned at her, saying "Checking out a friend's restaurant?"

"I know, but- come on, that can't be the only reason."

"It is," he said truthfully. "I've seen your adverts on screen, you know."

"Well, that's why *he's* here," Pandora said, Marlon nodding. "Me and Marlon want to know if you know about some woman trying to take Mum away from us."

"What?"

Ted told the story as quickly as he could. By the time he finished Marlon and Pandora was bored to death, Pandora flatly asking "So do you know anything about that, then? I mean, I know Mum's seen you since she came back to life."

"She didn't tell me about this," Denise said truthfully. "Now, um... I really have to get back to my office."

"You're going?" Marlon said disappointedly, and Pandora kicked him.

"I've got a lot of paperwork to do," Denise lied, Ted nodding.

"Ok. Try and come back later?"

"I'll try."

"Oh, and Denise-"

Denise turned back nervously, Ted looking at her.

"You don't know whereabouts Dreamer is, do you?"

She's in my office with the baby you don't know anything about.

"No," Denise said, shaking her head. "You know nobody knows where Paul lives, Ted. They've got people searching so they can torch the place down, but you know they'll never find him."

Ted could feel a migraine coming on.

"Ok. Thanks."

Denise turned and walked away, almost crashing into Bella the waitress.

"Bella! Watch where you're going! You could have dropped the food!"

"I'm sorry Miss Jessica," Bella said humbly, though she knew she wasn't the one who should be apologising. "I've got Miss Black's food-"

"Give it to me, give it to me- and don't say her name!" she hissed, Bella noticing Ted, Pandora and Marlon watching them curiously. She recognised them right away.

"Oh- I'm sorry," she said quickly, and meaning it this time. "I-"

"Take their orders," said Denise through gritted teeth, taking the plate and balancing it on her lower arm while she held the glass and packet of rich butter cookies in the other. "What are the cookies for, Bella?"

"For the baby," Bella said, blushing. "I thought he might like them."

"Baby?" Marlon whispered, Ted and Pandora shrugging.

"I didn't think of that," Denise said grudgingly. "Thanks, Bella."

"You're welcome."

"Did you say Miss Black?" Ted asked curiously, and they looked at him. Bella looked at Denise for help, but Denise didn't know what to say. Ted took that as a yes.

"Is Dreamer here, Denise?"

"No," she gushed. "Miss Black- she's an old lady- my mother's friend."

"What's her first name?" Pandora said flatly, not even looking at her.

"Callie," said Denise quickly, and Callie the waitress frowned at her from across the room. "Um... Callie Blacksmith. Black for short."

"Really," said Ted, staring at her. Denise swallowed, nodding.

"She's here with her baby grandson, and this is her food so I really have to get going. I hope you enjoy your time here at Jessica's!"

Before they could ask anything else she was gone.

Pandora, Marlon and Ted looked at each other, Pandora saying "Maybe it's just me. But Denise hasn't ever been that shifty before."

"No," said Ted thoughtfully, Marlon saying "Mum's in her office."

"Why do you say that?" Bella asked quickly, and they stared at her as if she was mad. Why would they tell the waitress their business?

"Can we make our orders please?" Pandora said as she looked at her coldly, and Bella blushed again.

"Of course. I'm sorry."

* * *

Denise made Dreamer eat every scrap of her meal before she told her that her other two children were out in the main restaurant with Ted.

"It's time for me to go anyway," Dreamer said, looking at the clock. "As long as Ted doesn't come barging in here, he doesn't have to know I was here. Keep your mouth closed, Denise."

"Trust me, I did. It was Bella the waitress who said your surname!"

"And Ted guessed I was here, didn't he?"

"Exactly! I swear he's psychic, Dreamer."

Ted listened at the door with Pandora and Marlon, eyes wide. She *was* here! Denise lied to them, the little…

"Ted's not psychic. He's just an excellent guesser."

Ted placed his hand on the doorknob angrily, but Pandora whispered "Knock, Dad!"

"Is the baby still hungry?" Denise asked concernedly, but Dreamer said "He just ate a whole packet of cookies, Denise. Don't give him anything else. And he's got sandwiches and fruit in his backpack."

Ted started to feel confused.

"What the hell is this thing about a baby?"

"They know we're listening," Marlon whispered, Pandora nodding as she said "They're play-acting."

Dreamer picked Julian up off the chair he was sitting in, playing with his teddy bear. Holding her close to him, she said "Say bye to Denise, baby."

Baby Julian smiled at Denise, waving shyly.

"He's so cute!" said Denise happily. "You have to bring him again."

"I didn't hear jack!" spat Marlon, making everyone freeze.

Dreamer quickly gave Denise an air kiss, whispering "Bye."

"Call me when you get home," Denise whispered back, and Dreamer nodded. Denise waited until she vanished with the baby before pulling open the door. "What the hell do you think you're doing, Ted?!"

"Restraining myself from slapping your lying little face!" snapped Ted, pushing past her and walking into the office. It was empty, as he knew it would be, but there was still an empty glass and plate on Denise's desk, with an empty packet of cookies.

"So she was here," Pandora said, folding her arms. "Why did you lie?"

"Look, if you want some answers I'm not the one you'll get them from." Denise closed the door behind Marlon, saying "I suggest you call Dreamer, ok? And if you can't get hold of her, call Agnes."

"Denise, don't do this." Ted was pleading with her now. "Everything was so right before Brown came barging in my house- and you know where

Dreamer is. I have to get her back."

"We have to get her back," Marlon corrected, glaring at him. "We."

Denise knew Ted was head over heels in love with her friend.

"Ted, things have changed."

"What do you mean?" said Pandora, suddenly nervous. "Changed?"

"Yes." Denise took a deep breath, then she shook her head. "It's not my place to say. You need to hear it from a relative."

That skipped over Ted's head. "Just tell me where she is!"

"I don't know where she's going," Denise said apologetically. "She *was* here, I'll give you that. From what I made out, she's got her own place now. She- she's not coming back to yours."

"What!"

"Why not?" said Marlon desperately, then he scowled. "And of all the acts you could've pulled with your stupid little waitress and our Mum, you had to do some baby act! What's your problem? You could've just made out she's got a new guy or something!"

Denise knew Marlon had inherited his temper from both Ted and Paul. Taking a deep breath, she spoke calmly.

"That's beside the point, Marlon. Your mother isn't coming home."

"I should kill you, you-"

"Marlon!" said Ted, grabbing his arm as he made to go to Denise. "Don't be so immature- do you want her to call the police on you?"

"Dad, this is getting to me! First James, now her- who's next?"

* * *

"Dreamer!" called Barbara, and Dreamer turned. "Over here."

"Just a minute," Dreamer said, the baby clinging to her fearfully. He didn't like the roar of the bus engines. "I need to buy a ticket."

"I've already bought it for you- come on, this way."

Barbara led the way, her husband at her side. Dreamer hesitated, then she followed her towards the coaches.

The driver yelped when Dreamer ascended the small staircase, not even acknowledging the ticket she held in her hand until a second later.

"Dreamer Black!" he gasped, taking his hat off. "Please, refund that ticket. You're a guest on my coach."

"I'd rather not refund it," Dreamer said politely. "But thanks even so."

"You're welcome, Ma'am. Take a seat. I'm Harry, your driver."

"Nice to meet you, Harry."

Barbara motioned for her to sit in the seat in front of her, but Dreamer smiled and shook her head.

"I just want to spend time alone with my son."

"Well said," said Barbara's husband, smiling at her. "I'm Hugh, by the way Dreamer. What's your son called?"

"Julian."

"He's a precious little thing," Barbara said, slightly disappointed that she didn't want to communicate. "Well, I'll see you when the ride is over, Dreamer. It'll be two hours or so."

"Ok."

* * *

Dreamer stared out the window, deep in thought. She knew she couldn't hide forever, especially when she had two other children to think about, along with their father.

Ted must be worried sick, she thought ruefully. *But I have to let him go. I'm not going back, I'm moving forwards. He'll never accept Baby Julian- and I don't think Pandora and Marlon will either. Papa foresaw it. I foresaw it. I have to let him go and move on.*

Baby Julian gazed up at her, wondering why Mummy wasn't doing anything. He nestled closer to her under his baby blanket, Dreamer looking down at him.

"I thought you were sleeping, sweetie."

"No sleepy yet," smiled Julian, and Dreamer tweaked his tiny nose.

"Well, when we get home you'll have some warm milk like Mama said, and then me and you will go to sleep and dream about cookies."

Julian shook his head, saying "I no want cook-cook. I want Mummy."

"I'm right here, baby." Dreamer stroked his hair, murmuring "I'm here."

* * *

Pandora stepped into her bedroom, Shadow squeaking at her impatiently.
"Quit bossing me around, Shadow!" she snapped, as her mobile rang.
Shadow fell silent as she picked it up, looking at the screen.
It read private number.
Glaring at the rabbit, she answered it.
"Hello?"
"Pandora, it's me."
"Me who?"
"James."
"What do you want?" Pandora asked coldly, sitting down on her bed.
"I need to see you."
"That's funny," she said sarcastically, "Because you couldn't wait to get away from me six days ago."
"Don't," said James painfully. "Don't. I need to see you… and Marlon."
"See Marlon first."
"I'm seeing him tomorrow. I think he's going to punch me."
"So do I," Pandora answered. "When do you want to see me?"
"Right now."
Pandora looked at the clock; it was half seven.
"Where?"
"The park."

* * *

Pandora zipped up her jacket as the wind blew, icy cold. James was gazing across the lake, his back towards her. Pandora stopped, wondering whether to just back away and go home again. He deserved it.
Then she decided to hear him out. She folded her arms, looking at him.
"Well?"
James whipped round, startled. He didn't even hear her arrive.
"I want to say sorry. I never should have ran with the others-"
"So you admit you was running, then." Pandora could feel her temper rising. "You won't blame it on your mother, no?"
"No. I wouldn't lie to you."
Pandora smiled in spite of how angry she wanted to be at him.
"At least you're honest with me. But you're still a friggin' coward."
"Pandora, you don't understand," James said desperately. "Come on, put yourself in my shoes. That was *Paul Black!* Didn't you hear what he was saying? He would've made us feel his wrath!"

"Maybe your mother would have," Pandora replied, scowling. "She was there to see *my* mother and grandmother get burnt to a crisp."
"I know-"
"You should've told her you was staying. You should've told her to let you out of the car when you saw us walking. Damn, James, you should've jumped out the car and rolled into the road," said Pandora wearily, and James chuckled. "It's not funny- it felt like you betrayed us."
James sobered up instantly, saying "I didn't... *mean* to betray you."
"Uh-huh."
"I was scared. Come on Pandora, he had *lightning* stabbing the ground."
"Good. I really wanted Brown to get hit," Pandora answered, making him smile again. "I don't know where he ran to, but I know for sure he'd better get out of the country. Because Paul's going to get him so badly."
James agreed with that. "You don't call him Grandpa, then?"
"James, the man looks like he's thirty and he's hundreds of years old. How can I call someone who looks like that Grandpa?"
"Mmm. Come here, 'Dora." He pulled her close to him. "I missed you."
"I missed you too," she mumbled, then she snapped out of it. "No. Don't! I'm not speaking to you until you apologise to my mother for running."
"Fine. Where is she?" James asked, knowing the answer already. Marlon had told him everything between texts and phone calls earlier.
"I don't know where she is," Pandora said, pulling herself out of his arms. "All I know is everything's been so weird."
"Mmm," James said again. "Let's sit down."
"What for?"
"Talk to me about it."
Pandora rolled her eyes. "I've already got a mentor."
"With any luck you won't need her anymore," James said softly, "Because I'm here to take over."
"She's my godmother, so I do need her. Oh yeah, and *she's* the one who rescued us when we was freezing in the cold. About ten minutes after you whizzed by with your stank mama."
"Oi!" said James angrily, and Pandora glared at him.
"What, you wanna say something in her defence?"
"Listen, Little Miss American-"
"No, *you* listen. I don't forgive you for running. And I shouldn't be here with you either, it doesn't feel right."
She was lying through her teeth, but he didn't have to know that. Pandora gave him a pointed stare before she turned and walked away.
"I'm going home."
"Pandora, wait!"
"Bye, James."

* * *

Dreamer sighed, flicking her wand one last time.
The designer sofa appeared in front of the plasma screen with two matching armchairs, cushions appearing to match them.
Finally. She was living in a very modern, designer home. Home!
Dreamer sank down on the sofa, then she remembered she had to fill her cupboards in the kitchen and call her parents, Denise and Miriam.

* * *

An hour later, Dreamer was lying snuggled under the duvet of her king-sized bed, her bedside lamp on. Lying there feeling totally at ease, she smiled. At least Baby Julian was fast asleep. She'd read him three stories before he finally nodded off, his tummy full of warm milk.
Dreamer hoped he'd sleep peacefully throughout the night. She was already looking forward to the morning, knowing Baby Julian would be the one to wake her. Pulling the duvet right over her head, Dreamer settled down for a good sleep. Sticking her hand out of the duvet, she snapped her fingers.
The lamp went out.

* * *

"Dreamer Black," said Marlon desperately, but the ball simply glowed a brighter blue than before. Ted stood behind him, biting his knuckles. They'd been trying this every night for almost three months now, but it wasn't working. Pandora entered the room, saying "No luck?"
"No," said Ted bitterly. "I bet Paul's behind all of this."
"So do I," Pandora said, "But that's not what I want to talk to you about."
"What is it?"
"Let's go in the living room," Pandora said flatly. "Come on, Dad."
Marlon followed curiously, wondering why she looked so scared.

* * *

"Remember Denise's dumb joke about a baby?" Ted nodded. "Look."
She handed him a magazine, pointing at a picture.
"That's Mum right there, in Mothercare World."
"Mothercare World?" Ted repeated disbelievingly, Marlon as well.
"What's Mum doing in Mothercare World?"
Pandora took back the magazine, reading aloud.

"Dreamer Black seems much happier after the alarming incident at Bryant Stadium, though still wary of ordinary people such as myself, Vera Smith, writer of Celebrity News. Here Dreamer is shopping for her baby in Mothercare World-"

"Her baby?" Marlon repeated, eyes wide. "What does that mean?"
"It's a load of crap," Pandora answered. "Mum hasn't had time to have a flipping baby. Maybe she's just… looking at the clothes?"
"Why would Mum look at baby clothes, hermit?"
"I don't know, camel mouth. Dad, what do you think?"
"I think," Ted said slowly, "That it doesn't make sense. Maybe someone saw her standing next to a baby and they immediately thought-"
"But remember, that started ages ago in Denise's restaurant," Pandora cut across. "And nobody knows where Mum lives either."
"I don't get it," said Marlon confusedly. "The baby thing was just an act-what's Mum carrying it on for? Why did she go to Mothercare?"
"I say we call Grandma Agnes and find out," Pandora replied. "Dad?"
Ted was trying to put the puzzle pieces together, but he was failing. Looking at his daughter, he nodded.

* * *

"I'm not telling you a thing," Agnes said calmly. "Ask her yourself."

"I would if I could friggin' get hold of her!"

"Don't you dare talk to me like that, Ted," Agnes said smoothly, and Ted swallowed as he apologised. He knew Paul was probably listening.

"I'm getting so frustrated, Agnes- I just want Dreamer back home."

"She has her own home now. She's not going back, she's moving forwards."

"You mean she's dumping me?"

"I'd prefer to say she has given you up. It sounds much nicer."

"Why, Grandma?" Pandora took the phone. "Why did she give us up?"

"Darling, I'm only talking about your father."

"Oh."

"Ok, look, she's given me up." Ted tried to remain calm. "I get that, Agnes. But what's all this about a baby?"

"When you find that out all of you will turn your backs on my child."

"I'd never turn my back on my mother," spat Marlon, Pandora as well. "You're talking crazy, Grandma."

"If you say so, honey. All of you listen to me." Agnes spoke calmly. "People know of Dreamer's whereabouts and the subject of a baby. Close friends. But they won't tell you. You have to find out on your own."

The line went dead, Pandora looking at Ted.

"Dad?"

"Damn right we'll find out on our own," said Ted through gritted teeth. So much for family sticking together!

Ted picked up the house phone, dialling the number he'd memorized in his head ever since he realised Dreamer wasn't going to come back.

"Dad?" said Pandora again. "Who are you calling?"

"I've got no choice, 'Dora." Ted spoke quietly. "If they won't tell us, we have to find out on our own." He took a deep breath, then he said "I'm hiring a private detective."

Pandora and Marlon smiled, satisfied.

"That's what I'm talking about."

* * *

"Sarge, are you ok?"

"I'm fine," snapped Brown, glaring at the officer. "Why?"

"Because you're shaking," the officer said flatly. "Are you cold?"

Cold with dread, yes.

"Bring a cup of tea to the Detention Room. I'll have it while I talk to Stile."

"Yes sir."

Brown climbed the stairs slowly, thinking fearfully.

Six days ago Stile had woken up in terrible pain, screaming his lungs out. Nobody could touch him, he was jerking up and down in his bed begging someone to stop- crying his eyes out... he was screaming right now.

"Paul, please! STOP!!"

Brown stopped dead in his tracks, heart racing. Though he already knew it was Paul Black who was behind torturing Damon, he hadn't heard him say the name before. All of the officers turned and ran, down the staircase Brown was coming up.

"Paul Black!"

"I knew it was him, I knew it!" yelled P.C. Jones as he pushed past Brown. "I knew he was biding his time until Dreamer came back!"

"Run, Sarge!"

Paul lowered his wand, staring through the wall at Dave Brown, the man who'd captured his wife and child and had them burnt at stake. Roughly pushing Damon aside, he stalked towards the door.

Brown knew he didn't have time to run. The door burst open, Paul emerging with his wand pointed directly at Brown's heart.

Brown backed two steps, mouthing wordlessly. Though he'd seen pictures, this was the first time seeing Paul Black in the flesh. And the man looked younger than him!

Face alight with cold fury, Paul hissed *"Granite."*

A stream of silver light slowly left his wand, snaking through the air towards Brown. Stepping backwards, Brown said "Please, no. Don't-"

Damon, weak and shaking, crawled across the floor to the door, collapsing by Paul's feet. Then he lifted his head, eyes widening.

Brown was still backing away from the silver light.

"Is that a... a curse?"

"You have a heart of stone," said Paul icily, flicking his wand. The light collided with Brown's chest, Brown freezing in his tracks. "You would have murdered my flesh and blood, Dave Brown."

Brown's eyes widened as he felt his body stiffen.

"Having a heart of stone is terrible," Paul continued deviously. "But then, it is just a saying. You don't *really* have a heart of stone." Paul smiled, an evil smile. "And now, I'm going to make that saying a reality."

Brown stared at him, unable to move. Bending his head a little, he stared at his feet- his black work boots, which felt so hard. And looked... grey.

I'm going to make that saying a reality.

"No! Please! *Aaaaaaaaaaargh!*"

Damon screamed as well, covering his eyes. He didn't care if he was a grown man- nobody should have to witness something so horrific.

Paul smiled, backing away to admire his artwork.

"This prison does need a little... designing. The statue of Dave Brown can be the first thing. Perhaps you can tell the new Sergeant to add some plants and vases, Damon."

"Please- just kill me." Damon was shaking so much he couldn't even get to his feet. "Kill me now- I don't want to live anymore."

"You poor thing," said Paul coldly. "Was Brown your lover, Damon?"

"No!"

"Then stop snivelling and get up."

Damon obeyed, face wet with tears. Paul suddenly grabbed him by the collar, slamming him into the wall right next to Brown's statue.

"Murder, Damon. It's not very nice, is it?"

"N-no- let me go!"

He was dangling high off the ground- Paul was so tall!

"You're going to pay for what you did to my daughter, Damon. Every night, when you close your eyes, you'll see the stone face of Dave Brown staring at you. Every time you misbehave, you'll pass his statue. You'll be sorry you ever touched my child and grandchild, believe me."

"I already am sorry," said Damon pleadingly. "I'm sorry, Paul!"

"I know," smirked Paul, "But now you'll be even more sorry."

He vanished, Damon dropping to the ground.

He didn't move from where he was, even when officers called his name one floor down. His name and Brown's... and only Damon answered.

* * *

"Mummy, I want cook-cook peas."
Dreamer smiled at him as he sat in his high chair.
"You didn't even eat all of your oatmeal, sweetie."
"I no like oaty. I want cook-cook!" Baby Julian giggled, adding "Peas."
"Breakfast first, cookies after."
Dreamer flipped the pancake in the air, catching it in the skillet again.
Julian clapped excitedly, saying "Again, Mummy!"
Dreamer was about to flip the pancake again for her son when she stopped, staring through the glass wall into her backyard at a black box- with a lens. She put the skillet down, the baby's smile fading.
"Mummy?"
"Eat up, baby." Dreamer spoke softly, staring right through the lens into the man's eyes. The baby recoiled, not liking her expression one bit.
Cruise gasped, daring to take a few more photos. He pressed stop on the recording button and gathered his things as he heard Baby Julian start wailing- he sounded like a choir boy hitting the high note.
Distracted, Dreamer looked at him.
"What's wrong, sweetie?"
"I no want oaty!" wailed Baby Julian, eyes filling. "I want cook-cook!"
"Shh," she said gently. "Take a few more bites for Mummy, baby."
"Will I get cook-cook?"
"Three," Dreamer promised with a smile. "Breakfast first, ok honey?"

* * *

Ted stared at Cruise's broad smile, saying "Done already?"

"Sir, I did say all I needed was one week." Cruise placed his DVD on the kitchen table, along with a few sheets of paper. "I'm done."

"Cool," said Marlon, but Cruise ignored him as he handed Ted the papers.

"That's Dreamer Black's address. I had a feeling she wasn't far away- and here's the name and address of everybody who went into her house- except her parents, of course."

Cruise shivered as he remembered bolting as fast as he could the minute he saw Paul Black and his wife enter the kitchen, which faced the back garden. He'd read about what happened to the other spy, who went missing and was never found. Cruise was *not* going to be next.

Ted read the names slowly, his jaw dropping as Pandora smiled at Marlon.

"Miriam?" he said incredulously. "Miriam knew about this?"

"Yes sir, she did." Cruise smirked, pleased with himself. He took it upon himself to follow Miriam home, finding out everything. "It turns out that Miriam Hughes is the er... mystery lady."

"What!" Pandora burst out, Marlon as well. *"Miriam?"*

"I've got all the evidence on this disk-"

"I don't believe this," Ted said weakly, as Pandora let out a stream of curses, Marlon with her.

"After I just got back from the office, after she asked me if I heard anything about my Mum! I'll kill her, Dad!"

"We'll do it together," said Marlon furiously. "With a shotgun, right?"

"I'd rather axe the little-"

"Marlon! Pandora!" said Ted sharply, looking at them. "Stop that talk."

Pandora and Marlon closed their mouths and simply looked at each other, no doubt carrying the conversation on inside their heads.

"What about this... baby thing?" Ted asked nervously, and Cruise hesitated. Then he said "It wasn't a joke, Mr Stone- the baby's real."

"You're kidding," said Pandora blankly. "It- it's not hers, though."

"Well, actually..." Cruise dithered before saying "It *is* hers."

"It can't be," said Ted, looking at him confusedly. "I mean, she hasn't had *time* to have a baby. This is the ninth month she's been back, almost tenth. She's been the same the whole time, so how-"

"I don't know how, but it's hers," Cruise said, head starting to hurt. "It's time to look at this DVD- I took the last photos this morning."

* * *

Pandora and Marlon stared at the screen, mouths hanging open. The baby was laughing as Dreamer tickled him, his face mirroring hers.

"They look just like each other," Cruise said nervously, looking at Ted. "He even has her eyes, Mr Stone. Dark green, like Christmas trees."

Ted said nothing, deep in shock. Cruise licked his lips before flicking through the photos one by one, Ted's eyes growing wider and wider. Dreamer cuddling the baby as he cried. Dreamer playing with the baby, laughing as he frowned at her stack of bricks being higher than his tiny body. Dreamer singing a lullaby as the baby fell asleep in her arms. Dreamer holding the baby in one arm as she spoke to Miriam. Miriam cooking happily for Dreamer while Dreamer fed the baby. Agnes, Paul and Dreamer seated at the kitchen table having lunch while the baby mashed his food with his little spoon, up in his high chair.

Cruise stopped, worried Ted's eyes would leave his head.

"Mr Stone?"

"Go on," Ted said hoarsely, looking at him. "Was that the last one?"

"There's only one more-"

"Show it," said Pandora, Marlon as well. Cruise obeyed, all of them staring at the photo of Miriam pulling a blanket over Dreamer as she slept, on the sofa. Dreamer looked real drained in that photo.

"What happened to her?" Ted demanded worriedly, Cruise quickly saying "The baby didn't sleep all night- so neither did she. She had to call her friend over because she had a terrible headache, and she was worried about her baby."

"It's not hers," spat Pandora, and Marlon nodded. "It can't be."

"It's not mine either," Ted said quietly, and they looked at him.

Deciding the silence was way too intense, Cruise went back to the main menu, saying "Here's the videos of the baby if you'd like to-"

"We don't want to see them," said Pandora, but Ted said "Play them." Cruise obeyed.

"Mummy, I want cook-cook peas."

Pandora's stomach tightened as Dreamer smiled at him. Judging by the awkward movements of her father and brother, they felt jealous too. Anyone could tell Dreamer adored the baby, whatever his name was.

"You didn't even eat all of your oatmeal, sweetie."

"I no like oaty. I want cook-cook!" the baby giggled, adding "Peas."

"Breakfast first, cookies after."

Ted saw red as the baby beamed at the love of his life.

"Turn it off," he said quietly, and Cruise looked at him.

"Don't you want proof that Miriam is the mystery lady?"

"I said turn it off! Now!"

Cruise obeyed quickly, Ted's face in his hands.

"I think you should see for yourself that Miriam Hughes-"

"We'll take your word for it," Pandora said, joining her father. Marlon was staring at the screen as if something was still on there.

Cruise straightened his collar as he said "I'll leave the DVD with you."

Ted took a deep breath, shoulders shaking. Cruise immediately felt pain as if he was somehow involved in this matter- it hurt to see a man cry.

"How much do you want for your work?" Ted asked, head bowed so he wouldn't have to look at him. "I'll write you a cheque."

Cruise opened his mouth, then he shook his head.

"Keep the money. I don't need it."

"Are you sure?"

"Yeah. I uh… I hope you sort everything out between you, Mr Stone."

Ted nodded as Cruise turned to leave, Marlon walking him to the door. After it shut forcefully, after Marlon came back into the living room, Ted said "I don't know what to say, you two."

"That is *not* her baby," hissed Pandora, as Marlon spat the same words out. "She must have adopted him, and then changed his eye colour."

Ted stared at her.

"Well it's possible," she said crossly, folding her arms. "Right?"

"It's hers, 'Dora." Ted's mind was spinning, his heart racing to keep up with it. He repeated himself as Marlon yelled it isn't. "It's hers."

"Dad, it can't be!" said Pandora frustratedly. "It takes nine months to-"

"I know, it's hurting my head. I can't work it out," said Ted miserably. "I really can't."

"Call Grandma Agnes and Paul," Marlon said, eyes filling. "Now, Dad!"

* * *

Ted made Agnes repeat the whole incredulous story three times before his world went black.

Pandora sat in a corner, unable to move as she stared at her father's lifeless body. Damon Stile? How? When? If that was his baby, and Dreamer was a month pregnant before she died, that meant she had an affair with Damon. But she died, so how could the baby be alive? Pandora's eyes filled as she tried to make sense of everything. Did Dreamer know what Damon was doing to her all along? Maybe she laughed with him about it, maybe-

"Stop!" screeched Agnes, appearing in a flash of red light with Paul. "Don't you dare think of my child in disgusting ways like that, Pandora! She didn't know for sure until the day she died!"

"For sure?" Pandora repeated, hurt. "So she thought he did stuff?"

"She dreamt," said Agnes furiously, as Paul knelt beside Ted. *"Dreamt,* child, do you hear me? She didn't know if they were just nightmares or something real, she was as confused as I was!"

"She didn't know until the day she died," Marlon said quietly, looking at his sister. "Trust me 'Dora, Mum would never have-"

"What about that baby?" Pandora said, biting the words out. Already she hated the beaming little brat. Marlon's expression became dark too. Agnes chose not to answer her, knowing that her words might somehow influence them to do something terrible to her baby grandson.

Ted groaned on the carpet, opening his eyes slowly.

"What happened?"

"You passed out," Paul said, hauling him up gently. "Hello again, Ted."

"Paul," Ted said weakly, then he remembered everything. "Tell me I was just dreaming, Paul- Agnes. Everything... it was just a dream."

"Now isn't the time for denial," Paul said curtly. "We're going to stay here with you until your anger wears out. Agnes will help calm you."

"You're going to stay with... no. No!" said Ted angrily. "You're the one who saved that baby in the first place-"

"You're telling me you would have let him die?"

"Yes!" said Ted frustratedly. "It was *nothing*. Just... nothing!"

"I agree, Ted." Paul spoke calmly. "But I knew it would become something- my youngest grandchild. I'm not surprised at you being angry with me, but surely, you can't possibly wish I left Julian to die."

"That's his name?" spat Pandora from her corner. *"Julian?"*

"He's a lovely baby boy," said Agnes lovingly. "Your brother."

Marlon exploded furiously, shouting "That brat is *not* our brother!"

"He's nothing where we're concerned!" said Pandora angrily. "Nothing!"
Ted was just as angry.

"He's nothing to me either!"

"Obviously," snapped Paul, temper rising. "Because he isn't yours!"

"We're going to stay with you, Ted." Agnes was the only one who was
still tranquil. "You, Marlon and Pandora need to calm down. We've
foreseen the things that will happen while you're angry. We're going to
wait until you are at peace again, and then take it from there."

"We're not going to college," Marlon said, glaring at Agnes. "We won't."

"Suit yourselves," Agnes answered. "Now, get showered and dressed for
bed, the pair of you. Come downstairs for a last mug of hot chocolate,
and then off to bed you go."

"Yes Grandma," muttered Pandora, suddenly feeling small. "Come on,
camel mouth."

Paul watched them go, rubbing his chin.

"Camel mouth, Ted?"

"They call each other names when the mood suits them," Ted explained,
head throbbing. He must have landed hard. "For Pandora, Marlon is
camel mouth and for Marlon, Pandora is hermit."

"Very amusing," Paul said with a small smile. "Do you feel calmer?"

"No," Ted confessed. He looked ok, but inside he was raging with hurt,
anger and fear. With that baby suddenly on the scene, where did that
leave him and Dreamer?

Upstairs, Pandora called Alice while Marlon dialled James's number.

Alice didn't know what to say, for the first time ever. Neither did James.

Pandora and Marlon both hung up frustratedly, tossing their mobiles on
their beds and leaving their rooms.

"James is a prat," Marlon said, looking at his sister. "He didn't-"

"Make it better, I know. Neither did Alice," Pandora said bitterly. "I'm
taking time off college. I don't care if I get thrown off the course."

"Ditto."

"Marlon, Pandora," called Agnes. "Come and have your tea, darlings."

Pandora's eyes filled as she looked at her brother.

"Mum always makes us a nice tea. With muffins and stuff."

Marlon's heart panged as he nodded. "Yeah, I know."

"I want to see her," Pandora said. "We'll get Paul to take us."

"*Ask* Paul to take you," Agnes scolded, at the foot of the stairs. "And call
your mother first, to see if she's up for seeing you."

Ted looked at her hopefully. "What's her number, Agnes?"

* * *

Baby Julian jumped in Dreamer's arms, eyes snapping open as the house phone rang.

"Mummy!"

Annoyed at whoever was calling so late, Dreamer kissed him before laying him down properly in her bed, whispering "Sleep, honey."

Julian laid down obediently, Dreamer pulling the duvet over him. She took her time, hoping the caller would hang up, but they didn't.

"Hello, good night. Dreamer speaking."

The person inhaled sharply, Dreamer frowning.

"Hello?"

Silence.

"You've woken my son up just after I put him to sleep," she said coldly, looking at Baby Julian as he fidgeted under the duvet. "He mightn't go back to sleep for a long time, thanks to you. I suggest you talk, or I'm going to send a charge of electricity down the line."

Paul burst out laughing. "Go it, little one!"

"Papa!" she said, surprised. "What's the matter? Why are you calling?"

"I'm not," Paul said, chuckling. "My former son-in-law is calling-"

"Ted??"

"With your children and mother at his house."

"Oh," said Dreamer, suddenly realising everything. "Um…"

"Dreamer, you didn't tell me you was pregnant," croaked Ted. "Why?"

"I thought- I thought- Papa, Mama, please bring my family to me."

Paul clasped Ted's arm while Agnes took Marlon's hand in one of hers and Pandora's hand in the other.

"We're on our way."

* * *

Dreamer pulled her hair back into a ponytail as Baby Julian hung onto her leg, scared.

"Knock-knock coming, Mummy. Big knock-knock."

"Don't be afraid, baby. Mummy won't let them do anything to you."

She could already feel the negative energy issuing from Ted, Marlon and Pandora- and they weren't even there yet. And Baby Julian could sense it too, the forceful knock which Ted would give-

BANG!!

Ted slammed his fist onto the door, Baby Julian screaming and bursting into tears.

"Mummy!"

Outside, Agnes slapped Ted hard across the face.

"Stop that, Ted! You've frightened the baby!"

Baby Julian was wailing with no intention of stopping, lights going on across the road. Barbara peeked out of her window, eyes widening at the sight of Agnes and Paul Black, with some other people.

"Who cares about the stupid baby?" spat Pandora, though she cringed as Julian discovered a new octave. "Can't Mum get him to shut up?"

Inside, Dreamer was trying to calm him down as she walked to the door.

"No!" yelled Baby Julian, tears falling. "No, Mummy! No open it!"

"It's Mama and Papa out there, honey. Don't you want to see them?"

"No!"

The baby struggled in her arms, but Dreamer didn't let him go.

"Come on sweetie, calm down for me. Calm down for Mummy, ok?"

She was so close to the front door everyone got ready for when she'd open it, but the baby screamed even more. Turning away from the door worriedly and walking with him into the kitchen, Dreamer placed him in his play crib. It was a giant cushiony box which Baby Julian normally enjoyed bouncing around and napping in, but now it felt like a prison.

"Mummy!"

"Hold on, honey- hold on." Dreamer could feel a migraine coming on, a big one. "Let me get the door."

"No!"

"Yes, baby. It's Paul-Paul and Nana, look!"

Paul strode in all business-like, marching up to the crib.

"What's all this noise for, son?"

"Paul-Paul," he wept, crawling to a corner and sitting there. "Paul-Paul!"

Pandora refused to acknowledge him as she hugged her mother tightly.

"I missed you so much!"

"I missed you too, sweetie." Dreamer kissed her forehead.

Marlon pulled his sister out of the way so he could get his hug too.

Ted stared at her hungrily, taking in her beautiful face. Two years his junior, Dreamer looked like she was twenty four maximum- a student. He knew she'd never look a day older, but she would grow more beautiful.

"How- how are you?" he asked weakly, and she nodded nervously.

"I'm fine."

"You're ok with…" he gestured at the crib hopelessly. "Your baby."

"Yes. Yes I am."

Ted could feel his anger draining away. He could never stay angry at Dreamer Black for long- and he wasn't sure if that was a good thing.

"Mummy," sobbed Baby Julian, making Dreamer turn. "Mummy!"

"I'm right here, honey. I won't let anything happen, I promise."

"What, does he think we'll kill him?" said Pandora tactlessly, and Dreamer looked at her thoughtfully.

"Is that what you're thinking, sweetie?"

"I- I- no," she said, shaking her head. "I just don't want anything to do with him."

"Me either," Marlon added stonily, and Dreamer looked at him as well.

"That's fine with me, Marlon. I knew you wouldn't, which is why I'm living here in my own home. Away from you."

Marlon and Pandora bristled under their mother's penetrating stare, feeling uncomfortable. The words *away from you* danced around their brains, both of them looking at each other. What did that mean?

Paul coughed loudly, distracting everyone. Clapping his hands, he said "How about we all have that tea Agnes almost served?"

"Yes, lets," Agnes said quickly, sensing the feelings her daughter was having. "Dreamer, stop those cruel thoughts and come to the table."

"Yes Mama," Dreamer answered, as Baby Julian sniffled in his crib. Walking over to the thing and smiling down at her son, she asked "Better now, sweetie?"

Baby Julian gazed up at her, eyes filling. He thought Mummy left him there and forgot about him, but he couldn't verbalize that thought. Instead he lifted his arms, Dreamer reaching down and picking him up.

"What do you want Mummy to give you for tea, baby?"

Baby Julian thought hard, screwing up his face as he thought. Pandora and Marlon watched him icily, sitting at the table slowly. They didn't take their eyes off him for a second. Ted looked at them, whispering "Calm down, you two."

They ignored him.

Julian thought about his dummy, his teddy bear and some other toys. Paul smiled as he watched him, Agnes flicking her wand repeatedly.

With each flick food appeared on the kitchen table, followed by drinks.

When everything was done, she smiled happily. Then she pouted at the baby, saying "Come now, darling, we've given you almost ten minutes." Dreamer thought he'd forgotten the question, so she repeated it.

Julian giggled, wiping his tears away. Then he said "Cook-cook."

"No," Paul said immediately, and Dreamer burst out laughing.

"Be nice, Papa."

"You spoil that child with cookies, little one." Paul folded his arms, looking at her. "There hasn't been a day since he met you he hasn't asked for cookies. Before he met you he didn't know what they were."

"Well, what did you give him?"

"Fruit and vegetables," Paul said, and Dreamer laughed again.

"Papa, you can't be serious."

"I certainly am," Paul said as he sat at the head of the table. "Right son?"

Baby Julian giggled, Dreamer placing him in his high chair. Pandora and Marlon glared up at him, Dreamer deciding to sit with him on her lap.

Ted sat opposite her so he could stare at her a while longer. Dreamer determinedly looked anywhere but at him, Julian reaching for a muffin.

"My one!"

Pandora had an urge to snatch the muffin quickly, but she held off. Dreamer glared at her and she recoiled, eyes immediately filling over. She couldn't remember a single time in her life when her mother looked at her like that.

"Sorry," she mumbled, Dreamer looking at Marlon as well.

Marlon held his hands up, saying "I'm not thinking about it."

"It?" Dreamer repeated, Agnes laying a hand on her arm warningly.

"Dreamer, don't. Stay calm, yes honey?"

"But Mama-"

"Little one," said Paul, and Dreamer looked at him. "Let it go."

"Let it go or let *them* go?" Dreamer answered casually, and Paul smirked.

"Both, little one."

"Paul!" said Agnes, glaring at him. "You're not supposed to egg her on."

"Can't I answer my child?" Paul answered, Agnes snapping "Not when you're encouraging her to close her heart on her family!"

"Well, if they're thinking cruel thoughts about the baby, then-"

"Be quiet," Agnes said coldly, as Pandora and Marlon stared at their knees. "Put yourself in their shoes, Paul. What would you do?"

"I'd be glad of another sibling," Paul answered coldly. "No lie, Agnes."

Agnes closed her mouth, knowing Paul was an only child like herself. After their parents found out what they were, when they were around thirteen, both pairs decided never to have any more children for fear they'd be as weird as their first.

Agnes and Paul were cast out on the street on the very same day, when

they found each other. It was on that day they vowed they'd have revenge on these stupid mortals who thought they were better than them because they couldn't do zilch, vowed to stick together no matter what happened.
Paul cleared his throat uncomfortably, knowing what she was thinking.
"Never mind Memory Lane, Agnes. Let's have this tea."
Baby Julian beamed at Ted, saying "Hello!"
Ted stared at him, not knowing what to do. He looked at Dreamer but she stared stonily over his shoulder, through the glass wall into the garden. Ted looked at Agnes and Paul, who glared at him.
"My grandson is talking to you, Ted."
"He's not anymore, look."
Baby Julian had lost interest in the stranger already, taking his muffin and breaking it into tiny pieces.
"Baby, you're making a mess," Dreamer said amusedly, and he giggled.
"I share, Mummy. See?" He picked up a piece, holding it out to Pandora. "Hello! Look, I share it!"
Pandora hesitated, then she held her hand out. Everyone smiled as Baby Julian dropped the piece in her hand, beaming at her.
Pandora stared at her baby brother, who stared back confusedly.
"You no like it?"
"I- I do," she said, looking down at her hand. "Thank you."
Pleased, Baby Julian picked up another piece and held it out to Marlon. Marlon leant across the table, Baby Julian dropping some in his hands.
"What you name?"
"Um... Marlon."
"Maaarlon," he repeated slowly, and Marlon nodded. Baby Julian looked at Pandora, asking "What *you* name?"
Nervous all of a sudden, Pandora mumbled "Pandora."
"Pa- Pa... Mummy?"
Everyone laughed, Dreamer saying "You can call her 'Dora, sweetie."
"Dorwa." Baby Julian giggled, repeating it. "Dorwa!"
Pandora smiled shakily at Dreamer, who smiled back at her.
"What are you thinking, honey?"
"He- he's kind of cute," Pandora said truthfully, and Marlon nodded.
Agnes beamed happily, clapping her hands as she said "I can feel the negative energy disappearing faster than water down a drain."
"So can I," Dreamer said quietly, as Julian squirmed in her lap. "Ted?"
Ted jumped, startled. "Yes Dreamer?"
"Why are you so quiet?"
"I... I was just thinking, that's all."
Baby Julian stared at him, then he said "What you name?"
Ted looked at Dreamer, as if asking her permission to answer.

"You don't need my permission to speak to him," Dreamer said, Paul as well. "Just answer him, or he'll ask you again later."
Ted looked back at Baby Julian, saying "Ted."
Baby Julian's face lit up. "Ted!"
Ted nodded as he pointed at Marlon, saying "Marlon." Then he looked at Pandora, saying "Dorwa." Then he beamed at Ted. "Ted!"
"He likes learning new things," Dreamer explained, when they looked at her with a small smile on their faces. "But the best time was when-"
"He discovered he had a mother," Paul said, and everyone looked at him.
Pandora, Marlon and Ted shifted guiltily in their seats, thinking the same thing. They hadn't thought for one second about what it must have been like for Dreamer, finding out she had another child.
"Um... how did you feel when you found out about the baby?" Ted asked cautiously, and Dreamer looked at him. She took a moment to answer.
"I was shocked at first."
"I can imagine," muttered Pandora, Dreamer continuing "But when I saw Baby Julian, I loved him more than anything in the whole world."
The hurt hit the three of them at the same time: they looked away from her. Dreamer smiled at them, saying *"Anything.* Not anyone."
The smiles that lit their faces surprised her; did they really think she'd stop loving them because of Baby Julian?
"You can't possibly think I'd stop loving you," Dreamer said, amazed. "That's ridiculous. You're supposed to stop loving *me. "*
"Never," Pandora said fiercely, Ted and Marlon as well.
Paul looked at the clock, saying "It's getting late, everyone."
Everyone's faces fell, Dreamer's as well. They didn't want to separate, not when everything had miraculously sorted itself out.
Pandora and Marlon scowled at Paul, wondering if he enjoyed spoiling the moment. Paul winked at them, saying "Actually, I was going to suggest you staying here with your mother. It's almost two a.m."
"Dad as well?" asked Marlon hopefully, and everyone looked at Dreamer. Dreamer nodded, saying "Ted as well."
Ted breathed out, relieved. Dreamer smiled at him, and he shyly smiled back. Then he asked "Do you have enough room?"
"I should have. I've got an upstairs."
"Ok then."
Almost an hour later the table was clear again, and Agnes and Paul were gone. Pandora and Marlon were in bed, Pandora asking to share with Marlon for one night. So Dreamer turned the double bed into two singles, waving her wand to move around everything. A bed stood on either side of the room, beds which they were now both asleep in.
Ted stood in the living room downstairs, waiting nervously. Dreamer was

tending to her baby, and what a cute little baby he was too, Ted thought ruefully. He wondered where he and Dreamer stood now. Everything seemed so right at the table, even with Baby Julian. Ted already liked the happy baby, which was weird since he thought it was hate at first sight when he saw the pictures and video clip Cruise showed him. But now...

Upstairs, Dreamer laid her son down in his crib, stroking his hair.

"Sweet dreams honey," she whispered, pulling his soft quilt over him. Baby Julian slept on, his tiny thumb in his mouth.

Dreamer left his tiny lamp on for him, taking a deep breath as she left the room and went downstairs. Now she had to see to Ted.

Dreamer felt butterflies in her stomach as she stared at his broad back. He was looking at a portrait of her when she was twenty, Agnes and Paul seated behind her. They looked much more impressive than the Royal Family, Ted thought with a small smile, then he sensed her behind him. Taking a deep breath, he turned to look at her.

Dreamer didn't even know what to say. Neither did Ted. They stared at each other for a good ten seconds, then Ted said "Um... hi."

"Hi," Dreamer said quietly, then she pulled herself together. "Um... upstairs. Pandora and Marlon's had their showers now, so you can have yours."

Ted nodded, saying "Ok."

"I've summoned some of your things from your house," Dreamer said nervously, wondering why he was staring at her so intensely. "They're in your room- um, the room opposite mine. That's the room on your left when you go up the stairs... Ted?" she said, as he continued to watch her. "What's the matter?"

"You're so beautiful," he said quietly, and Dreamer smiled.

"Thank you. The shower's waiting for you."

Ted smiled, asking "Am I sleeping on the sofa?"

"No- didn't you hear what I was saying?"

"I was admiring your every angle," he admitted as he moved closer. "What was you saying, Dreamer?"

"I... I was saying that- that your room is upstairs and..." Dreamer trailed off, staring at the milk-chocolate man she loved. Ted had a finely featured face that went well with the muscular body that came with it. His build gave the impression of a man who used his physical strength often, but Dreamer knew that Ted was as gentle as a mouse. His appearance intimidated his opponents in court, but if they knew him the way she did they would be more confident, not afraid of him one bit.

Ted knew what she was thinking. Dreamer watched those beautiful lips curve into a smirk, Ted saying "You like what you see, don't you?"

Dreamer almost nodded. Dragging her eyes away from him, she said

"You're very vain, Ted."

"Because of you. All I have to do is look into those emerald eyes…" His eyes scanned her face hungrily. "To know you love me as much as I love you." He stepped so close she grazed his torso. "I'm right, aren't I?"

Dreamer didn't answer. She hardly heard a word he said, simply gazing at the rows of perfect white teeth behind those lips.

"Aren't I?" Ted repeated softly, before he lowered his mouth to hers. To both of them something shifted in the universe, because the kiss felt like lightning jolts, shocking them all the way to the tips of their toes. Dreamer's arms curved around his neck, Ted lifting her off her feet as he pulled her closer. He was so focused on the tender kiss, he didn't hear Marlon and Pandora traipse downstairs. Neither did Dreamer.

Pandora stopped dead, backing and crashing into her brother.

Eyes closed, in their own world, Ted and Dreamer didn't react to the noise. Marlon grabbed Pandora by the arm and pulled her back upstairs, whispering "They don't know we was there. They don't have to."

"Ok, ok- just let go of me!" she hissed. "And thanks for waking me up for nothing, camel mouth!"

"Nothing!" he whispered, offended. "It was to talk to Mum! You know, midnight chat and stuff!"

"Well we're not going to have our midnight chat now, are we?" Pandora pulled away from her brother. "I'm going back to sleep."

When their door snapped shut, Dreamer frowned in her haze of lust and she paused the kiss that had her soul on fire.

"Did you hear that?" she murmured against Ted's mouth, Ted answering "It might be the baby."

"I'll check," Dreamer said, her voice low. "You'd better get your shower, Ted. I… I'll show you where your things are."

Ted nodded, heart racing as he let her go. Dreamer gazed at him for a moment, then she turned and left the living room.

"Follow me."

Ted obeyed, taking steady breaths to calm himself. So was Dreamer, but she hid that fact very well.

"The bathroom's right there."

She pointed to another door before turning and walking down the hallway, slipping right through the closed door at the end as if she was a ghost. Ted smiled, entering his glamorous room and picking up his towel. She had all of his things there already, laid out for him.

Dreamer sat on her bed, feeling there was a vast change in her and Ted's relationship. Never, she thought, had Ted ever made her feel that way with just a kiss.

* * *

Ted didn't dare go and talk to Dreamer again, knowing she was up. Though her kisses were always mind blowing, *that* one… Ted shook his head, still revelling in the electrical feeling. He hoped Dreamer would come and say goodnight. If it reached half two and she didn't, he would go to her instead.

* * *

Dreamer hesitated, then she knocked on his door.
Ted sat up quickly, saying "Come in."
Dreamer walked in slowly, a smile spreading across Ted's face.
"You ok?"
Dreamer nodded. "I had a quick shower, and… I made you a hot drink as well. It's downstairs with mine if you want it."
Ted was already on his feet.
"You didn't have to make me a hot drink before I go to bed."
Dreamer raised an eyebrow.
"I *always* make you a hot drink before you go to bed."
"Slipped my mind," he said amusedly, and she smiled.

* * *

"Are you going to work tomorrow?" asked Dreamer, but Ted said no.
"I've moved up in the firm," he said, and she gasped.
"You've been promoted? That's excellent, Ted!"
Ted smiled, saying "It didn't feel excellent at the time, what with you being gone and all." His smile grew. "But now it feels great."
Touched, Dreamer leant across the table and kissed him.
"What role do you play now?"
"I'm a private lawyer now; I don't have to rush to someone's aid as much as I used to. I'm earning fifty two thousand a year-"
"You're kidding!"
"Nope. That's how private I am. Not only that, but I'll be called all over Europe to help people. Three times a year I'll have to leave the country, it comes with the package." He smiled at her, taking her hand. "That means, my lovely, that I'll be taking you, Marlon, Pandora and Julian on holiday with me."
Dreamer's eyes filled as he kissed her hand.
"You don't mind Julian not being your son?"
"No," Ted admitted. "It bugged me at first, when I saw the pictures-"
"What pictures?" she said, staring at him. "I made sure my baby wasn't in any magazine photos, so how could there be pictures of him?"
"Well…" Ted hesitated. "I sort of hired a private detective to find you."
Dreamer leant back in her seat, surveying him through her green eyes.
"Really." Ted nodded. "Well now I'm going to hire a private lawyer besides yourself to sue you, Ted! How could you spy on me?"
"It wasn't spying, Dreamer. I missed you," he said calmly. "Nobody would tell me what was going on- Miriam acted like she knew nothing."
Dreamer averted her gaze to their hands, entwined on the kitchen table. Ted wondered if now was the time to give her his version of the Spanish Inquisition. She looked so innocent. His heart said no, but his mind screamed *yes!* He chose to go with his mind.
"Why didn't you tell me it was Miriam who was messing your head around?"
"I didn't want you to be mad at her," Dreamer said, looking anywhere but at him. "Don't be angry, Ted- let me explain how she feels."
Ted opened his mouth, then he closed it and nodded.
"I'm all ears."

* * *

"It's not like that!" he burst out, for the third time. Each time Dreamer explained Miriam to him, he had the same reaction. "Explain it again."
"Ted, I've explained it around four times now." Dreamer picked up her wand, tapping his and her mug at the side. The cold chocolate drink was instantly hot again, steam rising from each mug. "That's how she feels, yes? She feels like you stuck your foot in everything when I came back just like you did when we met- she thinks she'll be singled out again."
"It's not like that," Ted repeated. "Call her."
"Ted, it's gone four in the morning."
"Call her, Dreamer." Ted didn't care what time it was. "Now."
Dreamer obeyed slowly, picking up the house phone.

* * *

Miriam rolled out of bed, scrambling up and running for the phone. She knew it was Dreamer calling.
"Dreamer, is everything all right? Is Julian ok?"
"Everything's fine," Ted said, surprising her. "We need to talk."
"What are *you* doing there, Ted? Where's Dreamer?"
"Right next to me."

* * *

Miriam put the phone down half an hour later, all smiles.
She replayed Ted's soothing voice in her mind over and over, hardly able to believe it.
"Believe me, if you had just talked to me about this, it would have been sorted ages ago. I never knew you felt this way, Miriam. Trust me, Dreamer didn't say a thing all those years back. I just thought you was a distant friend in America she fell out with. And I had to hire a private detective, who found out you was the one corrupting her mind. But never mind that now- what's done is done. Dreamer's like a sister to you, right? Think of me as your brother-in-law. You're a part of this family, all right? You're a part of us. I want you to come out with us for dinner tonight, if you don't mind."
Miriam had said she didn't mind, asking what dinner was for.
"We're celebrating a new beginning with and for you, Baby Julian, Paul and Dreamer. I'll take you to a church if I have to, Miriam. You're in this family now. You don't only have Dreamer and Agnes, but me too now. We

223

are one, do you hear me? We're all going to stick together."

* * *

Ted held Dreamer close to him as she slept, afraid to let her go for fear all of this was just a dream. He would wake up to a house with no Dreamer, two depressed kids, and still in his position as a regular lawyer at work.
Ted looked down at the love of his life, looking so innocent and perfect as she dreamt of something that was making her mouth curve into a smile. Ted hoped it was him in her dream making her smile like that.
Unable to stop himself, he kissed her soft lips.
The effect worked better than any alarm clock Dreamer ever owned.
She smiled, running her hands through his curly hair as he lowered his head to kiss her neck.
"Don't you ever sleep, Teddy?"
"Sure," he mumbled against her skin, "Just not right now."

* * *

Baby Julian woke up almost four hours later, already giggling.
"Mummy," he called. "Mummy, Mummy!"
Silence.
Julian scratched his head, confused. Mummy *always* came when he woke up calling her. The baby took a tiny breath, then he called her again.
"Mummy!"
He waited to hear "coming honey", but there was just silence.
Baby Julian screamed blue murder when he realised Mummy wasn't in the house.
"Mummy!!"
Dreamer jumped, in the shower.
"Coming!" she called, but he couldn't hear her through the closed door.
Pandora stirred, opening her eyes as Marlon groaned "Go to him, 'Dora!"
"I'm going, idiot!"
"Mummy," sobbed Julian, hugging his teddy bear. "Mummy!"
Pandora took a deep breath, wondering if she was mad. She didn't like little kids. Especially when they were crying that hard. Then she reasoned that this was her baby brother, and she needed to comfort him. She immediately felt guilty as she remembered what she thought of him seconds before he gave her a piece of his chocolate muffin.
"Mummy," wailed Julian, as Dreamer dressed as quickly as she could.
Pandora took another deep breath before turning into the baby's room.
Baby Julian paused mid-scream, staring at her.

Pandora approached him slowly, asking "You ok?"

"Dorwa," he wept, reaching out to her. "I want Mummy!"

Marlon entered the room as she lifted him out of the crib.

"Is he all right?"

"Marlon," Baby Julian said, eyes filling over. Marlon smiled at him.

"What's up, baby brother. You all right?"

"No!"

"What's wrong?" asked Marlon, and Pandora rolled her eyes.

"Didn't you hear what he was saying?"

"Yeah, but… he's so cute when he talks in that baby voice."

"He is a baby, idiot."

"What's wrong Julian?" asked Marlon gently, and the baby sniffed before saying "I want Mummy."

Downstairs, Ted was waltzing around the kitchen making a spectacular breakfast. He couldn't hear a thing over the sizzling of the frying pan.

Dreamer pulled her robe on over her gown as Baby Julian whimpered, then burst into tears again. He didn't know Marlon and Pandora well enough to feel comfortable with them.

"Mummy!"

"I'm right here, baby." She turned into the room, Baby Julian shrieking happily as she took him off Pandora. "Are you ok?"

"Mummy!" he squealed, suddenly beaming. "Mummy!"

Pandora reached out cautiously, stroking his curly hair as he giggled.

"Mum, I… I'm sorry for-"

"It's ok, sweetie." Dreamer smiled at her. "Get your showers, both of you. I'll bathe Baby Julian in my room."

"I'll iron his clothes," Marlon offered quickly. "Where are they?"

"In his drawer, but you don't have to-"

"It's ok Mum, I want to." Marlon kissed her on the cheek. "I want to."

"I can make his breakfast," Pandora said. "What does he like?"

"Oatmeal," Dreamer said, but Julian said "Cook-cook!"

"Or Weetabix-"

"Cook-cook!"

"Or even Rice Krispies if he doesn't make a mess-"

"Cook-cook!"

"And if I'm making pancakes then-" Dreamer stopped, wondering what that delicious smell was. "Where's Ted, honey?"

"I'm not sure. Downstairs?" suggested Pandora, Marlon shrugging.

Dreamer decided to find out what the smell was later.

"Come on baby, it's time to get your bath."

* * *

When Dreamer carried Baby Julian downstairs and put him down, he ran into the kitchen where Pandora, Marlon and Ted was waiting.

The three of them couldn't help cooing at him lovingly, because he looked adorable in his tiny dungarees and blue t-shirt underneath. Dreamer followed slowly, Ted saying "He's so cute, Dreamer."

"Thank you. Wow," she said, as she looked at the table. "Did you-?"

"Yep," Ted said proudly. "I can cook, you know. Have a seat."

Dreamer picked Julian up and put him in his high chair, smiling as his face crumpled.

"Don't worry sweetie, you'll come down after you eat."

"Oaty?" asked Baby Julian, and Pandora smiled at him.

"Oaty with cook-cook chips and jam and sprinkles, look!"

Baby Julian squealed happily, staring at the colourful breakfast she set in front of him.

"Mummy, look! Dorwa done it!"

"Beats ironing clothes," Pandora said smugly, and Marlon pouted at her.

"No arguing," warned Ted, bringing the plates over. "Not today, kids."

Dreamer spooned some of the oatmeal, feeding it to her baby.

"Mmm!" said Julian happily, and Dreamer smiled at him.

"Say ta to 'Dora, sweetie."

"Ta, Dorwa! Ta!"

* * *

"Mum, please let us stay," begged Pandora, but Dreamer shook her head.
"You wanted to stay off college because things were rocky, honey.
Everything is sorted now, so there's no reason why you can't go."
She flicked her wand at the front door, which opened slowly.
Marlon and Pandora pouted as two rucksacks appeared, no doubt bearing
everything they needed for college.
Pandora sighed, picking up her black rucksack. She was dressed head to
foot in black: a black sweater, black jeans, black socks under black boots,
a black combat jacket with a matching black hat, scarf and gloves.
"Don't know why it's freezing like this in October," she muttered, kissing
Dreamer goodbye. "Come on, Marlon."
"You both go to Forest Academy?" Dreamer said interestedly, and they
nodded, Marlon kissing his mother on the cheek.
"Bye, Mum."
"Bye honey."
"Those children really love their mother," Barbara said from across the
road to her husband. Hugh smiled and nodded.
"Morning Dreamer!" he called, and Dreamer waved.
"Morning Hugh."
"How's Baby Julian?"
"He's fine."
"Dreamer, why don't you pop over for lunch?" Barbara called from her
front door, as Hugh got in his car. "Bring the baby along!"
"I'll see what I'm doing at lunch," Dreamer said, averting her gaze.
"All right then." Barbara wondered why Dreamer was still so withdrawn.
"I'll be in all day, so pop over whenever you're ready."
Hugh rolled down his window, asking "Where's the big kids going to?"
"College," Dreamer said, looking at him. "Forest Academy."
"I can give them a lift if they'd like," Hugh offered, and Dreamer looked
at Pandora and Marlon. Pandora's face remained blank, but Marlon's was
hopeful. Dreamer nodded, saying "Ok then. Thank you."
"Come on in," Hugh called, as Baby Julian's tiny feet pattered.
"Mummy, where Dorwa and Marlon go?"
"College, sweetie." Dreamer picked him up. "Say bye."
"Bye Dorwa!" called Baby Julian, beaming at her back. "Bye Marlon!"
Both of them turned and smiled, Pandora coming back over to kiss his
soft cheek while Marlon kissed the top of his head. Julian giggled,
slightly overwhelmed by the affection he was receiving.
"Be a good baby, ok?" Pandora said, and he nodded.

Hugh smiled, patient as ever. Barbara smiled too.

Ted came to the door as well, saying "Be good, ok you two? I don't want another phone call from your principal for the rest of the week."

Pandora and Marlon smirked at each other and got in Hugh's car.

"I mean it," Ted called. "I'll be calling in to check on you. And if I don't get a good response you can forget going out on Halloween."

Pandora and Marlon scowled at him, Pandora slamming the door behind her. She specifically told her father she was going to a graveyard on her own on Halloween, and he reluctantly agreed. Marlon was going to a party. Dreamer leant back against him as the car pulled away, asking "They've been misbehaving at college?"

"Only because you wasn't around. They missed you," Ted said, not remotely bothered about that anymore. "They was depressed."

"Oh." Dreamer's face fell. "I should have called them."

"Never mind that," Ted said quickly, hating the miserable look on her face. "What are we going to do today?"

"I don't know," she confessed, as Baby Julian squirmed in her arms. "It's nice that everything is sorted properly, but…"

Ted stared at her. There was a 'but' in their moment of bliss?

"But what, Dreamer?"

"Well, we have to be realistic," she mumbled, and Ted realised that they was standing at the front door still, Dreamer's neighbour watching them. Ted smiled politely and she smiled back, then he pulled Dreamer inside and closed the door.

"Mummy Mummy, I want to play bricks peas!" Baby Julian gazed at her happily, waiting for her to put him down and conjure his toys.

Dreamer did just that, flicking her wand carelessly. The toys rose in the air and zoomed into the living room, Dreamer putting her baby down so he could run after them

"Come play, Mummy!"

"Coming sweetie."

Ted blocked her way, saying "Explain what you mean by realistic."

"And Papa tells me *I'm* the dreamer," Dreamer muttered, looking at him. "Ted, last night was great, but-"

"Don't!" he snapped, making her jump. "Don't say it was a mistake."

"I wasn't going to." Dreamer looked into his eyes, calm as ever. "I was just going to say it was great, but we have to be realistic. You've got your house, and I've got mine. I'm not moving out of mine, Ted. It's my home, and I've come to love it here."

"In just two and a half months?"

Dreamer nodded. Ted rubbed his neck, thinking about that.

"Well, I could move here with the kids-"

"I'm not ready for that, Ted." Dreamer sighed. "Neither is my baby."
Ted knew this. He knew Julian would be startled to find three strangers suddenly on the scene.
"So… what are you saying? You want me to leave with the kids?"
"I say we wait until they come home, and then sort it all out."
Ted nodded, saying "Fine. But for now, can we enjoy our day?"
"Our day?"
"Celebrate us getting back together. Because," he said as he looked her right in the eyes, "Whether we live together or not, we *are* together."
Dreamer smiled.
"I'll accept that."

* * *

Pandora walked into class slowly, everyone looking at her.
"Hey Pandora!"
She didn't answer, dropping in her seat next to Alice.
"You hung up on me," Alice said sulkily, and Pandora looked at her.
"Good morning to you too, Alice. Jeez, lighten up. It's a nice day."
"Oh, I should lighten up? Why don't *you* enlighten me on your baby-"
"Shh! Break time."

* * *

"Can I come home with you?" begged Alice, but Pandora said no.
"Unless you're talking about my dad's house- and it's still no because I'm not going there. I'm going back to Mum's with Marlon-"
She broke off, noticing James talking to her brother. They hadn't spoken since she left him in the park two and a half months ago, and after Pandora repeatedly rejected James'ss calls, he stopped calling.
Alice nudged her, saying "Go make up with him."
"It's not me he needs to make up with, it's my mother."
James watched Pandora over Marlon's shoulder, suddenly oblivious to whatever Marlon was saying to him.
"We've got to practice for the game, so forget about the Halloween party."
"Mmm," James answered, as Pandora walked off, Alice in her wake.
"It doesn't matter anyway, there's still Christmas parties and stuff, right?"
"Uh-huh."
Pandora turned a corner, then she was gone. Alice looked back and smiled sympathetically, then she was gone too.
James scowled. Did she feel sorry for him or something? What did

Pandora tell her?

"And we need to work on our essays for the coach too- I can't believe there's a writing side to sports-" Marlon stopped, looking at him. "Bro, are you even *listening?*"

"What? Oh- yeah," lied James. "Yeah, I'm listening."

"Good, so *you* can tell Derek we're not going to the party."

"What?!" spluttered James. "Why not?"

"Because we're already behind on work," Marlon answered. "We need to catch up before we get kicked off the course."

James pouted.

* * *

"Make sure you make notes," their lecturer said firmly, staring right at Pandora. "Some of you don't seem to be taking Creative Studies seriously."

Pandora rolled her eyes as the lights went out, the film starting.

"Pandora, why don't you take him home?" Alice whispered in the dark. "I mean, that way you'll be ok again and-"

"We *are* ok," Pandora whispered back. "I'm just holding off talking to him until he apologises to my mother for being such a coward."

"And when he does?"

"Then we'll be back on track."

"Pandora!" barked Mr Works. "Stop talking and start working!"

Pandora glared at him, picking up her pen. She wrote down the title of the film, and the date. Alice followed suit, Pandora scowling at her.

Funny how she's the one who always whispers and copies my notes but I'm the one who gets shouted at.

Turning her paper over, Alice scribbled *'Shall I talk to him for you?'*

Pandora read her words slowly, remembering all too well when she saw James hug Alice outside her door at home. Her gut clenched.

'No, I'll talk to him myself.'

Alice nodded.

* * *

"Nap time, baby."
Baby Julian's eyes filled over as he looked at his toys, then at Dreamer.
"I no want nap, Mummy. Peas no nap?"
"Please *yes* nap, and play some more when you wake up."
Baby Julian thought about this, scratching his curly head. Then he reached up to his Mummy, Dreamer bending and picking him up.
"Good boy."
Ted wanted to follow, but he forced himself to stay put on the sofa. Dreamer stopped at the door and smiled at him, making his stomach flutter as she said "I won't be long."
Ted nodded. "Ok."
Baby Julian looked up at Dreamer curiously, then he looked at Ted.
Ted smiled, saying "I think he's onto something."
"Mummy, look!" The baby placed his hands on Dreamer's chest, then his little ear. "Boom, Mummy! Boom boom! What that boom, Mummy?"
"It's my heart, baby."
"It fast," said Baby Julian, transfixed. "It go fast, Mummy!"
Ted smirked, knowing her heart *would* be racing if he was around. Embarrassed, Dreamer said "I... let's get you to bed."
She left quickly, nearly running up the stairs.
Ted waited for a good ten minutes before laughing his head off. Dreamer descended the stairs slowly, her hand on her slender hip.
"You think that's funny, do you?"
"It's hilarious," Ted answered, grinning at her. "Wow, Dreamer. You looked so relaxed and normal, but then Baby Julian gave you away."
"He picks up on everything," said Dreamer lovingly, then she pouted. "I'm not sure that's a good thing."
Ted burst out laughing again, Dreamer smiling grudgingly.
"Come here, you." Ted pulled her into his arms. "Get ready for lunch."
"Lunch?"
"With Barbara, remember?"
"Oh Ted, I don't want to- I can't leave you by yourself-"
"Dreamer, the woman looked real disappointed when you tried shunning her off." Ted caressed her cheek with the back of his hand. "Go to her."
"I can't. Baby Julian's asleep now- I'm not waking him up just for-"
"Baby, I'm perfectly capable of babysitting for you."
Dreamer bit her lip. "I've never left him alone with a stranger before."
"I'm not a stranger, though."
"To him you are- Ted, stop it-"
"Say you'll go to lunch," Ted said, eyes sparkling as he pulled her closer.

"Or else I'll torture you in the sweetest way possible."
Dreamer inclined her head with a slow, seductive smile.
"I think I'll prefer the torture, to be honest with you."
"Oh yeah?"
"Yes."
"Ok, how about I torture you and *then* you go to lunch?"
"How about you come with me?" Dreamer countered. "I'll call Miriam to come over and watch the baby, and I'll call Barbara and let her know I'm coming in an hour."
"Ok," Ted said. "You know, Marlon and Pandora finish at half three."
"They should be here by half four then," Dreamer answered as she picked up the house phone. "By that time everyone should be relaxed. We can watch a film together before we go out to dinner."
"Dinner?"
"Dinner," Dreamer said, looking at him. "Remember Ted, in the early hours of this morning, you went dramatic on me."
"Dramatic?" Ted thought back to when Dreamer couldn't get enough of him, at sunrise. Remembering the expression on her face, he smirked at her. "I thought you liked it when I-"
"Ted!" Dreamer put the house phone down as he started laughing. "Stop being so- I'm talking about when you called Miriam!"
"Oh!" Ted slapped a hand to his forehead. "I totally forgot."
"Right, so I'll call Miriam quickly and then Barbara, then-"
"How long will it take for Miriam to get here?" Ted cut across, smirking.
"Three quarters of an hour minimum. Why?"
"That's all I need to deal with you, my lovely."
"No," Dreamer said flatly, but Ted ignored her as he walked towards her. "No, Ted!"
"Yes, Dreamer."

* * *

Baby Julian woke up to Mummy shrieking with laughter, Ted as well.
"Ted, stop it! We've got to go."
"I don't want to go anymore."
The doorbell rang.
"See, that's Miriam- let go of me." Dreamer pushed him away, laughing
as she went and opened the front door to her friend. "Hello Miriam."
"Dreamer," Miriam said, beaming at her. "How have you been?"
"Fine, fine- come inside."
Miriam noted that Dreamer was out of breath.
"Are you ok?"
"What? Oh- I'm fine."
"You're all out of breath, though."
"Because of Ted!" said Dreamer, laughing as Ted popped his head
around the door of the living room with a sly grin on his face.
"Hey Miriam. All set for dinner later on?"
"Um... yes, I brought a change of clothes in the car." Miriam smiled
nervously, then she looked at Dreamer. "Is Baby Julian asleep?"
"Yes," Dreamer said, as the baby called "Mummy!"
"Well, he was," Dreamer said grudgingly, as Julian called again.
"Mummy!"
"I'll go and get him," Miriam offered, and Dreamer nodded.
Dreamer listened as she picked up her wand, Julian shrieking happily.
"Minnyam!"
"Yep, he's in good hands," Ted said thoughtfully. "Ready?"
Dreamer nodded, placing her wand on her side and letting go. It slowly
slid out of sight, vanishing into thin air. Ted frowned at her.
"Where'd it go?"
"It's in an invisible pocket," Dreamer replied. "Shall we?"
"Yep."
Ted offered his arm, Dreamer taking it as she called "Bye, Miriam!"
"Have a nice time!" Miriam called, at the foot of the stairs with Baby
Julian in one arm. He sensed Mummy was going... with the stranger.
"Mummy, where you go?"
"Across the road, sweetie. To Barbara's house."
Baby Julian reached to her, mouth trembling. Dreamer's heart melted,
and she felt like cancelling lunch and staying with her baby. Stepping
closer, she took him off Miriam as tears trailed down his cheeks.
"Don't cry, baby. I'll be back soon."
"Soon?" he repeated, not knowing what that meant. "What soon mean?"

"I won't be long. Don't cry honey, you'll make Mummy cry too."
Baby Julian wiped his tears away, but his eyes filled again.
"Why don't we take him with us?" Ted suggested. "Miriam can let in Pandora and Marlon- if she doesn't want to come too?" he added hastily, when Dreamer glared at him. Miriam smiled and shook her head.
"I'll let in Pandora and Marlon for you. It's already a quarter to three."
"This is a very late lunch, then," Dreamer said, conjuring a tiny pair of trainers for Baby Julian. His tiny puff coat sailed out of his wardrobe, out of his room and downstairs, Dreamer catching it easily.
"Are you sure he needs that?" Ted asked. "I mean, it's only across the-"
"I can't risk him getting a cold, Ted."
Miriam took the trainers quickly, wanting to do it for her.
"Honestly Dreamer, you worry so much over him," she murmured, as Baby Julian giggled, squirming at her gentle touch on his feet.
Ted watched him with a small smile, marvelling at how much he looked like his mother.
"I bet you looked just like Julian when you was a baby, Dream."
Miriam looked at him as Dreamer said "I probably did. All done?"
"Yep," said Miriam, while she wondered if Ted had always called Dreamer 'Dream', just how *she* had always called him Teddy.
Baby Julian clung to Dreamer happily, Dreamer wiping his mouth.
"You shouldn't be drooling like that," she said, shaking her head at him as a dummy appeared. Baby Julian grabbed it happily, Dreamer looking into the eyes that mirrored her own. "No running around at Barbara's, ok honey? You can take your teddy with you."
"Back soon," Ted added to Miriam, who nodded.
"Mummy, what those?" asked Baby Julian, reaching for Dreamer's earrings. Dreamer caught his hand gently, saying "My jewellery, baby."
"Oh," he said, gazing at them. "They nice, Mummy."
"Thank you sweetie."
Miriam smiled, hugging herself as she watched Dreamer cross the road with her child in her arms, her lover at her side. Barbara opened the front door before Ted could even press the bell, eagerly ushering them inside. Miriam closed the door gently, smiling.
She couldn't wait to see Pandora again.

* * *

Pandora felt a little miserable as Alice linked arms with her. Though it hadn't been as if she'd been speaking to him constantly for ages, she kept remembering when her and James had been inseparable in primary school. And a bit of secondary school.

And that night they shared together on her sofa too, it filled the long gap of separation they experienced when they both fell apart.

"Pandora, are you even listening to me?" demanded Alice, pouting.

"I miss him," Pandora mumbled, and her face softened.

"Shall we go to the Sports Building? He should be finishing now."

"But I can't talk to him, can I, because Marlon's going to be there."

"I'll distract Marlon," Alice said quickly, and Pandora raised an eyebrow. Alice smiled, saying "What? I'm not even going to lie to you-"

"You like my brother."

"I think he's cute," Alice said, shrugging. "That's all."

"You know, normally I'd be mad at you, but I guess that's being a bit of a hypocrite," Pandora said. "I like his friend, he likes my friend-"

"Marlon can't stand me," Alice answered, and Pandora smirked.

"He acts like it because he doesn't want to get rejected. I can tell he likes you, he used to look at Janice the same way before I clocked."

"Mmm," Alice answered. "So is it ok to tell Marlon about you and-"

"No! He'll kill James," Pandora said, quickly filling her in about Marlon and his accurate crystal ball. "I had to scarper real quick."

"I get that, but up a tree?" Alice couldn't believe what she just heard. "Boy, you must be quick on your feet."

"I am," Pandora answered. "So... should we go to the Sports Building?"

"Yes, lets."

* * *

"Marlon, tell her I'm not interested!" James said angrily, as Cindy smirked at him. "We broke up ages ago-"

Marlon was confused. "But when I asked about her, you said-"

"I lied, ok bro? We broke up at least six months ago!"

"No wonder I haven't seen you," Marlon said to Cindy, smiling broadly as Alice and Pandora turned the corner. "Don't listen to him, he's been missing you. He told me he missed you about three days ago."

"I know he misses me, because I miss him too."

"Aaaah," said Marlon, amused as James smiled a little. "See, he's smiling! Cindy, how about we go out at the weekend?"

"Ok, sure. Marlon, aren't you going to grow?" Cindy laughed as she looked up at him. "You've been the same since high school!"

"Don't start on me!" Marlon said, making her laugh again. "Focus on your man, and slap him for staring at your- hey 'Dora!"

James whipped round as Cindy wrapped her arms around him.

"Pandora! What are you doing here?"

"Waiting for Marlon like I always do," Pandora said smoothly, Marlon saying "You remember Cindy, don't you 'Dora? James'ss girl!"

It's a wonder Cindy kept smiling, James thought nervously. The look Pandora gave her was so cold he swore the temperature went down.

"Hi."

"Hey Pandora!" said Cindy, smiling at her. "I haven't seen you in ages!"

Pandora shrugged. "I don't really speak to anyone from high school anymore." *Including you!* "How come you're here at Forest?"

"I just came to talk to my man," Cindy answered as she kissed James'ss neck. "He's been missing me, haven't you Jamie?"

Pandora raised an eyebrow at the nickname, James struggling to prise Cindy off him. She was pretty strong for someone under five feet. Cindy let him go, walking up to Pandora happily. James and Marlon frowned, looking at each other. Was Pandora really that tall?

"Wow, you're nearly as tall as James!" exclaimed Cindy, Pandora countering "You're nearly as *small* as-"

James coughed loudly, saying "Cindy! Let's go, ok?"

Wondering why Pandora was being so cold, Cindy turned and left.

Alice watched her sashay back to James, thoughtful.

"She's Cindy?" she whispered. "She's really pretty."

"She's a flea in a short skirt," Pandora answered, and Alice burst out laughing. Marlon struggled to keep a straight face for Cindy's sake, but even James was biting his lip to stop himself from laughing.

Cindy glared at Pandora, taking James'ss hand.

"I thought you'd be glad to see me again, Pandora!"

"I'm glad to see you've grown a centimetre," Pandora answered flatly, and James burst out laughing with Marlon, who said "Cindy, don't worry- she's not in a good mood or something. What happened, Pandora? Did a guy try and get your number?"

Pandora glared at him, Marlon apologising quickly.

"James, I'm gone. I'll see you later, Cindy."

"Bye," Cindy answered, James casually saying "Bye Alice, Pandora."

"Bye," they answered, Pandora's eyes resting on his for a moment before she turned and walked away, Marlon following her with Alice behind. Cindy watched them go, then she looked down at herself.

"Oh! She hates pink, I forgot! Pandora!" she called, and Pandora glanced over her shoulder at her as she walked, not even stopping. "I forgot about the pink, I'll wear blue next time! Is that ok?"

Pandora hadn't even acknowledged the colour until she mentioned it.

"Wear what you want, I'm not bothered."

"Well, I know you don't like pink and..." Cindy swung on James'ss arm as she spoke, holding tighter when James tried to pull away. Pandora stopped walking, watching the Barbie doll speak. "And I remember that time Janice came to school in pink, and you didn't speak to her for like... the whole day until she got home and took it off... how is she, anyway?"

Pandora's green eyes seemed to darken as she stared at her, Cindy's smile fading as James blurted "It's not what it looks like- I swear, it isn't-"

"What's not what it looks like?" Cindy said, looking up at him. "Pink?"

"Yes," he said quickly. "Pandora, pink is just a light form of red."

Pandora looked at him, pretending to be puzzled.

"Cindy, do you know what your man is talking about?"

"No," Cindy answered, then she reached up and tweaked his nose. "Stop being so silly, Jamie! Let's go and get something to eat."

James stared down at her. He couldn't remember *why* he had even dated the annoying little-

"Come on, Jamie! Jamie? James!" said Cindy, as he roughly detangled himself from her tiny body. "Be gentle with me!"

Pandora almost laughed: she barely came up to his chest.

Cindy saw her smirk, saying "We was once the same height, but then he just shot up like a tree- Jamie, what's the matter?"

"I've got to go," James answered, pushing her away from him and running down the corridor, past Pandora. "See ya!"

"Jamie, come back right now!" screeched Cindy, but James ignored her.

"See you later," Pandora said, amused. "Alice, I- Alice?"

She stared down the empty corridor, surprised. She thought Alice and Marlon stopped with her, but they were gone.

Pandora grimaced as she carried on walking, by herself. She didn't want to think about what those two were getting up to.

James waited impatiently, leaning against the wall. As soon as Pandora exited the Sports Building he grabbed her arm, saying "Do you always walk so slow? I mean, it looks good, but not when I'm freezing in the-"

Pandora silenced him with a soft kiss, surprising him.

"The next time I see Cindy on your arm, a dirty look won't be all she receives from me," she said quietly, making James smile.

"Aaah, was my Pandora jealous?"

"I wouldn't call it that," Pandora said thoughtfully, "Because I've seen you with loads of girls and I don't give a toss about them-"

"But Cindy's my ex," James said smugly. "So obviously you'd be upset."

"I'm not upset."

"But you was."

"I was not," Pandora said flatly, and he burst out laughing.

"If you say so. Come here."

* * *

"Marlon, the cameras!" gasped Alice, but Marlon ignored her.

"You kept away from me on purpose, didn't you Alice?"

"I didn't keep-"

His mouth was on hers again. When he released her, it took all of her willpower to push him away.

"We have to go back, Marlon- we left Pandora in there."

"She knows her way home-"

"Not home to Dreamer's!"

Marlon closed his mouth. Alice folded her arms, saying "Let's go."

Marlon pouted, then Alice smiled.

"After you kiss me again."

* * *

They walked the long way around the building, Alice ahead of Marlon.

"Alice, wait up!" he called, but Alice ignored him as she head a soft laugh. She just about recognised the laugh. Just about. Pandora hardly *smiled*, let alone laugh like she was doing now.

Alice's frown deepened. Laugh so softly like she was doing now?

She turned the corner, then she gasped.

It was Pandora all right, with her arms around James'ss neck as he lowered his mouth to hers.

"Alice, *wait!"*

"Pandora!" hissed Alice, but Pandora ignored her. "Marlon's coming!"

Right now, Pandora didn't care. Neither did James.

"James, stop! Let go of her!"

James ignored her as well.

Swearing, Alice dashed back inside the corridor, pushing Marlon in the chest. Marlon stumbled, surprised.

"What's wrong?"

"Pandora's gone home," lied Alice. "She just called, um… she's gone."

"She doesn't even know the way!" said Marlon, outraged as he started to walk through the door, but Alice pushed him back. "Alice, what-"

"Let's go and look down the building again."

"We've looked already!" Marlon said, but she wouldn't let him pass.

"Alice, stop being so silly- we've got to go home. I want to see Julian."

She contemplated his calm tone, then she heard James chuckle softly.

"How did you feel, Marlon?" she said quickly, and Marlon frowned.

"How did I feel about what?"

"About your baby brother."

"Alice, we'll talk about this another time-"

"Don't go out there!" she said, trying to pull him back, but he was too strong. "I mean it, Marlon! If you go out there you'll regret leaving Pandora on her own!"

Pandora smirked as Marlon asked what the hell she was talking about.

"Come on, let's get out of here."

Alice heard their footsteps pounding before she released a breath.

"Go on then," she said, ushering him forwards. "Go out."

Marlon stepped outside, looking around. There was no one there.

"Alice, you're really weird sometimes," he said as he looked at her. "I'll regret leaving 'Dora on her own if I come out- and see zilch?"

Alice smiled, shrugging.

"I was just seeing if you're one of those weedy guys who do everything their girls tell them to." Her smile grew. "I'm glad you aren't."

"Mmm. Come on, let's go before more classes end. I don't want the bus to be packed."

"I'd better go," Alice said, surprising him.

"Where're you going?"

"My father's picking me up," she said apologetically. "He'll be waiting in the car park like he always does."

Marlon pouted. "Why isn't he at the clinic?"

Alice kissed him before saying "Daddy owns the clinic, Marlon, so he can leave whenever he wants to."

"Uh- huh. Well, should I walk you to the-"

"No," said Alice quickly. "I don't know how he'll take me seeing you."

"Ok, I'll see you on Monday," Marlon said, kissing her on the cheek. "I'll call you later on."

"Make sure you put Julian on the phone," Alice said, as Pandora flounced towards them. Alice's jaw dropped, Marlon immediately stepping away from his sister's friend.

"I know already," Pandora said tonelessly. "I was going to get the bus, camel mouth, but then James drove by. I forgot he had a car, didn't you?"

"Yeah, I did!" Then Marlon frowned. "Wasn't he with his girl?"

Pandora smirked. "He *was* with his girl, up until... two seconds ago?" Alice smiled, shaking her head as she continued "But she's gone to get some friends of his, see if they want a lift home."

"Oh," said Marlon, not clocking on. "Well, come on then, let's see if he's got room to fit us in. Alice-"

"See you on Monday," Alice said, amused. "See you, Pandora."

"Bye Alice."

* * *

James took care not to speak to Pandora too much, simply asking about her course and how her lessons were today. Pandora made sure her answers were as deadpan as they would have been if James was still unfamiliar to her, like the day he asked how she was and she ran up to her bedroom.

Pandora smiled, thinking *those days are long gone.*

To Marlon, everything was normal. To James and Pandora, it felt weird and uncomfortable being so close yet so far apart.

"So uh... where now?" asked James, looking at Marlon. "We're here."

Marlon looked around, even though there was no point. He didn't even know the *name* of the town let alone the road Dreamer lived on.

"I'd better call Mum and ask."

* * *

Baby Julian bit his teddy's paw happily, sitting on Dreamer's lap.

"Are you sure that's all you want to eat?" Barbara asked anxiously as she looked from Dreamer to Ted and back, then she glanced down at their plates. "You've hardly touched anything."

"We'll be going out to dinner at seven," Ted said, smiling at her. "So..."

"Oh, why didn't you tell me?" said Barbara, pleased. "Romantic dinner?"

"Family dinner," Ted replied, flashing her a smile. "The whole family."

"Well, that's still lovely. I... you don't mean Agnes and Paul will be-"

"No," Dreamer said, smiling a little. "They won't be coming, Barbara. Papa would give everybody a heart attack, ditto Mama."

Barbara smiled back, Ted saying "What does Hugh do for a living?"

"He's a mechanic," Barbara said proudly. "He loves cars."

"Mummy, can I peas have cook-cook?"

"Not now, sweetie."

"Cook-cook?" Barbara asked, perplexed. "What's that?"

"Cookies," Dreamer explained, and the baby giggled. "He loves them."

As Barbara started to say she had plenty in her biscuit tin Dreamer's mobile went off, making her close her mouth.

"Dreamer speaking."

"Hi Mum!" said Marlon brightly. "We're lost!"

Dreamer rubbed her the back of her neck, Ted recognising the sign of a migraine coming on.

"I forgot you haven't been before- are you in town right now?"

"Yep."

241

"What road are you on?"

"Uh… Middleheart Road."

"That's real far, Marlon- how did you end up all the way there?"

"Um…" Dreamer waited. "We got a lift."

Dreamer sighed. "A lift."

"Well… we didn't know where we was going, so I thought we'd be better off in a car than a bus, because buses can't turn back round and stuff-"

"Stay where you are, honey. I'm coming to get you."

* * *

"She's coming to get us," said Marlon, smiling back at his sister. "Cool."

"Why don't you stand outside the car and wait for her?" James said. "If she's teleporting, it'll be easier for her to see you."

"Ok," Marlon said. "Come on, 'Dora."

"You go," Pandora answered flatly. "Wake me up when she gets here."

Marlon shook his head at her and got out of the car, James murmuring "You're not really going to sleep, are you?"

"No, but he doesn't need to know that," Pandora answered. "And when my Mum gets here, you're going to apologise to her."

James nodded determinedly. "Don't worry, I will."

* * *

Dreamer walked slowly, spotting James'ss car easily. Marlon straightened up, opening the car door swiftly.

"'Dora, Mum's-"

Pandora and James broke apart pronto, but it was too late.

Further down the road, Dreamer sighed. She wasn't in the mood for drama.

Marlon stared at his sister as if he was only seeing her for the first time. Pandora didn't know what to say. Neither did James.

"You and him?" said Marlon, heat rising. "My best mate?"

Pandora spoke uneasily. "Marlon, listen-"

Marlon slammed the door shut, Pandora grabbing her rucksack and getting out of the car as he stormed away.

"Marlon, wait!"

"Go to Hell, Pandora!"

"I'm sorry ok?"

"Yeah right! Trying to mess with my flipping head, acting like the crystal ball was lying to me, and- and- lying flat out in my face!" he spat, wheeling round as James left the car too. "He was with his girl two seconds ago or whatever the hell you said- I knew it, I flipping knew it!"

"Bro, calm down!" said James, diverting Marlon's attention. "It's not-"

Marlon's fist collided with his face before he could finish, James knocked off his feet.

"Marlon, don't!" cried Pandora, as James held his nose in pain. "Stop!"

"Get the hell back, Pandora!" spat Marlon as he kicked out, James doubling over, winded. "What was you thinking?"

"Marlon, don't hurt him!"

"He won't hurt after he's unconscious-"

"Enough," said Dreamer smoothly, her voice magically magnified as she walked towards them. "Get away from him, Marlon. You too, Pandora."

Marlon lashed out one more time before doing as he was told, Pandora making sure she was far away from her brother.

Dreamer held a hand out to James, James taking it quickly. With amazing strength for such a delicate woman, Dreamer pulled him to his feet.

"Are you all right, James?"

"Don't talk to him," Marlon said angrily, but Dreamer ignored him.

"I'm fine," James said weakly, holding his side. "I- Dreamer, I'm sorry for running off when Paul came. I should've stood my ground."

"Everybody's afraid of my father," Dreamer answered, smiling at him. "I wasn't surprised- in fact, I wasn't thinking of you at the time."

"Good," James said, a hand still over his nose. "And- and my mother-"

"It's fine, honey. Don't worry about it."

James hesitated, Dreamer repeating herself.

"Don't worry." Turning to her children, she held her hands out. Pandora and Marlon took one each, closing their eyes as Dreamer teleported.

* * *

"Where Mummy?" asked Baby Julian, perplexed as he looked up at Ted. Miriam picked him up lovingly, saying "She'll be home soon."

Dreamer appeared in a flash of white light, Pandora and Marlon with her.

"What's *she* doing here?" spat Marlon, Pandora as well.

Dreamer's face mirrored theirs as she said "Sit down."

"But-"

"Now," she said coldly, and all three of her children recoiled. Remembering the baby, Dreamer took a deep breath before saying "Miriam, take Baby Julian upstairs please."

Miriam nodded, getting up with the baby. As she expected, he started struggling in her arms, eyes filling as he said "I want Mummy!"

"Mummy's right here baby," Dreamer said, rubbing her neck as she smiled at him. "Let Miriam read you a story while I talk to Marlon and 'Dora, ok sweetie?"

Baby Julian hadn't even acknowledged the presence of his siblings until Mummy said their names. He shook his tiny head, face crumpling as he wailed "I want Mummy *now!*"

Ted's eyes averted to the carpet. He knew he should say something, but he didn't know what. Dreamer's head was starting to hurt as Miriam said "Let's show Mummy we can be brave, love. Are you a brave boy?"

Baby Julian nodded, eyes on Dreamer.

"Then let's go upstairs and show her we can be brave, ok?"

"Ok," he wept, Dreamer exhaling with relief.

"Thank you, Miriam."

"Anytime," Miriam replied, glad to get away from the horrid glares Marlon and Pandora were giving her as they sat on the sofa.

As soon as they were upstairs Dreamer turned to her children.

"Mum, I didn't mean to hit him," Marlon said, heat rising as he looked at his sister. Dreamer raised an eyebrow, Marlon recoiling.

"Well, I did mean to- but for a good reason, Mum! Him and Pandora was kissing in the car- he's my best mate- she's my sister-"

"I don't ever want to witness you physically harming someone ever again," Dreamer replied, looking at her eldest child. "I understand that you're angry, Marlon. But fighting isn't going to solve anything. Did Pandora attack Janice when she caught you kissing her?"

Marlon dropped his gaze, mumbling "No."

"And did she hurt Alice when she came to find you today?"

"No."

"So what makes you think you have the right to hurt James?"

"Mum, I- I didn't think-"

"I know," Dreamer said, tone softening. "Marlon, violence isn't the key to any problem."

"But Mum, James is my best friend-"

"Honey, you're being a hypocrite." Dreamer was amused now, and the small smile on her face showed it. "Janice was and Alice is Pandora's best friend. What you feel now is exactly how she felt. Not nice, is it?"

"But... but-"

"You need to talk with James," Dreamer told him, Pandora looking at her knees. Marlon shook his head angrily.

"I'm not speaking to that back-stabber ever again."

"Then talk to your sister," Ted said, wanting to be involved even though he knew Dreamer was perfectly capable of handling their children.

Marlon glared at Pandora, saying "No."

Dreamer sighed, saying "If you won't talk to James, then at least let James do the talking."

"I don't want anything to do with him!"

"For how long?" Dreamer said, and Marlon didn't answer.

Pandora felt real guilty.

"Marlon, I... I'm sorry-"

"Don't talk to me, Pandora. Go celebrate socialising once again."

Pandora's eyes filled over, Marlon refusing to look at her as she got up and left the room.

Dreamer sighed, saying "I'm not going out to dinner while they're like this. It's supposed to be a happy occasion- and I don't feel very happy."

Ted looked at Marlon, who visibly flinched.

"Dad, it's not my fault- blame Pandora, not me-"

I'm blaming both of you!

"Don't you have homework to do, Marlon?" Ted asked icily, and Marlon nodded. "Then go in the kitchen and start working on it."

Marlon obeyed as Baby Julian wailed from upstairs.

"Mummy!"

"Bring him down Miriam," called Dreamer, and Miriam obeyed.

As she walked to the staircase she heard a small sob, from the spare room. Miriam hesitated, then she went to the door to listen to her.

"Everything was fine. Why did I have to be greedy and kiss him again?"

"Well, at least Marlon knows now," Alice said gently. "I mean, it's better he knows. Besides, I didn't like lying to him either."

"You're just saying that because you're going out," wept Pandora. "What should I say to him, Alice? He looked at me like he hated me!"

"Marlon doesn't hate you," Alice answered, then a voice said "Alice, end the call in five minutes. I'm expecting a call at five thirty."

"Yes Daddy," said Alice politely, then she continued her talk. "He doesn't hate you, he's just angry and upset right now. At least you know where he's coming from, right? You've been through what he's going through."

"You sound like my godmother," Pandora said, smiling through her tears.

"Well, I've been around the clinic enough times to get the hang of it."

"Mummy!" yelled Baby Julian, making Pandora and Miriam jump.

Before Miriam could soothe the frustrated baby and get away from the door Pandora wrenched it open, eyes glistening with tears and anger.

"Were you listening to my conversation?"

"I just wanted to see if you was all right," Miriam said feebly, backing two steps as Pandora stepped forwards. "I wanted to help if I-"

"I don't need your help," spat Pandora. "Not after everything you've done."

"Pandora, you don't under-"

"I understand just fine, Miriam! You're a lesbian!"

"You take that back, Pandora!" cried Miriam, hurt. "I'm no such thing!"

"Well sniffing around my mother like a dog says something else!"

"I'm not sniffing!"

"Yes you are! What the hell are you doing here?"

"Mummy," wailed Julian, tears falling as he looked from Miriam to Pandora and back. He was scared. "Mummy!"

Miriam held him in her other arm as she said "I was invited!"

"Well we don't want you here, not after what you put my Dad through!"

"Your- Pandora, Ted's a grown man! And he doesn't mind me here-"

"This isn't his house anyway! I don't know how you can even look at us knowing what you did-"

"Ted," murmured Dreamer, eyes closed as she laid on the sofa. "Please go and get Baby Julian for me."

"Ok," Ted answered, taking her hand and kissing it. "Are you ok?"

"Not really, no. Marlon? Honey, are you ok?"

"Yes Mum," called Marlon from the kitchen, trying to sound cheerful. His voice was anything but. "I'm fine."

Pandora and Miriam's voices grew louder at the top of the staircase, Baby Julian sobbing harder and harder. Ted reluctantly left his beloved to stop the argument, and take the baby out of the angry atmosphere.

"Break it up," he called, clapping his hands as he walked up the stairs. Miriam and Pandora fell silent, but Baby Julian continued to cry.

"I want Mummy," he wept, and Miriam realised her shirt was damp.

"Oh love, I'm so sorry," she said gently, as Baby Julian sobbed into her shoulder. "I didn't mean to scare you, I-"

"Here Miriam, I'll take him," Ted said gently, reaching for the baby.

Miriam shook her head, saying "He hardly knows you, Ted-"
"Miriam, it's ok. I promise," Ted said, as she looked down at the baby. "Let me take him down to Dreamer."
Baby Julian reached for Ted as well, eyes filling over. Feeling a little betrayed, Miriam handed him over.
"Hey, little man," Ted said softly, holding him in one arm. "You ok?"
"I want Mummy," wept Julian, his green eyes full of anguish as he looked at the stairs. "I no like Minnyam and Dorwa anymore."
Pandora and Miriam glared at each other, Ted saying "Did they shout?"
"Yes, and I cry-" The baby burst into tears again. "I want Mummy!"
Pandora wondered whether she should apologise, then she decided not to. Instead she turned and went back into the spare room, slamming the door shut behind her.
Miriam realised she was cutting her palms her fists were clenched so tight. Taking a deep breath, she said "Ted, I'm sorry I shouted at her. But... she really-"
"Never mind," Ted said reassuringly. "Um... dinner's cancelled."
"I kind of realised."
"Come downstairs," Ted said, already walking down. "You too, 'Dora."
"I'm not coming."
"Now," called Ted, and Pandora sighed and got up.

* * *

Marlon smiled at Miriam, who blinked at him as Dreamer reached for her baby boy.

"Suddenly you like me again?" she said, under the voices of Ted and Dreamer, and Baby Julian's giggles as Dreamer tickled him lovingly.

Marlon shrugged, saying "If Mum and Dad forgive you, then I do too."

"Really."

"Yeah. And I don't forget when you helped us get back home."

Pandora walked in the living room slowly, Marlon and Miriam's smiles fading as she sat as far away from everyone as possible.

Dreamer didn't look with her eyes, instead feeling everyone's energy. Laying on her back, she lifted Baby Julian high in the air, looking up into his delighted face as he squealed excitedly.

"Mummy Mummy, I fly!" he said happily, flailing his tiny arms and legs. "Look, Marlon! I fly, see? I fly!"

Marlon smiled and nodded, Dreamer saying "Should I call Mama and Papa, Ted?"

"Uh…"

Before Ted could decide whether that was necessary Agnes and Paul Black appeared, taking their seats across the room.

"Let's begin, then."

"This is what I'd like to call a family meeting," Ted said nervously, and Agnes scolded "Dreamer, sit up."

Dreamer sighed, doing as she was told. Baby Julian beamed at Paul, Paul winking at him. Baby Julian giggled.

"Well, it's not exactly a *meeting* meeting, but… it's to do with the kids, and I um… Paul?" said Ted, swallowing. "Stop looking at me like that."

"Paul," said Agnes, swatting her husband on the arm. "Stop that."

Paul was annoyed. "I'm giving my full undivided attention to the boy, Agnes. Would you rather I make objects fly around the room?"

"Go on Ted," said Agnes, ignoring Paul's question. "Continue."

"Well, everyone's been reunited and such, and… well, we have to make some decisions about what happens next."

"Well said," said Paul, agreeing totally. Agnes nodded too, ditto Miriam.

"Dreamer and I had a talk," Ted said, looking at her. "She isn't moving out of her home for my benefit. I… I don't mind that."

Agnes smiled, knowing that Ted minded a whole lot more than he was letting on.

"So um… well, really and truly I uh…"

Dreamer smiled at him. She'd never seen Ted so nervous.

"Look, Marlon and Pandora- we're going back home. Baby Julian isn't used to you yet- isn't used to so many people in his home."

Ted waited for the blow, but none came. Pandora and Marlon didn't react to their father's declaration, not for a few seconds anyway.

"Can we like… arrange something?" Pandora asked tonelessly. "I mean, I want to stay with my mother."

"Yeah," said Marlon, looking at Dreamer pleadingly. "Mum?"

"How about they come on weekends, Dreamer?" Paul said, looking at his child. "Every other weekend isn't a bad idea."

"And they can visit on their days off," Agnes added, and Dreamer looked at Ted before saying "That sounds fine, Mama."

"What about Julian?" demanded Marlon, hurt. "How come he can stay?"

"Julian isn't Ted's son," Paul reminded him, and Marlon closed his mouth. Then he asked "What about you and Mum, Dad?"

"Don't worry about that," Dreamer said, a small smile on her face. "Everything's ok between me and your father."

"Promise?" asked Pandora dubiously, and Dreamer said "I promise."

Ted clapped his hands, feeling much better after getting that load off his chest.

"Well then, that's living arrangements sorted. Marlon, Pandora- it's your day off tomorrow. We'll go in the morning."

"You don't even have your car," Pandora pointed out, and Dreamer said "Miriam can drop you back home if it's all right with her."

"Tomorrow?" Miriam said, surprised. "Dreamer, I can't stay the night-"

"Why not?"

"Well, I…"

Miriam felt she'd outstayed her welcome. She didn't want to be around Pandora, anyway.

"Come on Miriam," coaxed Dreamer. "I'll make you hot chocolate."

"No, I'd rather-"

"Hot chocolate with a muffin."

"Dreamer-"

"Hot chocolate with a muffin and cookies."

"Cook-cook!" said Baby Julian happily, and Paul said "No, son."

"Peas?"

"No."

"Papa," started Dreamer, then she remembered Miriam. "Miriam, stay."

"I can't."

"Ok, hot chocolate with a muffin, cookies and a slice of apple pie."

"No, I really have to get going. I've got work tomorrow and-"

"That's even better, because Ted does too. You can drop him and the kids off on the way."

Miriam looked at Ted, who shrugged a shoulder.

"It's up to you."

"She's staying," Paul said, rising to his feet with Agnes. "Right Miriam?"

"Yes," she sighed, and Dreamer smiled.

"Papa scares you, doesn't he?"

"He scares everybody," muttered Marlon, and Paul smiled at him.

"That's right, my boy. I scare *everybody.*"

"It's not Halloween, Paul," Agnes said, amused as he laughed. "Come, let's go home."

Paul kissed Dreamer on the forehead, saying "Bye, little one."

"Goodbye Papa."

"We'll come by at the end of the week," Agnes said, kissing her as well.

Baby Julian lifted his arms happily, saying "Paul-Paul!"

"Hmm… this baby boy adores me," Paul stated, reaching down and scooping him up. "Don't you adore your grandpop, son?"

Baby Julian giggled, throwing his arms around Paul's neck.

"I'll take that as a yes," smiled Paul, and everyone laughed.

Marlon's mobile rang. Answering quickly, he said "Marlon."

"Hey," said Alice gently, and Marlon smiled. "Is everything ok?"

"No," he confessed, going into the kitchen. Pandora followed. "I saw my best mate snogging my little sister, that's newsflash one. The woman who helped wrecked my family is here- the mystery lady. Miriam."

"Miss Hughes? No way! Pandora didn't tell me that-"

"Yeah, well Pandora and her got into an argument upstairs-"

"I caught a bit of it. She was real angry."

"So was Miriam," Marlon answered. "You know, I've never heard her lose it before, especially with Pandora-"

Marlon broke off, sensing her behind him. Taking a deep breath, he fixed his face with his dirtiest look before turning around.

"What?"

"Marlon, we need to talk about… what you saw today."

"What, are you going to tell me I was hallucinating?" sneered Marlon. "Because seriously Pandora, you'll need to think of something else."

"Why are you being like this? I don't have a problem with you and Alice, and I didn't have much of a problem with you and Janice-"

"I wouldn't have cared if you did!"

"What's wrong with me going out with James?" said Pandora, hurt. "Marlon, you're overreacting. You're acting like-"

"Like what, 'Dora? Like I just witnessed one of the four people I love so much it hurts kiss one of the other four? Like it came as a massive blow because I see James as my brother, meaning I thought he saw you as a sister? Like I feel like all of it is really wrong?"

"But it's not wrong," Pandora said, then she took a step backwards as

Marlon stepped forwards, face murderous. Everybody was still talking happily in the living room- Dreamer, as usual, was the centre of attention. Nobody noticed that the kitchen door was closed.

"How the hell is it right?" spat Marlon, then he realised Alice was still on the line. "Um… can I call you back after I talk to my sister?"

"Sure," Alice said gently. "Marlon, she's right: James-"

Marlon hung up angrily, saying "She'll always side with you."

"Good, seeing as I knew her first," Pandora answered, her usual flat drawl returning. "Marlon, me and James-"

"I don't want to have this conversation, Pandora." Marlon slipped his phone in his pocket and turned away. "We'll talk later."

Pandora glared at him. "Don't pull your big brother act on me."

"I am your big brother," snapped Marlon, turning back round. "You'd better remember that from now on."

"Ok, look: how about I tell you to get stuffed?" Pandora said, heat rising. "I'm seeing James whether you like it or not."

"Then we have nothing to say to each other from now on," Marlon answered, making her stop short.

"What?"

"You heard me, 'Dora."

"Marlon, please- you can't do this to me." She was a little shocked, but she hardly showed it. "I need you just like I need Mum and Dad-"

Marlon shrugged, hating the hurt that was beginning to show on his sister's face as he said "Obviously you need James more than me."

"That's not true. I've always put family first, and you know it."

"Why did you kiss him, Pandora?" sighed Marlon, shoulder's falling.

He looked like a six-year-old being told Santa couldn't make it this year for Christmas. Pandora imagined Baby Julian looking just like that when he was six. "How long have you been hitting on each other?"

"Don't say it like that," Pandora said, cautiously moving closer to him. "Listen, since before Mum came back- before I met Alice-"

"That long?" said Marlon disbelievingly, but Pandora said no.

"Remember when James said hi I and I bolted upstairs?" Marlon nodded. "Well… he gave me his number that night, when you came back from wherever. He wanted to help me."

Marlon's memory was all too clear. He remembered James telling him to help Pandora while they were out too… they discussed it in the car…

"But I didn't talk to him, I swear," Pandora said, pleading in her eyes. "You have to believe me- I tried to destroy his number with my box."

"And it didn't work?" She said no. "Why the hell not?"

"Mum," said Pandora softly, looking at the kitchen door. "She wouldn't let the paper vanish- it was still there the next day. I had a feeling she was alive, but I didn't have any proof."

"Mmm," Marlon answered. "So… when did you talk to him, then?"

"When you blew his nose off. Seriously," she said, when he gaped at her. "I'm not denying I had a crush on him, because I really did. But I didn't use his number at all, or talk to him until his nose got blown off."

Marlon remembered Pandora's behaviour towards his friend.

"So that's why you was so cold to him- you liked him."

"What, did you think I'd act all giggly or something?"

"Most girls do," said Marlon, smiling, then his face fell. "'Dora-"

"It's ok," said Pandora quickly, knowing he was about to apologise. "Don't worry about it."

"Just act normal around each other when you're around me," Marlon said. "Please."

"Isn't that what we've been doing?" said Pandora, amused. "If it wasn't for the kiss you never would've guessed we were going out."

"True," he said grudgingly, then he moved closer to her. Reaching out, he pulled her into a hug and kissed her on the forehead. Pandora smiled as he held her, mumbling "I'm sorry I acted like a jerk today."

"It's all right."

"No it isn't," he said firmly. "Tomorrow, when we get back home, I'm going to call James and say sorry for trying to break his nose."

"Why don't you go visit him? He lives in the area now."

"Yeah. Yeah, I think I will."

* * *

"This feels nice," murmured Dreamer, as Ted massaged her shoulders downstairs in the living room. Miriam glanced up from her book, amused. "The massage?"

"No. Yes," she said, as Ted prodded her in the back. "Yes it does, but I'm talking about the children. They all went to bed smiling… happy."

"Looks like Marlon and 'Dora made up," Ted said, adding pressure to his hands. Dreamer was unsuccessful in stifling her moan, Ted smirking as Miriam glanced up again. Dreamer bit her lip, apologising.

"Maybe we should go to bed," suggested Miriam, but Dreamer and Ted both said no. They didn't feel tired one bit. Miriam pouted, feeling like she was the mother and they were her naughty teenage children.

"Bed," she said firmly. "Ted, you've got work in the morning- and so have I. Dreamer, you have to be properly awake when Baby Julian gets up- and if you stay up any later you won't be. Let's all have a hot drink, and then get ready for bed."

Ted and Dreamer sighed, Ted's hands falling to his sides as Dreamer said

"Yes Mama," in the sweetest voice imaginable.
Miriam smiled at them, saying "Good."
Ted and Dreamer smiled back.

* * *

"Dreamer... Dreamer..."

Dreamer clapped a hand to her mouth, ushering Miriam inside her bedroom and pointing at Ted. He was fast asleep, but his mouth was certainly awake.

"Yes, Dreamer- yes..."

Miriam's jaw dropped, and she hissed "Is he serious?"

Dreamer nodded, laughing she whispered "Oh, Teddy."

"Dreamer..."

"Teddy Bear..."

"Dreamer..."

"Yes," whispered Dreamer, and Ted whispered "Don't stop, Dream..."

Dreamer pulled Miriam forwards, whispering "Stay there."

"Dreamer, I can't!"

"Shh! Ted, baby," she whispered.

Ted smiled in his sleep. "You're so beautiful."

"Open your eyes and look at how beautiful I am, baby."

Ted squirmed in his sleep, lifting a hand to his brow as he obeyed. Everything was out of focus. Was he dreaming?

"Look at me," whispered Dreamer, and he blinked.

When Miriam slid into view, he opened his mouth and screamed.

"Aaaaargh!!"

Dreamer collapsed, laughing her head off as Ted scrambled away from his lover's best friend, tumbling off the other side of the bed.

The crash made Baby Julian snap awake, looking around fearfully. Pulling his tiny thumb out of his mouth, he asked "Mummy?"

Miriam tried not to, but soon she was laughing as much as Dreamer, who was using her as a shield to stop Ted from reaching her.

"Teddy, it wasn't my fault! You started it, talking in your sleep-"

"I was dreaming!" he said, outraged. "You took advantage of the dream!"

"I didn't mean to frighten you, Ted-" Dreamer struggled to stop laughing. "I was only joking with you. Your face!"

Miriam burst out laughing as well. She'd never seen Ted look so horrified in all the time she'd known him.

"I'd pay big money to see that again," she told Ted, who glared at her.

"Miriam, don't mention this to anyone at work, especially your boss."

"Tony would find it ever so funny- ok," she said amusedly, when Ted made throttling movements. "But when everyone asks me why I keep cracking up when there's nothing amusing happening-"

"Tell them you suffer from mental health or something."

Dreamer and Miriam burst out laughing again, Dreamer saying "What a wake up call, right Teddy?" Ted scowled at her. "It's soon seven o clock. Get your shower while I wake Marlon and Pandora. If you leave at eight you'll be back home at around nine, nine thirty."

Ted's face fell. "Do we have to go?"

"Yes," smiled Dreamer. "You and Miriam start work at eleven, and Marlon and Pandora need to go and see James."

"Right," he said glumly, as Baby Julian called "Mummy!"

"He's awake," smiled Dreamer, and Miriam said "The noise must have woken him up."

"Mummy, Mummy!"

"Coming sweetie," called Dreamer, and they heard him giggle.

"I'll go to him," Miriam offered, but Dreamer shook her head.

"It's ok, I'll go. Get yourself sorted out."

"Ok."

* * *

"I need some sticks," Pandora said, slumped on the sofa with her rucksack. Marlon looked at her.

"What for?"

"To hold my eyelids up," she answered, and he smiled.

Ted jogged down the stairs, looking flash in his business suit. Dreamer smiled at him as he entered the kitchen, Baby Julian waving excitedly.

"Hello!"

"Hey, little man. Did you eat all of your breakfast?"

"Yep!"

"Yes," Dreamer corrected gently, and Baby Julian said "Yeees."

Ted smiled, saying "You remember my name, don't you?"

"Yep! Yeees," he said, when Dreamer raised her eyebrow at him. "Ted!"

"Good boy," smiled Ted, and Baby Julian giggled.

"Where you go?"

"To work."

"Ohhh. Where Marlon and Dorwa go?"

"Home."

"To you house?"

"Yep."

"Yes," Baby Julian said shyly, and Ted and Dreamer laughed.

"Teddy, how am I supposed to teach him to talk properly if you're saying exactly what he's saying?"

"Sorry Dreamer. I forgot," smiled Ted, while the baby asked "Teddy?"

"My nickname," Ted smiled, but that big word skipped over Baby Julian's head. In minutes he was calling the friendly man Teddy instead, as if the name Ted never existed.

Miriam made sure she had everything before she came downstairs, jingling her keys.

"Ready to go?"

"Ready," called Ted, Marlon nodding. Pandora didn't react.

Ted straightened his collar, checking himself over.

"You look brilliant," Dreamer said softly, and Ted smiled at her.

"Thanks, Dream. Um… I'll call you at lunch, ok?"

"I go too," said Baby Julian, eyes filling. "Mummy, I go too!"

"You can't, honey. Ted's got a lot of work to do."

Baby Julian's face crumpled. Feeling his heart wrench at the sight of him weeping, Ted said "I can take him with me if you want-"

"He hasn't known you long enough to trust you, Ted." Dreamer smiled at him. "If you get as far as the door with him I'll be surprised."

Ted did get as far as the door. As soon as it opened Baby Julian twisted in his arms, screaming for his mother.

"Mummy!!"

Dreamer burst out laughing. "Don't you want to go, baby?"

"No!"

"Told you," Pandora said to Marlon. "You owe me two pounds."

Marlon handed the money over without a fuss, his mind full of what he was going to say to James when he saw him later on today.

Ted handed the baby back over, chucking his chin. Baby Julian giggled, Ted saying "See you soon, little man."

"Bye Teddy!"

* * *

Dreamer lay curled up on her bed, fast asleep. Baby Julian slept in her arms, snuggled comfortably against her chest.

Paul Black appeared at the foot of Dreamer's giant bed, looking at them thoughtfully.

"Spitting images of each other," he murmured, sitting down in Dreamer's armchair and smiling at his only child, and his youngest grandchild. "Spitting images."

* * *

James walked up the path nervously, spotting Marlon and Pandora talking further up. He stopped, sticking his hands in his pockets. Why should he talk to them? To get another punch in the nose?

Pandora watched him over Marlon's shoulder, James avoiding her eye.

"He's here," she told Marlon flatly, and Marlon looked around.

James stepped backwards, Marlon opening his mouth to tell him not to be such an idiot. Realising James was suddenly nervous of him, he looked at Pandora before saying "Call him, 'Dora."

"James," called Pandora, and Marlon cringed at how soft her voice was. "Come here- don't act like he's going to kill you."

"He wants to, though," James answered. "You can tell."

"Glad you can," Marlon said, and Pandora glared at him. Marlon quickly took a minute to take a breath, controlling his temper. "Listen bro, just come. I need to talk to you about... all of this."

James looked at Pandora, and Marlon snapped "How long have you known me, idiot? Suddenly you don't know if you can trust me?"

"I can," James said, offended as he walked over. He winced, holding his side. "You know I had to go to casualty, right?"

"What for?" demanded Marlon: Pandora bit the words back.

"You bruised my ribs when you slammed your size nines into them."

"I had every right," said Marlon, though he felt guilty. "Er... sorry."

"Sorry?" James repeated. "Thanks to you, I'll have to sit in the stands while the team goes head to head with Hertfordshire! I can't play football until everything's better again- but yeah, you can!"

"I won't play," Marlon said firmly. "They'll have to get another guy."

James shook his head, saying "No."

"No what?"

"You have to play. You know you're one of the best in the team."

"I'm one of the best because I know you've got my back!"

"Er, sorry to interrupt," Pandora said flatly, looking from her brother to

James and back. "But I didn't come here to hear you discuss ball, or wonder if you guys really are gay. Can we get back on the subject?"

"We're not gay," Marlon and James said together, and Pandora smirked.

"You said that too quickly."

"Ignore her," Marlon said to James, face growing hot. "Basically, I've decided to give you my blessings."

James burst out laughing. "Isn't your dad supposed to give the blessings?"

"Fine, I'll make this quick then." Marlon held his hand up, and started counting off his fingers. "One. Act normal around me and other people. Nobody needs to know you're hitting on my sister. She doesn't take publicity well." James nodded. "Two: I don't want to hear you go on about each other when you can't be together. That's just weird."

Pandora smiled, agreeing with that.

"Three: if you have an argument, don't talk to me about it. I was against this relationship from the start. Number four... I'm not a mentor. I don't want to listen to any problems you might be having. You want to talk, go find Miriam or-"

"Alice!" said James, smiling broadly as she neared them. "Hi!"

"Who's the guy?" muttered Marlon, and Pandora smirked.

"Her father, you idiot."

"Daddy, this is James Henbit," Alice said, beaming at her father. "He's one of my friends."

Tony nodded, shaking James's hand.

"And this is Marlon, Pandora's brother."

Tony smiled, clasping Marlon's hand as he said "I haven't seen you since you first came to the clinic. Good to see you, Marlon."

"You too," Marlon offered, and Tony's smile grew as he looked at Pandora.

"Pandora Black, you've got Miss Hughes very upset."

"Good," Pandora answered, and Tony laughed.

Suddenly he sobered up as he asked "How is... your mother?"

"Still with my father," Pandora said amusedly, and Tony pouted.

"Tell her that I'd like to call a meeting with her, if you please."

"You mean her, me and my father."

"No, I mean her alone."

"Daddy," said Alice warningly, as Marlon demanded "For what?"

"To speak about Pandora. Your father will be at work," Tony said, a little smugly. "And you shall be in college. Give this letter to Miss Black."

Pandora took the envelope, looking at it curiously.

"It's only to discuss whether you still need to be under the care of Miss Hughes," Tony said reassuringly, and Pandora said "No I don't."

"You can't be sure of that though," Tony said reasonably. "You're both steamed up, aren't you? While you both say you don't want anything to do with each other, in a week's time you could make up."

Alice frowned as Pandora and Marlon nodded, unsure if her father was up to something. She knew he desired Dreamer.

"And your mother knows Miriam better than Ted," Tony said, a little desperately as Pandora watched him. "It's better that she come."

"Fine. She'll have to bring my baby brother along," Pandora said with a shrug of her shoulder, and Tony nodded.

Anything to have her alone with me.

"What?" said Marlon sharply, and everyone looked at him. "What did you say?"

Everyone frowned at him. "He didn't say anything, Marlon."

"I swear he did," Marlon said, but they shook their heads.

"Daddy didn't say anything," Alice said, but Pandora looked her brother right in the eye, silent.

What did he say, Marlon? What was he thinking?

Marlon shot Tony a filthy look before answering, as silent as his sister.

He thought anything to have her alone with him. She can't go.

Yes she can. Let him try it on, Mum'll let him have it.

Are you sure?

Pandora nodded, Tony unnerved by the silence.

James grinned, asking "Are you doing some kind of telepathy?"

They didn't answer, Marlon repeating himself.

Are you sure, Pandora?

Yes.

But what if it backfires? What if Mum decides she wants him?

That's her business. As long as she comes clean with Dad so it doesn't hurt too much.

I thought you wanted Mum and Dad together?

I just want Mum happy. Don't you?

Mum's already happy, Marlon replied. *You know she is.*

"We'd better get going," Tony said, freaked out by the silence. Were they talking to each other in their heads?

Mum's unsure of herself right now. All she's sure of is Baby Julian.

What about us??

And us, I think. I don't think she'd go with Tony.

What if she does? The thought terrified Marlon. He didn't know life with Ted and Dreamer separate. Neither did Pandora, not much. *'Dora!*

I don't know, ok? We'll have to wait and see what happens.

But Alice is my girlfriend. I don't want her as a step-sister!

Don't think of her as any kind of relative, because she isn't. She's your girlfriend, leave it at that.

The conversation ended there, the siblings breaking free of their little spell.

"What was you saying?"

"That we need to get going," Tony said, Alice nodding.

"I'll call you guys later."

James stuck his thumbs in his pockets, asking "So… we're cool now?"

"What? Oh- yeah," said Marlon, nodding. "Yeah, we're cool."

"I'm going home," Pandora said, walking away. They looked at her in surprise, Marlon calling "What're you going home for?"

Pandora smirked as she looked back.

"To stay in my bedroom and pretend I don't exist."

Marlon and James burst out laughing as she smiled, continuing her walk.

"Those days are long gone, Pandora!"

Pandora waved a hand in reply.

* * *

Dreamer cuddled her son as he sat on her lap, watching a children's show.
Her eyes were on the screen, but she saw nothing.
Baby Julian giggled, Dreamer stroking his hair absent mindedly.
She needed her mother. She had no clue what she wanted anymore.
Agnes appeared, smiling gently. "Dreamer."
Dreamer shook her head, the baby sticking his thumb in his mouth.
"Is it nap time for Julian?" Agnes asked gently, and Dreamer nodded.
Half an hour later, when she came back downstairs, Paul appeared.
"Little one," he said gently, looking at her. "I did say you should have stayed with us a little longer. You're still very muddled up."
"Do you think it's the curse of the flames?" Dreamer asked, but Paul shook his head. Agnes sat down on the sofa, saying "It's not the curse of the flames, darling. It's the curse of your fear."
Dreamer was confused. "My fear?"
"What are you afraid of, little one?" Paul asked. "Ted?"
"I give my all to him, when I never have before." Dreamer sighed as she spoke. "When he came that night and we shared a kiss, I felt a tremendous change in our relationship. Yet…"
Agnes and Paul leant forwards. "Yet?"
"Yet I see myself hurting him one more time," Dreamer whispered. "One last time. And I can't avoid it happening."
"Why ever not?"
"Because… I want it to happen," Dreamer confessed. "I want to know if he has felt the change too. If he can forgive me anything like I can now forgive him anything."
Agnes and Paul thought about this, Dreamer continuing "I want to know if he loves me as much as I love him, if he wears his heart on his sleeve like I wear mine."
Paul rubbed his chin thoughtfully. "It is a test."
Dreamer nodded, Agnes saying "Well, it takes two. Why should you have all the fun, little one? Ted is always challenged by other beauties."
Dreamer nodded. "I know. I wonder, even though he promises I am his moon and stars, if he has ever been intimate with any."

* * *

"Mr. Stone?"

Ted looked up from his laptop, quickly minimizing Dreamer's photograph and opening up his notes on a client.

"Yes Brandy? What can I do for you?"

"I brought your coffee, sir. Along with a sandwich and cake."

Ted smiled at her. "Excellent. I only wanted a coffee, you know."

"I know, but I heard your stomach growl." Ted's PA, Brandy Shakes, walked over holding a tray with two of everything. "There you go."

"Thanks, Brandy. Is that your lunch?" She nodded. "Where will you eat?"

"In the cafeteria, sir. It's not so crowded around this time."

"Why don't you join me," Ted said, eyes on his laptop screen. "You'll have to come back up here anyway. It saves time."

Brandy's smile was so sweet it was difficult for Ted not to smile back.

"I'd like that very much, sir."

Ted nodded, Brandy sitting in front of him at his desk, watching him.

Ted, used to this behaviour from other women, ignored the sight.

But what a sight it was. And the memories!

Brandy smirked, thinking the same. "How is the lovely Dreamer Black?"

Ted shrugged. "She's fine."

He picked up his coffee as Brandy did, their hands brushing against each other. Ted refused to acknowledge her soft fingers.

Brandy tried to be innocent as ever. "Are you... back together?"

"Yes. I think so. Actually, yes we are."

Brandy sipped her coffee, watching him as he frowned in thought.

"Are you sure?"

"Why do you ask?" Ted answered, his voice as calm as he could get it.

"I just wanted to know if she knows about... our affair."

"It wasn't an affair," Ted said, heat rising. "She was dead. Damon Stile murdered her- she wasn't there. She was dead and gone."

Brandy shrugged. "She wasn't dead in the three months you couldn't find her."

Ted slammed his laptop down, making her jump. Then she smiled.

"I love your temper, Mr. Stone."

"Brandy, you can't keep doing this to me." Ted rubbed his brow, leaning back in his chair. "Everything we agree to forget you bring back up. Why do you do it?"

"Because I love you, Mr. Stone."

* * *

"Whoa," said James, Pandora behind him.

Marlon stared at the crystal ball disbelievingly. Ted had a girl on the side?

"You don't love me," Ted said wearily. "You love the fact that you scored with a powerful man."

Brandy leant forwards. "Up to four weeks ago."

"Brandy!"

"Yes Mr. Stone?" she said sweetly, and Ted scowled at her.

"Stop this. All of it- it stops today."

Brandy smiled, reaching for a sandwich as Ted took deep breaths.

"So you'll just forget what we had?"

"Yes."

"For how long." Brandy used her long nails to slice the hardened plastic as she spoke. "Until Dreamer vanishes again?"

"She's not going anywhere," Ted said angrily.

"Until you have an argument, then? Over the baby who isn't even yours?"

Ted didn't answer her.

"She knows our business," Marlon said furiously. "Why did he tell her?"

"He was probably frustrated because nobody told him anything," Pandora answered. "He had to let off some steam."

"To her?" said Marlon disgustedly. "Why mess with her of all the girls?"

"She is pretty fine," James admitted, and both Pandora and Marlon turned to glare at him. "Well... not as fine as Dreamer, anyway."

Pandora raised an eyebrow, James quickly saying "Or Pandora."

"Shut up," Pandora answered, and Marlon burst out laughing.

* * *

Ted arrived home in dampened spirits. Brandy refused to let him go.
"A kiss is just a kiss," he muttered to himself, sticking his key in the lock.
"Dad's home!" hissed Marlon, placing a hand on the crystal ball.
The image of Brandy Shakes, now talking to another woman, was replaced by swirling white mist.
"Kids?" called Ted, and Pandora and Marlon called "Upstairs, Dad!"
"With James!" James called. "Hello Mister Stone!"
"Hello James," Ted answered wearily. "Is everything ok now?"
"Yes sir!"
"Good. Be down for dinner in an hour, all of you."

* * *

Dreamer ate her food slowly, Agnes adding another spoon of rice to her plate as she said "Eat up, Dreamer."
Paul sliced his steak, deep in thought. Dreamer looked up at him as Agnes finally sat down after adding some tiny pieces of chicken to Baby Julian's bowl.
"Say ta, baby," Dreamer said without taking her eyes off her father, and Baby Julian said "Ta, Nana!"
"You're welcome, darling. Dreamer, why do you watch your father?"
"Papa looks as if he's having a vision," Dreamer replied. "Papa?"
"It's your lover, little one," Paul replied. "Ted."
"What about him?"
"He has indeed been intimate... with a certain Brandy Shakes?"
Dreamer's jaw dropped. "His personal assistant?"
"His *very* personal assistant," Paul said, eyes glinting with malice. "It seems as if she was his lover after you were murdered. His secret lover."
Dreamer felt her stomach contract with anger. "Secret?"
"Well, nobody sensed the woman's tactics. Not even you."
"How could she?" Agnes said angrily. "She was weak when she returned! Her power gradually returned, gradually!"
Paul ignored his wife, addressing his daughter only. "He went back to her when you left after returning, to stay with your mother once again. During the fiasco with Miriam."
Dreamer started to feel sick. "Papa, I really don't want to hear this-"
"And when you took Baby Julian home," Paul continued. "During the two to three months he couldn't find you, Brandy was there to comfort him. To act as if she understood exactly what he was feeling."
Paul looked Dreamer right in the eye. "To bed him."

Dreamer slid back from the table on her chair, Agnes standing up.

"Paul, that's enough."

"I'm not finished," Paul said curtly. "Only two hours ago she captured his lips, little one. What are you going to do about it?"

"Nothing," Dreamer said quietly, then she thought. "Pay him a visit."

"The children will be delighted to see you," Agnes said firmly, reminding her daughter that her children were there and would most likely witness a showdown.

Paul waved his hand, a beautiful face appearing above the kitchen table. A woman's face.

Dreamer stared at her pale skin and rosy cheeks, her big blue eyes, her blonde hair. Her lips were blood red, her smile confident.

Baby Julian whimpered, scared. He jumped as Ted's voice boomed around the kitchen.

"Why do you do it?"

Brandy's expression changed, her eyes clouding over with lust. Dreamer watched her face, sickened as her lips parted.

"Because I love you, Mr. Stone."

"You don't love me. You love the fact that you scored with a powerful man."

The face of Brandy smirked. "Up to four weeks ago."

"Brandy!"

"Yes Mr. Stone?" she said sweetly, and Dreamer cringed.

"Papa, I don't want to see or hear this."

Paul looked at her, then he snapped his fingers. Ted spoke again.

"Stop this. All of it- it stops today."

Brandy smiled. "So you'll just forget what we had?"

Dreamer backed from the table, Baby Julian twisting in his high chair to look at her.

"Mummy!"

"Papa, please-"

"Paul," said Agnes warningly, but Paul paid her no attention as he made Brandy repeat the line like a parrot.

"So you'll just forget what we had?"

"Yes."

"Papa, turn it off- take it away," begged Dreamer. "Papa!"

The face of Brandy seemed to stare right at her.

"For how long. Until Dreamer vanishes again?"

"She's not going anywhere," Ted said, anger evident in his voice.

Brandy rolled her eyes. "Until you have an argument, then? Over the baby who isn't even yours?"

Dreamer half hoped Ted would say Baby Julian was as good as, but he didn't answer. He shouldn't have to anyway.

The woman- his lover or whoever she was- she was right.

Baby Julian wasn't his child. He didn't even know Ted for starters.

Dreamer fought the tears back as Barbara's face faded.

Paul stared at his daughter, silently daring her to cry.

Dreamer swallowed, then she took a deep breath. "I won't."

"Indeed you won't," Paul replied, snapping his fingers.

The table cleared itself, Agnes pouting at him.

"I wanted to do it."

Paul chuckled. "You'll have many chances, Agnes, to clear a table."

Agnes smiled back.

Dreamer sighed, starting to feel depressed for no reason. Then she remembered Baby Julian. Just looking at her son made her smile, warmth spreading from the top of her head all the way to her toes.

"Whatever happens at least I still have you, right baby?" she said as she smiled at him, and the baby nodded.

* * *

"Dad, we know."

Ted glanced up at his kids. "Know what?"

"About you and your PA," Marlon said. "Why didn't you tell us?"

"She was a mistake," Ted said, and Pandora scowled at him.

"Yeah right. She was a mistake- that's why you secretly went out with her after Mum died, and you went back with her when Mum came back-"

* * *

"And he went courted her when Dreamer came to me for a week, and when she moved away with Julian," Agnes said angrily. "Paul, he isn't the angel we thought he was."

"Well, it's fair to say that he didn't know Dreamer would come back from the dead." Paul rubbed his chin as he spoke. "He had every right to try moving on, even if he felt like he betrayed Dreamer afterwards."

"Humph," said Agnes huffily. "And what about the other times?"

"Well... one could say he was still trying to move on."

"Paul!"

"Oh, fine, he had no right to kiss the woman today, but he did the other times. Ted and Dreamer were separate then, do you agree?"

"Yes," grumbled Agnes. "So it's only today he was wrong to do anything with that... that woman?"

"Well... I'm not certain," Paul confessed. "It depends on if he and

Dreamer indeed patched things up and were courting once again."
"And if they wasn't?"
"Then Ted is in the clear."

* * *

Baby Julian snuggled up to his mother as she slept, sucking his thumb.
He could hear Nana and Paul-Paul talking downstairs, but nothing made
sense to him. All he understood was that if he called they would come.
Dreamer frowned in her sleep, her mouth parting as she whispered
something. Her baby boy looked at her curiously.
"Mummy?"
Dreamer didn't answer, back in her dream. Baby Julian rolled over and
pushed himself into a sitting position with his tiny hands. His tiny breaths
could be heard quite clearly as he touched Dreamer's cheek.
The baby jumped as emotions coursed through him like water down a
drain, images flashing before his innocent little eyes.
"AAAHHH!!!!"
Paul leapt up, teleporting upstairs right away. Agnes was right behind
him.
"Dreamer!"
"Paul-Paul!" yelled Baby Julian, blue light swirling around him and his
mother. "Nana- Paul-Paul!"
Paul ran to the bedside and grabbed the baby- ZZZTT!!
The baby screamed again, Paul thrown backwards.
"Agnes, what is this?!"
Agnes pulled out her wand. "We must awaken Dreamer before she kills
her son!"
"With pleasure!" spat Paul, leaping up and aiming his wand at his
daughter's torso. *"Quantalamera!!"*
BANG!!
Dreamer snapped awake, gasping for breath. The swirling lights vanished
as she sat up, Baby Julian's tiny hand sliding off her face.
"What happened?"
Paul was angry enough to shake the life out of her, the baby trembling as
he marched over to the bed.
"Why don't you tell *us* that, little one! What did you dream of?"
"A duel," Dreamer said truthfully. "Between myself and Brandy Shakes."
"Did you cast a spell?" asked Agnes, and Dreamer nodded.
"It was very vivid."
"So vivid it almost came to life!" snapped Paul. "Julian lived the dream
with you- he felt the impact of the spell!"

"What!"

Dreamer turned to look at her baby, who was crying quietly.

"Oh honey, I'm sorry," she said gently, as Baby Julian lifted his arms to her. She picked him up, cradling him. "Did I scare you?"

Baby Julian snuggled into her, Dreamer wiping his tears away.

"And why were you asleep when the child was awake?" demanded Paul, and Dreamer scowled at him.

"Papa, Baby Julian fell asleep before I did. He must have woken as soon as he realised I wasn't speaking anymore."

"Hmm," Paul said. "Well, I think you should call Ted and find out what's going on with him and his assistant. Why did he kiss her today?"

"Let him call me," Dreamer answered. "If he's the man I think he is, he'll call and explain everything."

* * *

As soon as Pandora and Marlon left for college the next day, Ted picked up the house phone drowsily as thoughts raced through his head.
Dreamer knew about Brandy. He knew she knew, he could feel it in the air.
"Hello, good morning."
"Dream?"
Silence.
"Dreamer, please," Ted said desperately. "I need to talk to you."
"There's nothing to talk about," Dreamer said coolly. "Or is there?"
"Well… if you've forgotten it I don't need to bring it up again."
Dreamer smiled as she held the phone to her ear, Baby Julian on her hip.
"Yes, I've forgotten it. I've already forgiven you and forgotten it."
"Good. Can I see you?"
"Sure, drive up when you're ready."
"I can't," said Ted. He could just about stand up. "I'm not up to driving."
"Then… I'll teleport with the baby."
"Ok."
"See you in half an hour."
"Bye."

* * *

Dreamer appeared in the living room, expecting to see Ted on the sofa. He wasn't there.

"Ted?"

Silence.

Baby Julian hung onto her tightly, looking around curiously.

"Mummy, where we is?"

"Ted's house, baby. Ted," called Dreamer, and a quiet voice said "I'm in the kitchen."

Dreamer hesitated, then she stepped into the kitchen.

It was dark in there, the blinds shut tight, the lights off.

Ted sat at the kitchen table, head in his hands.

Dreamer stepped back out, placing Baby Julian in the living room.

"Stay here, baby. Play with Bear."

Baby Julian sat slowly, holding his teddy.

Dreamer entered the kitchen, pulling the doors closed behind her. Hesitantly looking at Ted first, she pulled the blinds open.

Sunlight flooded the kitchen, Ted wincing.

Dreamer stared at him. He looked withdrawn, his chocolate skin pasty looking. His eyes had dark circles under them.

"Have you been up all night?"

"Yes." His voice was ragged. "I've been up all night receiving calls from Brandy Shakes, worrying about how I'd tell you about her, wondering how far she'll go to make me hers, and scared stiff she'll ruin our relationship."

Dreamer didn't know what to say. She thought at first she'd attack him left, right and centre to ventilate her anger at his weakness. His weakening at the first woman who dared move to him when she knew very well who and what Dreamer was, but she hated seeing him like that.

"She won't ruin our relationship," she said gently. "I promise."

"What am I going to do? I can't face her everyday."

"I know," said Dreamer mischievously. "Where would you like her to go, Teddy? What do you wish happen to her when you go to work?"

"I'd rather she move to another office," sighed Ted. "It's better she's Caroline's assistant- they hate each other. I wish that was possible-"

Dreamer smirked, pulling out her golden wand.

"Your wish is my command."

* * *

"Don't go," Ted mumbled against his pillow, as Dreamer pulled his duvet over his shoulders. "I want to see you when I wake up…"
"You will," she assured him, Baby Julian giggling in her arms.
"Night-night, Teddy!"
"Day-day, Julian," yawned Ted, and Dreamer laughed.

* * *

Dreamer noticed an envelope on the living room table, a sealed envelope with her name on.
"For moi?" she said amusedly, picking up the envelope.
She held it to her close to her face, inhaling deeply. Drinking in the answers to her curiosity about who sent the letter.
Pandora's hands have been on it… Dreamer inhaled her child's strong feelings for James Henbit. Her love for her family. Her not-so-sure feelings towards Baby Julian and his arriving practically out of nowhere, changing things. And another person's emotions… a stranger's.
A male stranger's.
Dreamer frowned, looking at the envelope. He wasn't a person who was just sending her a regular appointment. The envelope reeked of lust aimed directly at her, lust which began before she was murdered and grew stronger over the years. Lust so strong it made her eyes water.
"Goodness," she murmured. "Who is this man?"
Baby Julian shivered in his sleep, Dreamer conjuring his baby blanket and spreading it over him as he dreamt on Ted's sofa.
Then she opened the letter.

* * *

James lifted Pandora high in the air, swinging her around. Pandora squealed like a little girl, her hands on his shoulders.
"James, put me down!"
"Say I can come to yours," James replied, laughing. "Your Dad won't mind me coming."
"You wear Dad out- he didn't sleep well last night. If you come over-"
"I won't even speak to him. I'll just go up to your room."
"You're not allowed in my room," said Pandora breathlessly, and James smiled at her.
"Fine, I'll pretend I'm going up to Marlon's room, and slip in yours."
"Well... Marlon won't appreciate you coming in my room either."
James pouted. "Do you always have to crush my ideas, Pandora?"
Pandora immediately disentangled herself from his strong arms, hurt.
"I didn't mean to, I'm just saying that they've got boundaries."
"Like I don't know already."
Then, seeing the look on her face, he softened.
"Don't look like that, Pan. I didn't mean to get grouchy."
Pandora shrugged. "It's ok."
"You don't always have to pretend you don't care, you know." James took her hand. "Sometimes you should let your feelings out."
"Not always."
"Why not?"
They walked towards the lake, holding hands.
"Because sometimes you have to keep things to yourself."
"You can tell me anything, Pandora."
"Fine," she said amusedly. "You look like an idiot wearing your hat back to front all the time, and I hate it when you stare at my mother like she's the only one in the frickin' room. You stink like a sewer after you play football, and I don't bother coming near you until late, because at least I know you've showered by then. I always wonder if you're bisexual, because you're amazing with me but the way you act with my brother is a bit worrying. And-"
"All right, I get it," grumbled James, and she burst out laughing.
"So I do keep it to myself. Can I have a kiss?"
"No."
Still, he lowered his mouth to hers, Pandora's arms curving around his neck.

* * *

Holding Baby Julian in one arm, Dreamer stared at the clinic.

"No go, Mummy." Julian looked up at her. "Peas?"

Dreamer nodded, saying "We'll call Miriam out, then."

Everyone inside was already alert at the appearance of Dreamer Black, Miriam hurriedly rushing out of her office and crashing into Tony.

Splash!

"Damn it, Miriam! Watch where you're going!" he said angrily, staring down at the coffee stain on his crisp white shirt.

Dreamer watched him amusedly as he cursed, trying to rub it out. Walking into the clinic with Baby Julian clinging to her like a monkey, she said "Miriam, there was no need to run to me like that."

Miriam smiled as she kissed Dreamer on the cheek, then the baby.

"How have you been, Dreamer? It's been ages!"

"Only a month," smiled Dreamer, and Miriam's smile grew.

"Is everything all right now? The living arrangements, I mean."

Dreamer nodded, smiling. "Marlon and Pandora are with me and Julian every second weekend, and I may go to theirs in the first if I feel like it."

"Excellent," beamed Miriam. "So I'm sure Pandora truly doesn't need to come back to the clinic?"

"Nonsense," said Tony from behind her, making her jump. "We mustn't jump to conclusions, Miriam-"

"I take it you are Antonio?" Dreamer asked smoothly, and Tony looked at her. It took a lot not to inhale at the sight. She was *beautiful*.

Dreamer smirked, knowing what he was thinking. Tony nodded, holding out a hand as he said "That's me. Alice, my daughter, is a friend of Pandora's-"

"I'm quite aware of that."

"Oh." Nervous, Tony ran a hand through his hair. "Well… uh…"

"Come in, Dreamer," Miriam said quickly. "You haven't seen the clinic yet."

"I doubt it will interest me," Dreamer answered, making her pout.

"You've gone all posh in less than five minutes."

"I'm just wondering why Antonio sent me a letter to discuss the wellbeing of my daughter," Dreamer answered with a shrug. "He could discuss with you, not me, if she still needs to come here."

"True," said Miriam curiously, looking at Tony. "Why didn't you just ask me, Tony?"

"I- um… well, I thought-"

Dreamer smiled as she watched him struggle to answer her best friend.

"Would you like to talk to me in your office, Antonio?"

"Yes," he said quickly. "Please."

"All right. Miriam? Will you wait here?"

"I have another client due in ten minutes, Dreamer." Miriam smiled apologetically. "Can I visit you this evening?"

"If you like. I'll see you later."

Dreamer followed Tony into his office, Tony taking a deep breath as he closed the door behind her.

* * *

"Antonio-"

"Please, call me Tony."

The man acted laid back but Dreamer knew he was nervous. She smiled at him as she said "Tony, then. Why didn't you just ask Miriam about my daughter?"

"I couldn't wait any- I mean... I had to meet you."

"I can tell," Dreamer answered, amused. Baby Julian sat on her lap quietly, sucking his dummy as he looked at Tony curiously. Tony fidgeted a little, then Dreamer said "So, Tony. Why were you so anxious to meet me?"

"Because I fell in love with you the moment I saw you, years ago." Tony drew a deep breath. "You was at one of Ted Stone's work gatherings. I was invited by my cousin."

Dreamer nodded, letting him continue.

"You looked stunning, Dreamer. You always do."

"Thank you."

Tony shook his head. "I knew I had to meet you, right there, right then. But I was afraid."

"Of?" asked Dreamer, then she pouted. "Of the fact I was a witch."

"It was silly and I hope you forgive me. I didn't have the guts to approach you at that party. I grew obsessed with the thought of you."

"I know." Dreamer was highly amused now, Tony saying "I was always lusting after you."

"Doesn't take a genius to work that out."

"Are... are you and Ted Stone... back together?"

Dreamer smiled. "Would it bother you if we were?"

Tony started to say no, then he nodded.

Baby Julian's stomach grumbled.

"That's my cue to leave," Dreamer said, Tony startled as she stood.

"You're going already?"

"I need to feed my son," Dreamer said, looking at him. "I can always return another time and we can finish our talk then."

"So long I've waited to meet you," Tony said hoarsely. "So long. You have no idea how much this means to me."

Dreamer nodded, then she left Tony's office.

* * *

"Yum!" said Baby Julian happily, as Dreamer fed him some delicious spicy and cheesy mashed potato. "It nice, Mummy!"

Ted trailed into the kitchen, yawning.

"Dream, you're still here? I thought you went after I fell asleep."

"I took a walk with Baby Julian," Dreamer answered, smiling at him. "You look much better."

Ted smiled back at her. "And you look gorgeous."

"Thank you Teddy."

Baby Julian beamed at Ted. "Hello Teddy!"

"Hey little man. You ok?"

"Yep!"

"Yes," Dreamer said as she prodded him gently, and Baby Julian giggled as he shyly said "Yes."

"Good stuff," smiled Ted. "Dream, how about we take him to the park?"

"Together?" asked Dreamer, and Ted nodded. "People will think we're a family."

"We are, silly." Ted smiled at her. "Feed Baby Julian and then we can go."

* * *

Pandora gazed across the lake, deep in thought as James and Marlon joked about behind her.

"Dorwa!" shrieked a happy voice, and Pandora turned and saw her baby brother in their mother's arms. "Dorwa!"

Dreamer set him down, Baby Julian running to her happily. Pandora knelt with her arms held out, Baby Julian throwing himself into them. Pandora scooped him up and cuddled him close, kissing him on the forehead.

"Hey, baby brother. You ok?"

Julian nodded, beaming as he saw his big brother. "Marlon!"

Marlon joined them, James calling "I'll call you both later!"

Pandora handed Julian over to Marlon, who hugged and kissed him as well. Some passersby smiled as they watched, some others gazing at Dreamer as she walked, Ted beside her.

"Let's sit by the lake," he suggested, and Dreamer nodded.

* * *

Dreamer helped Baby Julian break some bread she conjured into tiny pieces, showing him how to throw them to the ducks and swans in the lake.

Baby Julian threw the bread and clapped happily, Dreamer holding his tiny hand.

"Look, Mummy! Look!"

"I see it, baby." Dreamer smiled down at her son. "Throw some more."

"I feed the duckies, Dorwa!" Julian beamed at his big sister as she sat, and she smiled at him. "I feed them!"

"Dad, is Mum and Julian staying for dinner?" asked Marlon almost desperately, and Ted answered "I didn't ask."

"Ask her!"

"I will when she comes back. Let Baby Julian feed his ducks."

* * *

Baby Julian ran about happily, Dreamer lifting him up and cuddling him.

"Time to go, sweetie."

"Ask now!" hissed Pandora and Marlon, Ted hesitating as Dreamer neared them. "Go on, Dad!"

"Uh… Dreamer, would you and the baby like to stay for dinner?"

"And the night," said Marlon quickly, and Ted slapped him on the back of the head. "Ow!"

"You don't have to stay the night, Dreamer," said Ted, and Dreamer replied "I'd love to."

"You would?" Ted's heart leapt as she smiled and nodded. "Really?"

"Yes, Ted. Ready to go?"

"Definitely!"

* * *

Baby Julian slept soundly, cuddling his teddy. Dreamer laid next to him, deep in thought.
Ted watched from the doorway for a while, then he whispered "Dreamer."
Dreamer looked at him. "Yes Ted?"
"Do you fancy a hot drink before bed?"
"Of course."
Dreamer stroked Julian's curly hair as she slowly got up, joining Ted's side. Ted took her hand, and they went downstairs.

* * *

"I miss you so much sometimes."
"I feel the same," Dreamer admitted softly as she held her cup. "But at least we're together."
"Can you share my bed, Dream?" Ted asked quietly. "I want to hold you close to me. That's another thing I miss about us living together."
"Well, why don't you come with Marlon and Pandora on the weekends?" suggested Dreamer. "Instead of you staying here alone?"
"You wouldn't mind?"
"Of course not."
Ted smiled at her, relieved. "All right then."
They sipped in silence, Ted holding Dreamer's hand.
After a while Dreamer said "And yes, I will share your bed."
Ted smiled at her. "Let's go up, then."

* * *

Ted held Dreamer close to him as they lay in bed, deep in thought.

"Dream?"

"Mmm?"

"You know Christmas is coming up. I really want us all to be together, to have a magical Christmas, all of us. Agnes and Paul too."

"That sounds wonderful," Dreamer said softly, and Ted smiled.

"If you don't want to come here for Christmas, we can come to yours. Anywhere you feel comfortable."

Dreamer nodded, snuggling closer to him. "I'd prefer having us at mine."

"Great. I'll buy the tree and decorations and the presents." Ted kissed her on the forehead. "You just relax and let your man do the work."

Dreamer thought about Antonio and her parents, and decided to forget testing Ted. They were at a place in their relationship they'd never been before, and she loved it. She would never do anything to betray him again.

Never.

* * *

Ted woke up to Baby Julian's giggles as he said "Teddy!"
Ted smiled, muttering "Hey, little man. You ok?"
Dreamer looked at Julian, who shyly said "Yes."
"Good boy, baby." Dreamer kissed Baby Julian. "Ready for breakfast?"
"Yes Mummy. Teddy come too?"
"Of course."
Ted smiled and got out of bed, asking "What time is it, Dream?"
"Just gone ten. Marlon and Pandora are waiting for us at the table."
"Give me ten minutes. I'll be there."
Dreamer smiled at him. "I don't think they're going to wait another minute to eat their breakfast, Ted. But ok. I'll tell them."
"Bye Teddy!" said Julian happily, and Ted smiled at him.
"See you in a bit."

* * *

Dreamer sat at the table with Julian in her lap, saying "Your father'll be ten minutes, but if you're really hungry you can start eating your food."
Pandora picked up her fork immediately, making Marlon burst out laughing.
"Pandora, seriously- can't you wait ten minutes?"
"No," she replied flatly, and Dreamer smiled amusedly as Marlon laughed again. "I'm starving."
"So am I, but I still want to wait for Dad."
"You do that." Pandora forked a sausage and took a bite. "Usually you scoff your food before anyone anyway."
"Yeah, but I don't want to look like a pig in front of my baby brother."
"He'll find out you're a pig real soon," Pandora replied amusedly, making Dreamer laugh. "It's something you realise."
"All right, fine. I'll eat mine," said Marlon, picking up his fork, and Baby Julian said "I eat too!"
Marlon and Pandora laughed as Ted came into the kitchen, pouting.
"So none of my kids want to wait for their Dad to come before they eat?"
"No," Marlon and Pandora said amusedly, and Baby Julian beamed at Ted, a big smile on his tiny face.
Everyone froze, staring at the baby.
He looked just like Ted as he smiled at him- just like him! Dreamer stared at Julian as well, mind already whirring like Ted's was.
"Take... um... Pandora, take Julian while I talk to your father in the living room."

Pandora knew what they were going to discuss and so did Marlon. She reached for Julian, gently taking him from their mother.

Julian squirmed in her arms as his eyes filled over, and she said "It's ok, Julian. Mummy needs to talk to Teddy, ok?"

"Ok," he said, and she gently wiped his tears away.

Dreamer pulled Ted's kitchen doors closed behind her, heart racing as she turned to Ted, who said "Dreamer, think hard. Could Julian be mine?"

Before Dreamer could answer Agnes and Paul appeared, Dreamer scared as she said "Papa? What do you know?"

"As much as you, little one." Paul was unnerved as well. "It's a possibility Baby Julian could be Ted's son. But I am not sure."

"So there's a possibility." Ted exhaled as he looked at Dreamer. "Dream, think about the dates. He could be my son."

"He could be," Dreamer admitted quietly, and Ted's eyes filled over.

"That small time I spent hating Julian when he could be mine- I can't forgive myself-"

Dreamer placed a finger on his lips, shushing him gently. "Don't worry about it."

"But-"

"We'll get a DNA test for you and Julian, at the hospital."

"Bear in mind it will take a week for the results to come," Agnes said grimly. "It will be a gruelling week for all of us."

"Let's go now," Ted said, and they looked at him. "I have to know as soon as possible- we can't delay the test. Please, Dreamer. Let's go now."

Dreamer nodded. "Papa, Mama- please stay with Pandora and Marlon until we get back."

Agnes and Paul nodded. "Of course."

Dreamer took a deep breath before she went back into the kitchen, saying "Come, baby."

Julian reached for her happily, and Dreamer gently took him from Pandora.

"We're going out with Teddy, ok?"

"Ok," Julian said happily, and Pandora said "Mum?"

"It's fine," Dreamer said softly. "Everything will be ok."

"What if the baby's Dad's?" Pandora asked quietly. "Will it be ok?"

"Of course it will."

"And what if he isn't?" Marlon asked as quietly as his sister had. "Will it still be ok?"

"Of course," Dreamer repeated. "Everything has been fine so far even though we all thought Julian wasn't Ted's. We put it behind us, remember?"

Marlon and Pandora nodded, then Pandora said "Good luck."

"Thank you sweetie."

Dreamer gently put on Julian's tiny puff coat and shoes, then his little hat. "Don't you look cute."

Julian beamed up at his mother, and she kissed him on the forehead.

"Ready, Ted?"

"I'm ready," Ted replied hoarsely, and she realised how nervous he was as he said "Dreamer- me and you- I mean if the test is negative... will we-"

"Don't worry," she said softly. "No matter what happens, I promise me and you will be ok."

Ted breathed out, relieved as Julian fidgeted in Dreamer's arms. Then he said "Let's go."

* * *

Five days later...

Ted couldn't stop pacing the living room. The hospital had told him and Dreamer the results would take five to seven working days to be received. However, the letter would be sent to Dreamer's home, not his.

Pandora and Marlon came home from college with James and Alice, Alice saying "Hi Mr. Stone!"

"Hello Alice," Ted said, distracted for a split second as they all put their bags down. Then, remembering that James was Pandora's boyfriend and Alice was Marlon's girlfriend, he said "No switching with James when you go to Pandora's room, Alice. If I check on you and find James in there instead-"

"That won't happen sir, I promise," smiled Alice. "Come on Pandora."

Ted took to pacing his living room again as they all went upstairs.

* * *

"So he could be Ted's," whispered Miriam, Denise awestruck as Dreamer held the envelope. "Open it, Dreamer!"

"I can't." Dreamer shook her head. "Not without Ted being here."

"Do you want me to call him?"

"Yes please."

Denise pulled out her mobile quickly before Miriam had a chance and called Ted, saying "Ted? It's Denise. Come to Dreamer's as soon as you can, and bring Pandora and Marlon. No, nothing's happened- well, something has. Dreamer needs you here with her."

"Both of you need to go," Dreamer said, as Denise ended the call. "I'll call you both in a few days and we'll definitely see each other."

"You promise?" said Miriam, and Dreamer nodded.

"I promise."

* * *

"Dad, slow down!"

Ted didn't slow the car until he pulled up outside Dreamer's house, leaping out of the car and hurrying up to her front door.

Pandora and Marlon ran after him as Dreamer opened it, Ted taking a moment to breathe. As calmly as he could, he said "Did the results come?"

"Yes," she said quietly. "Come inside, all of you. It's freezing."

Baby Julian shrieked happily when he saw his big brother and sister.

"Dorwa!" he ran to Pandora, who scooped him up and cuddled him, then handed him to Marlon. "Hello Marlon!"

"Hey Julian. You ok?"

"Yep! Yes," he said shyly as Dreamer smiled at him, and everyone laughed. "Teddy!"

Baby Julian reached for Ted, who smiled and took him from Marlon.

"Hey, little man. Did you miss us?"

"Don't know," said Julian shyly, and everyone laughed again, Dreamer saying "Pandora, Marlon, take Julian upstairs to the play room. He has a lot of toys in there and there's a television you can watch, just while I talk to your father."

Pandora and Marlon nodded, leaving the room with Julian, who cried "Mummy!"

"I'll be up soon, baby. I just need to talk to Teddy, ok?"

"Ok," Julian said, eyes filling, and Dreamer blew him a kiss. "Soon?"

"Soon," Dreamer promised. "I'll be up soon."

"Dreamer," said Ted quietly, and she joined him in the living area. "I haven't thought of anything else all week. I haven't even been able to sleep properly- I kept waking up in the night and then I couldn't sleep until dawn. And then I had work, where I couldn't concentrate-"

Dreamer snapped her fingers and the envelope sailed through the air towards her.

"Do you want to do it, Ted?"

"No," he admitted. "I'm scared, Dream. Scared stiff."

"There's nothing to be scared of," Dreamer said softly. "Things won't change if Julian isn't your son."

"And if he is my son, that changes everything," Ted said just as softly. "I won't miss out on spending time with him, Dreamer. I love him."

Dreamer nodded, then she slowly opened the letter and pulled out the paper, eyes scanning the page fast. Ted waited with bated breath, then he gathered the worst as her eyes filled over.

"Dream?" She looked at him. "What does it say?"

Dreamer swallowed as tears trailed down her face, then she placed the letter on the coffee table before she took a deep breath, Ted saying "Dreamer, talk to me. I'm not the father, am I? It's all right, you can say it- I promise I don't mind-"

Paul and Agnes appeared in a flash of blue light, and Ted was startled to see tears sliding down Agnes's face too.

"Little one," said Paul firmly as he looked at Dreamer. "Pull yourself together and talk to your lover." He looked at his wife, then he said "You too, Agnes. Pull yourself together."

Ted knew they knew what the results were. "Is it bad news? I'm not the father, am I?"

"It's good news," whispered Agnes, Paul saying "Pretty excellent news."

Ted looked at Dreamer, hardly daring to believe it. "Dreamer?"

"Look at the letter," she whispered, and Ted obeyed, reading fast.

His heart began pounding as he gasped "I don't believe it!"

"Ninety nine point nine percent," whispered Dreamer, and Paul wiped her tears away as he said "He's yours, Ted."

"He's mine?" Ted repeated amazedly, and they nodded.

"He's your son."

Ted let out a big cheer, Paul as well as Agnes kissed Dreamer, Pandora and Marlon charging down the stairs with Julian.

"What's going on?" demanded Pandora, and Ted said "He's mine, 'Dora! Julian- he's my son!"

"Seriously?" said Pandora amazedly, when Marlon punched the air with joy. "He's our full brother?"

"Yes," Dreamer said softly, taking Baby Julian from Pandora.

"Hey little man," Ted said softly, looking at Julian, and Julian said "Hello Teddy!"

"Not Teddy, baby." Dreamer smiled at her youngest son. "Daddy."

"Daddy?" Julian repeated curiously, and Dreamer nodded.

"He's your Daddy."

"Teddy my Daddy?" asked Julian, and Dreamer softly said yes.

"Come give Daddy a hug," Ted said as his eyes filled over, and Julian reached for him, beaming. Tears trailed down Ted's face as he held Julian to him, stroking his curly hair.

Pandora and Marlon's eyes filled as well as they watched the moving sight, Ted holding out an arm to Dreamer. She came closer, and he pulled her close, kissing her forehead.

"So we're definitely going to be all together for Christmas?"

"Of course," she said softly. "I promise."

Marlon cheered again, Pandora smiling as Ted put Julian down so he could kiss their mother properly. She couldn't help saying "This is brilliant."

"Super brilliant," smiled Paul. "We will leave you now, little one, to spend time with your family. You'll see us at the weekend."

"Yes Papa," Dreamer said as she broke the kiss, and Paul and Agnes vanished.

Ted exhaled, feeling like he would burst with joy as Baby Julian reached for one of his toys.

"This is amazing."

Dreamer smiled as well, Marlon beaming as he asked "So are we going to live together now? There's no reason for us not to."

"That's totally up to your mother," Ted replied as he put his arm around Dreamer. "Whenever she's ready, we will."

Baby Julian was making his toy horse ride around the carpet by itself, beaming as Dreamer said "Are you still against magic, Ted? Baby Julian is too little to control his power, and I can't stop being a witch."

"Of course I'm not against it," Ted said warmly. "After that fiasco with the police and the stadium, how could I be? I love you for what you are, Dreamer, and I'd never wish that you'd change."

Dreamer smiled at him. "I love you, Ted Stone."

"And I love you, Dreamer Black."

"Don't get all mushy," Pandora said, scowling as Ted smiled at her mother dreamily. "You'll make me chuck up."

Dreamer and Ted burst out laughing, Marlon saying "I'm hungry. What's for dinner, Mum?"

"What do you fancy, darling?"

"Spicy chicken and rice," Pandora said before Marlon could reply, and Ted said "Sounds great. You want me to make it, Dream?"

"If you'd like," Dreamer replied, taking a deep breath. She felt so relieved about the DNA results and so happy as well. Now she could truly put the memory of Damon Stile behind her, properly. They all could.

* * *

Ted gently stroked Dreamer's hair as she slept, smiling happily.

"I love you," he whispered, and Dreamer smiled as she murmured "I love you more."

"Well I counter that with an I love you double more."

Dreamer opened her eyes to look at him, then she said "Triple."

"Quadruple," Ted said instantly, and he laughed as she pouted. "You can't win this, Dreamer. I love you more than you'll ever know."

"The same goes for me, Teddy." Dreamer kissed him. "Shall we get up?"

"Nah. Well, not until Julian wakes anyway." Ted sighed contentedly, then he looked at her. "Can we put the whole memory of Damon Stile to bed? Once and for all?"

"Of course," Dreamer said softly. "I want to tell the same to Pandora."

Dreamer's bedroom door opened, and they saw Pandora creep in nervously.

"Morning," she mumbled, and Ted and Dreamer said "Morning."

"I was sort of listening," Pandora said cautiously. "But only when Mum asked if you should get up, Dad. I was coming before that, and-"

"It's ok, 'Dora. Don't worry about it." Ted smiled at her. "Want to snuggle down with us?"

Pandora's face lit up and she looked every bit a six-year-old. "Can I?"

"Of course," smiled Dreamer, and Pandora stepped out of her slippers before she ran and joined her parents in bed, snuggling down in between them.

"I heard what you said about Damon Stile," she mumbled. "Can we really put him behind us now that we know he has no connection to us?"

"Yes," Dreamer said softly. "Pandora, I know he frightens you and he has for years. Even since being in prison. I don't want you to feel that way anymore."

"I can't help it," whispered Pandora. "He could escape from prison and get me again. Or hurt you like before, or kill you again-"

"Shh," Dreamer said soothingly, and Ted noticed she had her golden wand in her hand. "He won't, Pandora. I promise you."

An almost invisible blue mist slowly unfurled from the tip of Dreamer's wand, heading straight for Pandora's face, into her mouth, up her nose...

Pandora's eyes grew heavier, and soon she was fast asleep.

"Dreamer?" said Ted anxiously. "What are you doing?"

"I'm going to erase Pandora's memory of Damon Stile," Dreamer replied, and his jaw dropped.

"You can do that?"

"Of course I can. We'll have our old Pandora back, the Pandora who is confident and not scared of socialising," Dreamer said. "She can call her old friends and patch it up with them. I know they'll be shocked and pleased to hear from her after such a long time."

Ted nodded. "Do it. Do Marlon's as well- and anyone they told about Damon- flip, erase Damon's memory of her as well, Dream."

"Of us," Dreamer corrected softly. "All of us."

Ted nodded, then he said "Then do me. I don't want to remember him either."

"I'll need Papa and Mama's help," Dreamer started, and then she stopped when her parents appeared before her bed, smiling at her.

"Little one," smiled Paul. "This may be the best idea you have come up with in a very long time."

"Will you help me?" asked Dreamer, and Agnes said "Of course we will, darling. In fact, you and Ted should go to back to sleep."

"What? But I need to-"

Paul simply touched Dreamer's forehead, and she slumped on her pillows, fast asleep. Amazed, Ted said "You can do magic without your wand, Paul?"

"Of course," said Paul, a little smugly. "Well, we started off doing magic without our wands anyway. When we hit eleven, our wands appeared for us and helped boost our abilities."

"Can Dreamer do magic without her wand?" asked Ted, and Paul repeated himself: "Of course."

"Nice," said Ted. "And-"

"Your questions will have to wait, Ted. Agnes and I have a lot of memory wiping to do."

Before Ted would reply Paul touched his head as well, and he fell backwards, fast asleep.

Paul smiled at Agnes. "Let's get this over with once and for all."

* * *

"Mummy!"

Dreamer snapped awake, startled as she saw Baby Julian's tiny face close to hers. Ted was just waking up as well.

Pandora stood with Marlon, a bright smile on her face as she said "Afternoon."

"Afternoon??" Dreamer repeated incredulously as she looked at the clock: it was gone three p.m. "Why didn't you wake us, either of you?"

"You looked like you was having a good dream," smiled Pandora. "We sorted Julian for you. He's had his breakfast and lunch already, and I bathed him. He was making the water bubble and the rubber ducks change colour."

"Baby wizard in the making," smiled Ted, Julian reaching for him happily. "Hey, little man."

"Hello Daddy!"

"We'd better get up," Dreamer said, shaking her head. "Why was I asleep for so long?"

"No idea," shrugged Ted as he held the baby, then he stood up with him one arm. Dreamer couldn't help eying her man's muscles appreciatively, and Marlon grinned as he noticed the look on her face.

"We can take Julian for you again, Mum, if you don't want to get up yet." Dreamer's face grew hot as he grinned at her knowingly, and she said "I'm getting up, sweetie. I really fancy pancakes."

"I'll make them," Ted said, smiling at her. "Take Julian while I get a shower."

Dreamer took their tiny son, smiling as well.

"Does anyone feel like a massive weight has been lifted off their shoulders?" asked Pandora, and they looked at her. "I feel like... real settled and content- and like a thousand percent more confident. Like I can socialise again with no worries. I want to contact my old friends and see how they are. Oh, and call James too."

"I feel it too," said Marlon. "Maybe something happened that changed us or something."

"Definitely," said Dreamer quietly. "But I don't know what it is."

"Well Grandma Agnes would definitely know-"

"And she isn't going to spill," Agnes said amusedly as she appeared, Paul as well. "It was a positive force, Dreamer, a force you yourself came up with."

"I did?" said Dreamer blankly. "But I don't remember-"

"Of course you don't," Paul said flatly. "I made sure you wouldn't."

"You meddled with my mind?! Papa, that's not fair!" Outraged, Dreamer got to her feet and glared at her father. "You can't do that!"

"I already have," smirked Paul. "Now, let's have some of those pancakes you wanted. Agnes can make them."

Dreamer was seething as she said "Fine."

"You upset our Mum," grinned Marlon, and Paul smiled back at him as he said "She will get over it, son. Come on, let's go downstairs."

* * *

Dreamer calmed down after finishing her mother's brilliant pancakes.

"I suppose whatever you did, it was for all of our own good."

"It was," Agnes said solemnly, and Dreamer said "All right. I'm not going to be angry over it anymore."

"Good."

Pandora got off her mobile happily, saying "Mum, me and my friends are going to have some kind of reunion in about two weeks in Westport. James is going to come too, and I'm bringing Alice to meet them."

"That's brilliant, sweetie." Dreamer smiled at her only girl, Ted as well. Then Ted said "I'm going to drop you and pick you up, 'Dora."

"Yes Dad," said Pandora resignedly, and Ted said "You can choose the time. I'll let you have that privilege."

"Great!"

* * *

Two weeks later...

Ted let himself and Pandora in, Ted saying "Quietly now. I think everyone's asleep."
"You wish," said Marlon, munching popcorn as he turned on the lights. "How was your reunion, 'Dora?"
"It was great." Pandora smiled broadly. "Everyone really liked Alice."
"Good." Marlon smiled back. "Mum and Julian are sleeping. I wanted to wait up for you."
"Aww. Thanks, big brother." Pandora hugged him before she put her bag down. "I'm going for a shower then I'm going to bed. I'm so tired. But it was totally worth it. Night!"
Smiling still, she made her way upstairs.

* * *

Ted slipped into bed next to the love of his life. "Dreamer?"
"Mmm?"
"I'm back."
"Great," Dreamer said shallowly, taking a deep breath before she opened her green eyes. "Did Pandora have a good time?"
"She had an excellent time," smiled Ted. "I haven't seen Pandora so happy in so long. Whatever your parents did, we have to thank them properly. We're all so content now."
Dreamer nodded, snuggling into him. "And Julian is speaking more fluently now as well. It's more curious questions these days than baby language."
Ted smiled. "I noticed that too. He's a happy toddler."
"We'd better go back to sleep," smiled Dreamer. "It's nearly three in the morning."
"Pandora asked me to pick her up at half one," said Ted apologetically. "Then I had to drop Alice and James home."
"It's no problem, Ted." Dreamer kissed him before she laid down properly. "Let's go to sleep."
Ted kissed her gently. "Night."

* * *

One month later…

Marlon leapt out of bed and ran to his bedroom window, looking out.
The streets were white with snow.
"Yes!!"
He dashed out of his room and ran across the landing to bang on his sister's door.
"Pandora!"
"What?" she said groggily as he burst into her bedroom, grinning. "Get lost, camel mouth!"
Marlon pulled the duvet off her happily, making her curse furiously as she sat up, trying to grab it back, but he danced away from her happily.
"It's Christmas, 'Dora!"
Pandora's expression cleared as they heard their baby brother call for Dreamer.
"Mummy!!"
Dreamer left her and Ted's room with Ted at her side, smiling.
"Merry Christmas Mum!" said Marlon brightly, and she said "Merry Christmas honey. Did you wake up Pandora?"
"Yes he did," scowled Pandora, then she smiled. "Merry Christmas!"
"Merry Christmas."
Baby Julian squealed happily from his crib, Dreamer scooping him up and cuddling him lovingly.
"Morning sweetie."
"Let's go open our presents," said Marlon excitedly, and Ted said "Not before you shower and have breakfast."
"But Dad-!!"
"Listen to your father," Dreamer said amusedly, and Marlon sighed his ok.

* * *

Ted smiled as he watched Dreamer help Baby Julian unwrap his last present. Pandora and Marlon smiled as they watched too, all of their presents already unwrapped.

Julian shrieked happily as he saw the army action figure, tugging at it happily so he could start playing immediately.

"Look, Mummy! Look!"

"It's lovely, baby. Say thank you to Daddy," smiled Dreamer, and Julian beamed as he scrambled to his feet and ran and hugged Ted's leg.

"Thank you Daddy!"

"You're welcome, Julian." Ted swept the tiny child up and hugged him. "Marlon, Pandora, why don't you take Julian into the garden and build a snowman?"

"Dress warmly though," Dreamer added, and Pandora nodded as she reached for her coat. Dreamer pulled on Julian's tiny puff coat and boots, then she put a woolly hat on his little head, a scarf on his neck, and tiny gloves on his hands. When she noticed them smiling at her, she pouted. "I have to be protective. I don't want him to fall ill. And the same goes for you two," she said, smiling at Pandora and Marlon. "Put on a hat, scarf and gloves please."

"Yes Mum."

* * *

Ted gently pressed a mug of hot chocolate into Dreamer's hands as she stood, watching her children play in the snow with a smile on her face. She said thank you softly, and Ted had a strong urge to kiss her.

"Ted?"

"Yes Dream?"

"I wouldn't have my life any other way," Dreamer said softly as she looked up at him, and he saw her eyes had filled over. "I'm so happy."

"So am I," he said quietly. "Dreamer... do you think the worst is definitely behind us?"

"Yes," she said gently. "We can look forward to everything good now, Ted. Even if we argue, I know we won't separate. Our love is too strong, stronger than it has ever been before. I truly believe everything can only get better. For all of us."

Dreamer meant every word she said, and Ted believed them.

And Dreamer was right.

Everything got better and better for the family and their friends, their problems long gone, left in the past.

Ted and Dreamer couldn't ask for anything better.

* *

Thank you for reading A Witch Like No Other!

Follow me on Twitter @misskelz90 and look out for posts about other available books and more!

You can also follow my Amazon Author Page if you search for me; "Makala Thomas".

I really hope you enjoyed reading this book but like any book, some will not like it and some will love it.

Be sure to leave a review!

Happy reading!

xxx Makala Thomas xxx

Other Titles by Makala Thomas

The Link: Matthew's Beginning

The Link: Colette's Beginning

The Link: Colette's Fame

The Link: Colette's Return

The Link: The Betrayal

The Link: Psycho Eruption

Integrity

The Angel (Who Knew Not Love)

Jeiklee

Count Angelo

A Witch Like No Other

Skylar Grey

Kenco: The Goddaughter

Kenco: The Return Of Her King

Krissie Taylor

Beast

Lost

Love Conquers All

The Stranger In The Woods

Unrequited Love

The Tail Of A Queen

Amaris

Gadget Girl

Contact Makala Thomas here:

Facebook Page:

The Diverse Works Of Makala Thomas

Twitter:

@MissKelz90

Email:

misskelz90@gmail.com